a sacred
Peace

Drifters, Book Eleven

SUSAN RODGERS

Somewhere there's a drifter
trying to find his way…
—Amanda Marshall (*I Believe In You*)

This book is for the drifters…
I believe in you.

Contents

Prologue

*S*handa Ellis was late. Her wardrobe fitting for *Sacred Peace,* Charlie Deacon and Charles Keating's contemporary gunslinger series shooting in and around Calgary, Alberta, was supposed to be a ten-thirty midmorning gig, but the dashboard clock on her Jeep was already pushing ten to eleven and she was still at least five minutes away.

"Last time I leave the main drag to hunt down a Starbucks in a city I'm not familiar with," she complained as she navigated the Wrangler around a slow-moving minivan.

A trim, perky blonde whose bouncy, short Marilyn Monroe curls framed a round face with porcelain skin and soft, moist brown eyes, Shanda was *Sacred Peace's* female lead. This would be her second big series. The first, a dystopian space odyssey shot in Vancouver, won her a legion of awards and jumpstarted a slew of offers. Jonathon McCloud was the reason Shanda finally signed onto the modern gunslinger show. The man was a legend, known for creative original plot lines, snappy dialogue, and attention to cinematographic detail. Didn't hurt to have powerful Charles Keating on board as one of the producers, either. Usually a music producer, in recent years he'd branched off into film and had apparently agreed to help Charlie Deacon get *Sacred Peace* shot.

Charlie Deacon. Hmm. The guy had made his name in film but he, like Shanda's other co-star Josh Sawyer, was in love with the TV series and wanted to see it get made. Shanda had met both men during the casting process to see if she was suited for the part. At the time, during a 'get-to-know-each-other' lunch meeting, Charlie had also cited consistency for his family

1

for a reason to make the contemporary western. He and his wife Jane had a young daughter, Stella, and a new baby boy, Lucas. There was hope *Sacred Peace* would 'hit' and Alberta could provide the family a home base—city living for Charlie on early morning or late night shoots, and Canmore, the mountain village of athletes and pure-of-heart environmentalists, as the family's main residence—for at least a few years to come.

Josh hadn't said much at that lunch meeting. Now, as Shanda steered onto an exit ramp and pointed the Jeep towards a distant building she recognized as the sound stage where she was overdue, she thought about the man who would be her love interest on the show. At the same time, her pulse quickened and her throat got suddenly dry. Josh was attractive, sure enough, but it wasn't his looks or his rating as People's 'Sexiest Man Alive' a few years back that got her heart racing. Instead, it was his reputation.

The Grammy fiasco was only a month old. Shanda had screened a few of the resulting YouTube videos at her grandmother's birthday party in Vancouver last week. She'd waited to watch them because she didn't want to color her notions about the guy or form any opinions about him based on media reports, but in the end her curiosity won out. The world of celebrity was fickle, the reporting often slanted, and for sure there was more to Josh's meltdown that day than she guessed the media was telling. Still…after viewing his rampage against some fan and his own security, and watching him inadvertently hit his wife in the meantime, Shanda had sat back, nauseated and apprehensive.

"You'd better stay on this fella's good side," her wise grandmother had said at the time. "Although I can't say it looks like your new job is going to be a lot of fun. You couldn't pay me enough to work with someone with a personality as unpredictable as that man's."

Pushing the unwelcome thoughts aside, Shanda finally steered a hard right and skidded to a stop in one of the cast and crew's assigned parking spots. Swallowing nervously, she muttered to herself, "I could have gone to L.A. I could have chosen New York. But nooo, I wanted to work with Charlie Deacon on Jonathon McCloud's new show." Wrenching the visor mirror down so she could apply some last minute lip-gloss, she grumbled, "I ought to be shot."

Grabbing her bag and the empty Starbucks cup, she hopped out of the Jeep.

There wasn't a lot of time to ponder Josh's dark reputation any further. One of the show's wardrobe assistants was at the door, holding it open for Shanda. Hurrying, she put on a fake smile and greeted the trendy young black man.

"Hi. Shanda Ellis," she said warmly, hoping that by ignoring the fact that she was a half hour late, her tardiness wouldn't be a 'thing.' Unfortunately though, as she dumped the Starbucks cup in a nearby garbage bin, a steady pressure on her bladder forced her to accept that she had to pee. Badly.

No choice. She was going to be even later for her appointment with wardrobe.

"Great start," she mumbled inwardly. Fixing a crooked stare and what she hoped was an endearing smile on the young assistant, she raised her eyebrows and drew herself to a halt in the long hallway outside the costume department.

"Ummm...?"

The guy stretched out a purple-sweatered arm, pointed, and frowned. "That way," he directed, anticipating the issue before Shanda really asked. "You might want to hurry. Rose has had Jonathon McCloud at her door twice in the last ten minutes. He wants final approval on your wardrobe."

"Damn Starbucks," Shanda moaned as she jogged down the hall to the appointed restroom door. "Like I need all that sugar anyway."

Five minutes later, she swept into wardrobe's large, bright room with her second plastered and rather inauthentic smile of the morning. Jonathon, waiting with arms crossed and snowy hair flowing over his shoulders, was clearly unimpressed until he made eye contact with his lead actor, at which point he pressed his lips together, forced a welcoming smile, and reached out a hand in greeting.

"Shanda. Welcome to Calgary. We're thrilled to have you on board. This is Rose, our Costume Designer. She was with me on *The Wyatt Boys* and on *Drifters* before that. Best in the biz, and awards up the yin-yang, so you're in good hands."

"Thank you, sir." Shanda waited while Rose took her bag and set it out of the way on the floor against the leg of a table.

A Caucasian woman in her mid-fifties, tattoos peeking from beneath the sleeves of her tight black sweater and grey hair swept up in a bun, Rose led Shanda into the changing area, where the first outfit was hanging from a hook in the small curtained space.

"Here, honey," she said briskly, physically turning Shanda at the shoulders and hauling off her baggy grey cardigan. "Pull off those black leggings and let's get you into the uniform to start."

The uniform in question was green and khaki. Although shot in Canada, the show centered around a small town American sheriff's office. Shanda was playing one of the officers—a new recruit, Olivia. Josh was the sheriff, Bobby, a man recovering from the murder of his wife, and Charlie was Hank, a local reporter. Eyeing the uniform's bland colors critically, Shanda hesitated, and fingered the green bomber jacket she'd often wear overtop.

"I'm already looking forward to the off-duty shots," she said.

"It's all the rage to look mundane, dear," Rose said with a frown as she stayed with Shanda and passed her clothes to hurry things along since they were already late. "The less makeup the better. Didn't you see Julia Roberts in that film she made a few years ago? I can't remember the name."

"That memorable, huh?" Shanda grinned. "I saw Reese Witherspoon in Wild. I do recall her 'au naturel' look in that film. She made up for it by being absolutely adorable in shorts and hiking boots."

"Your civilian clothes are attractive in this show." Rose, whose fragrant citrusy hand cream brought a tickle to Shanda's throat, hung up the loose striped top Shanda wore in today. "You have to be striking enough to catch your sheriff's eye, at least."

Shanda frowned, and stared downwards as she belted her pants. Rose caught the sudden tension in the raised shoulders and the new hard set to Shanda's jaw.

"What?" she asked kindly, using her foot to push a laced boot towards her cast.

"It's nothing. Just…"

"Josh Sawyer?"

Looking up as she stuck her toes into the boot, Shanda drew up her shoulders and huffed, "What was he like on *Drifters*? I heard he had some big breakdown on *The Wyatt Boys* and destroyed one of the sets."

"Do you always listen to rumors? And you ought to know by now not to research your co-stars on the Internet."

"Rose, Josh and I are in a lot of scenes together. I don't need to be miserable for the next six months. I took the part before the whole Grammys meltdown. I thought he was doing okay."

"He's an Oscar winning actor, honey. He's intense, but he's not normally cruel. You may recall Josh was going through a rough time during much of the *Wyatt Boys* shoot."

"I know, I know. I did my research. Which means I know Jonathon, his own father, fired him, so it must have gotten pretty bad on set. I just thought things were better now, that's all. The Grammys thing threw me."

"You will find that Josh will be very focused on his work and, if not overtly kind, then at least social. Although I admit, apart from a few quick fittings over the last few months, I haven't seen him much myself lately."

Rose bent to tie Shanda's boots while Shanda nudged on her jacket and admired the weight and appearance of it in the small dressing room mirror.

"So," Rose added, standing and giving Shanda a small push towards the curtained doorway, "I don't really know what to expect from him, but I know Jonathon well and I can't see him taking another chance on casting his son if Josh was still having addictions issues."

"Yes, but—" Raising a hand to move the curtain aside, Shanda spoke back over her shoulder to Rose, "Hasn't he been to rehab, like, twice?"

Turning to move forward, she stopped in her tracks.

"Four times, actually," Josh said quietly. Early for his eleven-thirty appointment with wardrobe, he was standing about six feet away, feet planted wide apart, and both hands stuck deep in the pockets of his tan leather jacket. He and Charlie had just arrived and greeted Jonathon. "The first two didn't stick. Or was it three? Can't say I remember those days well."

"Oh, shit." A quick red flush spread over Shanda's cheeks. Resting her weight on one leg, she let her gaze drift over to Charlie who, she was even more mortified to see, had gone a bit pale. Chewing on his bottom lip, he was staring at the floor. "Well, that about makes my morning perfect." She tossed the words into the room with careless abandon. How much worse could her introduction to this new series get?

5

"Makes mine even better," Josh immediately fired back. He looked behind her at Rose. "I can see you've got your hands full for the next bit. I'll come back in half an hour." Averting his eyes from his new co-star, he strode towards the entrance to the room and disappeared into the hallway.

"Oh, Jesus," Shanda groaned. Fixing Charlie in her sight, she met his eyes when he looked up. Holding her arms out to the sides, she stated matter-of-factly, "Just trying to get a feel for what I'm up against, that's all."

Jonathon was leaning on his butt against a long table peppered with ties, hats, worn leather gloves, and wool mitts. He remained quiet as Charlie spoke to Shanda. "You want to know what you're up against? You're up against a guy who just left his family in Vancouver and asked his wife not to bother moving out here anytime soon. For reasons you'd already understand if you had the news on at any point in the last few days. That's what—who—you're up against."

"Sweet. An angry guy. Good to know. Thanks, Charlie. Our love scenes should be downright magical."

Shrugging, Charlie said, "You asked." He turned to go find Josh to see if he could soothe the harsh reminder of his troubled past with some words of wisdom or hope. "But Shanda?" he tossed behind him. "Make your own assessment of Josh. After you've had a chance to see what a brilliant actor he is, and after you've experienced his generosity and kindness. Okay?"

"Fuckin' Starbucks," Shanda cursed under her breath. "All this for a caramel macchiato."

As Charlie left the room, she responded to Rose's gentle maneuvering of her body, and modeled for Jonathon, but found it almost impossible to meet the quiet man's eye.

"I'm sorry," she mumbled at the end of her session. "I guess I'm just nervous."

Jonathon angled his head towards her and tried to smile but it came out crooked. He took her hand and spoke directly to her with eyes like Josh's, all liquid brown and lit with sorrow. "So'm I," he said softly. "So'm I."

Chapter One

A loud discord on the piano was Jessie's way of saying 'F-you' to the song she was working on in the Robson Street studio.

"Ahhh!" she hollered to no one in particular after resting both forearms hard on the keys, and her forehead on the forearms, creating a second unruly noise that had Charles, who happened to be in the hallway outside chatting with Matt, ducking his head inside. Matt moved past him and stopped just inside the studio's door.

"Jessie?" Charles inquired.

Raising her head and arms from the keyboard, Jessie spun around on the small bench seat and stared at the men.

"I can't get it," she said. "I can't focus."

"Take a break, then," Charles insisted. "Go with her, Matt. Go get a coffee and come back in half an hour. Or go to your condo and work on the baby grand there."

"Charles, I've had three coffees today already. My brain's a speeding train. It's just missing all the stops, that's all." Rising, Jessie moved towards him and Matt. "The condo's not an option. My bed's much too comfy." With apologetic eyes, she took Charles' elbows and faced him. "You've got musicians booked for tomorrow and I've got nothing ready for them. I can't seem to make any headway on these tunes."

"I'll cancel the musicians. Take another few days to fine tune the songs."

"Charles! I'm stuck, okay? I need…I need another writer."

Matt had yet to say a word. He knew where this conversation was going before Jessie had even voiced the thought. Crunching on his bottom lip, he pondered the fiery woman in front of them, all messy ponytail, frustrated frown, and shifting feet.

Charles pondered the request. "I don't think that's a good idea, Jessie."

"Do you want mediocre or brilliant, Charles? You choose."

"*Sacred Peace* won't need the songs if my lead actor implodes, Jessie."

"Charles, Jacob is sitting around doing nothing besides waiting to see where this latest scandal is going to land us. He's in the city, you need songs, and I need help. I have no intention of jumping back into bed with him, against my will or otherwise. Besides," she added, raising her chin, "he's in love with Kayla."

Charles' eyes narrowed. "With or without Kayla in the picture, I am not yet ready to see Jacob in my environment, Jessie, either here or at home. Give me at least a few days to digest this latest crisis, will you?"

A quick stomp of her foot telegraphed Jessie's thoughts on the subject. "I've had months to digest it, and I'm sorry that this is new to you, Charles, but I need Jacob's collaboration on this tune. We're over it, it's time for the rest of you to get over it!"

"And when your husband—my actor—finds out you were in here recording with Jacob again?"

"He's not even talking to me at the moment, so ask me if I really care what Josh thinks." Fisting her hands at her sides, Jessie's eyes flashed fire.

Matt couldn't suppress a grin. Between the foot stomping and the childish ire in her pink cheeks, Jessie may as well have been six years old.

She noticed. "Ahhh! Stop it, Matt. Stop making fun of me."

"You're doing a fine job of that all by yourself, Jessie," he chuckled, sending a sideways look to Charles to assess his stress level. The man's face was a stoic usual pale instead of a nerve-popping red, so Matt relaxed.

Jessie caught the look and forced herself to calm down. Since Charles' heart attack, with the unavoidable exception of telling him about the Florida crisis, they were all being more careful to try to reduce his stress. Capitulating, she groaned. "Okay, fine. No Jacob. Go," she waved Charles off. "I'll get back to work."

With a final nod, Charles grumbled, "Let me know how it goes. Ulysses is bringing Deirdre down and we're off to the cardiac clinic for my checkup.

If you need me to cancel the session musicians for tomorrow, give me a shout. I'll be home later to sample Dylan and Carlotta's chocolate chip cookies."

"Fine," Jessie concurred. "But you may as well let Dee know that you guys will have the kids for the night because this is not going anywhere fast." Sauntering forward, she wrapped her arms around Charles and gave him a gentle hug and a light kiss on the cheek. "I love you. Pass this checkup with flying colors, please. In fact, I order you."

Her tender touch and worry worked. Charles allowed a small smile to sneak through his tough countenance. "I'm fine, Jessie. I'm feeling very well these days. I hope to get the all clear to fly to Calgary for the weekend." With a wave to Matt, he said, "Keep an eye on her. I don't need her driving off to Whistler under the pretense of working out a song." Back to Jessie he said, "We'll work with the engineer tomorrow to fine tune whatever issues you're having." With that, the Keating patriarch swept out of the door and down the hall to his office to gather his things.

A curious tilt to his head, Matt was left watching Jessie. She was smiling wholeheartedly.

"What?" he asked, casually scratching his chin as her smile widened enough to crack her jaw.

"Oh, I'm just happy you saved his life, that's all," she grinned. "No biggie."

A sad smile was Matt's response to that comment which, more than anything, brought up a memory that rather terrified him. "And?" he asked. "I know you, Jessie. There's more. What are you up to?"

Striding back over to the piano, Jessie grabbed her iPhone from where it rested next to the higher keys. Tapping in her password and then lightly hitting the phone App, she turned around and winked at Matt.

"No, Jessie," he told her, crossing the room and trying to grab the phone out of her hand. "There is no way to look at this and possibly think it's a good idea!"

Jessie staunchly air-palmed him.

Dropping down onto the cushioned piano bench, Matt hung his head.

"Jacob!" Jessie hollered into her phone, moving towards the far wall and sinking down onto the black leather couch with one leg casually folded underneath the other. "Tired of binge watching Netflix and feeling sorry for yourself yet?"

Matt couldn't hear Jacob's response, but reading Jessie's expression was easy enough. She lit up like a Christmas tree. "Damn," he muttered, shaking his head at her impulsive choice, which Matt felt in no way, shape or form would go over well with either Charles or Josh.

Jessie knew what he was thinking. Walking over to Matt after she disconnected with Jacob, she paused six feet away from him and tapped the phone lightly against her thigh.

"Spike," she said thoughtfully, "this wasn't a random decision. The rest of you need to learn to forgive and forget. I miss making music with Jacob. What we manage to create together is magical." Their son Dylan crossed both hers and Matt's minds. "Right now? With Josh still out in left field pissed at me? I need some magic."

I can give you some magic, crossed Matt's mind inadvertently, but he immediately blinked it away.

Still, it was like Jessie read his mind. A silly grin broke out on her face and she covered the last few feet between them and pulled him up from the piano seat into her arms. "C'mere," she teased. "Lose the jealousy, stop worrying, and trust me when I say this little songwriting session between me and Jacob will be strictly work-based. All business. No pleasure. We're done on that regard."

"You and Jacob will never be done, Jessie," Matt finally said in her ear, pressing her close to him and soaking up the friendly hug. "The two of you songwriting together will only serve to bring you back together. It'll be dangerous, and Josh will lose it."

"Matt," Jessie sighed, gently easing him away from her. "I'm so tired of Josh losing it over Jacob. I don't blame him, but I'm over it, okay? We need to move forward."

"And you working with Jacob is going to facilitate that how?"

"By us managing to have a working relationship that's safe and amicable, supervised if you prefer, and productive on top of that in terms of blowing these songs Charles needs out of the park."

"Songs that you write with Jacob that will provide the soundtrack for your husband's new series. Some of which will be love songs."

"For love scenes he will shoot with Shanda Ellis. Yes. This is a little messed up, I grant you that."

"When will Jacob be here?"

Like a mischievous schoolgirl, she ducked her chin as her eyes sparkled. "As soon as you go get him. Deal?"

At Matt's hesitation, Jessie threw up her arms. "Hey, I'm not going anywhere. I'm going to order us some dinner and organize a little agenda as to how we are going to tackle these tunes. Are you staying, Matt? To supervise? This one's gonna be an all nighter."

"Just what I need," he admonished her, "a night of watching you and Jacob make googly eyes at each other."

Jessie sighed. "Seriously. I suppose I should be grateful you're not worried that Jacob will try to violently impose himself on me if you leave us here alone."

"Are you?"

"Hardly. He's not in the same place emotionally that he was that night. He'll be on his best behavior. And when you and Charles arrive tomorrow, you will both forgive me because our songs will make millions and Charles' show will have a long, well-funded life."

Matt grabbed her phone and held it out to her.

"What?" Jessie asked.

"You need to call Carlotta and get her to put your children on the line before you sink into oblivion with your ex, then you need to call Josh and tell him what you're up to. No more secrets from your husband, Jessie."

"Some days, Matt, I feel like you're my husband, minus the mind-blowing sex. Bossy old thing."

Speechless, his frown deepened and he dropped the phone to his side.

Jessie's voice got quiet. "Josh hasn't spoken to me since he left, Matt." She held up three fingers. "That was three days ago. All I've gotten is a few random texts."

Matt found his voice, but it was a struggle. It came out raspy. "All the more reason to try him now and talk this through before he gets word that you're working with Jacob again."

"Fine," she grumbled, grabbing the phone out of his hand. "But I'm starting with Carlotta and the kids. I need some joy before I sink back into darkness."

"World's smallest violin playing just for you," Matt chided her, using his thumb and forefinger to imitate a bow being drawn across tiny strings. "Want some cheese with that whine?"

"Men," she griped, as she watched Matt swing around on the toe of a leather desert boot and take his impeccable self out of the studio. As the door *shuffed* closed behind him, Jessie wandered back over to the black leather couch and settled deeply into it, lying down and draping both feet over the arm closest to the center of the studio. She called the kids, sent them all kisses and said she'd see them tomorrow, and then she tapped Josh's name on her contacts list.

He answered on the third ring.

"Hey," she said, actually surprised that he was taking her call.

"Hey, Jessie," he said, his voice quiet but, well, there. "How's the song-writing going?"

Oh, we're going there right away, she thought, gulping nervously now that her husband was actually on the phone. "Kind of crappy, actually. Not so good. I'm, uh…I'm calling in a reinforcement." Squeezing her eyes shut, Jessie caught herself thinking *maybe Matt was right about this…oops. Me and my big ideas.*

"Jacob, I suppose." Josh sounded resigned. Tired.

At least he's not being combative, Jessie considered as she drew her knees back up towards the rest of her body, and stared at the ceiling. "I got stuck, Josh. He's here. It's business, that's all."

"Is it ever really business with you and Jacob?" Josh asked.

"We used to write together. It was never really a problem," she half-lied. "We just get lost in the music, in what we're doing."

"And…no part of you is still angry at him for what happened in Florida, I suppose. You being Jessie Wheeler and all, Mizz 'light and sunshine,' huh? The whole 'love one another, forgive one another' shtick?"

Jessie's voice softened. "Babe, I know how pissed you are. I understand why. But I've had some time to process what happened that night and I've also accepted my own responsibility in it. Jacob was in a bad place and I had a lot to do with it. We need to heal and move on."

"And…us?"

"I'm hoping that you will heal and move on too, Josh. Although I recognize that you need some time."

"I would prefer to have time where I am not picturing my wife in the studio with a man who raped her. Who still loves her. Who she still loves."

"I love one man, Josh, above and beyond all others. And that man is you. I wish you hadn't left mad."

Josh was silent for a moment. Jessie could hear a horse shuffling around, maybe Blue, munching on her feed. Josh was in the barn at the ranch, apparently. After a bit, he spoke. "I wish I hadn't left mad too. And I know why you didn't tell me the truth about what happened, Jessie. It's the same reason why everywhere I go I get stares and funny looks and see people whispering about me."

His voice was flat. Jessie could feel her radar perking up. "Josh? Are you okay?"

"It's going to be a long six months, Jessie. That's all. My co-star has the same hate-on for me that everyone else has, it seems."

"Shanda? She seemed real sweet at that fundraiser last year. I'm sure she'll be fine."

A heavy exhalation and a small *ppffftt* met Jessie's ears. "I'm just tired of it. That's all. All of it."

"Josh…"

"Yeah."

"Babe, you're scaring me. All of a sudden I wish I could just morph myself there and hold you."

"But…instead you're going to stare into Jacob's eyes all night long and maybe end up holding him."

"You need to trust me."

"Bought that cake, and ate it too. It was made of bullshit."

"Jesus, Josh. Jacob and I are both paying for our sins big time, okay? It's old news. I am promising you that nothing will happen tonight except freaking amazing tunes that will help catapult your new show to every top rating and awards show possible. You have to agree on that account. Jacob is one hell of a songwriter."

"Jacob is one hell of a guy, yeah, Jacob the musician, actor, and lover, apparently. I already thanked Kayla for the heads up on that last bit, and let's not forget the threesome y'all had in Scotland that time. Best orgasm of your life, I seem to recall."

"Oh, for God's sake. Are you ever gonna let that shit go?"

"Jessie, I told you. I'm just tired. I thought we were good, you and me. I thought we were climbing out of that deep, dark hole, but you know, if you added together all the months—months, not years—that we actually have been 'good,' you'd be shocked to find that they're pretty much equaled by the ones that have been bad. Counting these last few, I mean."

"What are you saying?"

Josh's voice was already dull, but it grew even more dusky and somber. "I'm saying that there's got to be a point when couples call it a day. And it likely starts around the time that things are bad more often than they're good."

"A lot of our bad was not our fault." Jessie swallowed bitterly, remembering.

"I know that, but I also know that between the two of us, we've made a lot of recent threats about leaving. More than once. We vacillate back and forth. One day it's me, the next it's you. We're riding on a pretty fucking skinny split rail fence here, Jess. And now you call to tell me that one of our main breaking points is about to spend the night locked in a studio with you."

Nauseous, Jessie closed her eyes and pressed a palm to her forehead. Her voice was thin. "I also seem to recall both of us saying we will never let go."

"Jessie, I don't want to let you go. I don't ever want to live my life without you in it ever again. For one thing, I would not be able to handle seeing you with anyone else again. Ever. Jacob or Matt or…or otherwise."

"Why do I sense a but in there?"

"Because there is. A big one. But I can't see living my life the way I'm living it right now, either. Worrying about you, about whether I'm good enough for you, about you being with Matt so much, and now Jacob again. I don't think I ever thought I was good enough for you."

"That's my role. You're playing my song now. We've both got to get over this self-pity crap."

"I can't help it. That's how I feel. My wife—" Josh's voice cracked finally, under the strain of the last few days, and Jessie's heart sank as she heard him start to cry, "My wife was raped. Basically. And she was too scared of me to tell me. Too scared of what I might do, of how I might react. What kind of person does that make me, Jessie?"

"Oh, Josh. It makes you one I love too much to hurt. That's who it makes you."

He struggled to speak. When the words finally came out, they were hoarse and forced. "That's not my take on it."

"Well then, change your thinking, babe." Desperate to make him feel less alone, less unworthy, Jessie added an earnest, "I love you. So much."

"I love you back. But, uh…look, I gotta go."

Jessie panicked. "No. Not yet. Please."

"Can't talk right now, Jess." Clearing his throat, Josh slouched by Blue's stall and eased his heavy spirit down to the barn floor. He hung his head and listened for his wife's breaths, as if they could inject some life back into his faltering heart.

Closing her eyes as she pictured the tragic, fleeting hurt dancing across her husband's chocolate brown eyes, Jessie rolled onto her side and laid her cheek on an elbow. "Okay. I know," she murmured.

"I'll call you tomorrow."

Her response was a whisper. "Okay."

After they disconnected, Jessie realized that Josh hadn't asked about the kids. And nor had he gotten angry, other than a few sad words that expressed his fears. Those things in themselves were worrying.

Grabbing a thick, soft patterned coverlet off the back of the couch to hug, Jessie chewed on a fingernail and tried not to let fear wash over her. But when Jacob arrived alone, after having been dropped off by Matt, she was only too glad to shut off her brain and sink into the graceful oblivion of music.

Chapter Two

The moon was high over Vancouver and about ready to give way to the sun by the time Jessie finally set her guitar in a padded stand and dragged Jacob down the hall to the thirty-first floor's kitchenette. Once there, she rummaged around in a cupboard for a bag of popcorn, which she placed in a microwave.

As it popped, Jacob filled the kettle and plugged it in. "Auxiliary percussion's the key to the chorus, Jessie," he was saying with an air of knowing authority. "We'll talk to Moe tomorrow and see what he thinks we should add."

"And I want strings. Violins. So they go like this…" Singing, Jessie raised one hand high in the air and brought the notes up accordingly to illustrate her point. "Cello will be the reverse, the bass line anchor. Like this."

Leaning back against the counter, Jacob grinned and watched his musical partner do what she did best—create gorgeous music.

"What?" Turning to check the timer on the popcorn, Jessie tried to avoid letting him see her smile. He caught it anyway.

"This is just cool," Jacob said, unable to refrain from returning the happy smile. "Considering your husband pretty much banished me from your life."

"Josh is just scared, Jacob. You know that." The mention of Josh brought Jessie's mood down pretty quickly.

"I know. I'm sorry."

"I called him. He knows you're here."

Moving forward, Jacob found a few clean mugs and set them on the counter. Jessie tossed a few thin, dark packages of Starbucks instant coffee at

16

him, which he clipped open with scissors while Jessie wrapped her hand around a cool bottle of Panama Jack's wine liqueur in the fridge and pushed it towards him.

"Can't see Josh being okay with it." Jacob was suddenly pensive.

"I'm tired of worrying about what everybody else thinks. About us, I mean. Look at what we've already accomplished tonight. This song is perfect for *Sacred Peace*."

Pouring hot water into the mugs, Jacob agreed. "It's definitely a lot harder edged than anything else we've ever done together."

"It's almost a Metallica ballad, eh Jacob?"

"Lots of pain in there, if that's what you mean." Holding out a hand, he accepted the Panama Jack's bottle from Jessie and twisted off the lid as she grabbed a spoon and gave each coffee a whirl. "The healing kind, I guess."

Sticking the spoon in her mouth, Jessie pushed on the bottom of the upside down liqueur bottle in Jacob's hands to urge more of the good stuff into her coffee.

"Can't wait to play it for Charles." Jessie dropped the spoon in the sink, removed the popcorn from the microwave, and accepted the mug Jacob pushed towards her. "Thanks." She waited for him to put the Panama Jack's back in the fridge, and then led the way down the hall. "*Sacred Peace* is dark. Josh's character is getting over his wife's murder. The whole premise centers around the secrets behind who killed her and why."

"How do you feel about Shanda Ellis playing opposite Josh? She's very beautiful."

"I wouldn't call her beautiful." Jessie took a seat on the leather couch and, cross-legged, faced Jacob at the other end. A serious yawn that brought tears to the corners of her eyes obscured her next few words. "She's...more...of the cute, perky girl-next-door type. Not exotic or glamorous, by any means. Thank God." Nadia crossed her mind and she grimaced. "Seems nice."

"Did you think about taking on the role?"

"Nope. One of us in that darkness is plenty."

"And Josh—love scenes—all that jazz?"

"Hey, I was spread eagled in Brussels with a man I don't know and who could barely speak English going at me. Then there was the truck cab scene.

Thought I was going to break my back, and let me just say thank God for Yoga." She used her chin to gesture to her side. "Hip flexors." Turning a little pink, she added, "It's part of the biz. You're an actor, Jacob, you know what it's like. We have to live with it."

"Um, I remember doing a few of those with you on *Mystic Nights* and finding them pretty damn awful." Jacob got comfy opposite Jessie and reached into the popcorn bag she held out to him. "I had blue balls for days afterwards." He colored but his eyes were alight.

"That's because you and I are crazy attracted to each other. It's a different story when it's just work. Josh will be okay. I hope." Sighing, recalling the earlier raw and painful conversation with her husband, Jessie sobered. Leaning back, she took a healthy swig of the liqueur-laced coffee. "Hey, Jacob?"

"Yep?" He, too, was yawning.

"Have you tried to reach Kayla?"

Jacob considered the question before answering. "No. I'm not quite sure how to go about that, if you want the truth."

"Is Casey expecting anything from you?"

"Nope. We ended good. She's cool."

"Can't see her and Kayla gelling well on this tour."

"My bad. Again." Staring at his mug, Jacob wrapped his fingers around it for warmth.

"I think you should go see her. What else do you have going on?"

"Nothing yet. I need to wait to see what Charles wants to do."

"He'll wait out the media storm and then send you out again. Likely start small and go from there."

"Deirdre wanted me to think about a film shooting here in Van but I'm not sure. That might be off the table now anyway." Glum, Jacob paused before letting his eyes drift up to Jessie's. "I'll never be able to make that up to you, Jessie. I still can't believe what I did. That I was capable of hurting you that way. You're a saint to even be here talking to me."

"It's not like you were a stranger, Jacob. Or that I didn't want you to begin with."

"No excuse."

"This is going to sound stupid, babe, but I've had enough unwanted sex in my lifetime to last ten lifetimes. I wasn't afraid of you. I was just afraid for my husband. And mad at myself for leading you on."

"Are you and Josh going to be okay?"

"We'll figure it out."

"You're worried."

"About him. Not how he feels about me, or how I feel about him. We just need to figure out how to meet in the middle and rise above the crap."

"Me being the crap."

"You couldn't be crap if you tried." Winking, Jessie handed him the pop corn bag. "You need to approach Kayla the same way. Let me tell you about these Sawyers. They need a lot of reassurance, but Jacob? Once they come around there's nothing else like it. Loving them, and being loved by them."

"Way to make me feel better."

"That's exactly what I'm doing here, Jacob." Jessie was all smiles now. She leaned forward and tapped him on the knee. "I'm telling you it's worth it, loving a Sawyer. It doesn't discount you and me or you and Talia, bless her heart. It's just different. Honey, you and Kayla could start a family. You'd be around ours so you'd have Dylan back in your life."

Tears pricked at her eyes as Jacob looked at her with a tiny hint of a smile on his face. Hope…

Childish Jessie came back. She almost bounced on the couch as she said, "Josh will see how happy you and Kayla make each other. He'll stop worrying about you and me, and he'll agree with you seeing Dylan again. The nasty media will slow down and get off our cases, Josh's show will be a hit, and everyone will be happy."

"You make it sound so easy, Jess. The whole happy-ever-after thing." Jacob's wry grin reached his eyes and lit up his cheeks, though. He tossed the pop-corn bag back across their laps. Jessie caught it with her spare hand, tucked the mug between her legs to steady it, and reached deep inside for a handful.

"It should be," she told him, munching on the popcorn as she talked. "Don't you think all of us deserve to be happy?"

"I think…I think it's more complicated than that, Jessie. I think there are too many layers of pain and fear to let it be that easy. I wish I was wrong about that." Jacob's voice was low and gruff.

Jessie's popcorn filled hand paused in mid-air. "What are you trying to say?"

"Josh, for one. He's not the same guy you married."

"How can he be? Jacob, he lost everything. He lost himself."

"Well, it worries me that he hasn't seemed to have found himself again yet. I'm not sure that he ever will. I think the part of him you loved died." He paused before adding, "Matt agrees. We talked about this on the way down from my place."

"Seriously, Jacob? So it's like, almost four in the morning and we're alone, so you're going to go down that road?"

"Hey. That's not what I—no. I'm not trying to get into your pants again, Jessie. I just…I'm still your friend, right? I'm still the guy who knows you best, apart from your husband. And I'm worried about you. About him."

"You've never made a secret of that, Jacob." Jessie lowered her tone as she took her last sip of the tasty coffee. Licking her lips to get the last bit of alcoholic sweetness off them, she pointed the mug at Jacob. "And you're no longer the guy who knows me best. You haven't been around a lot, remember? Two years with the beautiful Talia?" She said the last bit with the reverence Talia's memory deserved.

"Uh. Matt, huh? Okay. I guess that actually makes me feel a little better."

"Um…why?" A wet sheen covered Jessie's eyes because she was well aware of what Jacob was trying to tell her, and it was chilling.

"Because, Jessie." Jacob set down his mug and climbed over to Jessie's side of the couch. He took her mug and set it aside, then pulled her down alongside him. Facing her, he said, "You know I've always been afraid Josh would lose it again. Well, he did, at the Grammys. He's barely speaking to you right now, and you told me he's asked you not to go out to the ranch next weekend. I'm glad you've got someone on your side ready to pick up the pieces, that's all. Matt's been picking up your pieces for a lot of years now. I know he'll be there for you."

Jessie was shaking her head from side to side. "This is what you don't get, Jacob. Josh and I said vows to each other. It doesn't matter how low he goes or how bad he cracks. Yeah, I'm gonna get mad sometimes—I was pissed at him at the Grammys. But I love him. I will never give up on him even if he…

even if it happens like before, when I went to New York. He is, and always will be, the love of my life. I'm willing to give him his space now, after him just finding out about Florida, because I know he needs it. But Jacob? Not for long. Not for long."

Uncertain, she blinked and looked away from the piercing blue eyes that often, in the past, sank her. When she met Jacob's gaze again, his eyebrows were raised in curiosity.

"What?" he asked.

"I told him… at the Grammys, I told Josh…that I might leave him. But I was just scared, and angry. I could never leave him. Ever. I didn't want to the first time."

Softening, Jacob touched her cheek. He spoke quietly. "God, Jess, what I would give to have that kind of love from you. The forever kind."

Jessie was leaning on one elbow now, facing him. "I'm not that great a prize, Ryan. Obviously. Look how messed up Josh is over me. But that doesn't mean I'll let him go easy if he decides to bolt. And," she tapped him on the arm, "you should go after Kayla with the same kind of love and hope. Surprise her at one of the tour stops and get her back."

"Fine," Jacob grumped, with a small half-smile. "I'll try. But Jessie?" Wrapping his arms around her, Jacob pulled his old girl close and breathed in the lavender of her hair. He yawned. "I'm still glad you have Matt around to watch out for you."

"Oh, Lordy," he heard her whisper as she melted into him and closed her eyes. "I am too, Jacob. And I am glad that you have me. I'm gonna keep an eye on you, babe. You are not alone. Ever."

"Luv u, kid. Now be quiet and let me get some shuteye before the band gets here at eight."

Laughing, Jessie snuggled into Jacob's arms and fell asleep with the comfort of feeling his body close to her in a way that was neither threatening nor consumed with desire, which would have been uncomfortable and awkward for both. It wasn't as if the fire was out; their fire would never be completely extinguished. Instead, it was burning at a low, safe level that both hoped they could trust, and which they were trying to put aside for the benefit of others.

When Matt arrived at six to make use of the Keating gym, which was on a lower floor, he couldn't resist peeking in at them to see how the night was going. All the way up in the elevator he told himself it was stupid to check in because of Jacob and Jessie's shared history, although he wasn't worried about violence because he, too, was aware Jacob was not the same broken man from that fateful Florida day. Simply, he just didn't want to find the two singers in some kind of compromised position.

Pushing the door to the studio open, Matt wasn't surprised to find it quiet. Even these two superstars would recognize the need to slow down and take a break before the onslaught of another very full day. Glancing to the dimly lit couch, he had to pause and consider what he found—two old lovers, fully dressed, wrapped up in each other's arms offering a kind of trusted comfort and closeness that was sorely needed in each of their lives.

Unable to help himself, Matt wished he was the one holding Jessie. But he sighed and backed out of the space knowing that Jacob now had one up on him. Jacob could recline in Jessie's arms without lust, without the fear that came with strong desire based on enduring love. It had been a hard, hard lesson for Jacob, to learn to let go, and it had ended with the crossing of a very violent, dark line.

Matt wasn't there yet, at the letting go part. His love for Jessie was earned over many years of devotion and care, and it had yet to be consummated.

He had no idea of the earlier conversation between Jacob and Jessie, about Jacob's relief that Matt would be there for Jessie should Josh hit rock bottom again. If he had, he would have blushed and backed away quicker. Matt didn't need to hear that wish expressed. To him it was a given. He would be there for Jessie always. There was something about being needed, about having a place where he knew he fit. It was just too bad it hurt so much to be there.

Chapter Three

Later, Charles and Matt stood in the studio and watched their musicians assemble. Jessie had literally skipped down the hallway earlier to get them. "Get the rest of the staff too," she directed them. "This one's worth taking a break for."

They'd heard that before. Stupid grins were plastered on both Matt's and Charles' faces as they knocked on doors all the way down the long hallway and called to the Keating staff to join them in the studio. It was one p.m. and the new song had been fine-tuned and worked until it was presentation ready. With Jacob's and Jessie's yawns as evidence, this tune had been put through the grinder.

Magda even joined them, locking the front glass door and taping a note to it stating that she'd be 'back in ten.'

The first clue Charles and Matt had that this song would be different was Jessie's cat-ate-the-canary grin and the electric guitar she hoisted over her shoulder, a rarity for her as, most times, she favored either singing with the Gibson or just with Jacob's accompaniment.

Shrugging, fatigued eyes alight, she told them, "We wanted to change things up. *Sacred Peace* has dark moments that need a deeper energy than some of our usual stuff. We rounded this tune out with the help of everyone in the band. So it's not just ours. We hope you'll like it."

Her wide smile in Jacob's direction almost stopped Charles' heart for the second time. For one thing, Charles was still pissed at having found Jacob in his building, period, much less in his studio, when he got to work that morning. But here was Jessie, the victim of the boy's crime, not in any way being a doormat to Jacob's wants and needs, but instead radiating understanding, light and forgiveness.

"I constantly learn from her." Glancing over at Matt, who was also shaking his head at this woman in front of him—Jessie was now starting to lead the band in by finger picking a heavy electric melody on the guitar—Charles frowned. "Matt, why is Jessie always so happy when this boy is by her side?"

"You ought to know by now, Charles," Matt said agreeably, "that it's not just the boy. It's creating and playing the music that does this to her."

The room quickly got too loud for Charles to attempt a response. Putting his producer hat on, he tilted his head and deconstructed, in his mind, the song as it was being played, tweaking it here and there and adding visuals from the planned production design and storyline of the series to see where the song might fit.

Escalating gradually, the piece was almost a metal ballad. After about thirty seconds, Jacob came in with lead guitar, resting it against his thigh as he bent his knee for support and picked out the right notes to give the tune height and depth and a perfectly saturated melody made up of the right kind of pain to match Jessie's lyrics. The small, assembled crowd quickly determined the song was a telling of how Jessie felt about her place in the world watching a man she loved struggle in his own harsh reality.

As usual, Jessie left nothing behind when she sang. She gave the world everything she had to give, without compromise or fear of judgment, and Jacob echoed her intent in his guitar playing, which was at times so thrilling and perfect that Charles had to close his eyes and lift his face to the sky beyond the ceiling of their richly tapestried, sound insulated studio. Even Matt held his breath as Jacob's guitar sang in pitched precision, and while Jessie strummed the rhythm and poured her soul out next to him.

As the rock ballad eased down from its climax into a fine-tuned well-rehearsed conclusion, Matt just stared at Jessie in wonder. She did what she always did, coming out of the song from some far away place where it had taken her and held her captive, but she added a nervous side step as she let go of the guitar and let it swing at her hips, and she wiped her bare arm across her forehead to absorb some of the sweat the song's heated energy drew from her body.

After holding an extended final note that had the gathered folks cheering and the drummer throwing both sticks jubilantly in the air, Jacob was at Jessie's side in a second. Like he often did after they played a song together, he whispered something in her ear that made Jessie laugh and, as she took off her guitar, she held it aloft and reached for him, brushing her lips against his in friendship as old intimacies took hold.

Matt and Charles both sobered at that, but pushed it aside as the overpowering effect of what they'd just heard took priority.

Jessie grabbed Jacob's hand and turned to the band. "We are one helluva team," she told them, leaving them wondering whether she meant all of them or just her and Jacob. "What d'ya think?" she asked Charles, swinging back around to him all sweet and excited and childlike.

Stepping forward, Charles pocketed one hand in his grey Armani pants and allowed a hint of a smile to sneak out of a corner of his lips. "I think I'm okay with Jacob hanging out here for the next few weeks as long as you're okay with it," he said. "But in the light of day, and between the hours of eight and eight. Earlier if possible. I fell asleep before Dylan did last night. It wasn't pretty when I woke up. I can only take so much crayon art on my walls."

"We have that chalkboard wall for him, Charles…" Sobering, Jessie drifted off. "Unless…"

"We were in my office. At least he chose a blue crayon."

"He's missing his daddy," she whispered, as musicians and staff started to leave the studio quietly with thumbs up signs pointed in Jessie and Jacob's direction.

Both Jacob and Matt recoiled at Jessie's comment and, when she realized what she'd said, Jessie gasped and looked over at Jacob. "Oh, shit," she moaned. "Sorry, babe. You know what I mean."

"I know *who* you mean," Jacob huffed, but after the high of hanging out and songwriting with Jessie all night, he wasn't in the mood to be sentimental. He was in problem solving mode. Reaching out a hand to her, he grasped her fingers and said, "Come on. Let's go see the kids for a few hours. We'll come back here later and start on song number two." Letting her fingers drift out of his grasp, Jacob moved away and picked up his guitar from the nearby stand where he'd left it.

Ducking her head, Jessie shoved her thumbs in the back pockets of her jeans and nodded. "Kay," she said, and aimed her baby blues at Matt. "You in?"

"Jessie…" Unsure, Charles shook his head.

"He has the right to see his son." Facing him, she sighed heavily. "We don't need to tell Josh everything. Do we?"

"You're forgetting that your children all know how to talk, Jessie. Including Dylan, in his own baby way."

"The older two are at school. Dylan will forget by the time he talks to Josh. And maybe I can calm Josh down by the time he clues in."

"Jesus, you." The raw hostility in Matt's voice took Jessie by surprise.

"Matt?" she asked him, tweaking her eyebrows into curious curves.

"Your ego, Jessie. You need to park it and stop doing everything backwards. It's like you think there are no repercussions to your actions. You ignore the wishes of people who love you by barging ahead and doing things you know will hurt them, then you wonder why you have a mess to clean up afterwards."

He looked over at Jacob, who had put his guitar away in its case and was sauntering over to them with both hands shoved nervously in his jeans pockets. To him, Matt said, "I know you want to see Dylan, Jacob. Of course you do. But we need to do this the right way. With Josh on board first."

The look on Jessie's face was disconcerting to Matt when he glanced back over at her. She was eyeing him with a twist to her lips and confusion in her eyes that, once he figured out what she was thinking, had Matt frown and glare back at her. He'd seen that look before.

"No," he said, the word clearly floating up to cyberspace as she ignored it with a slight toss of her curls.

"Matt," she drawled, "I'm tired. Jacob's tired. He did me a huge favor coming over here and working out this song with me. Now, the studio's in capable hands. After their break these guys can lay some tracks while Jacob and I take our little break. The least I can do is thank Jacob by letting him see his son. And yes, I will deal with the fallout the second my husband actually agrees to see me again."

"And this will help. Going behind Josh's back, I mean."

Tears stung Jessie's eyes as she stared hard at her friend. "Must I remind you that you are my security, Matt? And my driver? You're not my goddamned conscience."

Leaning towards her, Matt spoke nose to nose. Stiffening, he started to tremble in anger. Jessie had to stifle a flicker of desire when she inadvertently reached out her hand and let it rest against his hard stomach. It didn't help when his musky aftershave caught her nostrils. Swallowing, she closed her eyes for a second and blinked them open as Matt spoke, hot fire flashing in pink flushed dots on his cheeks.

"Jessie?" he bristled. "How about I just say fuck—you and we call this little interchange even, okay? Unless you want me walking out of here and never coming back."

"Don't threaten me, Matt. Don't you dare fucking threaten me."

If he could have, Matt would have given her a shove and cursed his way out the door, but as it was, he simply stuck to the cursing. Jessie caught the word, "princess," but the rest of his rant was elusive to her ears. She did, however, grasp his message quite clearly as he stormed out.

"Jesus Christ," she exclaimed after he left, swinging around to Jacob, who was rather coolly watching her. "I get so fucking tired of everyone weighing in on my life. It's my goddamned life!"

"Lover's spat?" Jacob's quiet words were tinged with something akin to regret and longing.

"What? Jesus, Jacob, no! Don't start that rumor. Please! Matt just occasionally forgets his place."

Charles was still in the room, watching with cautionary interest. He spoke, his voice surprising Jessie, who had rather forgotten he was even there, since the band and recording engineers had all vacated the space and gone on break. Charles, too, was careful, subdued. "We're going to lose him, Jessie," he said blankly.

"What? Who, Matt? Or are you talking about Josh?"

"Both, the way you're going about things," he told her, and looked over at Jacob to apologize. "I'm sorry, Jacob. I'm with Matt on this one. Maybe you should try reaching out to Josh to see if you can persuade him to let you see Dylan on the up and up. He's likely cooled down a bit by now." With a clear layer of disappointment just before he swung open the studio door to seek out Matt, to the astounded Jessie he added, "You owe Matt an apology. Preferably now." The door settled into an open position behind him.

"Oh, for Christ's sake," she muttered, hanging her head. "I'm sorry, Jacob."

He pointed to the door. "Umm, not me," he said. "I had no real illusions about seeing Dylan today. It was just wishful thinking. It's Matt you need to apologize to."

"Dylan's your son. This isn't fair. Fucking Josh." Crossing her arms, Jessie leaned back against the sound booth and swiped at a frustrated tear.

Softening, Jacob lifted a large curl and pushed it tenderly behind her ear. Jessie took his hand and brushed her lips against the back of it.

"It's okay," he said with a small smile. "I just have two Sawyers to win over, that's all. Maybe winning the girl will earn me the guy. And then I'll have access to the little guy again."

"I guess it's good that you at least want to see Dylan," she sniffed. "For a while you didn't."

"You can thank Kayla for the new me," Jacob grinned. "I like your happy ending from last night, Jess. I can see the possibilities now. I couldn't before. But," he tapped her lightly on the arm, "you need to win your Sawyer back over one of these days too. And Matt, in the immediate future." Holding out his baby finger, he teased her with their old standby. "Pinky swear," he suggested, offering her his finger. "Pinky swear that we will win back our Sawyers and make this work somehow. For everyone."

"It was Matt," she said, hooking Jacob's pinky in her own and vigorously shaking it. At his knitted eyebrows she added, "Who Charles was talking about. He really does have to go, Jacob. I'm not going to have my rock much longer."

"It's that serious?" Jacob shifted his feet and tenderly brushed the curl back again. It was as unruly as its owner.

"I'm lonely," she whispered, hooking her fingers behind his belt. "And you're off the market."

Electric desire, elusive during the long night of working together and even lying down and sleeping arm in arm, shattered Jacob's body the second Jessie's eyes searched his, as if the combination of the look, the fingers hooking themselves behind his belt, and the admitted sadness, all buoyed by exhaustion and creative success in the incredible composition they wrote and performed together, had sparked it.

Slowly, Jacob removed Jessie's hands from his belt and, swallowing past new cobwebs in his throat, he stepped back and shook his head from side to side. "No." It was barely even a murmur. "You play this game, Jessie. I don't even know if you realize you do it. No wonder Josh is such a fucking mess." There was a blue blaze in Jacob's eyes now, as if the lust Jessie telegraphed to him had landed there and was burning brightly. Jacob pointed to himself. "With me, with Matt…do you know what I think sometimes? About you?"

Jessie's answer was a finger that she ran over her top and then bottom lip. Defiant, she faced him and waited for him to hurt her. The confused look on Jacob's face was one she knew well, his usual puppy dog sorrow; it was accented by an adorable body in tight black jeans and a grey T-shirt that she loved and missed and wanted to hold against her.

"I think," he started, "that you started young and now you can't stop. You've learned to substitute your body for love. You think I'll love you more if you give yourself to me. As if your body's some key you need to turn in order to get in."

"That's nice, Jacob," she managed, trying unsuccessfully not to have to swipe at another tear. "Thanks for reminding me of my lovely and yet very colorful past."

"Don't you think that's part of the attraction for us?" he questioned cruelly. "For me and Matt? Knowing your past?"

"The pictures," she breathed.

"Videos," he said quietly. Knowingly. "I found some. I've seen a few. I recognized you."

"You must have looked closely," she responded, not at all surprised that at least some of the old films had made their way into cyberspace. Her words were swollen with hurt at Caryn or Eric for likely placing them there and lying about it, and Jacob for seeking them out. "I suppose there were a few body parts you recognized."

"You think Matt hasn't found the movies too? Maybe even Charles?"

"Who the hell do you think you are, Jacob? We just created an amazing song together. I don't know why you would want to do this to me when we're finally becoming friends again."

"Because I am your friend, Jessie," he proclaimed. "I'm your friend, not your lover anymore. But I'm a red-blooded male who likes sex, as do most guys I know. As I'm sure Matt does. You tease and you touch—you're always holding my hand, or his. I've seen you. Even in front of Josh, you and I always kissed before we went on stage, long before we ever got together in New York. It's like you got so used to touching and being touched that you no longer realize where the line in the sand is drawn. I've got news for you. It was likely cute when you were a kid, and maybe you're trying to substitute us for your dad, on some crazy weird level, but Jess?" Jacob shook his head again. "Unless you're planning to go to bed with me again, of your own free will, or with Matt, it needs to stop. The touching. The playfulness. It needs to stop. And I'm saying this because I crossed that line with you myself. It started on Boxing Day in the nursery at La Casa and it spiraled out of control in Florida. And I can see that Matt's struggling with it too."

"I don't understand." Like a scared child awaiting punishment, Jessie crossed her arms over her chest and widened her stance. "What are you trying to say, Jacob? Just spit it out."

"I'm saying back off, Jessie. Back off from me, at least in terms of your blatant 'poor me, I'm lonely' overtures. And back the fuck off from Matt before you break his heart too, or before he abandons you in favor of being with a woman he can actually have. Because guess what, kid? I'm lonely too. And Matt's lonely. We're all fucking lonely. And Josh? With a woman like you in his life? One who craves touch the way you do? I'll bet the loneliest guy of all is your husband."

With that, Jacob left the studio. As the door *shuffed* behind him, Jessie was left in the semi-darkness. Bowing her head, she sank to the ground and pressed the heels of her palms into her eyes. Anything to shove the pain of Jacob's truths back inside.

Outside in the hallway, Jacob paused after he left the studio. Alone, Matt was leaning against the wall, rolling an unlit cigarette around and around between his thumb and forefinger.

"I can't leave her," he mumbled to Jacob while he stared at the unlit smoke. "You're already out the door and, like we said on the way down here yesterday,

I agree that a good solid chunk of Josh's soul that died when Jessie and the kids disappeared is never coming back. A part of him died that day and by all accounts I don't see it being reborn." Stricken, he looked over at Jacob. "How can I leave her?"

"You heard," Jacob muttered, planting both hands on his hips.

"Door was open." Matt placed the cigarette between his lips and savored the taste. The anticipation.

"It's true." Jacob faced Matt and contemplated what he'd just said to the mother of his son. "She's always touching you, in those, you know, kind of erotic places. Grabbing your belt, or laying a hand on your stomach when she talks to you. Then she turns an ankle over and puffs up her chest and loses herself in your eyes. Like she's capturing you. Roping you in. She used to do that to me too, back when we were on *Mystic Nights*. It drove me around the bend." Looking away, he added, "It drives me around the bend. Makes it too damn easy to touch her back, or to…start something, you know?"

"Charles has a few theories about that." Matt glanced over to the studio door to make sure it was closed. It was a double door meant to block out—or lock in—sound, so once it was closed Matt was certain Jessie could not hear. He continued. "She lost a lot of her childhood the day her father died. She was twelve. So Charles figures she's hung on to a lot of those childish mannerisms, the holding hands part anyway, as a way of holding onto her father, I guess."

"That's not a stretch, Matt. I know that. I just said that inside."

"She doesn't mean for it to be sexual. We just take it that way."

"Because of her past. The porn films."

"Erotica, she would say. Not hard core porn."

"Whatever." A thought crossed Jacob's mind. "Have you seen them? Those old films?"

Coloring, Matt shifted his gaze to the floor. "No. And out of respect for Jessie I don't intend to."

"She went under her mother's name. Emily Wheeler. I found a few late one night after smoking some good weed. Years ago now, back when we were doing *Mystic Nights* and Josh had looked up that Caryn chick. It didn't do me any good. We used to fight a lot then. We were doing love scenes on the show and believe me, that didn't help our case any."

"I won't be looking them up, Jacob. The photographs were enough. The look in her eyes…it was like seeing inside her soul."

Jacob paused and, apart from the high-heeled footsteps of Magda moving towards them with a stack of paper in her hand, and a happy buzz from the photocopy room she'd just left, the hallway was relatively quiet.

"You know, Matt? I'm hoping you don't leave her. But I'm also hoping it's because I knocked some sense into her." He started moving away, towards Charles' office. Jacob had to sort out a proper truce with the man who controlled his career so he could figure out his future. So he could sort out when and how he would try to see Kayla. "Because this lonely thing can get a guy and a gal into trouble they don't need. The kind of trouble that can sink a guy. Or a gal."

Tossing a last look over his shoulder towards Matt, Jacob was sorry to see how bent over and tired the man appeared. He stopped. "You okay, Matt?"

"Not even close," Matt sighed. "I need to find me a good woman. Maybe we should go back down south."

"Ah. Empty, meaningless sex." Jacob's voice got quiet as, nearby, the heavy door to the studio was slowly opened. "All that gets a man is more lonely," he said almost inaudibly. "Been there, done that. Bought that T-shirt. Wait for me, will you Matt? I need to make my peace with the old man."

Slinking into the hallway, Jessie gave Jacob's back a third finger salute before she turned to Matt and drew up her shoulders. Spying the unlit smoke between his lips, she yanked it out and held it up to him. "Glad to see I am nothing but a harbinger of peace and good health for all of my male friends," she wisecracked lightly, although the remark was sodden through with the old, familiar self-loathing.

Matt recognized her tone immediately. Straightening against the wall, he challenged her. "It's not lit. No harm will come to me by this cigarette."

"Ah," Jessie said, putting the smoke between her own lips and twisting around to sidle off towards the kitchen, where an accessible outdoor deck was often used for employees who needed either fresh air or a smoke. "Coming?" Wheeling back around so she faced him, albeit walking backwards the whole time, Jessie added, "It's just one time, Matt. One smoke."

"One time, huh?" he muttered, using his foot to shove himself away from the wall so he could propel himself into some kind of forward motion and follow her.

Outside, leaning against the rail above the windscreen, Jessie shivered. "Guess my tank top isn't quite warm enough for Vancouver's rainy grey days," she said. "Just for hot studio work."

In silence, Matt took off his jacket—his old standby today, a blue linen blazer—and wrapped it around Jessie. He let his hands linger on her shoulders so he could massage her and try to warm her up.

"For the record," she spoke quietly as she lit up the smoke with a lighter she'd grabbed from the kitchen on the way through, "this is you touching me. Not the other way around. Jacob's an ass," she sulked, and took a long, slow drag.

"Jacob's right on some counts." Taking the cigarette from her, Matt pivoted around and leaned against the windscreen so he could sideways-face Jessie as he smoked.

"Which counts?" she asked hotly. "Or do I really want to know?"

"Jessie, you can be a righteous spoiled bitch when you want to be. And I don't mind telling you that. But you've also got this power that over the years I had decided comes from your music. It wasn't until recently I determined that it's also the whole wild enigma relating to your past."

"Ah. Matt speaks his mind. Jessie fucking shuts up and sinks into a hole in the ground. Or vaults over this windscreen and flies to the city street below."

"Can you cut the dramatics?" Exhaling slowly, Matt turned a little more sideways, took another drag, and handed the smoke back to the incensed superstar at his side. "Jessie, when it all comes down to it, I suppose it doesn't matter where your power over me comes from. I just know it's there. And it scares the hell out of me."

"Well, Matt, if it helps, it scares the hell out of me too." Inhaling deeply, she blew a succession of smoke circles. The white wisps disappeared into the early afternoon and floated off somewhere towards the leafy green oasis of nearby Stanley Park to the northwest. "You have power too, you know," she said with a calculated coolness dragged up from years of self-preservation. "Hence my nasty shot at you back in the studio." She ducked her head and brushed the toe of her boot against the bottom rail. "I'm sorry, Matt. That was super shitty of me."

"It was up there," he agreed, "with some of your better daggers over the years."

"There haven't been too many, though, right? And isn't it that whole thing like, lash out at your friends and family because they're the ones that can take it?"

Soundless, he studied her boot and the muscled, shapely leg that was moving it.

Jessie stopped the movement and peeked over at him. She handed him back the smoke, and he finished it and stubbed it out in a nearby receptacle.

"Matt?" Jessie asked quietly, turning her face towards him.

Facing her, he put both hands on his hips and drew up the courage to tell her what he thought she needed to hear. "That's the thing, Jessie," he said. "I can't take it anymore. I'm losing my mind over here. You're pissing away your marriage and holding my hand and touching my stomach and letting me spend time with your kids and it's driving me crazy."

"Ahhhh," she lamented, twisting fully around to face him. "Seems all my friends are out to get me today. All I need now is a nice bright phone call from my depressed husband, the one man I am apparently allowed to touch and to sex into oblivion but who, at the moment, is not particularly interested in either marital pursuit. Then this miserable long fucking day will be complete."

"Look, I met a woman at Elysian Coffee last week. I'll give her a call. I'll take a few days off. Maybe that will cool me off a bit."

A tiny light flicked on in Jessie's eyes but it was bright and moist. "You don't want to go. To leave me, I mean."

"No. I don't."

Jessie bit her bottom lip and pondered this man who stood before her in a body hugging white button down shirt that clearly showed off his hard work at the gym, and muscled forearms that she ached to touch.

"Huh. Jacob and his theories," she declared staunchly. "We will finish this one day, Matt. You and me. You know how I know?"

Floored, Matt was speechless. "I won't go there with you." The words had emerged quickly, too quickly, and were accented with a shuffled movement that did nothing to erase the sizzling jolt of power that stunned Matt for the ache it left behind.

"Oh, yes you will," Jessie told him with a sudden snap of her fingers. "Like this. So fast. And the reason I know is because in your head…" She started to brush by him but stopped when they were face to face. "In your head you're already there. And if y'all think my past gives me some kind of electric dominion over men, then I can also tell you it gives me experience. And in my experience, Matt, men who fantasize about it are the easiest prey."

Changing her tune, her eyes flashed with pain.

She was the old Jessie again, the one hurt by what everyone thought about her. "Look at you," she scolded in his general direction. "You stand there all righteous and tell me you won't go where I was forced to go with men against my will many times. Deuce McCall, and my stepfather, remember? And where I occasionally had to go in order to make money in the hope that one day I could leave the Downtown Eastside. I can see in your eyes, Matt, that you are no different than anyone else. Than Jacob or Charlie or Josh or even Charles or anyone who has had his share of women at times when they probably shouldn't have. Who watch porn and who hire young girls to satisfy their needs. You were faithful to Julie? I sure as hell hope so, physically at least. In your head?" She shook her head vehemently. "I doubt it. Was it me you dreamed about touching all these years? Did you go hunting for my films?"

"Jessie," he pleaded, "stop this. You're taking what Jacob said too far." In his heart, Matt was sickened because he'd heard Charles say the very same things he and Jacob had agreed about her, that Jessie's past set her apart. That it made her more able and willing to cross the line in the dirt that married people were not supposed to cross.

But what sickened Matt even more was that he wanted her to.

He couldn't look her in the eye.

"Stick to the films, Matt," she whispered angrily now, sparks flashing across her eyes like fireworks. "I'll do my part. I'll stop touching you. I'll start right now. In fact, I'll even stop speaking to you, and I'll start riding in the back of the Audi again. You all wondered why I was so quiet when Charles and Dee first started pimping me out to make them a fortune? Because I didn't trust anybody, that's why. None of you. No men, and no women. I thought I could for a while, but I guess I was wrong."

She started to move past him but Matt's voice, spoken to the wind in front of him, stopped her.

"So you've got your theory for why I want you, Jessie." Wheeling slowly around, he kept his hands staunchly on his hips while she waited for him to continue. "But what you've failed to do is explain why you want me back. Or are we going to use your past as an excuse for that too?"

Her lips parted in confusion. But she didn't deny the ache to take comfort in the arms of this man, whose pockets she practically lived out of. Whose safe presence in her life had evolved and changed into something that crackled and threatened with the seemingly constant upheaval of her life and marriage. "That's Jacob's theory. It's not mine," she replied softly. "Take that as you will, Matt."

And she swept back into the kitchen, smiled brightly at Magda as she passed, and left the building on her own, forgetting that she had Matt's blazer on but grateful for the bit of warmth it offered as the heavens opened and a cold, wet rain soaked her. Jessie crossed Robson Street, caught a bus to North Vancouver, and got herself anonymously to La Casa before the others even realized she'd completely ducked out on them.

That evening was a quiet one at La Casa. The kids stayed there overnight and Jessie went home after her oldest, Emily-Grace, drifted off to sleep, her hand tucked in her grandmother's elegant fingers. Tomorrow would be another long day. Tomorrow Jessie would lay the vocals for the new song, and start working on another.

She would start at eight a.m.

Normal working hours.

A welcome coup for a reformed whore.

Chapter Four

The first day of shooting *Sacred Peace* set a precedent for the early part of the series. Six hours after their 7 a.m. call time, cast and crew took lunch as per union guidelines. That was nothing new. They'd been served 'substantials'—western sandwiches, today—part way through the morning to tide them over, plus there was a fully stocked craft table and breakfast for those who wanted more sustenance, so waiting six hours for a big sit down meal was all well and good.

The precedent was Josh's thing. Head down, at lunch he took his tray and a bottle of water and went back to his cast trailer for a solitary meal.

Charlie was in the lunch line behind Shanda. Together, they watched Josh weave between two hungry grips that were flirting with a woman from wardrobe, and make his way out of the expansive lunchroom alone.

As she turned back from watching Josh go, Shanda caught Charlie's concerned gaze. "He's quite the loner," she said. "With the exception of questioning the director, he never said a word on set."

"He'll be okay when Jessie gets here." Charlie handed her a tray and they started to move through the buffet line.

"When's she coming?"

"Not sure. She's recording our soundtrack. I suppose we'll have to see how long that takes." Charlie was stretching the truth but it didn't concern him. Part of Shanda's success and 'buy-in' for the series was partly dependent on her relationship with her main co-star.

Taking a right turn, Shanda posed a question that had been dancing around her mind. "Why didn't you take the lead, Charlie? It's your show. Why'd you take a supporting role and give the lead to Josh?"

"You see him this morning?" Licking his fingers because he'd inadvertently stuck a finger in his pasta sauce, Charlie raised his eyebrows at Shanda. "He's brilliant."

"Well, yeah. As an actor, he makes interesting choices. Little things like turning his chair around and suggesting he start with his back to the camera? Stuff like that makes him compelling, sets him apart, I guess."

"Shanda…Josh also has the capacity to connect deeper emotionally than some of us do. I suppose you could say it's part of his charm."

"Charm?" Raising her eyebrows, she followed Charlie to a table. As she set down her tray and dropped into a seat, she added, reprimanding him slightly, "Is that what they're calling it these days? That kind of intensity, I mean. That's an odd choice of word for him."

Charlie dug into his lasagna. "You don't think he's charming?"

Pointing her fork at him, Shanda replied, "You're charming. He's… disconcerting."

"Cut him some slack, Shanda."

"I just mean I haven't got him figured out yet. And I'd kind of like to have him figured out by the time we have to shoot our first love scene."

"That's not much of a love scene." A sly smile illuminated the truth. "It's more like a lust scene. I should know. I asked the writers to give it another pass to make it more…compelling."

"Compelling?" Scrunching up her cute, perky nose, Shanda paused, her fork halfway to her mouth. "Would you care to illuminate me? I have yet to see that script."

"You won't for another two weeks. It's in episode three."

"Charlie. Talk. Please."

Sitting back, Charlie pondered the attractive blonde he, Charles and Jonathon had agreed would play best across from Josh in *Sacred Peace*. Who would look good on screen next to Josh, and who could handle the story's intensity. "It's kinda hot and heavy," he confessed.

"Oh, great." Shanda's fork clattered to her tray and she covered her eyes. "I just love modern television." Peeking between her fingers at him, she studied Charlie carefully. "His wife will be okay with this, right?"

A leaden cloud washed over Charlie's pretty boy looks. "Josh has done lots of sex scenes. So has Jessie."

"But they're on the outs. Because of what happened with Jacob Ryan."

Charlie hesitated before speaking. But this girl seemed trustworthy and was certainly well liked in the industry. He leaned forward and scooped up another bite of his lunch before he spoke again. "They're on the outs to a point. Josh is angry. He's trying to figure out where he fits with her. She's not the easiest person—"

Cutting him off, Shanda jumped his line with, "Oh, I thought Jessie Wheeler was super easygoing. I've never heard a bad thing about her, really. Well," she shrugged, "not in the film world, I mean. The, um, main film world. Or in the TV world, like with *Drifters, Mystic Nights...*" She let her thoughts drift off.

"She is. She's great to work with. That's not what I meant. I just mean that she can be stubborn, childish, impulsive. Disrespectful of the rules established for her safety, that kind of thing."

"Oh. Oh, I suppose. At her level, yes, she'd have to be careful, but you'd think after what's happened to her..."

"She got a bit better for a while but she gets tired of the whole security thing."

"Ok. All right. Well," Shanda responded amicably, "I hope they get their shit sorted out or this is going to be a long six months."

"You have a guy in your life, Shanda?" Charlie asked carefully.

"No, I do not. Nor do I have a girl. Although I prefer the former. But don't worry, Charlie, Josh isn't my type, nor is it my style to swoop in and try to rescue sexy men with damaged egos. I seriously just want to make a mind-blowing series, and my chemistry with Josh is going to have to be a part of that. Me going to set nervous and scared is going to show on camera. I should talk to a producer about that—well, hey!" She poked him in the arm with her fork. "Seems to me I just did!"

"Ouch. Easy. Down, girl." Holding his fork out to Shanda, Charlie raised an eyebrow as if he wanted to challenge her to a sword-fight. Lifting her fork higher as a truce, Shanda half-smiled and backed off. "Fine," Charlie grinned. "I'll talk to my buddy Josh."

"Tell him he and I can go for coffee or something. We need to get to know each other at least a little bit. I need to see just how angry he is so I can figure out what buttons I can push on camera without getting my head knocked off."

With that, she forked in the last bit of her salad, finished off her vegetarian lasagna, and stood. "Sooner the better, Charlie, if you don't mind."

"I'm on it," he assured her. A thousand gloomy thoughts were vaulting around his mind, so Charlie sat for a while longer after Shanda vacated the chair opposite. Grim, he finally rose and took his tray off to the assigned deposit area, where a member of the lunch crew took it from him and chastised him for not eating his whole meal.

"Be nice to actually be treated like the boss," he grumped. "This set's already way too casual."

Shanda's insistence that he talk to Josh rankled him. Josh was a personal friend whose struggles Charlie knew well; whose struggles Charlie often faced alongside him. Apart from a few crazy years, like when Charlie himself was Jessie's partner, or just after Wes Sawyer shot his misguided child porn video that featured a reluctant Josh, the guys had been friends since grade school. It would be easier to look into those angry, sad eyes and tell the guy to just go home to Vancouver and make friends with his wife, than try to be Josh's boss and tell him to get his shit together because his co-star was terrified of him.

Crossing the courtyard outside the sound stage, Charlie rapped on Josh's trailer door. The airy screen door was closed but the outer door was clamped back against the trailer. "Good sign," Charlie muttered as he heard Josh mumble, "S'open."

Swinging open the screen door, Charlie hopped up the metal steps and faced his friend inside. He swung himself into the bench seat opposite Josh at the trailer's small dining table.

Josh sat back and regarded him with calm apprehension.

"How'd you feel about your first morning?" Charlie started.

Shrugging, Josh pushed a script to his left, where it rested by his lunch tray. He'd been going over the next scene. "Fine. You?"

Charlie jumped right in. "How'd you like working with Shanda?"

"She's okay." Josh focused harder on his buddy. His eyes narrowed. "Why?"

"Don't get defensive, Sawyer."

"What's up, Charlie? I know you."

Grabbing a pencil from where it lay on top of Josh's script, Charlie stared at it while he twisted it around his fingers. "Let's just say she's concerned."

Throwing up his arms, Josh recoiled. "Everybody's concerned. It's me, remember? Everybody's walking on eggshells around me. The guy at craft service this morning, that Newfoundlander, what's his name?"

"Greg."

"Yeah, Greg. The skinny guy. He was shaking so hard when he gave me my eggs and bacon I thought he was gonna drop the whole plate."

Charlie leaned back and guffawed loudly. "Because you're Josh Sawyer, that's why. An Oscar winning actor. Of course he's terrified of you!"

"He's scared I'm going to complain that the eggs were runny or something, and beat the shit out of him."

"Were they?"

"Were they what?"

"Runny."

"Were what runny?"

"The eggs! Get with the program, Sawyer." Grinning, Charlie grabbed Josh's script and absently studied it. After a moment, he let it fall to the table. Looking up, he met Josh's eyes. A serious gaze settled over him.

"No. The eggs were fine."

"Good. I wouldn't want to have to fire the guy. Every show needs a Newfoundlander on it to manage the social life of the cast and crew."

Letting one corner of his lip turn up at that, Josh picked up the script and tossed it at his friend. "So why are you really here, Charlie?"

"Truth?"

"Truth."

"Shanda. You know women, they worry about worrying. Well, she's already freaking out about the love scene in episode three. She wants to get to know you before it comes up, for her comfort level or some crap, she said. Might help if you ate lunch with us and stuff. Little things."

"Love scene, huh?"

"Yep. We've both done those. Never fun, uncomfortable as hell, but no big deal. I don't think she's done a lot of them."

"What, they didn't have sex in space? On her last show?"

Skirting that comment, Charlie offered, "She'd just feel more comfortable, I think, if she felt you were accessible. Someone she can relax around."

"Fine. I'll talk to her."

"Take her out for coffee or something, Josh. Spend some time with her."

Twisting sideways, Josh focused his gaze on a spot on the floor. He rifled his fingers through his hair before absently scratching his chin with his thumb and forefinger. Without looking up at Charlie he said, "She single?"

The hairs on the back of Charlie's neck stood up. Straightening, he regarded Josh carefully. "Not that it matters to you, but yes. She's single."

"I just kind of wish she wasn't, that's all."

"You have to work with her for a long time, Josh." Charlie's voice was cautious in a friendly sort of way. "You need to get your wife out here, buddy. You need some lovin.'"

"I'm not Jessie." The words were raspy. When Josh finally looked up at Charlie, he was somewhat defiant. "I'm not planning to cheat on my partner."

"Was that dig at Jessie really necessary, Josh? Really? And if you aren't planning to step out on her, why do you care if Shanda is or is not single?"

"I suppose I can have a little fun. On set, I mean."

Charlie's intelligent eyes darkened. "No," he said. "Don't do anything stupid. Not on my show."

"Charlie…" Josh was reflective, distant. "Don't you ever just want to lie close to a woman and not feel like your whole world is dependent on whether or not she's in it with you? Don't you ever just not want to feel that fear anymore?"

Staring at him, Charlie inhaled deeply. "One breath at a time, Josh. I know you've had a shitty time in the past, but you can't spend your entire life worrying about the future."

Josh held up two fingers. "I've been through it, Charlie. Twice. Twice I lost her. And my kids, you might recall."

"I know, buddy. We all know." The horrific memories twisted around

Charlie's gut. He had to make an effort to keep a tiny wince from slipping past the grit in his throat.

His voice dusky, Josh continued. "It's just that this last little while, since the whole Jacob thing at Christmas, all that snuck up on me again. I thought I was okay. I thought I was over it, the fear. Of losing her. Sometimes it's just too much. Sometimes it's all just too much. I feel like…like I'm paper thin, you know? Like I just need to hold someone who has no power over me, so I don't disappear. Someone I'm not afraid of losing."

"Fine. Then take that from Shanda, Josh, if you need it, on set where it's safe. Where it's your character, Bobby, holding hers, Olivia. Where nobody will get hurt. And buddy?" Charlie moved to go, but after he stood he waited at the door for Josh to look at him. To ask.

"What?" Josh finally said.

"Why would you want to spend even one night without her? Without Jessie? Without your kids? After losing her—them—before?"

"Didn't you hear me, Charlie? It hurts too much when I'm with her. It destroys me. Holding her is never enough. If I could just…climb inside her and stay there…maybe it would be enough."

"Because you think you're going to have to let her go at some point." Charlie's words were hushed. Reverent. Respectful of Josh's old losses.

"Something like that. 'My shadow declineth. I am withered. Like grass.'"

"Scripture?"

"I'm tired, Charlie. So fucking tired."

It was a few minutes before Charlie could speak. "I'm going to see if Trudy can come down for a bit, okay Josh?"

"Sure. Yeah, okay." But Josh's heart wasn't in it. It was everything he could do to get out of bed in the mornings. What kept him going was the horse, Blue, and this new character in this new world into which he could disappear. The real world still hurt. He'd thought it would be okay, but it wasn't. Josh had rarely felt more alone. At least when he was insulating himself with beer and drugs, he could numb the pain. Now he was constantly gutted with an increasingly larger ache, and the larger it got, the further it took him from Jessie, from the kids, from reality, from home. Even Kayla was no longer talking to him, or emailing or even texting silly emoticons, like she used to.

I need to get a grip, he chastised himself as Charlie's footsteps faded into the grass outside. *I need to find a way through this new darkness.*

Josh grabbed the script from the table, leafed to the afternoon's scene, and tried to focus on a world that didn't, in all reality, even exist.

~ ~

All that long afternoon, Charlie watched his good friend struggle off set. It was as if Josh didn't have it in him anymore to even try to make small talk with the cast and crew. There was no light in his eyes. The usually warm—albeit sad—eyes were dark and blank.

In front of the camera was a different story. Josh was a talented actor who could easily take on the traits and characters of a person other than himself. Intense and skilled, he built a wall between his real persona and the character he was playing, Bobby, and it served him well in terms of compartmentalizing his day, but did nothing to engender new friendships.

At one point in late afternoon, Shanda approached Josh at the craft service table.

Charlie watched with interest. He couldn't hear what they were saying, but from where he was standing by the cast chairs, Charlie could see Josh's eyes clearly. Josh didn't lose focus. He appeared interested and he listened carefully and, to his credit, he even mustered up a tiny smile for his co-star. But there was still something missing in those luminous chocolate brown eyes, and Charlie knew its name.

Jessie.

Afterwards, Shanda walked towards Charlie. Her legs were shaking, but she didn't tell him that. Instead, she just leaned into his ear and whispered something that had Charlie melting into the nearest chair after she left.

"About Josh?" she said to Charlie. "You're wrong. Everybody's wrong. He's not angry. He's just sad." And she moved away, her boots heavy on the wooden floor of the Sheriff's office set.

After he collapsed in the chair, Charlie turned his head towards Josh.

Josh was watching him. He stopped munching on an apple to wonder what Shanda said about him that had Charlie pale and looking at him as if he'd seen a ghost.

Sad? Charlie was thinking as he met Josh's curious eyes. *No shit, Dick Tracy. The man's still lost.*

Which made a new ache form in his heart at Charlie's next thought.

And so, by comparison, is Jessie.

Chapter Five

Jessie flicked on her blinker to turn left onto Robson. She was late this morning because she'd taken the time to drive David and Emily-Grace to West Point Grey Academy, tailed capably by Sam in a nondescript champagne colored sedan. With the soundtrack-recording project in full gear, she'd been happy to let Sam take the kids himself all week but today she was still feeling the fallout from what felt like personal attacks against her earlier in the week, and she wanted the extra time with her children.

"My kids are my priority," she griped as she eased her SUV into the Keating Building's underground parking garage. "They have to be."

The thought brought instant tears. Josh was distant, physically and emotionally, and Jessie was working long hours. The kids were well loved and cared for at La Casa, but they were missing their parents. At the school, Emily-Grace had hung onto her mother and refused to let go until the teacher took her hand and walked her away, sending Jessie a reproachful 'I-know-you're-a-star-but-you-suck-as-a-parent' stare first. Earlier, David had held on tightly too. At least he had let her go with a hug but Jessie's heart was heavy when she turned one last time and spied his big Josh-eyes watching her from beneath his longish chestnut-blonde hair.

"I love you," she had signed to him in the way she often sent her love to Josh after a performance, with a finger to the eye, a hand over her heart, and a graceful flourish starting with two fingers on her lips, and moving outwards. His little face had lit up then, and he sent her his barely five-year-old version back, which brought a bit of light back into Jessie's heart too, but it didn't last since Emily-Grace had a harder time letting go.

Now, as she turned off the ignition in the Keating building's parking garage and paused before gathering her things, Jessie pondered Dylan. This morning, he was inconsolable. Jessie had missed his bedtime last night, and by the time she'd gotten back to North Van from the UBC home this morning, he was having a temper tantrum over his breakfast, and both Carlotta and Dee were beside themselves. Charles was long gone to the office, so at least sparing him the stress was a relief, but Jessie could hear Dylan's screams the second she opened the SUV door.

Inside, he vaulted into her arms and wouldn't let go.

"Dee?" she asked, her lips pressed into a thin, concerned line. "Did something happen?"

"I don't know," Deirdre said, dropping into a high stool and cutting David's French toast for him. "He woke up in quite a state. He keeps asking for Daddy."

"Oh." Jessie held her little boy tight and wiped sweaty dark curls away from his forehead. He was quaking, and had buried his face in her shoulder. "What is it, little guy?" she asked him. "You're missing Daddy, huh? Momma's missing Daddy too. I think we all are."

"Dylan had a bad dweam, Momma," David told her with an air of authority that had Jessie crack a tiny smile despite the austerity of the moment. "He woke up cwying in the middle of the night and got in bed with me. But he wanted you or Daddy."

"Oh." Jessie couldn't meet Deirdre's quiet stare, then.

Always alert to Jessie's moods, Carlotta touched her shoulder lightly before busying herself tidying up the kitchen.

With a heavy sigh, Jessie took her youngest out to the hallway and walked him around back to the home studio. Plopping down on a round wooden stool with him in her arms, she had no choice but to offer what comfort she could, in words and through touch.

"Sweetheart," she said, pushing him away from her and melting at the tragic cobalt blue eyes that peered back at her through wet eyelashes. "I know you miss your daddy. We'll see him soon, okay?"

"I wanna see Daddy now." The little fingers worked themselves into knots.

Pulling out her phone, Jessie glanced at the time. "I'm not sure what

Daddy's call time is this morning, but why don't I see if we can get him on the phone for you, okay Dylan?"

At the little boy's nod, she tapped on Josh's name and waited, breath held, for him to take the call. He did, thankfully.

"Hey, Josh. Do you have a minute? Someone had a bad dream and needs to hear your voice."

"Yeah, Jess, is it Dylan?"

"You know it, babe." Holding the phone to Dylan's ear, Jessie smiled sadly and mouthed *Daddy*. She could hear Josh talking to their son but couldn't quite make out what he was saying. What broke her heart, though, were the hiccupy sobs emanating from Dylan as he listened and nodded.

"Daddy," he said, trying to grab the phone from Jessie when she put it back to her own ear.

"Momma needs a word, okay honey?" she told him and he resorted to his earlier finger twitching and, from his position on her lap, simply watched her.

"He's missing you," she said softly.

"I'm missing him too," Josh managed. He was a little out of breath.

"Where are you? You're walking."

"At the ranch. I have a late call this morning so I'm taking Blue out for a ride before I have to leave."

"Be careful, okay? I get nervous when you go riding alone. Didn't some girl get jumped by a cougar there once?"

"I've got my shotgun," Josh assured her. "I'll be fine."

"She was cross country skiing, I think."

"Listen, Jess, I don't have a lot of time. Is Dylan settling okay?"

Jessie eyed her son and smiled at him. He managed a small smile back and leaned into her so he could better hear his daddy's voice. "He's just fine, Josh. Adorable as ever."

"Hmmpph."

Ignoring the dig she knew was meant for her because of Dylan's resemblance to Jacob, Jessie puffed up her chest for strength and asked about the shoot.

"It's fine," Josh told her. "How's our soundtrack coming along?" The usual undercurrent of hostility was coloring his quiet voice.

"Two down, three to go," she answered. "We should finish number three tomorrow, at least our part in it. The studio musicians and engineers will be at it all weekend."

"How's lover boy?"

Swallowing past the bitterness suddenly clouding her throat, Jessie said, "Jacob and I are barely speaking, if that makes you feel any better. It's just work."

Josh was at the barn now. At that bit of news, he paused and listened carefully. "What are you fighting about this time?"

"Oh, just me and everything I do wrong. No biggie."

"Relating to? Can't see this being a music thing."

"Nope. We're pretty compatible in that department." She softened. "I just got reamed over the coals for my body language, apparently. That ought to make you happy to hear. Jacob's not taking any chances. He put me in my place quite succinctly, and so did Matt, just so you know. This girl is apparently way too touchy-feely."

"Why don't I find that comforting?"

"It's just over, Josh. No more crossing lines or greying lines or whatever you want to call it. I just want to stop being stupid and come be with you."

"We'll talk later, okay?" Cutting her off, Josh stared at Blue and shook his head in wonder. *My wife's a handful.*

"Oh—okay?"

"I don't have time to listen to all your lover boy woes right now, Jess. Me and my girl are going out for some nature therapy." Lovingly running his free hand over the horse's mane, Josh felt his shoulders relax. They tensed up again immediately, though, at Jessie's next razor sharp words.

"You treat that fucking horse like she's your goddamned mistress, Josh. She gets more of your time than I do."

Josh was silent as he took that in. When he finally spoke, Jessie was already regretting her words. "You still have Dylan with you, Jess?"

"Ahhhh. Yes." She sighed and looked at her son. "You may as well know now that your mother is less than perfect, Dylan," she said into the receiver. "In fact, she's pretty fucked up most of the time."

"For God's sake, Jessie. Cool it. He's just a little kid."

49

"I read somewhere that swearing is good for you. It releases tension."

"Then you oughtta be pretty chill, Jess." Josh quieted. "Just try to ease up around the kids, okay?"

"I will if you will."

Groaning, Josh grabbed the stall door and stared at his feet. "I'm not there. I can swear all I want."

"Yes, you've got lots of freedom, big boy. Enjoy it while it—"

Crossly cutting her off, Josh tossed in, "Why would I want you to come here? All we've been doing lately is fighting."

"Not fighting, Josh. Communicating. Discussing."

"No," he growled. "Fighting."

"Charlie called me last night. He said Trudy's flying in to see you."

"She is. Yes."

"Good. When?"

"She'll be here later today."

"Okay. Well that's good, then. Isn't it?"

"Look, Jessie. Call me tonight. We'll have more time to chat."

"All right, fine." A noise at the doorway caught Jessie's attention. Dee, signaling her to hurry. "School beckons anyway. Be safe riding that new mistress of yours."

Surprising both of them, the comment drew small chuckles.

"Blue's easy. She's a faithful companion."

"You suck. I love you."

At that, Josh managed a grin and ran a hand over the horse's soft neck. "Love you back. Hugs to the kids, Jessie."

"And to me?" she asked quietly, closing her eyes and holding her breath.

Josh couldn't help himself. He closed his eyes too and said, "Biggest one for you. Always."

Relief fluttered through Jessie's body. "Okay. Thanks, Josh. Have a really great day, okay, babe?"

"You too. Make some beautiful music."

"I will. Bye."

"Bye."

After they disconnected, Jessie smiled at Dylan and stood, adjusting him on her hip as she walked. Tweaking his nose with her thumb and forefinger she said, "Your Momma has paid more to the Sawyer family swear jar than she's paid the tax man over the years. And that's saying a lot."

The comment earned her a wide smile from her youngest child.

Now, as she made her way to the elevator in the Keating building, Jessie reflected on the conversation with her husband. By the time she reached the thirty-first floor, she had made a decision. Bouncing into the studio, she found Charles in the sound booth going over tracks with his top engineer. Jacob was alongside, unshaven, arms crossed and plaid shirt hanging out over his jeans, as if he'd been at the studio for hours already. Everyone looked up when Jessie trucked in and leaned against the doorway.

"Charles," she asked, dropping her bag to her side, "when are you flying to Calgary?"

"Tomorrow," he said, straightening up from the mixing board, hesitant and growing nervous. "Why?"

"What time?"

"Five. Ish."

"Good. I'm coming with you."

"You should be here for the weekend, Jessie. For your kids."

"My kids will be better served by me making friends with their father." Eyes flashing, she emphasized the word father and sent Jacob an antagonistic invisible bullet.

He responded with a downturn to his pressed lips and a spiteful narrowing of his eyes.

"Next weekend," Charles insisted. "Not this weekend, Jessie. Josh is shooting all day Saturday anyway."

Pouting, she glared at him.

Exhaling loudly, Jacob turned away.

Charles drew up his shoulders and frowned at his impulsive star. "My wife is tired, Carlotta needs a few days off, Sam needs the weekend off, Matt is taking a few weeks—"

"What?" Her heart started to race. "I thought he was just taking a few days."

"He met someone."

"Oh." Jessie picked at a broken fingernail while she digested that.

"You can stay at La Casa if you want, to give the kids some continuity. And you can have Dan at your beck and call if you want to go out. But we're a bit short handed. You'll be cooking your own meals and taking care of the kids."

"I'll be taking them home, is what I'll be doing." Fiery red splotches popped out on Jessie's cheeks. "And cursing you, Charlie, Jonathon, and my husband for your stupid series. You could have at least shot it in Vancouver! I think I'll quit this ridiculous business and become a—a schoolteacher! Or something."

Even Jacob chuckled under his breath at the idea of Jessie teaching school. Catching her eye, he grinned while she fumed.

With a mighty howl, Jessie flipped around on her heel and violently threw her bag on the leather couch at the far end. "Let's get to work then," she hollered back at them. "I'm leaving work at five, like normal people do!"

In the sound booth, Charles grunted and nodded at his engineer. "Sorry, Mitch," he apologized. "She's not been herself these past few days."

"Princess, much?" Jacob added, saying what Charles was thinking but didn't have the heart to say.

"Get to work, you," Charles growled. "And don't raise her ire any further, if you know what's good for you."

At Jacob's playful grin, Charles relaxed, and there were no further outbursts or issues that day, or for the remainder of the recording sessions. Matt didn't come back, and Jessie didn't get to Calgary for another two weekends, because the stomach flu hit her household one child at a time, and then got her good too, so by the time she saw Josh again, she was tired, frustrated, and very, very lonely.

Chapter Six

Meanwhile, on set, Shanda was feeling a bit better about her relationship with her co-star. Josh was coming around a bit, and thank God, because she was about to shoot their first heavy love scene. It was happening the day before Jessie would finally arrive in Calgary on the jet with Charles. The excitement preceding Jessie's arrival had been ramping up more each day as the week went on, as the local crew waited in breathless anticipation to meet Jessie Wheeler-Sawyer for the first time. Josh, however, was growing more anxious as time passed, and prepping for the love scene with his nervous co-star hadn't helped suppress his nerves.

Charlie caught up to him on his way to set. "Shanda's a wreck," he cautioned. "Take it easy on her."

"Hey, I didn't write this shit. You did."

"I just guided the re-write on it. And you're going to be the one, you know…" Charlie made an obscene motion with his hand that clearly illustrated the scene's intentions. "Doing the bonking."

"Lucky me."

"Hey, a lot of men would give their left nut to be with this beautiful woman."

"Not with twenty crew standing around watching, every one of them saying to themselves, 'Oh, so that's why Jessie Wheeler prefers Jacob Ryan.' These are not my favorite scenes to shoot, Charlie."

A vague memory of that long ago day on *Drifters* came to mind, when Jessie had been encouraged by the director to 'push the scene along.' Josh frowned and slapped his excerpted script sides against his thigh as he walked.

"Just get into character and hold her close, buddy," Charlie said. "You told me you were looking forward to that part of it, at least."

"Holding some chick I owe nothing to? Too bad I don't get to finish the job."

"I'm not going to dignify that with a remark. Break a leg, Sawyer."

"Yeah, producer buddy, I'd rather you don't watch this, all right?"

"I'm not missing you in action! Maybe I'll finally figure out why the hell Jessie left me for you."

"Funny guy. Take a hike. Get lost."

Charlie kept walking and clapped Josh on the shoulder. "I'm staying for blocking. I'll leave you to your own devices after that, when shit gets real, as they say, and I'll clear the set for you as well. With the exception of, you know, like camera. And maybe sound. If that's okay with you."

"You're hilarious, Charlie. So glad to have you as my boss."

"And…maybe set dec. Not sure about wardrobe, you might not need those guys."

"Ha ha."

They were on set then, and while they waited for the A.D. to call blocking, Josh found a new shadow warming up to his opposite side. Shanda's light touch landed on his arm.

"Hi, Josh," she said, trying to keep her voice from shaking.

"Hey," he replied, with a quick glance in her direction followed by a peek down to the script sides, which he rolled into a tube shape and fingered nervously.

"We got this," she stated with more confidence than she felt. "You and me. No prob."

"It doesn't really get any easier, does it?" Honesty seemed like a good way to go into the tough scene.

"For some actors, maybe. But I think for the ones with no ego who want to do it right, love scenes can still be tense."

Josh glanced sideways at her. "No ego, huh? So you're feeling a little better about me these days?"

She shrugged. "Everyone here worships you. I haven't seen any reason not to join the club." A small finger started twisting a ringlet in her short blonde curls. Josh did a double take.

Shanda noticed and lowered her finger, not realizing the nervous habit was also something Jessie did. Her face flushed a light pink and she looked away.

Josh couldn't suppress a small smile.

"What?" she asked him when she dared look back up.

"Nothing," Josh said, and settled his gaze on the director to see if he could guess what the guy was thinking for this scene. "It's just...my wife does that. A lot. When she's nervous."

"I guess I'm nervous."

"That makes two of us."

They shared a moment then, the two of them in a bubble that set them apart from everyone else on set. Josh reached down and wrapped his fingers around hers. Brushing his thumb against her warm skin, he was surprised to feel a slight tremor shoot up his legs and land in his groin.

Shanda, too, sucked in a tiny breath at his touch.

At the same time, under their breaths, both groaned inwardly. Physical attraction for characters like these was a necessity—there had to be a chemistry between them in order for the show to work, but romantic entanglements were frowned upon.

Good thing this is just a physical thing, Josh caught himself thinking, echoing Shanda's thoughts as well.

Interrupting their thoughts, the A.D. called them and, to Charlie's raised eyebrows, Josh walked Shanda onto the set with his fingers locked in hers. They settled in to see what the director had in mind for the scene.

They would shoot a wide master first, and then come in for close-ups. It would be a long day. The writing called for Shanda's character to show up unannounced at 'Bobby's' (aka Josh's) house, a log cabin in the woods. Set dec would build up a fire as background, and since they were shooting on a darkened sound stage, lighting would be geared to reflect nighttime, with moonlight and just a table lamp, as well as the small fire, for illumination. The 'action' would take place in the main living space.

Different directors approach love scenes in diverse ways. This man, a forty-something grey-haired guy with a stubborn jaw they knew as Randy, had already proven to be someone who liked to let the camera roll while his actors freely interpret the scripted action. But he was clear about one thing—he wanted this scene to be intensely passionate.

Josh and Shanda would be dramatizing the first physical connection between their characters. Josh's 'Bobby' was an angry divorced man who recently lost a wife to murder. When Shanda's 'Officer Olivia' shows up at his door, and previously ignited sparks catch and become flame, Bobby isn't interested in making eye contact. He's simply interested in sex, in a physical release of his torment.

No eye contact? Just a warm body to hold, to pleasure? Josh was all over this.

When, a few hours later after blocking and then lighting, the A.D. finally called "Picture's up," the director started with an easy shot—Shanda's Olivia coming to the door. An hour later they moved onto the love scene.

By then, both actors were feeling a little less nervous, although they had yet to start the tough stuff. As professionals, both were 'warmed up' from the first hour of shooting, and were feeling very comfortable in their characters' skins. So things transpired naturally, in a way that surprised both Josh and Shanda, and Charlie too, who stood half behind the props guy with both arms crossed and his producer's hat on, and watched without Josh noticing his presence on set.

The actors connected quickly, with a force nobody saw coming.

After "Action" was called, Josh started with a kiss preceded by one hand pressing on his co-star's lower back and the other raking back her hair. His movements were fast and almost desperate, as per the script. Easily losing himself in Bobby, and in Bobby's world, he tongued the woman in front of him and sucked on her bottom lip until he tasted blood. Sneaking up on him, real desire caught him unawares and made him gasp when he slipped a hand up underneath Shanda's top and ran fingers around her bra strap, undoing it with one quick movement. Josh brought both her top and her bra up over her head and sank to his knees, using his tongue to leave a hot, damp trail down the center of her chest and abdomen, stopping to suckle her nipples and massage both breasts as he moved.

Shanda let him take the lead; he wanted to, anyway, and his actions took any concern for her own authentic performance out of the shot because

Josh's mouth on her body was hot and electric. Gasping, throwing her head back when he undid her jeans and roughly yanked down the zipper, Shanda almost collapsed when Josh's tongue landed in a place usually reserved for couples without twenty silent crew on the perimeter, watching.

"Oh, Jesus," she cried, unscripted and shocked, as instant waves of pleasure floated up her body. Using her fingers to rifle Josh's hair back so she could watch him move against her, she was helpless, hostage in her body, as her hips started their own rhythmic movements.

From the sidelines, Charlie was frozen. Even he didn't expect this from his actor and friend. Yeah, they'd told Josh to make it desperate and real, but generally the actual acts were reserved for close-ups, with 'props' to facilitate ease amongst actors. Josh was *there*, and he wasn't holding back. Shanda was losing it, but she was in the game now too, and had Josh's T-shirt up and over his head in one quick movement, which only succeeded in ramping up her interest in how this was playing out, because suddenly this incredible man was half-naked before her, and her hands ached to explore every inch of him—his muscled shoulders, his strong back, his abs and chest.

But she was quickly in danger of coming right then and there, so she lifted his chin and, with eyes now glazed over with actual longing, she urged Josh back to his feet. There was a moment between them then, when their eyes met and something flickered between them that said *I need you and I trust you.*

Josh lifted his co-star, turned her, and shoved her back up against a wall. A dark light in his eyes apologized to her before he flipped Shanda around and used one hand to push her face hard into the wall. With his other hand, there was a quick movement and he yanked her jeans and panties down to her knees. She was gasping hard by then, widening her stance as much as she could for him, cursing the jeans around her knees and wanting him; yet the rough surface of the set wall was scratching her face, which Shanda, in her unrealistic state, knew the camera wouldn't like when they went in for close-ups because they would have to start at the top of the scene and there was no blood then.

Now Josh was undoing his own belt, and then she could feel him against her, his hips moving hard and propelling her against the wall with hard, quick thrusts. He had the wherewithal not to go in, but it didn't entirely matter to either one of them at the time. Josh's fingers were around her belly, down where his tongue was earlier, and despite herself, Shanda orgasmed in front of the crew.

"Jesus," Charlie cursed as he watched. Wiping a palm against his sweaty forehead, he turned his head away but felt compelled to see where this would end. The director had yet to call "Cut" and, with a quick glance in his direction, Charlie saw that it wasn't going to be happening anytime soon. The guy was letting the scene play out.

On set, Josh faked an orgasm to match the scene and bring it to a close. It hurt like hell, but he gave the mortified and breathless Shanda a few more hard thrusts before he let the two of them settle. She had melted back into his arms somewhat, and Josh had lowered his top hand to wrap around her waist and keep her from collapsing. His second hand stayed where he could continue to move his fingers, with his breath hot on her neck, to massage her and let her enjoy her orgasm.

She made no attempt to pull him away, and instead arched her back and turned her face away from the camera. After a moment, she placed a hand over his and lightly brushed a thumb over his moving fingers.

In the end, Josh urged her back around to face him. When their eyes met, hers were moist and scared. His were hard as slate.

They were in a standoff then, gasping, their breath ragged but slowing until Josh finally let a little of his old light back in and pulled her towards him. Crushing her breasts against his bare chest, he lightly massaged her back and buried his face in the short, unfamiliar hair until he could get himself under some kind of control. Shanda let him hold her, and she held him in turn, and both wished they were anywhere but on the set of a TV show, pretending to be people they weren't, and knowing that the people they were, were who really came through on this day.

Randy finally, mercifully, called "Cut."

Charlie banished the crew momentarily, and followed Randy onto the set.

Shanda couldn't meet his eye as she pulled up her jeans and accepted her top and bra from wardrobe before they vacated the space.

Josh put on his T-shirt and sent his friend an *I dare you* stare.

"What the hell was that?" Charlie demanded from him before Randy had a chance to speak. But he knew what it was. Charlie knew damn well. Josh was exorcising some demons here today. He didn't give a shit about the crew or about Shanda. He wanted a woman's body up against his, convulsing around his fingers, and this was a safe place where he could make that happen. The actions weren't against Shanda's will, per se, but they were still rough and demanding, and went too far as far as Charlie was concerned.

"You taking your revenge, Josh?" Charlie was demanding an answer, and he intended to get it. "Against Jessie or against Jacob? I told you to hold her, a little desperate lust, yeah, but not to fuck her blind in front of the crew and leave her bleeding."

"Oh, shit," Shanda breathed, standing back and taking in the two good friends' first on-set fight. "Is that what that was? Revenge?"

Randy touched her arm and signaled that she should move aside but she shook him off.

"This involves me," she told him, and gave Josh's bicep a hard shove. "Okay," she started, her voice trembling, her mind racing. "You are something else, and I'd be happy to continue this off set, any time," she laughed precariously, in a high-pitched weird falsetto, "but this was a bit much. I had a fucking orgasm, Josh!"

"And that's a bad thing why?" Josh asked, cocky and unapologetic.

"Duh, in front of the crew, on the master take. Jesus!"

Charlie broke in. "Josh, this is going to be a long day. Respect your co-star and your director and let's do this right from here on in. With wardrobe and props to help facilitate Shanda's comfort level. You got that?"

With a light shrug, Josh bit his lip and planted his hands on his hips. "Whatever you say, boss." Locking his eyes into Charlie's, he didn't blink until Charlie had to look away.

"I say you overstepped Shanda's boundaries today. And you better watch yourself." Glancing at Shanda, who was touching her cheek and realizing that she was actually bleeding from light scratches, Charlie deflated and Randy cursed. "Aw, geez," Charlie groaned, and turned. "Makeup!" he hollered, and the key from the on-set makeup department dashed in. "Help her out, will you?" he asked, and fired one last long look at Josh before leaving. In his head was an unwanted image of Josh and Jessie together. "So that's why Jessie chose you instead of me." A tiny grin curled up the corner of his lip, but it faded when he realized Josh was not smiling.

Charlie turned and stormed off the set.

Exhaling warily, Josh pivoted slowly around to Shanda, who was finding a seat on a high stool makeup had positioned nearby. His jaw worked as he tried to find the words.

In the end, she spoke for him. "I would ask if that was anger or whether it was lust, but since you've never really seemed interested in me until today I would gather it had shit all to do with me."

"I'm sorry," Josh finally said. "You're an attractive woman, Shanda. I lost it."

"Trying to make a point?" she asked quietly.

"Not to you," he answered honestly.

"Charlie was here. You wanted that to get back to your wife. Like…look at me. I am still in control. I still have power over women."

"Charlie wasn't supposed to be here."

"He's a producer. You knew he would be here. Jonathon was here too, in case you were wondering. I think he wisely took his white rage off set before Randy called cut."

"This wasn't about power over women, Shanda."

"Then would you mind telling me what it was?"

Makeup swabbed delicately at her scratches, which stung enough to make Shanda wince.

"I guess I needed it. To feel it." Josh's voice was dusky.

"To feel what? What it's like to rape a woman?"

Josh blinked. "That wasn't rape," he spit at her. "Rape is when a man pounds a woman with his fist and subdues her. When she fights back and screams 'no.'"

"Josh, I'm sorry you and Jessie are having a tough time right now, and that someone forcing himself on her has got you so angry and so sad." Reaching for his hand, Shanda was sorry to find that Josh was trembling. His eyes were floating, too. "But honey, keep it off the set, okay?" The makeup girl moved discreetly away to find some cover-up in her bag as Shanda spoke. "It doesn't belong here. Rough doesn't mean free access to my body for your personal exorcism."

Slipping off the stool, she sidled away, leaving Josh standing alone in the fake pale moonlight and wondering what the hell just happened.

Jonathon was nearby now.

"Josh," he called, as Josh strode off set. "A word, son."

Turning slowly to face him, Josh pointed a finger in his face. "Don't… call me that. Ever again." And he left the set.

Charlie trod over to Jonathon and, together, they watched their lead actor stomp off towards the soundstage's exit. "Well," he said matter-of-factly, "this day's going to be a helluva lot longer than we originally thought."

"When's Jessie get here?" Jon asked darkly.

"Tomorrow evening."

"Not soon enough for me." Jon started to walk towards the director, who was scratching his head. "I hope she can settle him down."

Charlie's voice stopped him. "Don't get your hopes up, Jon. They're trying to find each other in the wilderness these days."

Jon stopped moving and pondered that. He moved on without a response.

"Josh, you ass," Charlie muttered, hoping that Josh wouldn't pull a diva move and barricade himself in his trailer for the rest of the day. As he looked around for Randy, Charlie spotted the camera operator. He nodded at him and said, "So, Jordan, you get that or what?" And a wide grin split his face in two. "It's gonna make for great TV, no?"

Overhearing the comment, Shanda bristled at the remark, but she took it all in stride, and tried not to let her body sizzle as it anticipated her co-star's hands back on her skin for the close-ups, and his lips moving over her body.

"I'm sooooo in trouble," she moaned inwardly, and moved towards the craft table for a bottle of ice-cold water.

Chapter Seven

*J*acob was planning to land in Prince Edward Island on a commercial flight, despite a warning from Matt, whom Jacob was having a late afternoon coffee with the day before he was to leave the west coast.

"You're flying commercial? Wear a black baseball hat down over your eyes and a blazer or something, Jacob. Don't go looking like yourself."

"Yeah, I suppose I might get attacked by a gang of Jessie's fans if I take a chance on looking like me, huh? Young moms and teenage girls? I've heard that rolling pins can be lethal. They still use those for baking?"

The flippant comments earned a withering look from Matt. "You're not everyone's favorite star right now, Jacob." Matt wasn't being hurtful, just honest. They were sitting outside Elysian's West Broadway café, at small round tables, watching the traffic fly by. In the last five minutes two ambulances had roared past, sirens blazing and lights flashing. Neither man even stirred. Emergency vehicles were a fact of life in Vancouver.

"I'm not proud of myself, Matt." Jacob was drinking a flat white today. He sipped cautiously, enjoying the velvety feel of the smooth drink, while Matt stuck to peppermint tea to smooth a rumbly and unhappy stomach. "That was a bad time overall." Staring at his cup, Jacob twisted it around and avoided Matt's thoughtful silence.

After a bit, Matt spoke. "You're doing better, Jacob. Standing up to Jessie was a big step."

"Ha!" Jacob frowned. "Standing up to Jessie was one of the hardest things I've ever done."

"How'd the rest of the recording go?"

62

"It was just work. She barely spoke to me." Jacob leaned back in his chair and hung an arm casually over the back. "I don't think she realizes what she does, Matt. The touching. Or how it affects people. Sometimes she's just like a little kid."

"That's part of her charm, that wide-eyed innocence. She's a quandary. An incredible talent, but she has a certain naiveté that just makes you want to wrap her in your arms and keep the harsh world from hurting her."

"At the risk of getting hurt ourselves. Yeah, that's Jessie."

"At the same time, despite being battle-worn and weary, she's a war vet. A survivor with strength you wouldn't expect."

Jacob crossed an ankle over a knee and studied Matt. The older man was focused on his teacup, lost in some memory of Jessie that obviously brought back a certain level of pain. Matt's eyes had darkened, and his gaze was singular and absorbed.

"Matt?" Jacob asked. "What about this new woman Charles mentioned you're seeing? Is she helping dull the ache?"

"Miranda." Looking up, Matt shrugged. "She's the whole package, Jacob. Intelligent, attractive, successful…"

"She runs her own business?"

"More than one. The most well known is a restaurant in Gastown. She's partners with some famous chef from India."

"Sounds like there might be some perks."

"I can dine out when and where I want. I don't need those kinds of perks."

"Ah."

"Ah what?"

"I sense a but."

"It's new, that's all. Miranda is a powerhouse and I'm not sure I'm ready for that yet. It hasn't been that long since Julie and I went our separate ways."

"You and Julie started going your separate ways the day you started working for Charles Keating, Matt." Jacob's words were a harsh truth. They stung.

"We had some good years. Some great times. Katy's amazing."

"Good. So best of luck with Miranda, then. And if she doesn't stick, then at least try to get some decent sex out of your fling in the meantime."

Matt fired Jacob a *Seriously?* glare. "Your generation really worries me,

Jacob. Dating a woman is not about finding a bed partner. It's about respect and common interests and…" Spying Jacob's lighthearted grin, he chuckled. "All right. You had me."

"I'm only joking to a point, Matt. There's nothing like a woman you trust and love to hold and fall asleep next to at night."

"I think that's part of the problem with this latest thing with Jessie," Matt replied. He glanced at Jacob. "It's bizarre talking to you about her."

"I find it comforting," Jacob said quietly, lifting his cup and taking a sip. "Talking about Jessie with someone who knows her as well as you do, I mean. I've kept Little Miss Sorrow inside for so long. So what's part of the problem, Matt?"

Frustrated with his thoughts and worries about Jessie of late, Matt huffed and flipped his chair around to better face the street and its noisy traffic, complete with beeping horns and the occasional skidding tires.

"It's knowing I've had her back for so long and realizing that it's probably all coming to an end but not wanting to let it end because I know she still needs me. These last few weeks have been hell. She's so messed up over Josh and trying to find a safe place to land with him that I know she's hurting." Matt stared at a woman who was walking by with a small white dog held in a baby carrier at her chest, but he didn't really see her. He was lost in Jessie. "I swear sometimes I can feel how bad she hurts. I know when she's having a bad day or a bad moment. She just pops into my head with a whole bagful of sadness. And now…"

He looked back over at Jacob. "Well, who does she have now? To talk to? You? Not over this last while. Charlie and Jane are in Alberta, Steve's working in the States and Sophie's with him. Just three little kids, that's all Jessie's really got. Susanne ditched her, and Jessie's not close to Dan or Sam, or Ulysses, although he's always with Deirdre anyways."

"Arnie?" Jacob asked hopefully. "She's close to him."

"He's in Calgary keeping an eye on Josh and making sure he gets to meetings."

"So she's alone, apart from Dee and Carlotta, I guess. And apart from phone calls or emails to her *Drifters* friends, like Maggie and Sue-Lyn."

"I'm sure she's fine overall. But she must be feeling pretty isolated. Jessie's not your ordinary gal, she can't just pop out to the grocery store or to a movie when she wants to. Katy babysits for her, but then it takes two security, one for Katy and the kids and one for Jessie."

"She goes alone to movies, Matt. We used to sneak out a lot."

"Before the truth came out about Morgan and Nadia, yes. But lately, alone with all of the kids, she doesn't generally go out…no, she's pretty isolated. I know it's lonely for her."

"Too much time to think."

"That's about it."

"Well, personally I hope she stays the hell away from the grocery stores. Did you see the new People magazine today?"

Matt's radar perked up. He tensed. "No. Why?"

"Front cover is Jessie and Josh, and a thumbnail of his co-star. The article was about Jessie catching him with her. Shanda Ellis, is it?"

Shaking his head, Matt relaxed. "That never happened. I heard from Arnie that Josh and Shanda shared quite the raunchy love scene yesterday, but Charlie and Arnie, who're watching him pretty closely, agree there's no evidence of anything going on between Josh and Shanda." Drumming his fingers against the table, he added, "Apparently the love scene was rough enough that Charlie and Jonathon haven't had the nerve to tell Charles yet."

"Huh. Go, Josh," Jacob half-grinned until Matt gave him the evil eye. Referencing the negation of any kind of affair between Josh and Shanda, Jacob said, "Well, that's a relief. Although I can't imagine how those kinds of articles impact the kids."

"There have been a lot of chats in the Sawyer household about Josh and Jessie's fame. The kids are growing up in a hurry, but they've got lots of love to help them manage life."

"From Jessie. There's nothing Josh can do if he's not there."

"You're worried about Dylan."

"Hell, yeah. I'm worried about all of them. It's stupid. I'm here, I should be able to see the kids."

"Have you tried reaching out to Josh?"

"Not yet." Sitting back with his coffee resting on his lap now, Jacob added,

"I need to see how this weekend goes with Kayla. I'll use that as my barometer for reaching out to her brother."

"Are you optimistic?"

"I really don't know, Matt. I haven't got a clue what to expect from her. Anger, for sure, but once she calms down, I don't know."

"Well, I wish you well, Jacob."

"What about you? Are you going back to work?"

"I don't know. Not for long, likely, if I do. I'm thinking of asking Charles to let me go."

"Asking Charles? Or…Jessie?"

Matt was quiet. Bending over his knees, he rested his elbows on his thighs. "I won't be asking Jessie. I'll just be telling her."

"You'll kill her. You'll break her heart. Especially if things go sour with Josh."

"She's a grown woman. She'll manage. I think she expects it, anyway."

"She's a child who needs security she can trust. Don't do it, Matt. Don't leave her. Not now, anyway. Wait til things settle down. You've got Miranda and all that amazing Indian food. The ache for Jessie will go away."

"Will it?" Matt focused his eyes on Jacob. "I just replace her with someone else, is that it? Is that how it works?"

"Ha." Chuckling, Jacob looked away. "Yeah. Fuck you, Matt. I'm going off to the east coast to rescue a girl who needs me. Who I hope wants me. You can wallow in self-pity all you want to." Screeching back his chair, he set his cup down on the table with a hard crack. "But I can tell you this. When it comes to Jessie, all you get is pain. When all is said and done, that's all she has to give. Just ask Josh. He'll tell you."

Jacob hooked his thumbs over his jeans pockets and watched his friend take that in. "She's a big grey sky that only lets the sun in through the occasional little crack. But I don't need to tell you that, Matt. I have a feeling you already know. I'm sorry."

Wheeling around, whistling, Jacob sauntered off down busy West Broadway towards the nearby Cambie Skytrain station. Ducking his chin, he pulled his jacket collar up around his ears so no one would recognize him.

"Great." Matt sat for a while and finished his tea before he, too, stood and faced the traffic. He went the opposite way from Jacob, popping into a large bookstore on the next block to grab a few new reads before unlocking his Audi and heading home.

"Never read so many books in my life," he grumbled as he eased into traffic behind yet another speeding ambulance. As he drove, he thought about calling Jessie when he got home. But when push came to shove, after he dropped his new books on his kitchen island, he forced his finger to land on Miranda's name on his contacts list instead. The red-haired beauty was his age and his type.

And she was available.

The powerful entrepreneur answered on the first ring, her voice confident and imbued with a welcome warmth. "Hello, Matt."

"Hi, Miranda," he replied, relieved to have a bright new focus in his life to replace the shadows that lurked in his soul everywhere Jessie was concerned. "I have a hankering for Indian cuisine. How's your evening shaping up?"

"Better now." Matt could feel her smile through the phone. "Seven?"

They agreed to meet at her restaurant, but when Matt hung up he found himself filled with a weariness he knew came from missing his usual Keating/Sawyer routine. Jessie would be on her way to Calgary with Charles shortly, and he damn well wished he were going along. *I should be going,* he told himself with an angry grunt. *She needs me.*

Pondering what Jacob said earlier, Matt comforted himself with the notion that Miranda was a delicious looking woman with a perfect, robust figure, and there would likely be some of what Jacob called 'perks' tonight, after the intimate wine-enhanced Indian cuisine.

Forcing Jessie from his mind, Matt sat down at the computer and answered an email from his brother, Michael, who was currently on tour in Europe with his superstar wife, Kelly.

But Jessie popped back in. Matt couldn't help himself. He did a Google search for the new People magazine, and lost himself in the haunting front cover. There was Jessie, with Josh beside her—a photo from the Grammy day before things went haywire. The thumbnail picture featured Shanda, but Matt couldn't focus on her. He disappeared in the sad, scared eyes of the woman he'd grown to deeply love and cherish over time, and wished he knew how she was doing, what she was thinking, and whether or not she was missing him.

Chapter Eight

She was seething over the magazine article, is what Jessie was doing and thinking. "I caught Josh cheating on me? How could I have caught him with Shanda Ellis?" Jessie was fuming as she and Charles strode towards the gold-trimmed Keating jet. "I haven't seen my husband in weeks!"

As she smoldered her way into her usual wide leather seat, Charles' phone rang. Jessie didn't tune into the conversation until she heard a sentence that raised her antennae.

"So...Jessie gets assaulted by her ex-lover and Josh gets even by giving his co-star a very public and rough but unwanted orgasm. And leaves her bleeding. On our set." Charles was blistering mad.

On the other end of the line, Jessie knew, was Jonathon. She could hear his quiet fury echo through the phone, not so much in words, but definitely in tone.

The comforting hum of the Keating jet did nothing to settle Jessie's brain or heart as the stark reality of what was behind Charles' angry words sank in. When he got off the phone, she stared at him in stunned shock and surprise.

"Bleeding?" she managed, the magazine article forgotten.

Charles gestured to his cheek. "Her face," he answered, to her unspoken relief. "Shoved her up against a wall, apparently."

Sickened, because she felt there was more to this than Charles was telling, as evidenced by the angry flush on his face, Jessie retorted, "That doesn't bode well for me showing up on set, does it, Charles?"

"They got through the rest of the day okay," he muttered. "Whatever it was, Josh got it out of his system early on, at least."

"And Shanda?"

"Apparently she's embarrassed but okay overall. She's a pretty even-tempered girl, according to the reports coming back from Jonathon and Charlie."

"That oughtta make her a smash hit with everyone." Pouting, Jessie sighed and ran a hand through her curls when Charles fixed his gaze on her.

"Don't push his buttons this weekend, Jessie," he demanded.

"Yeah, I get it, and not for the next five months or for the rest of your seasons, but when Josh is on hiatus from *Sacred Peace* I'm welcome to go get screwed over by Jacob again, is that it?"

"Look, I understand you're upset and likely rather anxious over this weekend, seeing Josh again, and that article didn't help, but don't make any hasty decisions or stir his pot. Try to be civil and make things work."

Incensed, Jessie cringed. "That's your advice to me? Don't make any hasty decisions or piss Josh off? What about me? Where do I fit in all of this? I've got nobody left, and now my husband is trying to get back at me by very publicly screwing his co-star!"

"At least he's not sneaking around behind your back. We know the magazine is wrong."

"Oh, that's helpful. And don't be too sure. Sounds to me like they were pretty into each other. She didn't stop him. Right?"

"I suppose if she was upset she would have."

"Uh huh. Yep. Jesus." Disgusted, Jessie ran a finger around the rim of the coffee mug Victoria handed her and wondered which of Josh's famous tumultuous moods she would be dealing with at the airport.

In twenty minutes they were on the ground, but discerning Josh's current temperament would have to wait. He wasn't there.

As the jet taxied to its private gate, Jessie was deflated to spy Charlie, not Josh, waiting for them with a driver and a black SUV in tow.

Knowing she'd be upset, Charlie held out a child's multi-colored sucker as a truce. "Take it," he insisted, and she sulked but obliged. "I stole it out of one of those take home bag thingies from a birthday party Stella went to last weekend."

"And how're Jane and Stella and new little Lucas?"

"All well and happy. Loud. And life on set is good, in case you're asking.

Most times. C'mere." Charlie grabbed Jessie's shoulders and peered into her eyes. He was smiling happily, but beneath the attempt at jocularity Jessie sensed a layer of worry. "You good?" he asked her.

"Puh." Annoyed, she added, "Not hardly likely. What's this latest shit?"

Charles approached them then and shook Charlie's outstretched hand. "Son," he said amicably but in a businesslike fashion, and Jessie rolled her eyes and parroted the word *son*.

Catching the look, Charlie said hi to Charles, grinned, and wrapped an arm tightly around Jessie's shoulders as he led her to the SUV. "Your husband's brilliant," he said. "He just had a moment of weakness, that's all."

"And you're using it."

"Hell, yeah. It's friggin' awesome TV."

"You producers suck. You'll pimp out your kids to get what you want for what you consider good television."

"Easy, girl. Down. It's all good. Josh and I had a talk and Shanda's cool with everything so let's start this over again and try to have a good weekend, okay? It'll fly by."

On the way to the soundstage, Jessie sank down into her plush leather seat and listened to Charlie and Charles rattle on about details relating to their series. Her ears perked up when she heard Charlie say the dailies were incredible. Their premiere episode was in post, being edited, and Jessie and Jacob's new heavy ballad had already been added as the theme song.

"What I've seen so far is magic," Charlie was telling Charles. "Josh and Shanda have an intense chemistry that really lights up the screen."

"Lovely," Jessie glowered, crossing her arms defiantly in front of her chest as the SUV approached the *Sacred Peace* building.

Josh was working when she arrived. Unbeknownst to him, Jessie took up a quiet spot to watch from, in exactly the same spot from where Charlie had watched the rough love scene unfold the day before. The production was shooting a 'morning after' scene now, and Jessie's mood didn't improve when she saw her husband's co-star wearing one of his shirts. This one belonged to the production but it was a cream long-sleeved Henley, and Josh had plenty of those. Worse, all Shanda was wearing underneath was skimpy panties, and as she carried a coffee mug to Josh at the kitchen table and snuggled her arms around his neck, Jessie felt a shiver run up her spine. Next, Shanda dropped onto his lap and started to tease her character's new man by running a finger around his lips and kissing him. It wasn't a stretch for Jessie to know that Josh would be reacting physically to having this cute, perky woman in his arms.

Charlie approached and draped an arm loosely around her neck. "Relax, girl child," he soothed. "There's nothing going on between them."

"Duh, he gave her an orgasm. Was that, like, orgasm by immaculate touch?"

Charlie chuckled. "Nope, that was really something. I finally clued in to why you left me for him. I thought I was good in the sack, but Lordy, child."

"So not funny, Charlie."

Softening, he turned her face towards him and was saddened to see a wet mist settling across the sea-pearl eyes he adored. "Jessie, please. You need to relax and sort things out with Josh this weekend. The two of you are bombs ready to explode."

"Charlie, I just came off a chunk of time alone with three sick kids. And I spent a chunk of that time on the bathroom floor myself. I missed my husband's birthday and just found out he's basically screwing his co-star."

"He isn't. Trust me."

"He's got his hands all over her!"

"Yeah, as of this moment you're banished from the set. No more wives allowed on my set." Charlie made a motion to turn her away from Josh and Shanda but she refused to let him. He tried a new tack. An investigative one. "I'm sure you had Matt around at home to give you a hand."

"Matt's gone. He disappeared into oblivion with some hot new woman. I haven't seen him since he and Jacob and I had words back when we first started recording. He's likely spending his days in bed. And not alone."

"I didn't know that. I'm sorry."

"Ha! For what? Because everyone's gone and left me alone?"

"I'm not going to ask about Jacob."

"We've barely spoken. He's hopping a plane for the east coast tomorrow morning to go see if Kayla will talk to him."

"So you are alone. No wonder you're so cranky. Finger not doing the job?"

Jessie had a sharp retort ready and waiting for him but then the director called "Action" again and they were forced into silence while Jessie watched her husband snuggle the beautiful Shanda.

At, "Cut, that's the keeper," she stepped away from the set and waited. Nervous enough, Jessie didn't want her reunion with Josh to be public, but as it was, there were crew all over the place, so she didn't have much choice. She moved to the opposite wall from the craft service table in the hopes that the crew would all head for craft and end up far away.

Josh was expecting Jessie. He left the kitchen set and watched Shanda make her way towards the door so she could rest in her trailer, outside the building, before he wandered over to his wife.

"Hey," he said by way of greeting, but didn't reach for her. Instead, he kept his hands shoved deep in his jeans pockets.

Jessie was guarded, apprehensive. Extending an arm, she placed her palm against Josh's chest, against where she felt his heart would be. Glum, she let her eyes drift from there up to his face. Josh let a hand rise and cover hers on his chest.

"You're breaking my heart," she told him. "Again."

He studied her, his face lined with crags and worry. "I just can't deal," he started. "The only thing I can handle right now is this crazy fictional world I'm living in. And it's all an illusion, I know that. It's not real. Olivia's not—"

He bit his tongue.

"Ah," Jessie retorted, catching on. "Olivia's not real, is that it? But you're wishing she was. Or do you mean the actress playing her? That being the gorgeous blonde who was just straddling your lap in her panties. Shanda."

"I honestly don't know what I'm wishing, Jess. All I know is that when it gets so bad that it hurts to breathe, and I just want to curl up and die because I can't go down that dark road again, with booze and shit, that it feels good to sink into another world."

"Because the one your wife and kids live in is too hard to bear."

Grabbing the wrist against his chest, Josh pulled his wife close. He pressed his forehead to hers, and wrapped both arms around her waist. "All I know," he managed, his voice husky, "is that I feel bad. Every day. Like the whole world is just all grey clouds. I feel like I'm on the outside looking in. Always. I'm having a hard time with reality. I'm preferring unreality."

"What did Trudy say?"

Josh sighed. "She said it's not uncommon to feel this way. After everything we've been through…coming off addictions…she said the first few years I was just thawing out. Like when you're a kid and you go skating and your skates are too tight because your mother is scared your feet are gonna get cold and so she makes you wear too many socks. And so your toes freeze. You know that feeling when they start thawing out? How fucking bad it hurts?"

"Yeah, babe, I do." Jessie lifted her palm and laid it against her husband's cheek. "I know it hurts."

"Trudy said with…with everything that happened…with Jacob…and even him losing Talia…that my system basically just went back into shock and all that old fear came rushing back. Of losing you. Of being so scared again that I can't see two hours into the future without panicking."

"Did she give you something? To help?"

He shook his head. "N-no. No. Not a good idea. Not for me."

"Okay," Jessie agreed. Melting into his body, she said, "We'll be okay. You just need your family down here with you."

Josh's body tensed. "I don't know if I'm ready for that yet, Jessie."

"Why not?" Tears pricked her eyes. *Please stop pushing me away. Please.*

"I don't know how to explain it."

"Try, goddamnit."

Backing away a step so he could meet her eyes, Josh said, "I can barely drag myself to set these days. How am I supposed to take care of you and the kids?"

"So this is what it all comes down to?" she whispered. "All those days in that dark basement praying praying praying to get out so I can see you again…so I can hold you again…and first I gotta get through Nadia's brick wall and then through yours, and now we're back to square one again. Is this what recovering from addictions does to people? They get depressed and scared and can't take anything prescribed to lessen the pain? So they go back to drinking or smoking or inhaling or whatever?"

"I won't do that. I promise you. Charlie makes sure Arnie gets me to meetings."

"But I need to be with you. I need to be here too. I take care of you the best. And I'm so fucking lonely, Josh. Don't keep pushing me away."

"Or what, Jessie?" Josh wasn't angry now. He was just tired and sad.

"I dunno. I really don't."

"I do. And if that's what you need, then I won't stand in your way. I know I'm not here for you right now. I'm barely here for myself." Josh started backing away.

Jessie straightened and forced her chin up. "We've got the weekend," she told him. "And I intend to show you how much I love you. To bring us back onto the right side of that split rail fence you talked about before."

"All right," he said quietly. "The weekend. Let's do it." Josh reached for her hand, and tried to offer her a small smile. It came out crooked and forced. Jessie sank into herself but took his hand, and they left the sound-stage together.

That night, after dinner with the cast and crew, and after wandering around the ranch house and touching everything Josh may have touched, trying to gather his energy back into her soul, Jessie clutched Josh's white T-shirt in both fists and backed him into the bedroom. He didn't pull away, as she feared he might.

Jessie forced him onto the bed first, on his back, and she laid her body over his, tenting him in her arms and loving him the only way she felt she knew how. Jacob's and Matt's words bounced around in her brain and hurt like hell, but Jessie knew how to make a man feel good and she damn well needed to reconnect with her husband. Making love was a way to help him. The physical joining of their bodies was not a lustful act—it was a bloody necessary spiritual connection.

"Babe," she moaned in his ear as, fully clothed, she moved her hips against him, "let me just love you. Okay? Just let me have this."

Josh wasn't stopping her so Jessie wasn't sure why she was saying the words. She felt like she was begging. *Maybe I am*, she thought as his arms stretched around her back and ground her body against his. *Maybe I need to beg. That's who I am, a beggar. For sex. For a connection to this man I love beyond all others. Does that make me a whore?*

Josh could guess her feelings. Her thoughts bounced across to him, and telegraphed themselves across those diaphanous blue eyes he ached for when he touched himself in his sleep. Unable to stand it, that he had a lot to do with his wife's need to beg him for love, he moved out from under her and straddled her instead.

"You want this?" he said to her, gruff and insistent. "You want it the way I want to give it to you? Rough and angry? Is that what you want? Like Jacob?"

She froze. "Yeah," she breathed. "If that's what it'll take for you to let that shit go, then yes. Hit me, Josh. Is that what you want to do? You want to hit me?" Her words were cool, and bit off with barely concealed fury and frustration.

"You're begging me," he told her, grabbing her wrists and splaying them out to the sides so she was unable to move.

"To let me love you," she whispered as a wet tear escaped from the corner of her right eye. "Not for sex. It's not the same thing."

Something flashed across his eyes then, and Josh remembered what it felt like to be with Shanda on set yesterday, unable to finish what he started. This woman below him was familiar and yet almost a stranger, it seemed. Bending to her, he held onto her wrists and ran his tongue over her lips. He went at her the same way he went at Shanda, with deliberate, quick movements and hands that shook. Josh took Jessie hard and rough without foreplay, and he grabbed her hand and positioned her fingers so she could derive whatever pleasure she wanted from their coupling on her own.

When he was done, he moved away and laid on his back next to her while Jessie rolled onto her side away from him and wrapped her arms around her belly to keep herself from screaming or falling apart or both. After a bit, they took turns in the washroom, Josh first, and when Jessie came back to bed, he was gone.

Searching the house for him, she was about to give up when she spied an empty coat hook. Glancing below, Jessie noticed that Josh's boots were missing.

There was a flashlight on the ledge above the hooks, ready for quick access if needed. Grabbing it, she didn't bother putting a sweater or jacket on, and left the house, letting the screen door slam behind her.

He was in the barn, stretched out on a blanket in front of Blue's stall, almost asleep. There was a thick, smelly horse blanket nearby. "What the hell," Jessie mumbled, and reached for it. Lying down in front of her husband, she pulled the blanket up over their shivering bodies, and relaxed when his arm snaked around her middle and he curled his body into hers.

"I love you," she whispered hopefully into the moonlit semi-darkness as Blue snuffled above and behind them.

"Love you back," Josh murmured sleepily, and breathed in the lavender scent of her hair. "Little one."

That's all it took. Those two words; that simple endearment. Jessie finally crumbled, and sobbed while her husband held her, until she was all cried out, and she drifted off to sleep.

Chapter Nine

 $\mathcal{A}$ few days later, the production was shooting on location, which meant lunch in the great outdoors under the canopy of a large white tent.

Scanning it when she entered, Shanda eyed the men in the far corner and purposely, after she went through the buffet line, chose a table at the complete opposite end. Josh was part of the guys' gang today, rather unusually, since he almost always ate alone in his trailer, and Shanda was wholeheartedly avoiding him. Charles, Charlie and Jonathon were crowded around Josh, hunched over the table. The men were hunkered down chatting about something or other production related, and Shanda had no interest in interfering in whatever important issue they were discussing.

Just as she bit into a slice of gluten free garlic toast, a low buzz in the room intensified. An excitement, of sorts, took hold. Glancing up, Shanda watched as Jessie Wheeler-Sawyer padded quietly in, wearing, to Shanda's surprise, a beat up pair of Converse Chucks on her feet. Yellow plaid, with smiley faces on the toes.

Jessie was apparently accustomed to stares and attention. Either that or she simply didn't catch the energy bouncing across the room between cast and extras that were not generally used to the presence of a star of Jessie's stature in their space. Childishly licking her fingers one at a time as she passed through the buffet line eating her garlic bread as she moved—greasy, buttery, hence the finger licking—she ended with a nervous turn and looked around for somewhere to sit.

Shanda watched as Jessie picked up the posse of men in the corner, all of whom Jessie knew well. But judging by the woman's rigid posture when she spotted them, Shanda had a feeling she would look elsewhere for a seat. Twisting around, Shanda couldn't help but look behind her at Josh to see whether he was being welcoming to his wife. It was no secret on the set that he and Jessie were struggling during this weekend visit. Today was Monday, and yesterday had been a day off work. Greg, the craft service Newfie, had arranged a social outing—the cast and crew had gone bowling—and Jessie and Josh had hardly spoken to each other the entire afternoon.

Josh was watching his wife, indeed, with a mixture of sorrow and regret, Shanda thought. Turning back around, she looked up to spy Jessie tossing her curls and pressing her lips together as she looked away from him.

Jessie's anxious, roaming eyes landed on Shanda.

She took a few steps forward and said nervously, "Ummmm…"

With her foot, Shanda pushed the chair opposite her out. Jessie accepted the wordless invitation, deposited her tray on the table, and dropped into the proffered seat.

"Thanks," she mumbled. "I never know where to sit at these things. Especially when I'm not part of the cast."

"No worries." Shanda's voice was tense, edgy.

Jessie noticed and glanced up. The woman's doe-y brown eyes took her by surprise. They were gentle, like Blue's, and kind. Jessie relaxed and picked up her fork.

"The guys are into it over there," she observed with a nod towards the men. "Not my idea of an easygoing lunch."

"Yes, I suppose they're taking advantage of Charles Keating's presence. He looks great, by the way."

Jessie smiled. "He's doing well. His wife Deirdre, myself, and their maid Carlotta ride his ass a lot. He's completely outnumbered. The man doesn't have a chance."

"I'm glad for you. I know what he means to you, Jessie."

"I suppose the whole world does. Take my advice, Shanda. If you value your privacy, stay in Canadian TV and don't ever take parts in American films."

"The fame thing?"

"I'm guessing you're already learning."

Shanda shrugged and tore a bite-sized piece off her garlic bread. "I'm sure it's ten thousand times worse at your level. And Josh's."

At the mention of her husband's name, Jessie just nodded. Arnie had come into the room and was sitting a ways down from her with some of the crew. She gestured towards him. "We rarely go anywhere without security. It's hell, scheduling. And it's a constant worry with the kids."

"I know." Shanda was completely understanding, the kind of woman Jessie felt herself drawn to. Whom she immediately felt comfortable with, as if she could tell her anything. Almost a Maggie type, but less motherly and more girlish, with her bouncy blonde curls and Meg Ryan face. "I can't even wrap my mind around what you guys have been through," she was saying. "Sorry. Maybe I shouldn't have brought that up."

"It's okay. I kinda started it." Jessie's eyes lit up with a slightly forced but friendly ambience, and Shanda allowed a small grin back.

Behind them, Josh was watching with interest. It was nice to see Jessie interacting with another woman on set, and Josh knew by now that Shanda was a kind, sweet person. It made sense that Jessie would navigate to her. Arnie was nearby, keeping an eye on things, and Josh found himself rather captivated by his famous wife for the first time in a while. Being in the lunch tent with her but observing from a distance gave him the opportunity to study Jessie at length.

The old plaid Chucks. It wasn't a stretch that Jessie had brought those on the trip. They were her comfort shoes. They told him legions about where her mind was these days as she tried to reconnect with him. Josh would have chuckled if he was feeling more like his old self, but as it was he could barely muster a half-grin.

Jessie seemed happy enough as she chatted with Shanda, almost normal, in fact. But underneath that wide smile was a layer of dread. At the end of lunch, Josh would walk her to the black SUV that had delivered her to the set, and he would let her go, back to Vancouver, back to their children. When would she be back? When would they face each other again? Neither had a clue. The only thing they both knew for certain was that Morgan and Nadia still haunted them. Neither Josh nor Jessie wanted to let go of each other; it seemed like Morgan had buried their magic and their trust in some deep hole with the body of his wife.

Now, it was apparent Jessie's conversation with Shanda had taken a turn. And it seemed to be about him, Josh surmised, when Jessie's eyes suddenly darted over to him. His lips parted when their old electricity fired across the room. *ZZZZZZpppp.* Like a bolt of lightning, it came out of the blue and wrapped itself around his heart, shocking him. Shifting his butt on the hard plastic seat, he gripped his fork tightly and watched his wife.

Shanda had brought up the love scene.

"Do they ever get easier?" she was asking Jessie.

"Not always," Jessie responded carefully. "Depends on who you're working with, actor, director, that sort of thing. The vibe on set. Are people grumpy, is the sound team fighting? It's different every time. Every show is different."

Shanda wasn't sure how to respond to that. She decided to move her spinach around with her fork and conjure up another question to steer them down a new path and make her appear less like an amateur dork. Her brain raced ahead though, and jumped in with, "Do you ever feel anything? During love scenes?" Immediately she chastised herself, but bravely forced her gaze up to Jessie anyway.

Unclear about the woman's intentions, Jessie sucked in a small breath. "Only from my character's perspective," she said, leaving out her first love scene with Josh and how incredible that had been back in the *Drifters* days, when she pissed him off by wrapping her hand around him and gently adding pressure, for the sake of the scene. "Did you, on Friday?" she added. A second later she said quickly, "Apart from the physical reaction, I mean?"

"You heard about that." Shanda, mortified, ducked her head and set down her fork. She wiped sweaty palms on the thighs of her jeans.

"I'm not impressed with my husband, if you want the truth, Shanda."

"Jury's still out from my perspective." The pretty brown eyes searched Jessie's. There was something there…a nervous apprehension… "I won't lie to you. It was pretty hot."

Seriously. And you're telling me this before I get on a plane and leave my husband alone with you for the next five months. Jessie swallowed. "So you felt something."

Wiping her palms more vigorously, Shanda licked her lips and stuttered out an answer to this woman she admired and respected dearly. "Y-yes. I did. I…do. Surprised me."

Floored, Jessie set down her fork with a small ting while, off in the corner, Josh straightened. Eyes wide, she looked left and met his curious gaze, then tossed her curls again and glanced back at her lunch mate.

"Do me a favor?" Jessie grabbed her knife and gripped it tightly.

"Y-yeah. 'Course." Waiting, Shanda held her breath.

"Don't fall in love with him. Please." The request was simple, subdued. Jessie's eyes were floating. She said it again in an even lower tone, although her eyes were more earnest the second time around and her voice was struggling to be heard past the lump in her throat.

"Don't…fall in love with him. Okay, Shanda?"

It was Shanda's turn to choke up. She tried to make light but skirted the real issue as she did. "You don't need to worry about him. He's only got eyes for you."

"I'm not worried about him," Jessie lied. She was damn well worried but felt in her heart that Josh would likely only go there if Shanda tempted him. Her unspoken words chilled Shanda.

"I'm not that person," Shanda said in response. "That's not me."

"Funny thing," Jessie said, pushing back her chair and rising. "I didn't think I was that person, either. Until it happened."

Opposite her, Shanda panicked. She vaulted up. "No, Jessie, please. That wasn't my intention, to cause trouble or to…to warn you or something. I just…" Struggling, she stomped her feet lightly and said, "It's just that he's the kind of man whose sadness you want to peel away. Layer by layer, you know? Until he feels good again."

Blinking back tears, Jessie turned her hand inward and pointed to herself. "I'm his sadness," she whispered.

"I'm…I'm sorry, Jessie."

"Me too. You want to peel me away? I'll make it easy for you, Shanda. I'm catching a jet plane outta Dodge in half an hour."

In the corner, Charlie, who was seated next to Josh, had also picked up on some tension between the women. When both he and Josh didn't respond to something Jonathon said, Charles and Jon too, twisted around to see what was up.

"Catfight," Charlie intoned.

Josh stood and looked across the table at Charles. "We'll meet you outside," he said, and headed up the center aisle between tables to pause by his wife, who, eyes locked on Shanda, was clearly close to tears. Looking over his shoulder at Shanda, Josh was surprised to see a similar expression on her face. She angled her head to meet his eye, and quickly looked away, embarrassed at what he might see, at what he might detect lingering beneath the surface.

"Excuse me," she said, and moved to go.

"Shanda," Jessie said loudly. It worked. Shanda stopped and listened. "I know what it's like to love someone I'm not supposed to have. I'm sorry. I know how much it sucks."

Mortified, Shanda bowed her head and left the dining tent. Jessie steeled up her courage and lost herself in Josh's liquid eyes.

Confused at the remark, he cocked his head and tried to catch his breath. "Someone you're not supposed to have?"

"She's crazy about you. Your co-star wants you."

"Jessie?"

"You, babe," she told him, swiping at a tear. "You, you fucking asshole. On *Drifters*. When I was engaged to Charlie. It was hell."

A certain peace settled over Josh's face and he let one corner of his lip curve upward. "It sucked pretty good, didn't it?"

"Yeah." Sniffling, Jessie took his elbow and pulled him close. "She's falling in love with you," she breathed into his neck. "And I'm on my way out the door with no idea when I'll even see you again. I can't stand it."

"Hey," Josh said, pushing her away from him. "Let's not do this here, okay Jess? Let's go outside."

Taking her hand, he led her out of the main open flap of the large tent and towards the nearby parking lot. Once there, Josh pushed her gently up against the side of his truck and tented his arms on both sides of her. "Now," he said. "What's the problem?"

"I can't go. I can't leave you." Jessie stomped her foot in protest.

Josh chuckled quietly. "Damn, you're cute when you do that."

"I mean it, Josh." Gathering his denim jacket in her fists, Jessie bent her head and buried her face in his chest. "How do I walk away from you knowing how she feels about you? And what about you? Do you have feelings for her?"

"Jessie," Josh started, lifting her chin so she would look at him, "if Shanda told you that, then I'm guessing she wasn't doing it as a threat."

"Then why?"

"She's a little freaked out, maybe. I don't know. That love scene threw both of us."

The ground gave way beneath Jessie's feet. Her world started to spin. "You've got to be kidding me."

"What?"

"You've got feelings for her too. Everything we've been through and you're going to dump me for your co-star?"

"It's been known to happen." Josh laughed and tenderly touched his wife's face with his thumb. "Never," he determined. "If we decide it's over it will be because we decide it's over. Not because I want someone else."

"You used to say you would never leave me. I see that your stance has changed."

"No, Jessie, nothing's changed." Josh got quiet. "Go home and let me do my work here. I'll keep talking to Trudy and try to figure out how to work through all this shit Morgan and Nadia buried us in. Take care of the kids and when I feel like I can deal you can bring them here and we'll go one day at a time."

"You're leaving me with hope? I guess that's a good sign."

"There is always hope, right Jessie? That's what you told me that day outside Charlie's club." Bending towards her, Josh placed his lips over hers and kissed her. It turned into a long, tender kiss that had both wishing for more time.

Charles and Charlie were just leaving the tent. Both were respectfully quiet as they watched Jessie sigh her body into her husband's and watched Josh wrap both arms around her shoulders and press her against him.

"They'll be okay," Charles said as if he were trying to convince himself. "They're figuring it out."

Wandering towards their drive, he called to them. "Sorry, Jessie. We need to go."

It took Josh and Jessie a few seconds to unwind. They melted in each other's eyes at the thought of this new separation.

"Sometimes it hurts," Josh murmured to her, leaving his body tented over hers, his arms bent at the elbows and forearms leaning against the truck. "Loving you."

"A lot of the time, it seems," she answered honestly, swiping her sleeve under her nose and sniffling.

His gentle smile warmed her heart. "It's worth it though, you know? I think I figured that much out this weekend, just watching you. Just being with you. Without the kids around to muddy the water, I mean."

"Of course it's worth it," she told him with a sad but rather diabolical grin. "I'm worth millions."

Josh laughed outright at that. "I knew I should have done a film instead of this cheap Canadian series. It might take me a while to catch up to you."

Jessie punched him lightly in the stomach and took his hand to lead him over to Charles and Charlie. "Come on. Break my heart again."

There, Charles made an error that threw their sacred peace into a tailspin. Shaking Josh's hand firmly he said, "We've got a bit more work to do on the soundtrack, Josh, then we'll wrap the first episode up with a tidy little bow and send it to you for a viewing. Good? Just give us a few more days. I'm sure you'll be pleased."

Josh grimaced. "I'm never a fan of watching myself," he admitted.

In response, Charles jumped in with a quick, "No worries. If you don't want to watch it, just listen to the soundtrack. Jacob and Jessie wrote some incredible music together. I've decided to release their tunes as a whole new separate album as well."

As Josh crumpled from the shock of what that would mean—promotional opportunities, touring, likely another track or two—Charles climbed into the SUV.

Josh turned to Jessie. Judging by her defensive stance, she wasn't surprised. "You knew?" he asked her. "You knew about this?"

"We already recorded the album, Josh. This is not a surprise to you." Panicking, Jessie was quick to see that there was more to this arrangement that bothered Josh than what she was seeing. Shaking her head, she threw her arms out to the sides. "What? Why is this a problem?"

"He's like a cancer," Josh steamed. "I can't get rid of him. That's why it's a problem. You and Jacob recording songs for the show is one thing. Going out on tour again…" He shook his head slowly from side to side.

"Who said anything about a tour? Besides the *Sacred Peace* promo tour, that is? Which you will be on!"

"Go home, Jessie. I'll call you, okay?" With a final long look, and then a gentle chaste kiss on the cheek, Josh spun around and walked away, taking the musky, earthy essence Jessie loved along with him.

"I cannot believe how badly this weekend has ended," she growled at Charlie as she slipped into the SUV and he closed the door behind her. "I think I'll just go steal Jacob's sailboat or something and sail off into the sunset."

Chilled at that, Charlie frowned and leaned both elbows on her open window. "You haven't learned yet that running away is not the answer?"

"Sometimes, Charlie," Jessie grimaced as a ponytailed female driver got in and started the vehicle, "I can tell you that running away is the *only* answer. Bye. Luv you. Take care of him, will you? And keep him the hell away from Shanda."

"That'll be tough," Charlie mused as he let go of the window and watched her go. "They're in almost every scene together." The last part was said under his breath, but Jessie caught the essence.

She closed her eyes and sank deeper into her seat, and drove the entire set of right hand fingernails into the back of her left hand.

Opening her eyes as they exited the parking lot, Jessie caught sight of Josh one last time. He was leaning on the split rail fence Jonathon liked to surround his parking lots with. Facing her from the other side, Josh had one foot on the bottom rail, and was resting his chin on his two folded forearms, which were relaxing on the top rail. The longish piece of hair Jessie always loved to tuck behind his ear was loose and fluttering in the wind. Just as she was about to lose sight of him, Jessie caught her breath. Shanda had come up behind him and, as Josh turned to her, she lifted her hand and pushed that rogue piece of hair behind his ear.

Breathless and doing her best not to have a full-blown anxiety attack, Jessie closed her eyes again. *It's like I'm Charlie and she is me, only this is not Drifters and Josh and I have three children,* she thought. *And this sucks.*

The *Sacred Peace* base camp was soon far behind them. Josh and Charlie and Shanda were already becoming memories of a weird and difficult weekend. What awaited Jessie in the future, in Vancouver in a few hours? The children. That was something. But no Josh, no Jacob, no Matt, no Steve, no Charlie…no *Drifters* friends, no sure and perfect love. Just holes and hurt.

I've come full circle. I'm back where I started.

But then her phone rang and, when Jessie answered, a sweet voice cried, "Momma, guess what? Alfie brought his turtle to school today!"

Jessie chided herself. Wallowing in self-pity would get her nowhere. This beautiful little girl on the line awaited her in Vancouver, as did the child's two perfect little brothers. Life was good and full with the three Sawyer children in it.

Pushing Josh from her mind, Jessie lit up. "That must have been exciting, honey. What was the turtle's name?"

"Smiley!" Emily-Grace roared. "Isn't that the best name ever, Momma? For a turtle?"

She was obviously in a fit of seven-year-old hysterics, and it was catching. Laughing, Jessie talked with her daughter until she got on the jet, and even then until Victoria brought her coffee and the stairs swung up into the jet's belly.

Then they were airborne, Jessie and Charles, and although nothing with Josh had really been solved, there were some good moments to cherish, and there was, as he said himself, always hope.

Tomorrow, dawn would come and bring with it a new day, to help stomp out an old, and very painful, past.

Chapter Ten

The Saturday Jessie was in Calgary, Jacob had boarded a late night commercial redeye for the east coast, which, after a lengthy Toronto stopover, landed him in Prince Edward Island, Jessie's childhood home, at noon on Sunday. The last time Jacob was on the island was for Jessie and Josh's barefoot beachfront wedding. Glancing around the tiny airport as he lifted his bag off the carousel, he speculated that the place had a certain charm. The indifferent fiberglass black and white dairy cow guarding the departures exit was certainly endearing. Jacob wondered how many kids had fallen off while getting their pictures snapped by exhausted parents.

Outside, a lingering scan spotted mounds of snow here and there, marking time on a washed out muddy spring landscape. Vancouver had long been snow-free; in fact the city's famous gorgeous pale pink cherry blossoms were the only snowy detritus on the sidewalks these days. But P.E.I. still had snow. Shocking.

Jacob's twenty-something man-bunned driver skidded up to the curb as Jacob considered why anybody would want to live on an island that had snow so much of the year.

The driver was a musician Jacob had shared the stage with the night of the Sawyer-Wheeler wedding. Waving a hand at Jacob, he jumped out and circled around the back of his truck. "Wasn't sure I'd recognize you," he grinned. "But you look the same as you did on your last album cover."

"Good thing you're the only one who thinks so," Jacob shot back amicably, handing the guy his bag so he could drop it in the narrow back seat of his white Toyota pick-up. "Good to see you again, Chris."

"You too, man. You've done all right. No issues on the way down, then? I gather you usually fly by private charter."

"My boss has a jet. Avoids a lot of waiting around and makes for a comfortable flight, but it's hell on the carbon footprint." Sliding into the cab, Jacob thanked the guy for picking him up. "Glad we stayed in touch after the wedding," he said. "That was a great night for music. One of the best. Your island knows how to party."

"It wasn't so great in other ways though, eh? It didn't surprise any of us that you eventually hooked up with Jessie Wheeler."

"Took care of her, is more like it," Jacob mumbled, aiming his gaze out of the window at the damp beige landscape. "She's always a mess."

"A beautiful mess." Chris put the truck in drive and inched forward behind a slow-moving taxicab. "She's really something. People around here still talk about that wedding as if it was the royal wedding. Jessie was very kind to everyone. She's well loved."

"You can say that again." Jacob half-smiled despite the twist in his gut at the hard memory of Jessie marrying Josh once and for all, cozied up to the guy at the beach saying vows they seemed to be having a difficult time keeping.

"So…Summerside? The Harbourfront Theater? That's where your friend's dance troupe will be performing tonight?"

"Yep. Rehearsal and sound check start in an hour, according to my source." Jacob yawned widely. "Ouch," he said as his jaw cracked. Absently, he rubbed it with his hand.

"Red-eye, huh? No jet available for this trip?"

"Yes to the red-eye, and the jet was parked in Calgary last I checked. Josh is shooting a new TV series there. Jessie flew in to see him." A glum comment followed. "Not that my boss would have let me take the jet anyway. Despite recent musical magic, I haven't entirely worked my way into his good graces yet."

Respectfully, Chris let that one slide although he knew damn well Jacob was referencing recent rather inglorious headlines about his rough treatment of Jessie in Florida not so long ago. "Okay. Well, how about we get you some coffee before we head out of the city. Good enough?"

"Make it a double espresso and we're good." Jacob switched gears. "Hey, any of your friends coming up to this show? I saw it in Vancouver. It's something else."

"I don't know. I doubt it. We have this thing here where the road to Summerside is longer than the road to Charlottetown. Small city versus big city kind of thing."

At Jacob's confused look, Chris added, "Nobody ever goes to Summerside. But those folks all come down here. To shop, or for meetings, whatever. It's kind of an island joke." He half-slapped Jacob's arm. "Hey, how about I post the show on Facebook and see if I can stir up some buds. If you say it's good, I believe you." He hesitated. "Am I allowed to say you're going to be there?"

"Ahhh…" Matt's kind, wise eyes passed through Jacob's vision. "I guess not. My security bud would not approve."

"Wisely. I think you'd be mobbed. The girls from up west don't have much besides the two b's to keep them entertained. Bowling and bingo. Although I hear the hockey's pretty good." Laughing brightly, Chris circled through a small rotary and took an exit leading into a small city of 35 000. "So you don't drive or you just prefer not to have to?"

"I didn't for a long time," Jacob replied, raking tired fingers through his hair. "I did get my license eventually, but I don't get the opportunity to drive much so I'm not that comfortable with it. I don't need a car in the cities."

Chris sent him a sideways look. "I can't see you taking the bus. You're at the top of the music game. And you're a solid actor. And now…" He bit his tongue.

"Yeah, I fucked up." Jacob grew morose. "We may as well get that out of the way right now."

"No man, I'm sorry about Talia. Everybody is. I think everyone gets that things just got a little weird with your ex, that's all."

"Good thing," Jacob sighed, unwilling to go into it with this guy who was really not much more than a stranger. But that was the peculiar thing about celebrity. Everyone always thought they knew him, and Jessie and Josh too. When really, no one knew them at all.

After running through a Starbucks drive-thru, Chris pointed the truck in the opposite direction, towards an even smaller city with a quaint name—Summerside.

"Sure hope it's summery there now," Jacob shivered as he sucked on his jet-fueled espresso. "I can't believe you guys still have snow."

"Yeah it sucks, it's April," Chris agreed. "Last year we had so much snow in four months that there were still pockets of it around in June. In shady places where it took forever to melt."

"Ugh. Think I'll stick to Vancouver."

Fifty minutes later they were at the theater, a 526-seat performing arts theater where Kayla's troupe of Downtown Eastside dancers and musicians were presenting their largely B boyz based show tonight. Wiping sweaty palms on his jacket, Jacob saw that the low, contemporary taupe building housing the theater had a very obvious glass-doored front entrance as well as an easy-to-spot stage door to its right. "I wonder if I can get in the cast entrance," he speculated. "I'm used to finding my way around backstage."

"Should I just meet you back here, Jacob?" Chris asked.

"Get your buddies and come to the show. Text me and I'll leave you as many tickets as you need, unless it's sold out. Although I will warn you that I don't know what kind of reception I'm facing right now. I might not be welcome at the show myself."

Chris raised his eyebrows as Jacob retrieved his bag and rested a hand on Chris' open driver's side window. "So you're seeing this friend?" Chris asked, with a nod towards the massive tour bus parked in the lot nearby. "It's a romantic thing?"

Hesitant, Jacob pondered all the earlier concerns he'd raised with Kayla when they first got together. The angry Jessie-Jacob fans, the time for sadness and mourning that Talia's fans would need. But Chris had a pleasant down-home Prince Edward Island demeanor. He seemed like the kind of guy who could be trusted.

"I'm not seeing her at this point," Jacob admitted truthfully. "But I'd like to be."

Chris was quiet. He raised a thumb to his mouth and bit on a nail as he considered that. "I was a big fan of Talia's," he finally said. "Country music's pretty big here—we have a huge outdoor concert on the north shore every summer. In Cavendish, near the beach. I think she was even supposed to play here this summer. But I guess she'd want you to move on, huh?"

Nosy much? Jacob thought, but he let it go. This guy was kind enough to pick him up at the airport and drive him to Summerside. He fished in his back pocket for his wallet and started drawing out some bills. "Talia was a very special person, Chris," he said. "We had a lot of fun together and I'm never quite gonna believe that she's gone. But she is. And she's never coming back." Extending a hand to Chris, he held out the money. "This girl is someone I've known for a long time but never really considered as a partner until we spent some time together and realized we'd be good together. Talia and I were already going down different paths."

"And Jessie and you are done, huh?"

"We just recorded a new album together. So we kept the important part of what we had. Take the money, will ya?"

Throwing up his hands, Chris said, "I don't want your money, man. I'm happy to drive you."

"This truck's ten years old. Take the money, Chris." Jacob dropped the bills on Chris' lap and started backing away. "You island people. Get your priorities straight."

"No," Chris laughed. "Get yours straight. There's more to life than money."

"Thank God for that." Jacob held up his phone. "Text me with numbers if you want to come to the show. I'll see you tonight."

As Chris motored away with a few beeps and a wave, Jacob pondered which door to take. In the end he went with his first gut instinct and headed to the right, to the stage door. It was unlocked, as he figured it would be since there were smokers in the dance troupe and likely on the local crew who'd be taking puffs outside, so he pulled it open and stepped out of the sunny spring day and into a blue-tinged semi-darkness. Around him to the right were the relics of many long forgotten shows—sets and lights and stands and stools. A long hall at the far end opposite him likely led, in his experience, to dressing rooms. The black-painted stage area was to the immediate left, facing the 'house' further left, where comfortable blue-grey seats awaited patrons.

It took a minute for his eyes to adjust; in the end, Jacob's ears picked up a recognizable tune long before he saw any of the familiar Vancouver crowd.

The tune wasn't his; it was one of Jessie's that the back-up band was covering. The group was rehearsing the opening number. Sliding quietly into the darkened wing by the stage, Jacob picked up Casey and the band before he let his eyes adapt to the stage lights, underneath which Kayla and the entire dance troupe were rehearsing the number.

Jacob sucked in a breath when he saw Kayla. Lost in the music as always when she danced, she was moving with a fluid motion in synchronicity with the bodies floating around her. The tempo of the tune picked up, and her movements intensified. The troupe didn't need the rehearsal, Jacob thought. They were already moving with the practiced ease of a group who had lived, worked and danced together in harmony for months, starting with the workshops and moving onto the tour.

As the song drew to a close, the dancers stepped out of the magic and returned to their normal selves, stretching and listening and waiting and laughing.

Kayla raised a hand and held it across her forehead to block out the stage light. She spoke to the sound guy working from a booth behind eighteen rows of inclined cushioned seats. When she'd raised the hand, her tight tank top came up a few inches and Jacob found his gaze lowering to her exposed belly, and the tight abs he knew were begging for his touch.

He swallowed, and forced his eyes away.

Momentarily, Kayla called for the next number. As she did, the dancers mobilized. The ones not dancing to this piece padded off stage. Some made their way stage left, where Jacob was only partially hidden. Kayla was one of those. Two dancers who Jacob had gotten to know in the fall when he and Talia were visiting the workshops, screamed and leapt into his arms when they saw him. Over the shoulders of one generous hugger he met Kayla's astonished and shocked disapproval.

"Jacob," she stuttered. "Ummm…"

Taking a step back, she gestured to the drum set at the back of the stage, where Casey was easing into the rhythm of the piece now being rehearsed. "She's back there. She'll be a bit." Her eyes were narrowing and her lips twitching. The two dancers picked up on the tension, and left with small hugs and promises to see Jacob later.

"I'm not here to see Casey." Holding his breath as he awaited Kayla's digestion of that truth, Jacob paused. She wasn't running—that was a start.

Confused flickers ran across Kayla's stubborn brown Sawyer eyes before she spoke. "Jacob, I don't…I don't…"

"I'm sorry, Kayla," he tried, pocketing his hands in his jeans pockets and shrinking his body into his denim jacket. "I lost my shit in Vancouver. Your brother…not that I'm blaming Josh, I take responsibility for being an ass, but he scared the shit out of me. I think I wanted to hurt him. Not you. I was so, so stupid."

"So out of the blue you land on my turf weeks later and apologize? What the hell is this?"

"I needed to see you."

Rendered speechless by the simple declaration, Kayla tried to move but her feet wouldn't go. After a minute, she stammered, "Need a good screw, huh? Balls turning blue hanging around Jessie? I heard you two were recording together again."

Wisely, Jacob chose to ignore that comment. It left its sting, anyway. "What song are you doing now? For your solo?" he asked in a husky voice. "I can't imagine you're still dancing to my ballad."

Kayla melted. Those sad blue puppy dog eyes haunted her in her sleep. And here they were before her, all pouty and moist and in the adorable, huggable body of the sweet man she loved, in his tight jeans and, today, a loose flannel button-up shirt with sleeves that hung down over the knuckles of the hands she ached to hold against her body. Blinking back any threat of tears, she answered him. "Adele. *When We Were Young*."

"Ah," he said, and quoted the lyrics. "It was just like a movie…it was just like a song."

"Exactly. Fantasy." Brushing by him, she almost gasped when she caught a hint of Jacob's green apple scent. It screamed *home*. It imbued Kayla's body with a cozy, safe, warm memory, and it offered reams of comfort. Just past him, she closed her eyes and stilled.

Jacob grabbed a well-toned arm and leaned into her. "I came all this way to see you," he murmured into her left ear as she leaned her right shoulder against a wall and bowed her head. "I didn't expect for you to jump up and down when you saw me. But please, Kayla. Can we at least have dinner?"

"I have a show," she mumbled, without opening her eyes. "I don't eat much before shows."

"You don't eat much at all," he remembered, picturing tiny salads, and half-burgers he'd grilled on the sailboat.

"Go home, Jacob," she said softly, turning to him. "I can't do this with you."

Letting go of her arm, Jacob kept his feet planted. He was half leaning towards her still, his face a mask of uncertainty, his lips parting with words that remained unspoken, so inadequate would they be to express his sorrow over what he did to her in Vancouver.

Kayla didn't move either. Wiping a hand over her mouth, as a nervous reaction, she couldn't bring herself to move completely past him out of his space. "Did something happen with Jessie?" she finally managed to quietly ask. "Is that really why you're here?"

The blue eyes settled into their warmest, most loving blue. "You want to know what happened with Jessie? She told me love was worth fighting for. That's what happened. She told me to come get you."

"Jesus," Kayla said, both knees going weak. Her broken heart begged her to believe him, but her mind screamed *Run! Don't fall for this shit.* "Jessie's no expert on love. You ought to know that by now."

"Please, Kayla," Jacob begged. "Just talk to me. Please."

"Not now," she said, eyes filling. "I have a show. You shouldn't have come, Jacob. You're wasting your time." Pushing her lithe dancer's body away from the wall, she lightly elbowed him out of her way, marched down the narrow hallway, and disappeared into a dressing room.

Jacob watched her go, but he didn't leave. Instead, he sidled into the wings at stage left and tried to focus on the rest of the rehearsal. Kayla danced in other numbers, including the touching Adele ballad, but avoided Jacob each time she took or left the stage by exiting in the opposite wing, at stage right.

At the end of the show, Casey stopped in front of Jacob with a cat-that-swallowed-the-canary grin.

"Jacob," she smiled simply in greeting before embracing him tightly.

"Hey, you," he grinned back at her, holding her at arm's length to study the beautiful face with the high cheekbones and exquisite dark eyes. "Looking good, Casey."

"It's all the sex," she laughed, and winked. "I'm seein' Benjie now."

"I'm glad." Jacob gave her a second squeeze. "I hope you're insisting that he treats you right. Like I taught you."

"He's a dream. One of the good ones."

"And he's one of Jessie's permanent dancers. That can't hurt you."

Her smile flipped over. "What you did to her…I still can't believe it. The way you were with me…" She let the words drift away.

"I wasn't myself, Case." *Jesus, is everyone going to remember nothing about me except what I did to Jessie?* Jacob caught himself thinking. "And Jessie and I have a complicated history. Things got out of hand."

"You don't need to defend yourself with me, Jacob." Casey grabbed for his hand and held on. "I know about things that can get complicated and out of hand."

"Some day you're going to tell me your story, Casey."

Her frown darkened and the light in her eyes disappeared entirely. "Do ya have a supper date?" she asked. "I'm done here. I got a couple hours. Benjie's stayin' to help rejig one of the dances since Ariel got the flu."

His eyes flicked over to Kayla who, while in a small group of chatty dancers, was watching him chat with Casey.

Casey turned to see who he was looking at. "She'll come around if ya keep tryin.' But maybe not today." A diabolical grin lit up her cheeks again. "So let's go get food. There's a Subway across the street. Got any smokes?"

"Nope. But I could use one."

"There's a gas station just down the road. Let's take a walk."

Throwing a final woeful look at Kayla, Jacob followed Casey out of the backstage door into the cool Prince Edward Island spring day. Steering right, they sauntered across the parking lot and down the street to a nearby Irving gas station, where Jacob bought a pack of Players to share with his young friend. They smoked two each on the walk to the Subway.

"If you're gonna smoke, you need to pay a little extra and get Dunhills," he told her. "You can get them at specialty smoke shops. No additives. Virginia leaf tobacco. Quality paper. The best." He pointed his last cigarette at her and squinted. "But you really oughtta quit if you want to start drumming in the big leagues. Your heart and lungs won't be able to take it."

Disagreeing, she almost whined. "Lots of good drummers smoke."

"I see I have an awful lot left to teach you, Case. So you're gonna smoke cause others smoke, and drink too, I guess, and after twenty years—or less," he frowned, thinking of Josh, "you'll end up in rehab." Shaking his head, he opened the door of Subway for her. "Nope. We need to start you off right. Yoga and smoothies. Wheat grass. No greasy cheeseburgers and French fries." He winked.

Laughing, Casey hooked an arm in his elbow. "Fine. I'll start with avocado and spinach on my sub. That work for you, hozer?"

Lifting his arm and wrapping it loosely around her shoulders, Jacob ordered his sandwich and waited for Casey to order hers. They had them toasted and went through the process of adding veggies before Jacob paid for them and joined Casey at a four-seater table in front of the window.

Casey leaned her elbows on the table, and licked her fingers between bites as she filled him in on the more dramatic moments of the tour. Happily, Jacob took note that the sullen, angry girl he'd met in Vancouver was now a bundle of light. *That's what Kayla did for her,* he thought. *She gave her confidence. She gave her happiness.*

But soon Casey divulged a dark story that had Jacob feeling that her success and happiness were even harder won than he could have imagined.

"I hitchhiked to Vancouver after six weeks of walkin,'" she was telling him as she scrunched up her paper sandwich wrapper. "I had learned a shit ton about the woods when I was a kid. I hunted rabbits and squirrels for food."

"You lived on a reservation?"

"Yeah. Near Williams Lake. It was good for a while. A lot of outdoor livin' near a river. You can't beat it."

"Where'd you learn to drum?"

She shrugged. "Some music program that passed through the reserve. I just kept at it after the instructors pulled out. YouTube learnin,' mostly."

"There's a lot to be said for pounding out your frustration on an instrument," Jacob said tenderly, understanding the deeper pain he spied in Casey's eyes as she shared this intimate part of herself with him.

"It's better than on a person." From underneath dark eyelashes that were protecting luminescent eyes, Casey peeked up at him.

"Is that why you left home?" Jacob queried carefully. "Someone was hurting you?"

The eyes sank into an old despair as crappy memories came rushing back. "Not so much me. My mother." She paused. "Jacob?"

"Yeah?"

"I know what that white rage is that people talk about. Is that what happened to you? With Jessie?"

Astounded at the girl's capacity to read him in a way that no one else besides maybe Jessie, and perhaps even Kayla, really understood, Jacob had to shift in his seat and struggle to get his emotions under control. Casey's simple empathy washed over him like a light spring rain. He forced his lips to move.

"Y-yes." It was barely a whisper. "What happened to take you there? You're still just a kid."

Focusing on the table and on the sandwich wrapper she kept squishing between her fingers, Casey's eyes went almost blank. The words she spoke were frank, and devoid of emotion. "I got tired of him—my stepfather—beatin' my mother. He took her to the bathroom and dunked her head in the toilet. He was drownin' her. I swear to God she was dead when…" She stopped, and stared at Jacob, but he was pretty sure she wasn't seeing him. She was seeing a small frame home on a British Columbia First Nations reservation.

"So you…?"

"They had a shotgun under the bed. I got it. I shot him. And then I shot her so she wouldn't have to suffer anymore."

Large, slow tears started to slide down Casey's cheeks. Lost in the horrific memory, she either didn't realize she and Jacob were in a public place, or else she simply didn't care. "I took the shotgun and I left. I stopped by the tribal police office on my way out and I told my stepbrother because he was—is—the police chief. I knew he wouldn't care. I know he was glad."

Incredulous, Jacob asked quietly, "He let you go?"

"Yeah."

"Have you gone back? Or called him?"

"No. But I know he wrote it up as a murder-suicide. I read about it when I got to Vancouver. I'm home free."

"Oh, Casey," Jacob sighed, leaning forward and laying his hand over hers. "With that kind of history, you'll never be home free. Not in your heart, and not in your soul."

"Music helps," she said as her body shook at his simple understanding and the genuine gesture of love that came along with it.

"Yes," he agreed, with a tiny forced smile. "Music is the key, kiddo."

Casey leaned back and studied her friend. "I'm okay now," she said honestly. "I've made peace with what I did. My mother wasn't nothin' special. She died a long time ago, in her heart."

"That happens sometimes. I'm sorry, Casey."

"Yeah, well…You ain't gonna tell nobody, are you, Jacob?"

"Nope. You and me got each other's backs, kiddo. Right?"

"Right."

Jacob would have offered to pinky swear with her, but that old tradition seemed to be his and Jessie's sacred thing, so he forced himself to stay quiet on that regard.

When they left ten minutes later, Jacob stopped Casey just outside, at the bottom of the small wooden staircase that led up to the Subway Restaurant. "You keep my number," he told her. "I will always be here for you, Casey. Consider me a big brother, okay?"

"We had sex, Jacob," she giggled in a schoolgirl way, the light slowly coming back into her eyes. "I can't be thinkin' of you as my brother."

"A good friend then." He grinned stupidly at her. "Always, okay kid?"

"Okay." One last hug and they moved out of the small parking lot, across a quiet intersection in the sleepy city, and into the main parking lot of the theater across the way. Gathered outside the stage door were the smokers, so Jacob and Casey joined them. A few minutes later, as he stubbed out his smoke, Jacob's cell bleeped at him.

"Twenty-five tickets for tonight," he read to the assembled dancers and musicians. "My friend Chris is bringing up a crowd from Charlottetown. Where's the box office?"

Pointing him to the main doors, Casey asked, "Where you stayin' tonight, Jacob?"

His nervous glance landed on the bus, and Jacob raised his eyebrows hopefully.

"It's freezing," Casey said. "Stay with me and Benjie, okay? He won't care. The more the merrier, in his eyes." She laughed.

"Yeah, uh…I'll see, Case. Maybe. Thanks." Jacob didn't even blink at the offer. "I'm hoping Kayla will let me ride on the bus with you guys back to Vancouver. Do you think she'll go for it?"

"I think you'll need to bring a lot more than twenty-five new peeps to the show to get her to agree to that," she teased, and pushed him towards the main door. "Go get your tickets. I wanna hear ya cheerin.' See ya after, okay?"

"You'll hear me." Jacob gave the group a wave and sauntered off to buy his tickets.

The only part of the show he struggled with was Kayla's solo dance. The struggle related to his heart—the dance was exquisite. Kayla knew he was there, in the audience. Jacob supposed that had something to do with the reason she didn't smile at the end, or try to look out into the darkness. Instead, she simply bowed her head and tiptoed off the stage.

The Charlottetown crew was boisterous and thrilled and surprised to be in the company of Jacob Ryan, and of Josh Sawyer's pretty but downbeat sister. After the show they made the short trek to the Loyalist Lakeview Inn just across the street, and partied in Benjie and Casey's hotel room until management got annoyed and sent them back east.

After they tore off in seven separate vehicles, Jacob took advantage of the quiet and sought out Kayla, who had stuck her head in the door of Benjie and Casey's room a few times, but hadn't stayed. She wasn't hard to find— she was smoking outside the small hotel's main door. Grabbing the cigarette from between her lips, Jacob took a hefty drag and handed it back to her.

"You dancers and your smokes," he criticized amicably. "How do you manage?"

"I only smoke when I'm pissed," she bit off. "On this tour, that's been just about every day. Thank you for that."

Shuffling his feet, Jacob crunched a last bit of old snow under his boot.

The imprint his boot left was striped and dirty. "I didn't come here to hurt you all over again, Kayla."

"I can't imagine any other reason." She was shivering, so Jacob took off his denim jacket and laid it over her shoulders.

Turning her to face him, he took the butt of the cigarette from between her fingers and extinguished it in a nearby receptacle. "Kayla, look at me," he said, lifting her chin. Jacob smiled sorrowfully at the sadness and worry in her eyes. "I'm not looking for sex. I'm not even looking for a warm bed. I'm just looking for you, a girl who I know feels music the same way I do."

"The same way Jessie does," she whispered mournfully up at him, her shoulders sinking.

"Jessie is no longer a part of this conversation," he determined. "You know how messed up she is in your brother. She's off my radar, except for work, Kayla. I promise you that." Adjusting his stance, Jacob took her silence as hope. "Look," he tried, "let me ride with you to finish out this tour. By that I mean on the bus," he grinned sheepishly as his cheeks flamed pink. "I have a few more months off, then I start on a film and some promotional stuff for the new album. I really want to spend my time off with you. At a distance, if that's what you want, until I can earn your trust back."

"I don't know. I'm scared." The Sawyer eyes were floating. "You just showing up here…it's been kind of a shock. I'm not sure I'm not dreaming."

"The scared part? That makes two of us."

"Jessie sent you, huh? Of all people."

"Yep. She did. She got tired of me wallowing in self-pity."

Kayla stuck her fingers in her mouth and chewed on two nails at once. "What happened in Vancouver, Jacob? What'd Josh say to you?"

Jacob stared at his feet. "It doesn't matter."

"Was it Jessie? Or Dylan?"

"How about both?" he mumbled.

"So…I feel like I would be nothing more than a pawn for you. So you can stay close to them." Switching nervously to her baby finger, sucking on it, she added, "I've had a lot of long bus rides to think about this."

Hopefully, he smiled up at her. "You've considered us. As a couple, I mean. You thought about us."

Her shoulders sank. "I had lots of time to dream." She swallowed painfully. "Not that I ever expected you to show up here…or anywhere on my tour."

"I can't tell you what to think and what not to think, Kayla. All I can do is tell you how damn sorry I am for what I did, and beg you to try to trust me. To give me another shot."

"My brain says you don't deserve another shot." Unable to help herself, she yawned widely.

"Ah. I'm either boring you or I'm breaking you down."

"It's three a.m. I need to sleep."

He grinned. "You're making a lot of headway in that regard." Gesturing to her, he said, "You're not moving."

She grumbled incoherently but stayed put.

"So what's your heart say?" he asked her quietly, referencing their earlier discourse.

"I try not to listen to my heart. It just ends up—" She finished the sentence by blowing up her cheeks and shoving her palms against them so they deflated in a hurry, making a *pffft* sound as the air escaped.

"I came all the way here," he said softly. "That's gotta mean something."

Kayla regarded him with an air of curious disapproval. But underneath was a flicker of hope. A tiny flicker…of hope. "Jessie, huh?"

"Yup. Jessie. She's got this thing about Sawyers."

Poking her toe in the imprint Jacob left in the snow, twisting it, Kayla frowned. "What thing?"

"Something about Sawyers being worth loving." Jacob left out the Sawyer curse part, but his eyes lit up.

"By musicians. Crazy, moody, artsy, hopeless musicians."

Jacob laughed. "Not so hopeless. I don't think, anyway."

"The bus, then," she consented, to his jubilant relief. "But you have to sit where I can't see you."

"Okay." Jacob's heart did a little dance.

"No, uh, where I can see you. Uh…"

"How about next to you?" He asked it quietly, without expectation. But still, Jacob held his breath.

"How about we start with tonight?" she asked him, dropping her fingers into his. "Then we'll see where on the bus you fit."

A wide smile creased his cheeks. "You have a hierarchy on the bus?"

"Oh, yeah," she said as he held open the door and they made their way inside. "Dancers in the front, musicians at the back."

"And musicians who sit with dancers?"

"Hmm?"

"Benjie and Casey?"

"They sit in the back so they can make out and pretend nobody's watching."

"So we'll sit in the back too." His light laughter was infectious. Jacob turned Kayla's face up to his and let his lips brush softly across hers. She moaned and, for the second time that day, her knees gave way.

"Like I said," she breathed into his neck as she wrapped her arms around him. "We'll see how the night goes."

"I'm not worried." The elevator door slid open and Jacob led Kayla inside. They leaned against the back and studied each other. "Kids," he asked softly. "How many?"

As her happy laughter disappeared behind the *swoosh* of the elevator's closing door, Jacob pulled his girl to him, and let his body sigh into hers.

Chapter Eleven

Lighting was taking forever for the first scene after lunch, and the on-set hair, make-up and wardrobe crew were driving Josh nuts with their gossip about who on the crew was sleeping with who. Bored and more than a little disgusted, he decided to go for a wander around the built sets and find a quiet spot where he could go over his lines in peace. Passing Charlie at the craft table, he tapped him on the elbow with his rolled up script sides.

"Deacon. After you finish stuffing your face, run lines with me. I haven't got this one down yet."

"Where you gonna be?" Charlie was reaching for a bagel that popped up in the toaster.

"Somewhere thataway." Josh pointed his coiled sides towards the far end of the large soundstage.

"Give me ten. I'll find you."

Stepping over cables and dodging an electric carrying a heavy 1K light, Josh made his way to the back of the building. Tossing a coin between a bedroom set and a bar set, he chose the latter and set himself up on a round wooden bar stool. He set the day's excerpts on the counter and flipped to the right page, then leaned on his elbows with his hands interlaced lightly at the back of his head, and started reviewing lines.

A wall was missing at the entrance to the bar, removed for the easy manipulation of camera and gear. A light footstep came across the threshold. Josh twisted around to see who was also taking advantage of the quiet.

Shanda.

Straightening, he watched her wander in.

Since Jessie left four days earlier, he and his co-star had been carefully avoiding each other. The words exchanged in the lunchroom that day had left an awkward, stale taste. Shanda was embarrassed, and Josh was unsure what to make of Jessie's statement that Shanda had feelings for him. It seemed like this was a good time to clear the air.

Moving over the wooden floor, Shanda landed next to Josh and slid on to the bar stool to his left. Without thinking about it, she slipped an arm around his waist as a hello, then removed her arm and picked up his script sides.

"It's a long one," she said. "Two-and-a-half pages. This'll take you and Charlie most of the rest of the day the way the lighting crew is working."

"They've got two new dailies on today," Josh explained. "They're training. Slows things down."

"Oh well, I guess that's good," she replied. "Training, I mean. Calgary's booming and it looks like things are only getting better for film and TV in this province."

Nervous, Shanda ran a hand through her blonde locks and looked over at Josh. He caught the look and couldn't avoid a small flush that crept into his cheeks.

Sliding around on her stool, Shanda faced Josh more fully. "Josh, I owe you an apology for the other day. I guess I actually owe it to your wife but she's not here, so…" Puffing up her cheeks and exhaling slowly, Shanda let the sentence fade away.

With a wave of his hand, Josh cut in, "It's fine, Shanda. It's not a big deal."

"Jessie was upset when she left. I feel badly about that."

"You're a good person, Shanda. Don't waste a lot of time feeling bad about Jessie. She's a big girl. We're both used to certain…issues…popping up on the sets we work on."

"I'm sure you are." Hunching up her shoulders, Shanda struggled for something else to say, and gave up. As she slid off the stool, she grasped Josh's bicep for leverage, but instead of letting go when she was standing, she held on and said his name. Josh rotated his butt on the stool and faced her.

At the same time, with a mouthful of bagel, Charlie was making his way over the cables, looking for Josh so they could run lines. Outside the bar set, he heard Shanda's voice. Stopping, Charlie cocked his head to listen.

"So," Shanda was saying with a nervous laugh, "do you ever...face those issues head on? Like, uh...this is hard. Josh, I've never crushed on a co-star before. This is totally weird for me. Especially considering how scared I was of working with you. I almost didn't take the job because of you."

"I'm a good guy, Shanda. As long as I can stay clean I can stay a good guy. No, I don't mess around when I'm away from my wife. Even for pretty blondes like yourself."

Outside, Charlie relaxed and emitted a small *huh*. The last thing Josh and Jessie needed was for this thing with Shanda to get out of hand. He started to move, but glanced in the window as he passed it. Inside, he could see Shanda and Josh in close proximity, Shanda standing in front of Josh in tight leggings and a long flowing top, and Josh in his sheriff's khakis, the shirt open at the neck and tail hanging out over his pants since they wouldn't be shooting for a while and he'd have tons of time to fix up his wardrobe later.

What surprised Charlie was that what he was seeing didn't match what he'd just heard. Josh's arm was raised and he was running his fingers through Shanda's short blonde curls. She was lifting her hand and placing it over his, and moving his hand down to her cheek. At the same time, she moved closer to him, so she was standing directly in front of his bar stool, in between his legs.

"But you want to this time," Charlie heard her say. "I can feel it. I can see it in your eyes."

On the dim set, Josh swallowed. "That doesn't mean I'm going to act on it. I'm not, Shanda. I can't. Maybe...maybe if things were different." But Josh glanced down at those nervous pink lips and couldn't stop himself from brushing his thumb over them. Desire shot up into his groin, and he closed his eyes. Small arms snaked around his body and, before he could blink, Shanda leaned into him and pressed her lips gently against his. Dropping his hand, Josh let it land on her narrow hip. His left hand was already on one hip, and he absently wondered how it got there since he didn't remember putting it there.

Responding to Shanda's kiss, Josh pressed her body closer to his, and let the electric feelings for his perky co-star completely blow his earlier statement to bits. Running his tongue over her lips, he moaned lightly when she opened her mouth wider to let him in. The kiss lasted a good thirty seconds before Josh got hold of his senses and gently pushed Shanda away.

Outside, Charlie was now cursing but he was frozen. He couldn't move now or they'd hear his footsteps and anyways, he was curious as to which way this little rendezvous would go. Angling his head to hear better, he listened.

"Shanda," Josh was saying quietly. "I can't. As much as I'd love to spend time with you and be with, well," he sighed, "someone not near as big a handful as my wife, I can't. I just can't. I really love her. I'm sorry. Jessie is everything to me. She always will be."

He still had his hands on Shanda's small hips. In kindness, Josh lifted his right hand and once again touched her cheek. A tiny tear was forming in Shanda's right eye. He thumbed it away.

"She doesn't have to know," Shanda breathed hopefully.

"You're not that person, Shanda. And I don't want to be that person either."

Choosing another tack, Shanda tried, "Look, I know things aren't so great with you guys right now."

Josh groaned and sat back. Dropping his hands from her body, he scratched his chin. "I love how the whole world always knows our business. Shanda, even if things got to the point of no return with Jessie and me, you wouldn't want me, okay? For a few nights, a week, a month, maybe. But after that?" He shook his head. "The last time I lost her I lost myself too. I'm still trying to find my way back. I'm not your guy. I'm sorry."

"I just mean if things get bad, you know…and you need a shoulder. Mine're pretty skinny but they work okay."

A slow upturn to Josh's lips brought a smile to his eyes as well. "Thanks," he said sincerely. "I mean that."

She smiled too, not nearly as brightly, and it was followed by a quick downturn of the smile, then Shanda reached her arms around Josh and pulled him close to her. "I just feel like you need this right now, you know?" she said. "Like you need to be held."

Josh had no answer for that, except, Charlie noted, for tightly squeezed eyes and a hold on Shanda that brought her body even closer to his. When he buried his face in her neck, Shanda knew that she was right. He needed to be held, he needed to be loved. What Josh didn't need was to be left alone.

"You're a very special man, Josh Sawyer," she told him as she started to back away, trying not to disappear into those liquid brown eyes that, now, were fighting to remain afloat. Josh wasn't letting go of her hand. There was something about being understood that made him want this woman to stay in his presence. In his life.

Pivoting slowly around, Shanda forced her legs to carry her to the edge of the set. She didn't turn around because she didn't want Josh to see the tears now flowing freely down her cheeks, and when she got around to the exterior wall, outside where he couldn't see her, she collapsed back against it, closed her eyes, and sank to the floor, burying her face in her arms as she moved, and struggling to keep her body from convulsing.

A shadow bent before her. Charlie. Lifting her chin, he murmured, "Rough, huh?"

She could only nod, and try to suppress sobs, but she ended up gasping anyway, embarrassed enough to try to turn her face away from him.

Charlie continued. "He's a good guy, Shanda. He's a helluva lot better man to Jessie than I ever was. And you're right, they're having a tough time right now. The last thing Josh needs is temptation. Please find a way to work with him without being the cause of more hurt between him and his wife. I'm begging you."

His words were spoken with a solemnity and veracity that Shanda recognized were founded on a lot of years of friendship with the Sawyers. A lot of years watching them suffer when all they really wanted to do was love one another.

"I will, Charlie," she promised him between unsuccessful attempts at keeping her sobs quiet. "But I have to tell you. I'm pretty sure I'm in love with him."

"Then it's going to be a long season." Keeping his gaze fixed on her, Charlie exhaled slowly. "Love really sucks when it's not reciprocated."

Grasping his hand, Shanda nodded. "I know," she sniffled. "And I guess you know too."

"And you were scared of him." Charlie grinned. "Told you he was one of the good ones." At that, he rose, grimacing at the crackling in his knees. "You're off for the rest of the day," he said. "Go hang out at a coffee shop or something before you become too well known and no longer have that luxury. This series is going to skyrocket you to the top, kid."

"I'm not sure I'm ready for that." She tried to smile and, to Charlie, it was a rainbow breaking through the storm.

""You'll be fine. Josh and I will help you through it. You just need thick skin, that's all."

"Thanks, Charlie." Extending a hand up to him, Shanda let him pull her upright. "I'll be okay. Thanks."

"I know you will." Gently hugging her, Charlie let her go with a soft kiss on the cheek. She wandered away to a dark corner to wipe away her mascara trails, leaving him with a backwards wave.

"Well, shit," Charlie muttered to himself as he watched her walk away. Turning, he made his way inside the bar set, where Josh was lost in thought, his hands on his thighs and his eyes locked on a crack in the floor. "Sawyer," Charlie scolded him. "Can you not keep at least one of your co-stars from falling in love with you?"

"Mm. You heard." Josh sat back and rested his elbows on the counter.

"You've got about five more months to avoid falling in love with her." Charlie slid onto the stool next to his friend and pulled his script sides out of his jacket pocket. "Think you can do it?"

"No." Josh rotated around to the bar and laid his head down on folded arms.

"You need to get Jessie and the kids moved out here, Josh. Jane needs them around, for one thing."

"Okay. I will. I swear."

"One hug from your wife and Shanda's cute little breasts will disappear from your radar forever."

"Great. I mean good."

Charlie rotated around on his stool and laid his script sides next to Josh's. "I used to be all for set romances until I learned first hand what they had the potential to destroy. I will always regret losing Jessie to you. And I won't stand back and let the two of you flounder because of my TV show."

Josh sensed a serious tone in the usually genial Charlie's voice. He turned his head and lifted his gaze to study Charlie. "It's not *Sacred Peace* that's got us messed up, Charlie. It's old shit that snuck up on me when Jacob decided to reappear in Jessie's life."

"But now it's distance and a super cute co-star."

"So, what? You're going to fire me?"

"Not you, Josh."

It took a second for that to sink in. "Shanda? You can't do that. She's amazing. And we're just getting started. She has a contract!"

"You are way too concerned about your co-star, Josh. Let's get to work. Lines to learn."

"Charlie…"

"I'm not going to fire her today, Josh. But I will if I see her getting between you and Jessie again. I will not see you lose Jessie. It's my personal mission."

A quick smile lit up Josh's face and danced across his eyes. Hazel flecks rising to the surface made him appear almost downright happy. "Okay," he agreed as he grabbed his script sides. "I'm for that. Thanks, Charlie."

"The kids. Jess. You call them tonight. But for now, we learn lines. Top of scene nine. Go."

With a light chuckle, Josh tented his elbows over the paper and looked for his place on the page. Charlie glanced over at him and felt a wave of affection—love, even—for this troubled guy who once stole his girl out from under him. Josh's hair was cascading over his cheek now, long enough to almost brush the counter, giving him an aura of childish innocence.

Charlie couldn't help himself. With Jessie's sad eyes floating across his mind, he reached next to him and gave his good friend a generous bro-squeeze. His voice gruff, he said, "Love you, Sawyer."

Surprised, Josh looked up at him, a slow smile creasing his face. "This Sawyer's getting lots of love today," he decreed. "And I gotta say, I kinda like it." A more serious tone colored his next words. "I love you back, Deacon. And…thanks."

Laughing, Charlie raised his arm to hook around Josh's neck, and he gave him a second squeeze. "Jesus," he declared, "we might get through this scene today. Between the new lighting guys and us yelling 'line' to the scriptee all afternoon, we just might make it home before dark."

"We better," Josh said. "I want to take a ride on Blue up to the creek this evening. Come on, you're up first. Stop being all mushy and read." But he had a grin the size of Alberta on his face and, for the first time in a long time, Josh felt lighthearted, and maybe even ready for Jessie and the kids to make the move to the ranch.

Chapter Twelve

In Vancouver, Jessie caught a break from a long week alone with the kids when Dee called and invited her to La Casa for dinner.

"Matt's bringing Miranda around. Carlotta's got a special meal planned."

"The prodigal has returned, huh? Is Carlotta killing a goat or something? Tell her I know where she can get a sharp dagger if she needs it."

A loud huff came over the line from North Van. "Jessie, I swear. Some days I don't quite know how to take you."

"You can't tell me this isn't a test, Dee. You and Charles want to see if we can bring Matt back into the fold to babysit me without the two of us killing each other."

Deirdre was clearly exasperated. "Matt's our very dear friend, Jessie. We want to meet this new woman he's been dating. Now, are you in or are you not? Katy has offered to stay the night at your place, and Dan will do periodic checks around the exterior of the house."

"I suppose. Although I don't know if I can find a toga to wear at this late notice."

"Well, find something nice. Matt says Miranda enjoys dressing up for dinner. Leave the dirty cowboy boots and those ratty old sneakers at home."

"Blah," was Jessie's solemn answer. "Can't wait. See you tonight, Dee." Glum, she disconnected and sat at her kitchen island pondering Dylan, who was raising his arms up to her, his little fingers stretching as far as he could make them go.

"Up, Momma. Up!"

"You little monkey." Bending over to scoop him up, Jessie studied the blue eyes and wondered where Jacob was. Even though they hadn't talked more than just business in a while, she used one finger to text him, while using the other hand to give Dylan a banana she took from a blue Trout River, P.E.I. pottery bowl in the center of the kitchen island. The bowl was a wedding gift from their kindly South Rustico landlady during that tumultuous island summer. Jessie found it a good reminder for staying grateful and grounded as much as possible.

"Jacob, what are you up to?" she intoned quietly as Dylan sat in pure contentment on his mother's lap and started on his banana.

A text came back immediately.

On the tour bus with Kayla, just left Montreal

"Oh, shit! Wow. Okay, Dylan, well I guess one of your daddies is doing okay. I wonder how the other one is?"

She typed in a text to Josh, but none came back. "He's got a long scene today," she told Dylan, who aimed his baby-innocent eyes up at her. She melted and kissed his soft cheek. "Your daddy. Who I hope we all get to see soon. Come on, Dylan. You and me are going shopping. Momma needs to look absolutely dazzling for Matt's new woman tonight." Sliding off the stool, she set her son down and said, "Let's go do the potty and then we'll hit the road. Hey, buddy, why don't we take the Mustang today? It's gorgeous out there."

Shoving aside what Matt would think of the idea, which would be *Why don't you call a bit more attention to yourself,* she *pshawed* him and prepared for a trip downtown, with her two-year-old son in a car seat in the back of the open convertible.

"Whhhheeeeee!" they shouted together, riding down Fourth in Kitsilano as the bright sunshine, the gorgeous pale pink cherry blossoms lining the streets, and a sense of rebellious freedom conjoined to raise Jessie's spirits immeasurably. "Hey Dylan, you have so much to look forward to!"

Her son's laughter was contagious, and Jessie cranked up the stereo and laugh-sang to him as she drove. There was no Matt today, Sam was watching the older kids' school, Arnie was in Calgary with Josh, and Dan was resting before his night shift tonight. After promising Ulysses she would stay home to avoid any possible public outcries from angry Jacob—Josh fans, Jessie was stubbornly determined to enjoy a freedom she didn't often get.

"We'll be fine," she told her son, adjusting the rearview mirror so she could see him better. "You like 'Walk Off The Earth,' right?" she asked him in all seriousness, before stopping at a red light and choosing the Canadian band's popular tune *Hold On (the Break)*. "LOVE this guy's voice. He reminds me of, um, one of your daddies. Listen, Dylan!" And she sang all the way down to Pacific Centre, where Jessie parked in the underground parkade, retrieved her busy son, and realized she had forgotten his stroller.

Heart sinking, she muttered, "We never do this alone, just the two of us. I suppose you'll want snacks too, huh?" Then, shrugging her shoulders, she carried him to the elevator, ducking her head whenever she passed anyone. After a bit, realizing everybody was too interested in their phones and in their own lives to be bothered with her, Jessie relaxed. "We're good, little fella," she said, and Dylan grinned and buried his face in his mother's neck.

In the mall, Jessie found a kind Asian sales clerk who loved children to help keep an eye on Dylan while she tried on dresses in the shop of one of her favorite designers. She chose a stunning rose-grey silk mini-dress with a semi-plunging halter neckline and a revealing 'side-boob' silhouette. "This oughtta wow him. I mean her," she thought as she rotated her hips to see what the dress looked like from all possible angles. The saleslady brought her matching stiletto heels, and Dylan too, who was getting grumpy.

"Ah, already you don't like shopping." Jessie smiled lovingly at his mad face. "Let me change, and then you and me will rock the food court."

Checking the time, she decided she had a good hour left before she would have to head back to meet Emily-Grace and David at West Point Grey.

"Wonder how your daddy's day is going? Wonder if he will like this dress… mmmm…I like it, Dylan. I guess that's enough for me."

She used a credit card to pay at the counter, happy that the woman who waited on her didn't seem to have a sweet clue who she was. The woman just wanted the $ 5300 Jessie's purchase wrought. Jessie didn't blink an eye.

By then, Dylan was becoming quite a handful, pulling at his mother's fingers and becoming very whiny and uncooperative. "You sure are not like my other two," Jessie grumbled, trying not to lose her patience with him as he decided to stop at one of the benches in the mall.

Refusing to move, he stomped his feet and let out a mighty howl.

Kneeling before him, Jessie asked, "What is it, Dylan? Why are you so mad?"

"Hungy," he told her, fire blazing in his Jacob-eyes as he tossed off her hands at his waist.

"Oh," Jessie said. "I guess it is that time. We're on our way to the food court. Come on."

Her face whooshed red when she realized his tantrum was attracting the wrong kinds of stares. Two nearby giggly teenagers screwed up their courage and approached.

"Can we get a selfie?" the first one, a freckled redhead, asked. "And can you sign my, um, my shopping bag or receipt or something? That's all I've got."

"Uh, no pictures girls, sorry," Jessie answered nervously, thinking of how angry Charles would be at her for her unsecure downtown trip if he saw random pics posted on social media. Then, she bit her lip and said, "You know what? Screw it. Let's do pics."

It was a half hour later before she finally put a stop to autographs and photos and picked up Dylan, who was by then crying at all the 'Oh, this is Jacob Ryan's son' attention that Jessie could see was confusing the hell out of him.

"I'm sorry, baby." Ducking her head, she nodded at the displeased uniformed mall security flanking the fans, to thank them for helping disperse the crowd that had gathered around her. "Food. Let's go."

The local security was actively communicating via tiny headsets and mics as she looped her purchase bag over one wrist and started striding quickly away. Not surprisingly, a larger crowd was gathering. Twitter was once again giving her away. Before Jessie reached the escalator to slide her and Dylan down to the food court, a dour faced grey-haired black uniformed man wearing a cap with 'security' emblazoned above the brim, tapped her on the shoulder.

"I'm sorry, Mizz Wheeler, or Sawyer," he said. "Word's out that you are here. I need to escort you to your vehicle."

Jessie's jubilant mood crashed. Dylan was wriggling in her arms and screaming now, wanting down. He started kicking her.

"Dylan! Hang on, baby," she demanded before turning her eyes to the man. "I just need to get something for my son to eat. We kinda bypassed lunch. I won't be a minute, okay?"

"I'm sorry, Ma'am."

As if to prove his point, a group of four teens approached.

"Aren't ya'll supposed to be in school?" Jessie asked them, frustration tingeing her voice. "I apologize, but I need to get my son some food." Pushing her way through them, ignoring their disappointed pleas, Jessie was also pointedly ignoring the man from security. But she started to panic when Dylan's frantic wriggling form slipped from her grasp and landed, butt first, on the floor. To Jessie's utter embarrassment and chagrin, he started kicking a metal garbage can, again and again and again.

"Oh, fuck," she breathed, aware that her parenting skills were about to be on 'Twitter display' for the whole world to see. "Sweetheart," she tried, bending down to him. "This is not helping."

Picking Dylan up again, tears in her eyes, she turned back around to the guy from security who she was trying to dodge. "Okay," she exhaled, as Dylan kicked her again. "Ouch. Fuck, Dylan! You win. You both win. I'll take the escort."

Ten minutes later she was on her way out of the parkade with a Vancouver City Police escort, which let her off at the UBC house with a beep and a wave.

Dylan was inconsolable by then, and Jessie was shaking and cranky. Texting Sam to ask him to bring Emily-Grace and David home, she made her way to the kitchen and prepared a late lunch for her hungry son. By the time Emily-Grace and David were delivered by Sam, who held up his phone and frowned at her as a Twitter video played out the afternoon's drama, Dylan was asleep in her arms, all roses and sunshine and little boy love.

""Yeah, Sam, I know. I suck." Jessie held up her shopping bag and smiled, a mischievous glint in her eye. "But I got one helluva dress for tonight."

"You better hope it's drop dead gorgeous," he answered with a wry grin. "Because Matt was on the other end of this phone earlier, cursing up a storm. He's not impressed."

Blushing, Jessie shot back, "No worries. He will be."

The cryptic comment left Sam slightly confused, but the relief that Jessie and Dylan were home safe and sound far outweighed his concern. Grabbing a banana, he peeled it and went off in search of David and Emily-Grace so they could toss around a Nerf football before Katy's expected arrival in late afternoon.

Chapter Thirteen

That night, Josh and Charlie wrapped at about the same time Jessie slipped the exquisite dress over her shoulders and, with kisses all around for her children, stepped lightly up the flagstone walk to the silver Lexus. She still hadn't received a text from Josh, which pissed her off so much that she turned off her cell phone and left it on the dash of the SUV during her evening at La Casa.

"Stunning," Dan exclaimed as she was climbing into the vehicle. Scanning her from head to toe, but in an appreciative manner, not in any way a sleazy one, was why Dan was still around after all these years. "I guess the trip to Pacific Centre was worth the trouble, huh Jessie?"

"It will be," she answered brightly. "Between you and me, I'm hoping this dress and the presence of Matt's new woman will keep Matt and Charles from going down my throat for today's little shopping trip."

In the end, Deirdre's words were the most cutting. Spoken from the safety of the kitchen, she took Jessie aside and didn't hold back, although her message was delivered in a harsh whisper.

"Jessie, *normal* women don't tend to skip lunch to take two year olds shopping. Did you lose your mind?"

"Deirdre Keating," Jessie started in a huff, "what I choose to do with my two year old is my business. If I want to shop, I'll shop."

"You better hope you make friends with Matt again tonight, then, because this is not going to happen again in future. You will not go into the city—to public places—unsupervised, with your child in tow! Not while there's still all this hype over Josh's behavior at the Grammys, and Jacob's little faux pas."

"Oh, is that what rape is called these days? A faux pas? Jesus, Dee." With that, Jessie sucked up her courage, adjusted the spectacular dress on her body, and marched into the front room, where Matt and Miranda were lingering casually by the large fireplace under the warmth of the Paul Peel painting, being entertained by Charles, who was explaining to Miranda where he acquired the piece.

Thankfully, Miranda was an interested and attentive listener. She kept her eyes trained on Charles as he spoke, while Matt turned his head to greet Jessie. So Miranda didn't see the blaze of passion and desire that crossed her boyfriend's face when Matt spotted Jessie in the spectacular dress. Jessie did, though, and although it was exactly the reaction she sought from Matt, the fire his dusky eyes lit inside her own body threw her.

I'm just lonely, she intoned inwardly. *I'm lonely and scared that Josh is going to go down some dark road with Shanda Ellis. I spend all my days with kids and I need to feel like a woman again. So I'm damn well going to feel like a woman.*

Taking a glass of wine from Carlotta's kindly outstretched fingers, she angled her head and pressed her lips together to show Matt that she knew how friggin' stunning she looked in the new dress and heels. Locking her haughty, yearning eyes into his, Jessie tipped back the glass of light and refreshing Pinot Grigio and took a healthy swig.

"Oh, you little bitch," Matt murmured under his breath. "We're going to play that game, are we, Jessie?" And he turned and touched Miranda's arm.

"Miranda? Sorry, Charles, may I borrow this lovely lady for a moment?"

Jessie faced Miranda with the poise and grace she'd learned over years of meeting politicians, celebrities, and googly fans. "Miranda." Plastering a smile on her face that Matt immediately recognized as somewhat false, Jessie didn't wait for him to introduce her. "How lovely to finally meet you." She extended a hand.

Miranda was gracious in return, but she wasn't stupid. She caught on right away, mostly because Matt could not take his eyes off the woman who was supposedly his client. "Lovely to meet you too, Jessie." Accepting Jessie's hand, Miranda grasped her fingers with an elegance befitting her position as the owner of a number of successful Vancouver businesses. "I've been a fan for a very long time."

Ah, is that a dig? Jessie wondered. Out loud she said, "Thank you. And I hear you have a little restaurant or something?"

Oh, for Heaven's sake, Matt fumed.

Miranda, to her credit, took it well. "I do. You should come by. Matt can attest to the quality of the food. He's been my guest many times now."

As Jessie rather coolly let her gaze drift over Miranda's choice of clothing and the attractive body within that clothing, Matt watched her with increasing curiosity. He knew Jessie well enough to discern that she was uncomfortable. The way she was now holding onto the stem of her wine glass, with one set of graceful fingers laid over the others, the glass at mid-chest as if she needed something in between herself and Miranda; the way she silently appraised Miranda's expensive just-above-the-knee clingy cashmere dress, with its slimming waist tie and low cleavage, and the high black leather boots that clearly directed focus to her well-developed cyclist's calves; the way Jessie let her eyes anxiously flit to Miranda's flattering haircut and intelligent eyes…Matt knew the old record playing in Jessie's mind. *I am uneducated. I started my film career in erotic movies and photographs. I'm having trouble in my marriage. I'm alone. I'm lonely.*

Watching her process Miranda with a filter that came from being a teen runaway, and from being a victim of unwanted sex from the time she was twelve, softened his attitude at least a little towards Jessie tonight.

As if Jessie could read Matt's thoughts, she escaped the stilted conversation with Miranda when Charles joined in, and she settled her troubled gaze on Matt. Handsome in tight black dress pants accented with a small stylish silver buckled belt, a white dress shirt open at the neck and a black satin trimmed Dior-Homme dinner jacket overtop, with his hair gelled perfectly as usual to stand up on the top, she had to swallow hard to maintain any semblance of sanity in the presence of his girlfriend. Not having seen him since their harsh words a few weeks earlier made it especially difficult to be in his powerful presence at La Casa.

I need to talk to you, she breathed to herself and clutched the wine glass tighter. *I need to spend time with you. I miss my friend.*

Instead of answering, Matt broke into her thoughts with a quiet criticism that cut Charles off in mid-sentence. "Was that the reason you just had to go to the mall today, Jessie?" He pointed the nose of his wine glass in the general direction of her body.

Her response was edged so sharply she could have cleanly sliced a squash in one fell swoop. "I went to the mall to get out of the house," she bit off.

"Alone."

Is that worry in his eyes? Let it be worry. "What the hell do you care? You seem to have jumped ship."

That got him. It got all of them. From Charles came a low-voiced warning. "Jessie." It, too, was sharp and definitive.

Miranda caught her breath and looked over at her boyfriend, her eyes widening slightly.

Matt shifted his weight to his other leg. "This is not the time, Jessie," he admonished, the words slightly swollen with the emotion this little reunion was engendering.

Jessie glanced over at Miranda, who was now seriously clueing in to the sexual tension in the room.

"Matt?" Miranda questioned, as if to say *what the hell?*

Deirdre, who entered the room at just the right time and beckoned them to dinner, rescued them.

Charles rather wisely led the puzzled, voluptuous Miranda out into the grand wide hallway first.

Matt grasped Jessie's elbow and held her back.

Whipping her curled hair around to face him, she crunched childishly on her lip.

"Do you have a problem with me, Jessie?" he demanded, leaning into her, releasing his warm wine-infused breath seductively in her face. "If so, please don't take it out on Miranda."

"Finally getting laid, are we? You don't want me to get in your way?"

"Jesus Christ. You're such a fucking baby sometimes."

"I'm the baby? I'm not the one who ran off in a big sulk and forgot to come to work for the last few weeks."

"I've done enough overtime with all of you to earn a few weeks off, Jessie."

"Is that what this is? Spending time with me now? Overtime?"

"Look. When all is said and done I get a fucking paycheck from you, okay?"

With a wild elbow to the left, Jessie threw off his hold on her. "Just what I figured. I'm nothing to any of you but a goddamned paycheck. Still don't think I'm a whore, Matt?"

Wanting to storm away but completely unable to leave his presence, Jessie stood still on the new high shoes, her blood pounding in her ears.

Only the spark of anger that had ignited earlier and still remained shaded the hurt in Matt's eyes, which drifted down to Jessie's exquisite dress to spy the delicate bit of breast peeking out from the side of her rigid, toned body. One breast was scarred, from when Jessie was left cut and bleeding by Morgan's hand, back in Montreal a few years ago. It was everything Matt could do not to reach out and run the backs of his fingers over the raised skin, which he, at least in part, considered yet another of his mistakes in handling Jessie's safety.

Not unnoticed by the object of his desire, Matt's eyes wandered to the inviting half-moons peeking out from the dress' plunging neckline that led to tight abs. Jessie didn't discourage Matt's smoldering gaze—lifting a finger, she traced it slowly down between her breasts, and almost moaned when his eyes floated back upwards to meet hers.

Struggling to compose himself, he fought the rising pressure with a scathing retort. "Do I think you're a whore? In that dress? I don't have to think it, since it seems apparent you do that well enough on your own. Way to dress the part, Jessie."

Even Matt's ears were held hostage by Jessie's sizzling sexual energy tonight, by the sensual essence she telegraphed through the inviting soft *shush* of the short silk as she reacted to his mean jibe by taking a jarring step backwards.

The snipes they were tossing back and forth at each other like knives stopped at that dig, but only because Matt had the wherewithal to see Jessie collapse inward. She did it with a quick surprised inhale, a second sudden tottering step back, and a sagging of her naked shoulders.

Her gaze dropped to the floor. Matt saw her turn towards the main entrance as if she needed to avoid being in his sight and wanted an escape route.

"Don't," he said gruffly. "Don't leave."

The pretty blue eyes came back to him with another head toss. "Don't pretend you really care, Matt. I'm too old for games."

His comforting breath once again warmed her cheek when he moved forward and gathered her into a gentle hug. "You know I care, Jessie," he murmured. "Let's start again."

Ducking her head, Jessie let one arm slide around his waist, under his expensive dinner jacket, and she closed her eyes and pushed her hurt back into her belly where she felt it belonged. Inhaling deeply, she soaked up the light bristles on his cheek, the fresh soap and familiar aftershave smell of his body, the warmth and strength of his arms around her.

"You stupid dork," she whispered, as he relaxed his hold on her but left his hands on her waist. "How'm I supposed to do this? With you, without you?" Aiming both baby blues into her protector's caring eyes, she let one arm glide around to his belly and hooked her fingers low over his belt.

Gently, Matt removed the hand, but he held it lightly in his own fingers.

He put a halt to the sexual vibe with a quick question. "How was Josh last weekend, Jessie? Charles seems to think the two of you are working through things."

"Funny," she answered hotly. "The two of you seem completely unrelated. In my head. Like you're in completely different dimensions. Why is that? Is it distance? Is it because over the years I've spent way more time with you than I have with him?"

"It's because, Jessie, you're lonely and I'm here. That's all it is."

"Nope." She tilted her head in that cute way of hers and licked her lips before she bit down on the bottom one again. "It's because I know I'm losing you. That's why. So you're higher than Josh on the totem pole right now. You're in a different space. You're just one more person who is walking out of my life and leaving me alone. Because people can walk away from paychecks. Can't they, Matt?"

As that sank in, flush with disdain she added, "And I don't know what the hell's going on with Josh. Since you asked. His co-star's in love with him. Did you know that? We'll see how long he walks around with blue balls before he actually jumps on her."

"A good man can do that for a very long time, Jessie." Matt spoke to her back as Jessie quietly made her way to the hall.

She stopped and looked back at him. "Forever?" she breathed. "Can he do it forever? No," she answered her own question, and pointed her wine glass at him again. "Can he? Do you want to just lay down here on Deirdre's fancy rug and get it over with, Matt? Would you stay, then?"

Carlotta moved into Jessie's line of vision then. "They're waiting," she said kindly, well aware that the tension between Matt and Jessie was quickly unraveling what should have been a special evening for Matt and Miranda.

"No." The light in his eyes faded as Matt raised his chin just a little.

"So." Jessie lifted her wine glass and drained the last bit of the Pinot Grigio in one big swallow, as if she was instead sucking back her old Jim Beam. "You're leaving me no matter what." The implications of that sucked the life out of her.

"Yes." Matt had no other words—no explanation, no defense. He had nothing to offer her.

Watching him, memorizing him, Jessie fought a rising panic at the thought of living her life without her best friend in it, and she pivoted around on one high heel and stepped towards the dining room when, in fact, what she really wanted to do was hide in the restroom, clutch the porcelain sink, and melt into the floor.

A few moments later, Matt got his emotions under control and followed her, but wanting very much to do the very same thing.

Chapter Fourteen

By the time Josh got to the ranch, there was not a lot of daylight left. Twice during the afternoon's scene, he and Charlie had messed up their lines and broken out into fits of laughter and could not, no matter how hard they tried, get themselves under control until the first A.D. called a ten minute break and they went off to separate corners to compose themselves. Shooting with a friend—it was a blast, especially after the little showdown with sweet Shanda earlier in the day.

Feeling better than he had in a long while, Josh whistled during the drive up the lane to the clearing between the corral, barn and house, and eyed the horizon.

"I can fit a ride in," he said with confidence to the truck as he parked. The barn was close by, but he had to change first. Inside the low one-story house, Josh was surprised and pleased to find a note from Jessie's Aunt Evelyn saying she'd left a lasagna in the fridge for him. It came with directions to place it in the oven for an hour.

"Perfect," Josh said happily to the room. Sliding it into the oven, he put the timer on for the suggested hour and whistled his way into the bedroom to put on what he considered his riding jeans—a faded pair with a few interesting holes. He topped them with a thick plaid fleece jacket, a worn black cowboy hat, and an old pair of dust-brown western boots.

Almost at the barn, he realized he'd forgotten to text Jessie back. He'd meant to, all day, but between running lines with Charlie, shooting, rehearsing, and then driving, he just hadn't made the time. "Oh, well," he told himself. "No point in going back for the phone now. Daylight's on loan."

Inside the small barn, Josh unlocked a metal cabinet hidden in an unused stall. He pulled out a rifle, a short-barreled Winchester, and loaded it with ammunition taken from a box on the top shelf. Leaning it against the empty stall door for the time being, Josh pondered the cougars known to be a threat in the immediate vicinity. He was headed up the pass a little ways. Mounting a gun in a leather scabbard on his saddle was always a must, just in case.

The memory of Jessie's concerned voice brought a small smile to his lips.

"Hey, Blue," he said to his other girl as he opened the stall door and gave the horse a few gentle rubs on her neck before leading her out to saddle her. "I'll bet you're frothing at the bit for a little exercise, huh girl?"

She blinked back in her big, now docile way that she generally just reserved for Josh, who she loved unconditionally—the same way he loved her.

"You're so beautiful," he told her, his heart big and happy as he looked into those moist, doe-y eyes. "You're the kind of girl a man needs. Easy to please. You just need a good ride once in a while." Laughing at the double meaning of what he said, and coloring a little in the cheeks, Josh got to work saddling the horse.

Fifteen minutes later, he was on the trail.

In Vancouver, Jessie was getting more than a little drunk.

She was behaving much better, though. Matt surmised correctly that it was because Charles and Dee, who had practically adopted Jessie, were seated at the table, handing out warning glances and slight reprimands like bullets.

Matt was across from Jessie, with Miranda at his right. Charles sat at the far head of the table, in front of the open window with its light, billowy breeze, and Deirdre was next to him, on Jessie's left.

Overall, the conversation lightened up and was peppered with jokes and laughs, despite Jessie's rather cool, quiet presence at the table.

She found it hard not to stare at Matt who, she intuitively felt, had one foot out the door. *Because of me.* He was a good boyfriend to Miranda—attentive, laughed at the right times, touched her, teased her. It drove Jessie around the bend. She felt he was leaning into the sophisticated woman and whispering sweet nothings just to drive her, Jessie, completely nuts.

The more wine she drank, the more certain—and paranoid—she became. Still, she kept her cool. Charles and Deirdre would have found the sexual tension between Jessie and Matt quite entertaining, were they not aware, too, that it had come to a point of no return. No longer were the two able to function in any kind of healthy working relationship. Not if Jessie wanted to preserve her marriage to her troubled husband, at least. And she'd made it quite clear that she did.

Dessert was a tiramisu, one of Carlotta's special dishes. As Jessie dug in, she was aware that Matt was now watching her. They were on the last course. Dinner would be winding down soon. As Jessie spooned the last bite between her lips, she looked up at him, and her heart crashed to the floor. Matt had his right arm around Miranda's shoulders, his body turned into her. But his soft hazel-grey eyes were locked on Jessie. A soulful sorrow was at play there.

His goodbye. He was memorizing her, too.

Jessie's spoon clattered into her bowl, and she sat back and swallowed, gripped the edge of the table, and lost herself in his gaze. Everyone looked at her, and then at Matt. Fueled by the wine and the easygoing laughter during dinner, neither Jessie nor Matt could look away.

"Excuse me," Jessie finally said, lifting her linen napkin up onto the table. Charles stood and pulled her chair back for her. "Ladies' room," she mumbled, as Miranda sent a curious sideways glance over to Matt.

He looked away, and followed the sound of Jessie's heels down the hall until they disappeared.

In the washroom, Jessie sat on the toilet and sobbed. Wrapping her arms around her belly, she felt absolutely adrift and completely alone. Nothing seemed salvageable at the present time, nothing. Josh? Seemed like he had pulled the ball quite succinctly back into his court, leaving her feeling completely at a loss in terms of control over whether or not their marriage would pull out of its present funk. Her friends were away, and her longtime best friend was moving on, against both his and her wishes, but there was, quite frankly, no other choice.

In the dining room, when Matt looked back at Miranda, he saw sympathy in her eyes, but he groaned at the appearance of it, because it could only mean one thing. Pushing back his chair, he reached across the table and shook Charles' hand.

"Thank you for a wonderful evening, Charles." He nodded at Deirdre, who had the grace to try to hide her wistful smile from Miranda. "Lovely meal, Dee," he said, and took Miranda's hand to assist her in rising.

They left La Casa through its lovely arched front door, without waiting for Jessie so they could offer a cordial 'good night.'

Chapter Fifteen

Generally on the evening rides Josh didn't concern himself with worrying about the cougars, but tonight an eager, warm spring breeze rushed through the trees, and a glowing full moon was on its way up to beam an ecstatic white light into the Kananaskis. The wildlife in the area seemed all stirred up. The cougars' distant whines were punctuated with the occasional wildcat *screech*, and they were making Blue nervous. The horse's huffs and puffs were increasing in intensity, and her ears were flicking anxiously as she darted her head from side to side to study the blue-twilight landscape.

"Easy, girl," Josh's calm, husky voice encouraged her. "Let's go as far as the creek bed, then we'll turn around and head for home. I'd share my lasagna with you but somehow I don't think it's your thing. I could probably dig up a carrot or two, though, to sweeten up your feed. Next week you'll be riding with me to set so you can star in your own TV series. Whaddaya think of that?"

The horse's answer was a quick step to the left—more of a dance, actually. "Whoa! Easy, Blue. I need to actually stay in the saddle if both of us are going to get home before complete darkness."

Glancing around him, Josh felt an eerie chill creep up his spine. It tickled the hair at the base of his neck and caused him to narrow his eyes in curiosity. "Why do I get the feeling we're being watched, girl?" he asked the horse. "You feeling weirded out too?"

Slowly, he switched his grip on the reins to his left hand, and reached behind him. Laying his gloved hand on the stock of the rifle, he wrapped his fingers around it.

"We're okay," he told the horse. "Just a little bit further. Whatever's out here is likely more scared of us than we are of it. Ease on slowly. We're fine."

From the perimeter of the trail a squirrel bounded from one tree to the next. Blue reared up and twisted her body around, but Josh was an experienced rider. He stayed seated without any trouble, but he cursed at the squirrel. "A fucking squirrel? A glorified rat? That's what was watching us? Jesus, Blue, take it easy."

His heart was racing and he shook his head to clear the cobwebs. Then he urged the horse on down the narrow trail towards the sweet bliss of the moonlit creek.

La Casa's driveway was also awash with a melancholy moonlight when Matt walked Miranda to her Mercedes. She'd met him in North Van directly from work so he, too, had a vehicle in the circular driveway.

At her door, she turned around to him and forced a small smile. Matt placed his hands on her hips and asked quietly, "Come to my place?"

A light *pffftt* escaped her full lips. "Matt," she started, and his heart sank.

"Jessie," he said softly.

She sighed. "How long have you been in love with her?"

"It doesn't matter. She's not mine to love."

"Funny, Matt. Because it matters to me. Who I date needs to not be in love with someone else. Especially his superstar client."

"She's Jessie Wheeler." The answer was futile. It was a stretch. "A lot of men, and some women too, are in love with her."

"They don't know her. You do. And personally? My take on her is that she's a spoiled bitch."

Instantly, Matt's defenses deployed. "Jessie's going through a rough time, Miranda. She's confused about where she fits these days."

Miranda pulled on the driver's door behind her. It opened fluidly, but she paused before sliding inside. "I'm a successful woman, Matt. I run successful businesses. Multiple successful businesses. I can be choosy about who I fall in love with. I wish it could be you."

"Miranda…please. I'm leaving here. I'm quitting." Matt gestured to the beautiful Spanish villa spread out before them. But as he said the words, his stomach lurched. "I'm leaving Jessie," he added weakly. "I won't be working for her anymore. I won't be seeing her."

"You've been sleeping with her. For how long?"

"I haven't…" Matt took a minute to get his voice—that had been steadily rising in frustration—under control. "Miranda, I have not been sleeping with her. I have never slept with my employer."

"Maybe you should." She stiffened before easing into the sleek Mercedes. "Take her to bed and show her who's the boss. Maybe that will teach her a thing or two. Like how not to keep a husband who's apparently already slipping out of her grasp."

She slammed the door, but let the window down a notch as she started the car. "Goodbye, Matt. Please thank Carlotta for me. The food, at least, was very fine."

"This is not something that needs to be made public, Miranda," Matt cautioned as she put the vehicle in drive.

"What doesn't need to be made public?" she asked him. "Your feelings for that spoiled young rock star, or what a little slut she appears to be? Wow, does the public have the wrong take on her. Good night." And she circled the drive and slipped off into the darkness.

Striding over to his own car, Matt slammed a fist down hard on the roof. Leaning forward against the passenger side, with both hands resting on the now dented roof, he hung his head between his arms. Suddenly it was more obvious than ever that he needed to leave the Keating employ. "Damn," he cursed. "Just damn."

In the front entry, Jessie was astounded when Deirdre rather apologetically told her that Matt had left without saying goodbye. When she whined about it, Charles soundly growled her out.

"Jessie, you acted very childishly tonight. Miranda is a lovely woman. Matt deserves to have a woman like her in his life—"

"As opposed to the Keating puppet prostitute, is that it?" Jessie was in fine form. Turning one ankle over on its side, she glared stubbornly at Charles and dared him to kick her out.

Deirdre gasped. "Jessie, is that what you think?"

"Oh, come on." Turning on Dee, Jessie let the wine speak for her. "The two of you have made a bloody fortune off of me. You wouldn't have kept me in your home back in the day if I didn't deliver the goods."

"You're pushing your luck tonight, Jessie." Charles' voice was cool, low in pitch. A red bloom was spreading across his face and over the top of his balding head. "Go upstairs and sleep it off. Vancouver doesn't need any more angry drunks on its streets tonight."

"I had two glasses," she lied. "I'm fine. I'm not drunk, just angry."

"Why?" he asked her, almost shouting. "Why, because you can't have Matt, or because poor Josh is hell bent on protecting his heart these days? Why?"

"Because I'm sick and tired of being alone!" she cried. "Everyone's gone, off doing their thing, and I'm alone. And I don't know when that's going to change. If it ever does! Stupid Nadia and stupid Morgan! They ruined everything!" She was sobbing heartily now. Dee tried to grab her and pull her into her arms but Jessie rudely shoved her away and focused her anger back on Charles. "They ruined everything, Charles! Josh loved me so much before—before—Jacob—and the Langley house—and Nadia! Nothing's been the same since. Nothing. He's not the same. Josh doesn't even want to live in reality any more, did he tell you that? He'd rather just disappear inside *Sacred Peace* and be Bobby, fucking Shanda's Olivia! He'd rather be somebody that's not—my—husband!"

The sobs were great gulping ones now, almost overwhelming Jessie so that she teetered on the impossibly high heels. "I'm scared he's going to do something stupid," she admitted, fear sucking the breath out of her as she said the words out loud. "I'm scared he might try to hurt himself. I thought those days were over. I thought he was going to be okay."

"Oh, honey," Dee finally said, and held her, as Charles ran his tongue over his lips and faced his beautiful, frightened girl.

"Jessie," Charles said in a slightly more careful tone. "I know things have changed between you two. But Josh loves you. He's seeing Trudy, and Charlie said he had a really good day on set today. There was laughter today. He's doing better."

"Why, Charles? Did you ask yourself why he is doing better? Because I'm not there, that's why. I'm not there with him, cloaking him in sad memories!"

Shanda's comment came to mind—*I want to peel his layers of sadness away.* "He hasn't called or texted all day. If he's having a good day, it's fairly evident that I am not a part of that."

Moving to go, she pushed open the big mahogany door. Charles touched her arm. "Let me drive you," he said.

"No." She shook him off. "I mean it. I had two glasses, a while ago. I'm fine, Charles. I'll call you both tomorrow. Good night."

As she went to move through the door, he grabbed her and pulled her close. "I hope you don't really mean what you said. Yes, we made money, but I'd give it all back just to have you in our lives, Jessie. You and Josh and the kids."

"And Jacob," she sniffled. "Who is apparently with Kayla on the tour bus at this moment."

"Heard that." Charles smiled. "Our two mixed up kids. Will we ever get the two of you settled?"

"What would be the fun in that?" Deirdre asked, sneaking up for one last hug. "We love you, sweetheart. Drive safe."

As Jessie stepped out of the light of the front entryway and the door closed behind her, she stopped short. Matt's Audi was still there, not fifty feet away. And there, leaning against it, was Matt.

He wheeled around when he heard her heels, like a wild heartbeat slowing down, clacking slowly towards him on the asphalt.

Jessie stopped three feet in front of him. "Where's Miranda?" she asked, wiping the last of her new wet mascara trails off her cheeks.

Shrugging, he responded with a haughty, "Kitsilano by now? I have no idea."

"Oh." Crestfallen, Jessie slumped. "I'm such a bitch."

"She thought so."

"Lovely. Well, I suppose the old Wheeler reputation was about due for a new influx of degradation and torrid rumors."

"You gave the world a field day today, Jessie."

"All two-year-old boys have tantrums."

"Yes, but generally their mothers don't."

Jessie waved an arm towards the street beyond the Keating fence. "She leave because of me, Matt?"

His lips parted. He didn't know how to answer that question. Finally he just said a simple, "Yes," and eased himself back against the Audi, one knee bent and hands in his pockets.

"Are you going to see her again?"

He responded with a loud guffaw. "Are you kidding? No. She'd have me tarred and feathered and rousted out of the city behind a wild stallion if she could. No. Miranda's not impressed with me."

"Because of me."

He waited, working his jaw for the words. They emerged quietly honest. "Because I'm in love with you."

A choking feeling filled Jessie's throat but she spoke past it. "I know," she said. There was no question, standing there in the gorgeous rose-grey silk she bought to impress him, propped up by Pinot Grigio and an evening of uncomfortable chatter, that Jessie loved Matt back in a way that was true and sincere too, and powered by a desperate need for connection. Josh? He confused the hell out of her.

Twisting her fingers together in front of her stomach, letting her lips part and her head tilt to the side, she considered what to do. In the end, the deep ache she'd felt for Matt since the incident in Brussels, and her confusion over her husband's reticence to have her and the kids move to the ranch, won.

Matt knew the moment she made the decision. It crisscrossed her face like a lighthouse beacon, illuminating her eyes with *want*.

I want you, it said, and Matt stopped breathing.

As she covered the last few steps towards him, he let his hands rise and grasp her elbows as she slipped her fingers inside the swanky dinner jacket to rest them on the waist of his black pants. She didn't say anything, and neither did Matt, not with words, at least, but he met her eyes and held the charged gaze with a growing anticipation that electrified him.

"Can I?" he asked her, not stating completely what he wanted, but raising the fingers of his right hand and letting them hover until, at her gentle nod, he let the backs of them touch the half-moons of her breasts. Following the movement with his gaze, Matt brushed her there a few times, slowly, softly, almost moaning with the delicious feel of her and the way she arched her back and watched him. Without looking back up at her, Matt slid his fingers across her breast, across the nipple, to the exposed left side of the scarred breast.

Raising her hand, Jessie covered his fingers with her own, and nudged them inside the dress so his hand could cup her; so his thumb could brush itself over her nipple.

Looking up at her then, his mouth open in almost an innocent wonder, his eyes glazed and his body aching, Matt waited for Jessie's cue. She leaned her body into him and pressed her lips to the corners of his eyes, one at a time, and then to each cheek, before she let her tongue trail down to his lips. Instead of kissing him, she held his chin still and tongued him, melting when she felt his body tense and his fingers increase their movements against her breast.

His breath changed—it grew ragged, and as Jessie increased her pressure against his lips, kissing him hard now, she widened her stance and started, slowly, to move her hips against him. Moaning openly now, Matt removed his hand from her breast and wrapped it around her back. Pressing her hard against him, he started to tremble.

"Oh God, Matt," Jessie breathed in his ear now. "I want you. Please. I need this. I need you."

It didn't take any more encouragement than that. Matt reached behind him and flipped open the car door. Jessie ducked inside and he closed it, then skirted around the Audi and slipped in behind the wheel. Taking her hand after he started the car, he gathered enough presence of mind to see if she was serious, if she was ready.

Reading his thoughts, Jessie leaned back against the seat, arched her back, and squeezed his hand. "Yes," she whispered. "A thousand times, yes."

His small smile warmed her heart, and he turned the wheel and drove away from La Casa, leaving Jessie's Lexus behind. The radio was on low, spitting out some sweet late evening jazz recorded at The Cellar in Vancouver and, as they passed underneath the haunting streetlights, Jessie sank further into the cozy hominess of Matt's car and Matt's deeply loved and trusted company.

He took her to the condo he'd moved to after he and Julie split up. In the downtown area, it had underground parking. Sliding into his assigned spot, he looked over at Jessie, then opened his door, walked around the car, and opened the passenger door. Taking her hand, Matt helped her rise before wordlessly escorting her to the elevator.

His two-bedroom condo was on the tenth floor. Inside, Jessie took a good look around. It was decorated in contemporary manly blacks and greys and whites, by a man with care and taste for his surroundings. One wall was all windows, floor to ceiling, and had a couch positioned facing it, so Matt could sit and watch seaplanes land below on Burrard Inlet. The open concept kitchen was sterile almost—shiny, fitted with stainless steel appliances on a gleaming vanilla-colored polished stone floor.

Moving to the bar-style kitchen counter, Matt reached underneath for a bottle of wine. Using a corkscrew to open it, he watched her suck on a lip as she scanned his home.

In a moment, she looked over, all wide-eyed and nervous. "Ladies' room?" she whispered.

"Over there," he replied with a relaxed gesture towards the far wall, his voice dusky.

Hauling off the new heels as she walked, Jessie vanished into the washroom and closed the door behind her. Her phone was still at La Casa, on the dash of the Lexus. Pushing Josh out of her mind, she told her reflection that this was her goodbye to Matt, to a trusted, faithful friend who she loved dearly. She peed, washed her hands, wiped off the last of the black mascara trails on her cheeks, and opened the door.

Chapter Sixteen

Josh made it to the creek bed on Blue, but barely. The trouble was, when he got there, the stones bounding the small, shallow creek were slippery and, on a horse that was already skittish, they were immediate cause for concern.

The cougar—or cougars—seemed closer now. Blue knew they were there; she *shuffed* nervously and reared again, and Josh wisely decided to turn her around and start for the ranch. One last look at the gorgeous moonlight washing the creek's sins away, and he put enough pressure on the reins to get Blue to circle around. She didn't need a lot of convincing. The horse was dancing from side to side, struggling on the stones, and anxious to get home. She was moving too fast.

A loud screech from the left startled her, and Blue did a little leap that had her back facing the creek again.

"Jesus," Josh cursed, rising his seat up on the saddle so he could fire darting looks left, right, front, behind him. A swath of long hair got in his eyes when he reached behind him for the rifle. This time he went by feel, yanked it out of its leather scabbard, and swiped a sleeve across his eyes to clear his vision.

"Go," he urged Blue. "Go. Let's get the hell out of here."

And they started to move away.

⌒⌒⌒

Matt was standing behind the black couch when Jessie left the washroom. He moved towards her with a glass of wine, set his own wine down on a narrow, tall mahogany stand, and slipped off his dinner jacket.

Taking a sip of her wine, Jessie looked around, her eyes wide and interested.

"Jeepers, Matt," she said with the reverence her thoughts deserved. "In all of our years together, I've never been to your home. Not to your house, before, and certainly not here. That's kind of crazy."

"Kind of," he said, his voice trembling as he studied her.

"Matt," she said softly, noticing. "Honey, are you nervous? Or are you scared?"

The childlike way she asked the question threw Matt for a loop. "Scared," he whispered.

"Huh," she smiled, her eyes alight with a tiny, arduous flame that hid her own escalating nerves. Leaning over to the nearby stand, Jessie set down her wine glass. "No," she shook her head. "No being scared. Not tonight, baby. C'mere."

Starting at the top of his tight white dress shirt, which Jessie had fantasized many times about undoing, she slipped the button through the hole. Moving on down his chest and stomach, she repeated the procedure until she could slip her fingers underneath and spread open his shirt. Pressing her palms to his warm skin, she widened the shirt and bent her lips to the scar on his shoulder left by the bullet he'd taken for her a few years earlier.

"Sweet Matt," she purred, sucking a little on the scar, running her tongue over it, and then dropping her lips to his left nipple, "you took a bullet for me." Easily, she played around his nipples, teasing him with her tongue, licking and sucking, pleased when she felt his hand come behind her head to apply a little pressure.

Straightening, Jessie locked herself in his steady gaze and wrapped one hand around his belt buckle. "You ready?" she murmured to him, then brought her other hand down to unfasten the clasp. In a moment she had his belt open; soon the button of his pants was unfastened too. "Let me do this for you, Matt," she pleaded softly, palming his cheek and pressing her lips against his mouth. "Let me love you."

A choking moan escaped his lips as Jessie sank to her knees, and eased his pants just down over his hips. "Jessie," he gasped, afraid. They were way beyond the line in the sand now. There was no coming back from this.

With her fingers, Jessie cradled him and rubbed softly before she slipped him between her lips.

Overcome by the instant, almost debilitating pleasure of having her mouth and tongue massaging him in this very intimate way, Matt was at a momentary loss. It felt wrong, somehow…all those years of watching over her, over her family, of being angry at her, helping her, worrying over her, worrying over Josh when she was missing…twice…watching her on stage, so many times, so many shows…the music…her films…and here she was with her lips around his very private self in a very intimate manner, making him grow harder and harder, and urging pleasurable moans from his throat that Matt seemed to have no control over.

It was so exquisite, these waves of pleasure, that he felt his panic subside enough to have the presence of mind to know he wanted to watch her, to see those beautiful lips caress and kiss and love him this way. So Matt moved her hair aside and touched his fingers to her cheeks. As his hips started to involuntary move, he placed his palms flat against both sides of her face, and memorized this time with the woman he loved, knowing it was a one-time deal.

It was increasing, the pressure, and hearing her start to moan too was too much. After a few minutes, with a last strangled sound in his throat, Matt lifted Jessie at the elbows and wiped his thumb across her mouth. His eyes were tortured now, and his breathing was raspy and irregular, but he was into this new game of theirs now, and there was something he wanted, that he'd wanted for a long time from her, and that he intended to get.

Watching her—the way she was breathing now, her chest moving quickly in and out, her eyes half-lidded with desire, her back arching, and the small hands floating in the air, reaching for him—he grabbed Jessie's hands and lowered them to her sides.

"My turn," he insisted in a low voice, and reached both hands behind her neck.

To Jessie, it felt like it took forever, but soon she felt him pull at the wide silk ties of the halter dress, and they were loosened. Matt used both hands to slowly bring the ties down over her chest, and his eyes left hers and followed their trail as they creased the tops of her breasts. There, he paused, nervous again, but the ache in his groin needed release, and so he sucked in a breath and let both hands brush her nipples as the dress fell down her body.

He let it hang at her waist. It was tight enough at the hips to stay in place, but now her breasts were exposed, and he needed to put his lips to them.

Jessie covered his hands with hers and guided him, and he bent for a mouthful on her left breast, and sucked hard enough for her to gasp, before he couldn't stand the anticipation another second, and led her into his bedroom, which was directly behind her, adjoining the washroom.

Jessie laid down on Matt's big bed, on her back, and he eased down on his left side against her right side. Bending over her, he kissed her lips and tongued her until he had to move down her body and play at her breasts again; it was Jessie who finally took his hand and positioned the backs of his fingers up under her dress. Turning his hand, cupping her and playing there, Matt wanted to see her eyes, her body; he wanted and needed to know that his touch was electric to her, that it was hot, that she wanted him as badly as he wanted her.

Desperate for release, she arched her back and let out a sequence of small panting cries that told him quite clearly that she wanted the same thing he did. She spoke, too, laying a palm against his cheek as the words poured out. "Show me," she gasped. "Show me what you thought about. With me. What you wanted to…what you wanted to do. To me. All this time, Matt."

The simple request put him over the edge. Grasping her dress, he yanked at it until she raised herself up off the bed enough for him to pull it down past her ankles. Groaning with the exquisite anticipation of what she knew was to come, Jessie widened her legs for him, and the second Matt moved his lips to the outside of her panties, then pulled them off and put his tongue against her body, she arched her back and cried out.

When she started to lose it, he pushed himself hard into her, and thrust hard against her again and again, lost in the agony of his own sweet pleasure while Jessie crescendo'd into an intense orgasm that left her panting and bucking on the bed beneath him.

When it was over, and she lay spent and moaning, he moved inside her for a while yet, savoring the afterglow, kissing her tenderly, tenting her inside his arms, while inside her mind Jessie screamed, *THIS! THIS! THIS! This is what it's all about. This is why people have sex.* The safety of his arms, the love and trust in his eyes, the simple, beautiful way he touched his lips to hers, the way his muscular chest, shoulders and back tensed underneath her roving fingers…All of it was surreal to Jessie, whose love for this man who watched over her was complete, and rooted in a deep and special friendship.

"I love you," she whispered to him. "I love you, Matt."

"I know," he murmured, echoing her earlier comment, and anchoring it with a satisfied smile. "Now sleep, sweet girl. Sleep, and let me hold you. Just this one night. Let me hold you while you sleep."

Brushing her lips against his, and then running a finger over the lips that pleasured her so exquisitely just moments before, Jessie nodded. "Yes," she breathed. "Please."

Moving onto her side, she folded an arm underneath her head and let him get comfortable on his side next to her. Jessie wriggled into his body and fell asleep with her warm breath on his chest and her left hand resting on his right hip.

It was a long while before Matt let his eyes close over. Watching Jessie sleep was something he had done many times, on the Keating jet, in dressing rooms, in the studio on Robson. But never before had he been the man honored with the humble pleasure of simply holding her in his arms after making sweet love to her.

And never before had he been the man Jessie Wheeler loved.

Chapter Seventeen

The next loud screech from the cougar stalking them came the second the wild cat leapt for Blue's throat. The gaping jaws of the powerful cat ripped a jagged piece of flesh from the horse, whose terrified quick spin and arching back sent Josh flying.

Landing on his right shoulder, which cracked underneath his weight, he had sense enough to try to roll onto his back to escape the frantic movements of his horse, but Blue was insane with pain and fear, and although she tried to avoid her beloved rider, her back leg kicked his right calf. A crack pierced the cooling evening air as it splintered instantly.

Screaming, Josh buckled under the white lightning heat that seared up his body, and he involuntarily let go of the gun that he'd wrapped tightly in his fingers only moments earlier.

Breathing was like sucking in fire. His ribs cried foul—*are they cracked or are they broken*, shot through Josh's frantic mind in those first few terrible moments.

Crying, sobbing with the pain, he tried to twist around to eyeball the cougar, which he could hear somewhere behind him, growling menacingly. At Blue? At him?

Tears of agony streaming down his face, Josh vomited, managed to wipe his lips with his sleeve, and finagled his body around enough to clearly view the turmoil in front of him. Blue was mostly unmoving now, her proud head bowed as she made strangled horsey noises that communicated her suffering to her rider and to the big cat crouched, ready to pounce again, ten feet in front of her.

The closest thing to Josh was a fist-sized stone. Many, in fact. He grabbed one with his left hand and cried out with the pain that shot through his body when he threw it. Two more left his fingers before the cougar retreated about twenty feet away and coiled into pounce position, making threatening obscene catlike noises as it sat there.

"Oh, for fuck's sake," Josh cried, frantically trying to locate his gun. It was just about full dark now, and a quick assessment of his situation told him he was in serious trouble. The cougar had more fight in her, Josh was unable to move without supercharged blue bolts paralyzing his body with pain, and the rifle was where?

Oh, there it is, six feet away.

And Blue…Blue was beyond repair.

"Oh, Jesus," Josh moaned, as the horse struggled nearby. "No. No!"

The horse Josh had worked so hard to help, to train, the horse he loved deeply, with whom he and his kids spent so much time last fall and this winter…the horse with the sweet, sad, troubled Jessie eyes…was badly injured by the cougar crouched in front of her now. From where Josh lay on his side on the stones by the river, he could see wet skin flapping at the horse's throat. A fragment. A shiny, bloody, glow-in-the-moonlight omen of disaster.

"I'm sorry," Josh gulped. "I'm so, so sorry. Blue. Oh, God!" The horse was bleeding from the deep gash. She was in dire straits. The hard truth cut to the core.

I tried to help you, Josh said in his mind to her. *But I can't. I can't help you anymore. And right now I can't even help myself.*

As his racing mind settled, he considered his options. *Am I bleeding?* He knew he'd bleed out if the bone in his leg had broken through the skin. Glancing down, Josh managed, after numerous nauseating tries and a few slices with a knife he kept on his belt, to pull his jeans up enough to note that his leg was weirdly misshapen, but the bone hadn't appeared to have penetrated the skin. So that was good, at least.

Small mercies.

Accessing the rifle was a priority, obviously, since the big cat seemed intent on waiting for an opportunity to attack once again. But every movement sent blind pain ravaging up and down and throughout Josh's body. He tried to inch over to get the gun, and almost blacked out.

Josh had no phone. Jessie might try to call and wonder why the hell he wasn't answering, but Josh had let her go two days in a row sometimes without calling. Charlie would be with Jane and his children, twenty minutes away in Canmore, likely enjoying dinner now, and a snuggle with his beautiful wife. Arnie was staying at the condo in Calgary. He mostly only stuck with Josh in the city, when they went to AA meetings or to some of the community PR gigs Charles had set up for his actors. Charles was back in Vancouver, and Jonathon, who was only around the production part-time anyway, was distant, at best.

Nobody would be looking for Josh until he didn't show up for Saturday's call, which was not until the next day at 9 a.m.

It was going to be a hellish long night.

Chapter Eighteen

*A*round one in the morning, Jessie woke on her back to spy Matt slumbering peacefully next to her, one arm lazily looped around her body. He seemed so at peace, so content in sleep, that it hurt to lie there and watch him breathe in and out, knowing that what they shared last night would not—could not—continue.

Tentative, Jessie let her fingers brush his hair, the short gelled spikes that were so different from Josh's long hair. Stirring, Matt's eyes fluttered open. Jessie studied the wise light grey-hazel as Matt watched her in return. There was a serious bent to the way they peered at each other now. Like the crash after an alcoholic binge, it came from a sense of impending loss.

"Will you tell Josh?" he asked her, cradling his left arm around a pillow, at the same time recognizing that his beliefs about keeping secrets in a marriage were suddenly toast. They went out the door with his sense of honor.

The realization of what he'd done to Josh gutted him. He had to forcibly stifle a moan.

Jessie moved onto her side and lost herself in the gentle eyes that had cared for her and her family for so long. "I won't have to," she said. "He'll know."

"I'm sorry, Jessie. This isn't going to make things easier between you."

"I'm not sorry, Matt." Inching her body closer to him, she pressed her lips against his. They shared a sweet, intimate kiss before she sighed and inched back again. "I'll never be sorry."

"I already can't stand the thought of leaving you." Matt's fingers played in Jessie's hair, twisting a ringlet, which brought forth a sad smile. It was surreal that she was accessible to him like this now, for intimate touches and tender caresses.

"Where will you go?"

"Back to Kelly and Michael, maybe. Or to someone else they know of who needs security. I don't know yet."

"To someone who needs a guardian angel, you mean."

"It won't be the same."

"No. For me, either. Or for the kids. Matt?"

"Hmm?"

"When will I see you again?"

"I don't know, Jessie. At some big show, I suppose."

"Maybe we can keep this going," she asked hopefully.

He smiled at the way her face lit up, but his response was somber. "No. We can't."

Waiting a minute before she answered, Jessie's eyes filled. "I know."

"We have the rest of tonight."

Her voice was thick. "Thank God. Small mercies."

Reaching for her, Matt kissed Jessie with a bittersweet tenderness borne of goodbyes. "Don't forget me," he murmured. "Please."

"As if I could."

The remainder of the night alternated between making love and dozing lightly. When dawn broke, Matt's phone bleeped in the other room. He would have left it but then it rang, and soon there were more bleeps from text messages.

"Charles," he said to Jessie as he slipped out of bed, a wide yawn creasing his face. "I'm guessing he spotted your car. I should have texted him."

"Yeah," Jessie giggled. "And said what? Charles, I'm taking Jessie home to make sweet love to her all night long? I can't honestly say how I think he would take that."

"He's not going to be surprised."

"I guess not." Waiting, Jessie watched the doorway for when Matt would come back in. She could hear him messing about with a coffee pot in the kitchen. Moments later, he slipped back into bed on her left side, and snuggled her close.

"I wouldn't say he was panicked. I think he put two and two together anyway. But now he knows we spent the night together."

"And Dan? Katy might be worried that I didn't come home."

"I texted him from the kitchen last night. Not…this. Just that you had a bit much to drink and wouldn't be home til morning. Katy was staying overnight anyway."

"Yep. She's so great with the kids. But I guess I should get home, Matt. I wouldn't want to burn her out."

"She'll still be around for you, Jessie. Okay?"

"It's gonna hurt like hell every time I see her." The wet layer forming across Jessie's eyes deepened. She buried her face in Matt's chest and wrapped her arms under his, around his back. "I can't stand it."

He had no answer for her. One last time, Matt pulled Jessie to him. This time, their lovemaking was a slow build, a confident coupling that each savored for its highs and lows. Jessie eased her body on top of Matt's, and moved rhythmically over him, stealing kisses now and then until she clenched around him in another delicious orgasm.

In the shower, they held each other under the water and didn't speak. Steam encircled their bodies, creating a halo-like effect and offering a cleansing that both Matt and Jessie desperately sought, but which, like their short union, would not last.

In silence, holding hands, he walked her to the Audi, travel coffee mugs in their other hands. At La Casa, Jessie didn't go in to see Charles and Dee. Nor did Matt. She retrieved her SUV, checked her phone—not a single message from Josh—and, frustrated and emotional, tossed it on the passenger seat. Pointing the car towards the street, she followed Matt to her UBC house.

He stayed outside to talk to Dan while Jessie went in to see her children and Matt's daughter. Everyone was up, enjoying the usual teddy bear shaped pancakes.

"Oh, you lucky kids, Katy's teddy bear pancakes actually look like teddy bears. Not like mine or…um…daddy's, eh? Ours are just blobs." Jessie was trying to joke, but her heart was heavy. "Hi Katy. Hi babies." Moving around the kitchen island, she kissed the tops of the children's heads and was soon regaled with tales of their night with their favorite babysitter.

Slumping into the last empty stool at the island, Jessie studied Matt's daughter. Katy was a well adjusted eighteen year old whose interest in music was something she shared with Jessie. Petite, pretty, she sported a nose ring and often wore vintage fifties-style clothing with heavy black boots and thick socks. With the kids, she was patient and loving, and Jessie knew from Emily-Grace's tales of their special nights together that Katy took the time to read to the kids, to get them snacks, to listen to their endless stories.

Now, Jessie had to fight back tears as she watched the girl simply pour apple juice into the children's glasses.

Everything's changing, she thought. *Nothing will ever be the same again. Nothing's been the same since Nadia and Morgan.*

A few minutes later, Matt entered through the back door. He kissed his daughter's cheek and Jessie had to smile when he took the time to tousle each of her children's heads as well. He, too, was struggling with his emotions. She could tell by the way Matt avoided meeting her eyes, and the way he continuously licked his lips and crunched on them.

Katy had her own car. After a bit, she waved *so long* and, taking her guitar, left with a promise from Jessie for a guitar lesson later in the week. Dan had been released so it was no stretch for her to accept that her father would stick around the Sawyer home, likely for much of the day.

Normally when Matt or any of their security was around, they did not get involved in household activities, as per Josh and Jessie's request, although at times they did help with little things like grabbing the occasional snack or playing with the kids to help reduce any fear and make them seem like 'friends.' Today, though, Jessie fixed a silly smile on her face and invited Matt upstairs to help get the kids dressed.

"You can have Dylan," she grinned. "He's the toughest of the bunch. See if you can get him to sit still long enough to put pants on."

It was odd for Matt to join the kids upstairs, but they never blinked. David took him by the hand and right into the playroom, but Jessie picked her middle child up and turned him back towards the door.

"Clothes first," she admonished, and stopped to note, as David ran down the hall to his own room, that Matt was standing uncomfortably outside her and Josh's bedroom. With one finger, he pushed the door open, and she watched him.

"No," she said softly, shaking her head. "Don't go there, Matt. What happened with us was not about Josh and me. It was about you and me."

He was choking up. Wiping a hand across his eyes, Matt had to turn his head away from her. "I'm sorry," he said, to her or to the bedroom—to Josh—she wasn't sure.

"Oh, fuck this sucks," Jessie said, and collapsed in his arms. "Just go now," she said. "Go now."

Burying his face in her hair, Matt let a few tears come before he looked up to see Emily-Grace watching them. Pushing Jessie away, he said to the little girl, who was standing there with her choice of clothes for the day in her arms, "Come on, Emily-Grace. Come help Dylan pick out something cool to wear today."

And they got their day underway.

Chapter Nineteen

At one in the morning Alberta time, an hour ahead of Vancouver time, Josh finally managed to access the loaded rifle. It was an interminable quest, it seemed, inching along struggling to breathe past the jagged knives of broken ribs, dragging a useless shoulder and an even more useless leg. He passed out twice, each time demanding his body to keep going before the blackness took over, and failing at that simple task. What roused him each time was fear, and a crippling sorrow for the state of his horse, which he blamed on his stubborn stupidity at trying to get a ride in before nightfall.

There was a large boulder nearby. After grasping the heavy short-barreled Winchester in his left hand, Josh used it to provide enough leverage to get his broken body propped up somewhat against the boulder. The movements almost had him blacking out again, but he vomited again instead and fixed his gaze on the big cat that, almost like any ordinary housecat, was coolly watching him. The only thing giving away her animal instinct to kill was a menacing growl that occasionally came from deep in her throat, which scared the living shit out of Josh.

Blue was still close by as well. The horse was hurt too bad to take more than a few stuttery steps on the slippery stones. Grateful for her company, Josh avoided staring at the deep wound in her throat. His first glance had communicated the reason for the horse's distress now—blood was seeping from the open wound. Blue's head was hanging, and she seemed to be having trouble breathing and swallowing.

"Sweet Jesus, what a fucking mess." Sickened, Josh hefted the Winchester up to his left shoulder but screamed at the pain that shot through him when he tried to move his right arm. It was a full ten minutes before he got the gun hoisted and in a position that might have some effect on the big cat, who seemed to be waiting for the horse to die.

"Here, kitty kitty," Josh tried to joke and, with the rifle in a weird position against his one good shoulder, which was not the shoulder he usually used for support when firing, he aimed and squeezed the trigger.

And missed.

The horse jumped when the shot rang out. The cougar barely moved.

"What, you're not scared of guns, you big stupid animal?" The gun dropped to his side and Josh stared incredulously at the wildcat. "Go away," he demanded in a frightened whisper. "Go now. Please."

Fear rippled through his body at a new low growl from the cougar. "What?" he asked it, his voice swollen and slurred with pain and fatigue. "What are you trying to tell me?" Picturing Jessie and the kids, he wished now that he'd taken the time to call Jessie and tell her to bring the kids out, to move their family to the ranch once and for all. Shanda's overture had knocked some sense into him, and Charlie's words of wisdom and warning were also worth listening to. Temptation…it was part and parcel of many relationships, but Josh, who had already lost the woman he loved more than once, had vowed he would never lose her again.

"I came so close," he cried now, divulging his inner truths, his fears, to the cougar, to the trickling creek, to the dying horse. "I came so close to letting her go, to losing her forever. And now, what's it all coming down to? Am I going to die out here?"

The cougar was growling steadily now, and starting to inch forward on her belly. "Oh, shit," Josh groaned. Picturing her tearing his horse apart in front of him, killing Blue slowly, made him want to vomit again. Gasping, he worked at leveraging the rifle against his chest this time, as close as he could get it to his mangled shoulder. Somehow, sheer will, he later supposed, he got his finger around the trigger again, aimed as best he could, and squeezed.

And missed. Again.

The cougar hissed and started pacing in a small circle. Each time she came around, she stopped to survey the horse's condition.

"No!" Josh cried, mustering up as much energy as he could. "Just no.

Please, God. No." He raised the rifle one last time, and fired just as the cougar leapt back at Blue, who backed up and went down on her knees. Sobbing now, Josh's chest heaved with the effort to drop the heavy Winchester. His left arm sank to his side alongside it.

The cougar lay still. She would no longer be a threat, to him or to Blue. The horse turned her head to him. Moist, sad eyes begged him. They pleaded with him.

"I can't," he cried to her. "I can't."

A small *hfffff* accosted his heart, and launched Blue's pain into what little sense Josh felt he had left. Steel gripped his soul, and he did what he had hoped he would never have to do.

Josh raised the rifle one last time, held it aloft in quaking fingers, and shot his horse.

Sinking back against the boulder, he sobbed until the pain was too great to bear and the universe granted him the grace to sink into blackness; this he did with no more fight left in his body or in his spirit. Nearby, the cougar lay dead next to Josh's beloved horse, Blue. Next to all of them ran trickling, cool water in a blissful, serene creek, moving down into the little valley the way it always did, moving over polished stones and providing a natural serenity that Josh often sought, that he coveted with every breath. Tonight the creek sparkled under a doubtful moon, in front of which grey clouds drifted past. There would be rain by morning. A soft mist would start to fall before dawn, but it wouldn't last.

And by then, Josh would hardly care.

Chapter Twenty

Charlie was at work by ten to nine. He didn't start to worry about Josh until nine thirty. Even then, it was more of a mild *lazy ass, get your butt outta bed* kind of thing. But by ten thirty, Charlie was seriously concerned.

Jonathon was back in the city, on set today, in a huddle with the gaffer, director and cinematographer, discussing lighting details. Planning to fill Josh in on the action when he arrived, they'd waited for him, finally blocked his scene with his stand-in, and started lighting. But now there was no choice. The production would have to move on to another scene.

"Jon," Charlie said, as he approached the irate man who was standing, with his arms crossed, next to the camera. "I called Jessie's Aunt Evelyn to see if she could drop in on Josh, but she and Gary are in Calgary for the day. Jane's here too. I'm going to take a ride out to the ranch."

"Arnie can go. I need you here."

"You think Josh was drinking last night."

"Don't you?" Jonathon frowned and widened his stance as, on set, Shanda cornered the director for help understanding her character's motivation in the new scene.

"I don't know. He was good yesterday." Running a finger over his lip, Charlie scrutinized Shanda. *No way. No fucking way,* he told himself, before stepping onto the set and touching her elbow, interrupting her discussion with the director, a thirty-something who immediately shot Charlie the evil eye for interrupting his flow.

"Shanda," Charlie started as Jon watched, "were you with Josh last night?"

152

"I wish!" Scoping out Charlie's downcast expression, she added, "No! No, I wasn't. He's still not here?"

Instead of answering, Charlie whipped around and brushed by Josh's father. "He was okay when he left last night, Jon. He was feeling good and was planning to ask Jessie to get her butt to Alberta with the kids. If he's passed out drunk, then I want to be the one to kick his ass." Arnie was nearby, waiting for instructions from Charlie, who grabbed his elbow as he passed. "Arnie, let's roll."

As Arnie white-knuckled the steering wheel and pointed them west out of the sprawling city, Charlie pondered an earlier thought—that Josh might have called Jessie, and so she might have some idea where he was. Arnie was considering the possibility too, and mentioned it before Charlie got the chance to voice it.

"I can't call her," Charlie responded with a grimace, after going over the option a few dozen times in his head. "If she hasn't heard from him she'll just worry. Let's just hit the ranch and see what we find, Arnie."

It was pretty much noon by the time Arnie turned left off the highway and soon trundled up the gravel lane to the ranch.

Charlie cursed and pointed at Josh's metallic grey truck as Arnie swung a hard right and pulled up in front of the low rancher. "He's here. He better damn well be okay or I'm going to find a rifle and shoot the guy myself. I just might have to strangle him anyways for fucking up our shoot day."

Arnie grabbed his arm as Charlie started to open his door. "Charlie."

Twisting around, Charlie tried not to panic at the cool blue of Arnie's practiced and experienced, but deeply worried, eyes. Letting go of the car door, Charlie sat back and inhaled deeply.

"I'll go," Arnie said.

"He wouldn't do anything stupid, Arnie. I'm telling you, Josh was okay yesterday."

"I hope you're right," Arnie replied. "But I've been dealing with addictions for a very long time, Charlie, and Josh has not been in a good place for a good chunk of his life. Things have a way of catching up to a guy."

The idea of Josh either being passed out drunk or doing any kind of self-harm terrified Charlie. Jessie and the kids floated across his mind. "I need to go in," he determined as he stepped out of the car. "Josh is my friend. I can handle it. Let's go."

The screen door was unlocked. It *screeeked* eerily when Arnie pushed it open. Inside, the house seemed to be in order. Wandering over to the open concept kitchen, Charlie examined the cupboards and sink. Josh's phone was sitting rather unconcerned on the counter, but there were no new glaring messages on it. Running his fingers over a note on the island, Charlie picked it up and read it.

"Evelyn left him a lasagna." Glancing back to the sink as Arnie came out from the master bedroom with raised arms and a, "He's not here," Charlie took note of a bowl, likely from morning cereal, and a spoon. No plate or knife or fork. On a hunch, he opened the oven door to spy the full lasagna perched, waiting, on the middle rack. Yanking it out, Charlie dropped it onto the island. "Cooked but not eaten," he said. "Josh went for a ride. That was his goal yesterday, to get home before dark so he could take that crazy wild horse out. C'mon, Arnie."

Jogging across to the barn, Arnie and Charlie found Toby and Misty, Josh's other horses but, as expected, no Blue. Hurriedly giving them some feed, Charlie instructed Arnie on where to find running water for the horses. "Buckets, there," he ordered, pointing. "The ATVs," he said after the horses were fed and watered. "Josh likes his motorized toys as well as his four-legged ones. Let's borrow us some outdoor clothes from the house and hit the trail. City boy, you know how to drive an ATV?"

The urgency in his voice was sobering. Josh obviously went out for his ride last night, and it was deadly apparent he'd gotten into some kind of trouble. "He wouldn't miss call," Charlie hollered to Arnie as they sprinted across the clearing again. "And he's going to be pissed as hell after being out all night picturing that warm, cozy house and a homemade lasagna."

"We should call Charles," Arnie suggested hastily, grabbing Josh's black North Face jacket off a hook. A misty rain was starting up again.

"Not yet. Just Jon for now. If he wants to call Charles, fine." Charlie made the call, switched off his desert boots for a high pair of warm, water-resistant barn boots, and shoved a pair of Kodiaks towards Arnie. "See if these will fit. Your Nike runners won't last long in this mud and muck."

There were two ATVs. Charlie took Jessie's smaller one, after he and Arnie checked both for gas. The tanks were three-quarters full. Josh and Jessie had been out for a spin the previous weekend.

"I've been out with him but I don't have the lay of the land, Arnie. We're going blind here. I do know that the trail forks off in a few spots, and I'm no horse tracker, so we're likely going to have to go separate ways at some point." A thought struck him. "We should grab guns. Cougars. Bears."

"I've got mine," Arnie said, grimacing, as Charlie blanched.

"You carry that thing all the time?"

"Not all the time," Arnie answered evenly, firing up his machine. "You go get one if you want, but I'm off." With spinning tires and Jessie's trusting eyes in his mind, he pointed his ATV towards the wide nearby trail.

Charlie spun the smaller machine around towards the barn, and he leapt inside and grabbed the lock on the gun cabinet. "F this," he growled. It was locked. "What do I know about guns anyway?" But there had been reports of cougars in the area. He and Jane had been shocked to read in the local paper that some homeowners had seen the big cats stalking children who were waiting for school buses at the ends of driveways.

Josh had a work area in the back of the barn. Charlie grabbed a hammer and smashed open the lock. Scanning the interior of the cabinet, he noted immediately that the Winchester Josh always took with him into the woods was gone. There was another Winchester, a longer barreled rifle. After loading it, Charlie hoisted the strap over his chest, settled the gun diagonally across his back, and headed into the woods after Arnie.

Chapter Twenty-one

*E*mily-Grace and David had swimming lessons at two p.m. Matt and Jessie gathered up the kids and spent the session laughing and carrying on, pushing away their new reality as much as they could, wishing they could touch in public but knowing it was not an option. Occasionally, Jessie found her eyes wandering away from her children in the pool and over to Matt who, for most of the session, had Dylan on his lap—playful and happy at first, but then sleepy. Eventually, Dylan's eyes flitted closed and he napped against Matt's comfy chest.

"He looks good on you," Jessie murmured, as Matt colored and shifted the little guy in his arms.

Scanning the water again for David who, they were happy and nervous to note was a natural little fish in the pool, but who could not yet swim any distance unattended, Matt said without looking at Jessie, "Have you heard from Josh today?"

"No," Jessie answered, wringing her fingers. "Haven't tried him though, either."

"What about Charlie?"

"No, they're shooting today so I'm sure they're busy keeping Shanda entertained."

Wincing, Matt wondered at that comment. Jessie's overt jealousy of Shanda was sobering. Clearly, it was this insecurity that had helped propel her into his arms last night.

On the way home Matt grabbed pizza for the family, and they sat down to share it in front of the large screen TV in the media room. Again, Dylan ended up on Matt's lap. Eventually all three children drifted off to sleep as an animated movie played in front of them.

"He misses Josh," Jessie whispered, referencing Dylan's clinginess to Matt, and sorry if the comment hurt Matt's feelings but knowing in her heart that he would understand. She added an addendum that spiraled them off into another direction. "This feels so normal, Matt. Why? Why am I not missing Josh? Why am I so happy you're here instead of him?"

Matt emitted a low *pffftttt*. "Sometimes we just need a break from the hard stuff." He reached for her hand and brushed his thumb over her fingers.

"You mean from the sadness and the fights," she admitted, bending towards him for a long kiss. "Let's let these little ones nap. Want to sneak upstairs for a minute?"

Forcibly pushing aside a new wave of guilt, Matt let Jessie steer him into the guest bedroom upstairs. This was a dream; being with her this way was a dream.

Sitting on the edge of the bed, legs apart, Jessie treated Matt to the same special loving she gave him the night before. He cut her short this time, too, and hoisted her backwards as the pleasure of Jessie's soft mouth and tender fingers consumed him, making him desperate to tongue her and force her over the edge by driving himself inside the sensuous body he had so often told himself was not his to love. After roughly yanking her jeans down over her hips, Matt moved over Jessie with a steamy grin. "I love you, kid," he murmured as he pleasured her with his lips and tongue; as every muscle in his body went rigid; as low, throaty growls telegraphed his desire to take this woman and make her his for the short time he could have her, completely and without mercy.

When Matt's body gave itself fully over to Jessie with a force he didn't recall ever experiencing with Julie, he buried his face in her neck and tented her with his arms as he continued to convulse inside her, as he came down off the sweet pleasure wrought by loving her. She had come hard onto him too, and it took a few moments for Jessie to adjust her hearing past Matt's low moans and her own accelerated breathing to sense a phone bleeping somewhere. It was hers, down in the kitchen where she'd left it, and as Jessie calmed she could hear it plain as day.

It pissed her off.

"Friggin' thing," she groaned, and started laughing as Matt kept moving inside her, burying his lips underneath sweaty strands of Jessie's hair. Lightly, he brought her earlobe between his lips and sucked a little as he tried unsuccessfully to ignore the noisy phone, which seemed to both of them to be a harsh and unwanted dose of reality. "I hope it doesn't wake the kids," Jessie added nervously.

Matt's phone was in the pocket of the nylon aviator jacket he'd tossed on a chair by the kitchen island. Moments later, it started ringing too. Wrinkling his brow, he turned his head towards it, but stayed on top of his new lover, holding her in his arms so she could feel safe and loved for as long as he could gift those feelings to her.

"Charles again?" he asked with half-interest.

"I dunno. We'll get it in a sec, okay? Just let me enjoy this."

Twisting his lips into a sly curve, Matt slipped his hand down the now familiar belly and started moving his fingers over Jessie. Squirming, she let him play with her a while longer, and soon she was convulsing underneath him again.

"Oh God, this is Heaven," she breathed. "Stay in Vancouver, Matt. Don't go away. Ever."

The reminder sobered them. Quietly, Matt pulled away and strode towards the guest room's shower. "Come," he ordered, waggling a finger towards her. "Children, remember?"

"Again?" she teased, referencing his word choice.

Downstairs, Jessie's phone started up again. "Blah," she scowled, and followed him into the shower. "Somebody sure as hell wants something."

Melting into her steamy lover's embrace, Jessie clung to his chest and tried to quell a nervous, aching feeling in her belly. Matt couldn't stay here tonight, not in her bed with her, even if they slept in the spare bedroom. She knew what she—what they—were doing was, in so many ways, wrong, but it felt so right to connect with him this way.

"I'm so lonely," she breathed into his chest now. "Please, Matt. Stay. I can't fucking stand it. Josh and his stupidness. I fucking need you."

His answer was one long, last, beautiful, tender, perfect kiss. Gently nudging Jessie away from his body, Matt stepped out of the shower, dried himself off, and got dressed.

By the time Jessie was willing to vacate the hot, relaxing steam, Matt had checked his messages and made a call to Charles. Pale and trembling, he was waiting for Jessie at the bottom step.

Halfway down the stairs, Jessie saw the fear in his eyes and stopped. Like a stone, her heart hit the ground. "What? What is it, Matt?" Inside, her mind was already starting on a new treadmill of self-loathing. *I did this. I caused someone pain because I am not supposed to love this man. I am not supposed to be having sex with this man. In my husband's house. Oh, geez.*

Matt had to struggle to force the words from his lips. They came out cracked and blistered. "Jonathon called Charles. It's Josh, Jessie. He didn't show up for call this morning."

"What?"

As the implications of this new knowing slithered up her body like a snake, Jessie sank down onto the stairs. "Call would have been hours ago, Matt. It's five o'clock."

"Charlie and Arnie are out on your ATVs. They've been out all afternoon. They think Josh took his horse out last night and…" He couldn't finish.

She finished for him. "He didn't come home? After…last night? All… all night?"

They were both thinking the same thing. Matt looked away. He couldn't stand to see the agonized self-hate flickering across Jessie's eyes now. When he finally looked back, he cemented the insanity of the situation in which they now found themselves. "While we were together," he said quietly.

Turning her head towards the banister, Jessie grabbed it and melted her face into her arm. "I think I'm gonna be sick."

A small whine came from downstairs, from the media room. "That'll be Dylan," she managed. "He never sleeps long." Looking back up at Matt she added, "What now, Matt? What now?" The words were accompanied by a slow moving trickle of brand new tears.

Matt moved forward, kissed her on the forehead, and dialed Charlie.

Chapter Twenty-Two

*C*harlie didn't hear the phone ring, nor did he feel it vibrate in his pocket. Out this deep in the woods, when he'd stopped twice to check in with Arnie and Jon, he'd been surprised to find any reception, period. It was spotty—in some places there was reception—yet the messages he relayed were useless for their lack of information.

Josh could hear the ATVs. Twice they came close, but in his hurry last night to get to the creek and then home before dark, he had detoured off the main trail and taken a narrower path. As a result, he was not in his usual spot, and although he wasn't far from the main trail, he was still off the beaten path, per se, and not visible from any ATV that might have ended up at the creek via the main trail.

Last night when he left the barn on Blue's back, Josh was dressed warmly but the cool misty rain had long since soaked through his clothing. The dampness wasn't the biggest problem, though. The insidious pain and continuous blacking out frightened him almost as much as the snake-eyed coyote that had wandered up on the other side of the creek earlier, and regarded him with an air of curious disdain. She—or he—hadn't crossed the creek, though, and Josh surmised the gangly creature was just checking him out to be sure he was no threat to baby pups.

The ATVs were stopped now. Even in his hazy dreamlike state, Josh knew they were his machines—Jessie's had a smaller engine, so it sounded different. More like a sewing machine than a real machine, he often teased her. Now, in the worst pain of his life, bone cold and feverish at the same time, Josh slumped against the boulder and, in his more lucid moments, tried to will the ATVs to come near him. The odds were slim, at this point. Whoever was riding them would never find his narrow trail.

Letting his mind drift to Jessie and the kids, Josh started to pray a Hail Mary, alternating the bits he could dig up in the perpetual fog his brain seemed clouded by with thoughts of his beautiful, beloved mother, who passed away from cancer years ago.

On his second round, he got to 'full of grace,' before his eyes started to swim with little black dots again, and he passed out.

Charlie and Arnie had been back to the barn for gas already. When, late in the afternoon Charlie waved Arnie down at one intersection of the main trail, he was losing it. "Where have we not been, Arnie?"

Arnie hopped off his SUV, broke off a twig from a nearby tree, and started drawing a diagram in the dirt. "This is where I've been," he demonstrated quickly. "The only thing I can figure is Josh took the horse down the creek a ways."

"It would have been slippery as hell, Arnie. I can't see him taking the horse this far that late in the evening, up or down the creek, I mean. Walking on those stones in the dark would be like taking a horse onto an ice rink. You ever see Bambi, city boy?"

Accustomed to tense situations, many with very negative outcomes, Arnie easily read the frustration and fear in Charlie's voice. He thought the guy might actually have a complete meltdown, and Arnie knew why. Jessie and the kids, that's why. The Sawyer family had been through enough.

Standing back and scanning the area, which was populated by a dense assortment of trees and brush anywhere off the main trails, which were narrow this deep in the woods, he tried to think strategically.

"How do you feel about trying the creek anyway?" he asked. "We could go further down some of these trails, but like you said, Josh would have only come so far before hitting twilight and turning back. How long would that lasagna have taken to cook?"

"About an hour, tops," Charlie said. "Likely less. And he obviously set the timer, so…" The words faded as Charlie glanced down at his phone and saw that a call had come in from Matt. "Oh, Jesus," he gulped, and showed the phone to Arnie.

"It's okay," Arnie said. "Matt and Jessie aren't speaking these days so she likely still doesn't know unless Charles called her."

"And if he did, she'd be calling me. And she hasn't. All right, the creek it is. Go fifteen minutes west and I'll go east. We'll meet back here in half an hour. If one of us doesn't show up, we go in that direction because it means we've found him or...or something."

Arnie clapped Charlie on the shoulder. "We'll find him."

"Arnie, this is it. I'm calling search and rescue in half an hour. It'll be dark soon and Josh has got to be injured or he would've walked home. I'm not waiting any longer."

"Fair enough," Arnie agreed, jumped back onto the big ATV, and headed west.

Charlie went east. In ten minutes he saw the horse first, a chestnut lump, lying in deathly stillness on the polished stones. Nearby was a pile of something pale gold—a cougar. Also dead. Josh?

Stilling the machine, Charlie paused for a few seconds before he got up the guts to swing a leg over it. He didn't see Josh at first, and wondered if his friend had hit the trail and just gotten lost in the woods. Hoping for the best but fearing the worst, Charlie strode towards the dead horse.

His eye caught something to the left, something that didn't belong amongst the polished stones of the creek bed. The pointed toe of a cowboy boot.

Sucking in a breath, Charlie jogged the last twenty feet and bent down by his good friend.

"Hey, buddy. Josh. Wake up. Talk to me. Please." Heart racing, Charlie felt sick. Judging by the way Josh was slouched up against a boulder, he was badly hurt, or...

No. Just...no. I'm not going there.

Charlie shifted his position, dropping down on both knees on the hard stones, ignoring the quick pain that shot up his knees. A quick scan of Josh's body, and Charlie could see that his leg was likely broken. The right shoulder or arm was a mess too, according to the limp way it was hanging, and the right side of Josh's face was bruised and scraped. Leaning towards him, anxious to find a sign of life, any sign of life, Charlie touched the bruised chin.

"Buddy," he called loudly. "Josh, talk to me."

Josh's chest was moving. That was something.

Vaulting up, Charlie yanked out his phone and dialed 911, and almost threw the phone on the ground when, after the entire afternoon of searching with occasional decent reception, it now read *no service*.

"Fuck!" he screamed into the trees before pocketing his phone again. Already he was sick with dread. His friend had been out here in the cold overnight, maybe bleeding internally. And the cherished horse was dead. There was no realistic way to see Josh coming out of this intact. Even if he healed physically, the loss of the horse would kill him. The Winchester was at Josh's side. It was clearly evident that the shot that destroyed the horse had come from Josh himself.

A weak voice interrupted his frantic thoughts. Running distraught hands through his dark hair, Charlie turned and bent back down to Josh.

"What...took ya...so long?" Josh's eyes were slits that only remained open for a second. "Had a little...spin and toss action. Trouble...with a big cat."

Charlie touched his face again. "You're burning up, buddy," he said, trying to suppress the strong emotions that crisscrossed his face upon hearing Josh speak. "We have to get you out of here."

"I'd be...okay...with that."

"My fucking phone won't work out here, Josh. I have to head back down to the main trail. I gotta leave you for a bit."

Charlie's voice was fuzzy anyway. All Josh wanted to do was sleep. "Awwright," he slurred.

As Charlie stood to run back to the ATV, Josh, with his head still hanging, added a postscript. "Charlie."

"Yeah, man?"

"I had...to shoot...my horse. Blue." Josh would have cried but he had nothing left to give.

"I know," Charlie acknowledged with a low sigh. "She was a real good horse, Josh. You were right about her."

"She was...just scared...and lonely."

"You bet." Charlie whipped off the North Face coat he'd borrowed from

Josh's ranch house, and tucked it around his friend's shoulders. "Get warm. I'm getting us some help."

Ten minutes later, he ran into Arnie just as Arnie hit the main trail again. Charlie skidded to a stop and pointed down the trail. "He's down there. The horse is dead. Looks like she was ambushed by a cougar and Josh got thrown. I didn't have any cell service, we need to get an air ambulance in here right away, Arnie. Call Charles and Jon. I'm calling 911."

"You got it." Arnie didn't bother asking how badly Josh was hurt. Judging by Charlie's frantic instructions, there was some serious damage done.

The 911 operator gave Charlie some quick advice, basic stuff about keeping him warm and not moving him, before she let him go. When Charlie disclosed there was another guy with him, she directed one of them back down to the ranch. The nearby village of Canmore would be sending police and EMTs, who would come through the ranch to assist with the rescue effort. The air ambulance would be able to set down in the creek, using the phone's GPS for coordinates, but it could be an hour before it could be mobilized and land. Agreeing, Charlie was antsy to get back to Josh, so he gave Arnie his phone and spun back off down the creek bed. They'd deal with airlifting the still bodies of the horse and cougar out later.

Josh was no longer even remotely awake. It was as if he let go once he knew someone had found him, and disappeared inside himself. The wait for the helicopter was interminable. Charlie sat down next to Josh and positioned his body against him for warmth. As per the 911 operator's instructions, he didn't try to move him, and settled down to wait.

Chapter Twenty-Three

Jessie, too, fell silent. The only thing she said to Matt was, "Why couldn't I feel him? I can always feel him when he's hurting." She couldn't help but wonder if somehow Josh had switched off his part of their connection. Or maybe she had. Because of Matt.

Back to business, burying his own anguish over this new Sawyer trial, Matt connected with Charles again and, in a stilted voice, sorted out how to get Jessie to Calgary as soon as possible. To his credit, Charles understood that something sacred had passed between Jessie and Matt last night, and he didn't broach the subject. In his mind, and in Deirdre's too, they were two people desperate for connection, who truly did love each other on a very deep level, and who turned to each other in a time of need.

The children were ferried to La Casa by Ulysses. Katy met them there so she could help Carlotta watch over them, and Charles and Dee met Jessie and Matt at the jet.

"He'll be okay, honey," Deirdre told her, as Jessie fell into a seat. With nothing to say, and a numb percussion pounding in her ears, Jessie leaned a warm cheek against the cool window, wrapped both arms around her belly, swallowed past the steadily rising bile in her throat, and closed her eyes. Close by, Charles and Dee talked quietly, going over the little they knew about Josh's condition and what Charlie and Arnie figured had transpired.

Matt was the last on the jet. When he mounted the steps after a call to Katy to make sure she was settled at La Casa with the kids, he paused at the front of the aisle. Jessie, hearing his quick, nervous footsteps on the metal steps, forced her gaze over to him, and tightened both arms around her stomach.

Drawing both feet up to her seat, she tried to hug them instead, but no matter what she did there seemed to be no way to ease this new pain, to bring it more deeply inside her so she couldn't feel it.

With an apprehensive look to Charles and Dee, who were watching him, Matt dropped down into the wide leather seat next to Jessie and wrapped an arm around her. Curling up into a little ball, she buried herself in his side and wept.

Softly, he told her, "None of this is your fault, Jessie. You and I getting together did not somehow throw the universe off balance and cause Josh to get hurt."

She couldn't answer, so he held her close, put his feet up on an ottoman, and spent the short flight laying tender kisses on her forehead and tucking strands of damp hair back off her face.

Picked up at the airport by crew from *Sacred Peace's* transport team, they were delivered to the hospital to find Josh in surgery.

"He's in rough shape but he will recover," the general surgeon told them when she slipped out of surgery to fill them in. "Osteo's in with him now. He'll have some metal in both his shoulder and his tibia, and there are five cracked ribs that will cause him serious discomfort for a good few months. The dampness didn't do his lungs any good but we're medicating him. He will recover."

Relieved, Jessie just found herself nodding blankly. The only words that mattered to her were *he will recover*. At the same time, the only words bouncing around in her head and heart were a constant cacophony of self-loathing and confusion.

Josh spent the night in intensive care. When he was finally moved to a more accessible room the next day, he slept for hours and didn't see the endless cycle of friends who took turns at his bedside. Jessie stayed in a chair there, one foot tucked underneath her butt for the most part, chewing on her fingernails which, to her, seemed to be a better option than digging them into the backs of her hands.

A few times, Josh woke sick to his stomach, but he always settled back into the purple haze of drugged sleep. It wasn't until his second night in the hospital that he started to come around.

At eleven that night, Jessie left her chair to approach Matt who, standing outside the window to Josh's room, had been watching her for much of the day, his forehead bent to the glass and his hands in the pockets of his nylon aviator jacket.

Charlie was on his way down the hall with steaming coffee in one hand that was meant for Jessie. Arnie was in Josh's room, dozing in a chair in the corner by the door.

Jessie was facing Charlie, but she didn't see him. She was focused on Matt. All the long night before, and all day today, she and Matt had barely spoken. But she could see and feel the sorrow in his light hazel-grey eyes as he watched her from the window, and it was tearing her apart. Now, she reached for his left hand, pulled him close, and held on.

He buried his face in her neck and tried to breathe, but it was impossible. All Matt could bring in were great gulps of air that did nothing to settle him. Jessie, by now, was calm enough to offer comfort; she did this by whispering tender thoughts from her heart, generously mixed in with a number of *I love yous.*

Josh's bed faced the window. He could see them, but at that point neither knew he was awake. In his drugged and pained state, Josh tried to make sense of his wife embracing Matt so tightly, putting her palms to his cheeks and kissing the sides of his lips, his eyes. In the end, Josh tried to turn his face away, but the need to understand what he was seeing was overpowering.

Charlie froze. The coffee in his hand, he watched Jessie and Matt in their lovers' pose, and he pictured finding Josh with Shanda, kissing her but pulling away and telling her he loved his wife. Sliding through Charlie's mind next was the desperate search for Josh yesterday after realizing there had to be a good reason for him to miss his call time on *Sacred Peace*; finding him with a dead cougar nearby, badly injured and cold, with the horse he loved not six feet away, a jagged gash in her throat and a bullet from Josh's own rifle in her head.

Disgusted, Charlie had no patience for Jessie's theatrics on this night. He stormed towards her and grabbed her elbow, effectively forcing her to back up so rapidly that she almost tripped.

Matt, who was quick to realize that Charlie was the reason for Jessie's sudden movement, angled his head away from Charlie towards the window, looking up at the last second to spy Josh's eyes open and watching him. Straightening, Matt tried to speak, but it wasn't like Josh could hear him. Still, the words that escaped were, "I'm sorry."

Josh turned away, but there was comprehension in the heavy-lidded eyes. Matt shrank back from the window and sought Jessie's gaze.

She was trying to yank her elbow out of Charlie's fierce grip.

"Let me go!" she cried.

The coffee Charlie held in his other hand was dripping from its center steam hole. The hot liquid was burning his fingers but he ignored it. "Tell me I didn't see what I think I just saw, Jessie," he seethed. "Tell me you're not fucking Matt."

Helpless, Jessie stopped fighting him although her feet, in the usual brown boots, still moved a few steps backwards. Blistering tears of anger formed in her eyes. "One night," she fumed back at him. "One night. That's all we got."

"Why?" Charlie tossed the steaming coffee in the nearest garbage bin and wiped the hot beverage off his hand by swiping it across his jeans. "Why?" He was close to tears. "He was going to ask you to move here! Finally, you and the kids! Why would you want to fuck that up?"

Matt moved towards him. He touched Charlie's arm but Charlie threw him off so hard he elbowed Matt in the jaw. Clutching his jaw for a second, Matt released his hand, grabbed Charlie's arm and, with a quick RCMP law enforcement move, subdued him by bending his arm behind his back and yanking it upwards.

"Let go!" Charlie hollered. "Jesus, Matt!"

He was loud. Jessie glanced into Josh's room and met his quiet gaze. The liquid brown eyes startled her, and she jumped before pressing her lips together and wondering what he knew, what he'd figured out.

Matt wasn't done with Charlie. "It's not your business," he growled. "Drop it."

"Jessie is my business," Charlie retorted sharply.

Matt rebounded quickly. "Jessie hasn't been your business since the two of you ended your engagement, Charlie. You were done then, and you have no business sticking your nose in her life now, not where it concerns who she decides to spend time with."

"To fuck, you mean," Charlie countered hotly. "You mean who she decides to fuck."

"Charlie." Arnie was at the door. His voice was insistent. Charlie looked over at him, and then behind him. Seeing Josh's eyes on them, he crumbled.

"Oh, Jesus," he moaned. "Jesus, Matt, seriously? Jessie?" Forcing his arm out of Matt's grasp and backing away, rubbing his elbow, he spat, "The two of you deserve each other. Jessie, I thought I knew you. I thought you were better than this. I mean, I could see where Jacob threw you for a loop, but Matt? I don't get it. You and Josh…?" Throwing his arms out to the sides, he added, "He wants to make it work. He's trying."

"Charlie, the difference between you and me is that when you screwed around, all you cared about was sex. I care about love. What happened with Matt has nothing to do with Josh."

"The hell it doesn't. You're married!"

"Well, I've got news for you! I don't feel very married these days. I haven't since Christmas, and I sure as hell don't feel married living in Vancouver and begging my husband to let me come live with him, all the while knowing that the perky blonde co-star he spends every day with is in love with him!"

Something creased Charlie's face then—surprise? Jessie froze. "Did something happen between them?"

Charlie shrugged. "So what if it did?"

"Then I guess we're all good." Balling up her fists, Jessie crossed her arms and stared him down. "Go," she said to Charlie. "Get lost. I don't need you here right now, meddling in a life that no longer belongs to you."

Pointing a finger at her, getting close enough to jab it at her nose, Charlie said, "You make me sick. Your husband has been through hell. He's not drinking, he's not doing drugs, he's brilliant in *Sacred Peace* because he works damn hard at it, and yes he got into it with Shanda, but he walked away. Josh is the one who is trying to hang on to the two of you, and you just shit all over him. With your fucking security!"

At that, Arnie launched forward and gave Charlie a light shove. "I don't mean to be an ass, Charlie, but Josh is awake. He's hearing every damn thing you two are screaming at each other. Get lost. Now."

"You get lost," Charlie spat to Jessie instead. "You don't belong here."

A low growl escaped her lips. "Are you fucking kidding me, Charlie? You, of all people?"

His vicious stare could have curdled milk.

Arnie grasped Jessie's arm. "Come on. Let's walk," he insisted.

"Would everybody please stop touching me?" she cried, and shoved him away.

With one final look at Matt, her shoulders sank and she brushed by him, grabbing his hand and clinging onto his fingers until she got far enough away for their hold on each other to slip away.

With an apologetic look to Matt, Arnie followed her.

Matt closed his eyes, bent his head towards the floor, and said a silent prayer. When he looked back up, Charlie was watching him.

"What the hell were you thinking, Matt?" Charlie asked him, his voice still shaking, but somewhat more under control now that his princess super-star ex-fiancée was no longer present to push his buttons and piss him off.

"She's an amazing woman, Charlie. A lonely, scared woman who has suffered a lot in her lifetime."

"She's a spoiled child. And you can stop pretending you're riding in on some big white horse to save her, because the only person who can save her is herself." Deflating, Charlie added, "Look, Matt. You know better than anyone that these two are a mess without each other. That's never going to change. Do you want that? Ask Jacob how much it sucks."

In a hurt, husky voice Matt replied, "I've never had any illusions about being with her forever, Charlie. Never."

Studying him, Charlie's knees almost buckled. It hit him that Matt's feelings for his superstar charge were likely not new. Yet only now were those feelings being voiced. And apparently reciprocated.

Blinking, Charlie said, "I don't know what's going to happen here, Matt. Between these two. But I will tell you that I know how I want it to end."

"I want the same ending, Charlie. For Jessie. And for Josh."

It took Charlie a minute to gather his wits. His gaze never left Matt's face. Finally he said, "Why doesn't that surprise me?" Clasping Matt's shoulder he added a postscript. It came out hoarse. "I take back what I said earlier. You've always been Jessie's white knight."

Chapter Twenty-four

*L*ater that night, around three in the morning, the halls were quiet with the exception of a few nurses doing rounds and the occasional clink of metal on a tray, along with subdued laughter, from the nurses' station down the hall.

Jessie, still with Arnie, had curled up into a ball on a loveseat in a private waiting room and fallen into an uneasy sleep. Arnie was awake. There was a TV monitor mounted on the wall above Jessie, and he had it tuned into ESPN, but he wasn't really watching it. His chin kept dropping, but he was a light sleeper, and woke the second any noise from the hallway jarred him.

Earlier, Charlie had stayed with Josh, and Matt had gone for a long walk. Now, as Matt approached the large window, he noticed that Charlie, in the big chair at Josh's side, was snoring up a storm. Josh was struggling, though. Matt tensed, and jogged quickly inside when he saw that Josh needed to be sick.

Grabbing a plastic basin, Matt tucked it under his chin. "It's all right," he said, encouraging him. "You'll feel better after you get sick."

It was weird standing there helping Josh, who Matt knew like the back of his hand, knowing that only a few nights ago he was giving himself over body and soul to the man's wife.

Josh got the same vibe, but he was helpless in Matt's care.

After a bit, Josh settled back against the snowy pillow and groaned. "This sucks," he slurred, closing his eyes.

"Which part?" Matt mumbled as he moved to the small private washroom and emptied the basin's contents. Rinsing it, he sighed and glanced at his reflection in the mirror. What he saw looking back at him was a confused, sad, broken man.

Back in the room, Matt saw Josh's eyes, which were open again, following him as he moved to a rolling tray and set the basin down so it could be within easy reach if need be.

Josh answered his earlier question. "I take responsibility for messing up my body. I shouldn't have gone riding that far, that late. But there are limits as to how much responsibility I feel like I can take for the mess of my marriage."

"You need to stop pushing her away, Josh. If you want to stay married to her, you need to let her back in."

"Seems to me she doesn't want back in. Not really." Josh turned his head to the side. "I'm just so tired, Matt. Of everything. Of Jessie, of fighting to stay sober. Of life. Of everything." Blue's troubled eyes jumped into his head and Josh winced. Deuce McCall's old dagger sliced open his gut and twisted when Josh recalled the flap of skin hanging from Blue's throat, a steady flow of blood emptying the horse's life onto the creek's polished stones.

"Can I get you something? Ice chips or something?" Matt couldn't bring himself to leave this man who he knew Jessie loved above all others.

Josh was done in. Disgusted. He couldn't look at his old friend. "I don't want your help, Matt."

"Josh…I'm not sorry. She needed someone, and you weren't there. I'm not going to apologize for loving her."

"Please leave, Matt. Just go."

"I've got one last thing to say to you, Josh. Then I'll go. Promise me you'll listen." Since Josh didn't say anything, Matt continued. "Promise me you'll work things out with her. Promise me you'll take care of her. She needs you. She loves you."

Turning to Matt then, searching his eyes, Josh was sorry to see a deep pool of pain there. More than anyone else, with the exception of Charles and Dee, he knew how much the man cared for Jessie. He just never expected his love for her to end up in the bedroom.

"You're leaving," he murmured.

"Yeah. She knows it. She wants you. She's always wanted you."

"You've been fucking my wife but you're telling me she still wants me."

"Jesus, you two are stubborn." Matt leaned on the bedrail and studied Josh. "It was one night, Josh. That's what I got with her. One incredible, magical, amazing, surreal night, if you want the truth. And it wasn't nearly enough. But it has to be. Jessie is in love with you. You break each other's hearts again and again and again and yet you still love each other. Neither of you will ever be happy unless you are together. You and Jessie and Emily-Grace and David and Dylan."

"You love her."

Matt let out a small *mmpphh* sound. "Always. She's a stubborn, spoiled, obstinate little princess. How can you not love her?" He managed a tiny attempt at a smile, but his heart was breaking. "You know, when Charles first brought me to La Casa to meet her, she was this timid little thing with these big, sad eyes. I had dinner there a few times that first week and she never said a word. She just sat there and picked at her filet mignon or whatever and listened to everything that was being said around her but she rarely even made eye contact. Charlie was there one night. I remember watching him, thinking he had no clue what to do with her. How to talk to her. He was in complete awe back then. I think he still is, some days. Jessie's first film, the rom com she made with him in Curacao, was all over the place by then, and Jessie had recorded a few songs on its soundtrack. She was everywhere. Her face, her image…she was in demand. Every talk show wanted her, every stage demanded her presence."

"I remember," Josh considered quietly. "I saw that movie on the first anniversary of my mother's death. I was jealous as hell of Charlie for his career at the time. What I remember about Jessie was seeing her on Ellen and being amazed at how shy she was. And how…sweet and sad."

"She sang one of her first ballads on Ellen that day, one she later admitted she'd written for Sandy after he died. Charles and Dee were worried because she was so quiet and lost, it seemed, so alone…" Matt sighed. "I used to watch her and wonder what haunted her. Charlie did too. He really tried back then, to reach her. To get her to let him in. Josh…" Matt inhaled slowly. "Jessie never really let anyone in until you came along. Her confidence grew as far as performing and film work went, but even with Charles and Dee, and with me…she was so scared. Then you came along and she opened up like this beautiful rose in bloom."

"And you've been standing back watching her all along. Just waiting for your chance, huh Matt?"

"Josh, the first day at La Casa…the day I was brought in to meet her, Jessie had this aura about her. An energy. I didn't want the job. I knew I'd be a glorified babysitter a lot of the time. But by God, I couldn't walk away from those ice pale eyes. Even then, I could feel her screaming out for help. For someone to just be there for her, to be her rock. The weird thing is… we all wanted to be. All of us—Charles, Dee, Charlie. Carlotta, even. But nobody, least of all Charlie, could break down those walls, the ones that she built after Charleston, the ones she maintained after apparently being discarded by Caryn and Eric."

"Your point, Matt?" Intrigued, Josh wanted to know more, but the drugs and pain were pulling him back down into the deep abyss of sleep. He struggled to stay focused on this sacred tidbit from his wife's tough, sometimes sinister past.

"My point is that I had a lot of time to stand back and process Jessie, what made her tick, what hurt, what ached, what tore at her soul. I still remember the first time she ever hugged me. I was standing in the wings as always during one of her shows, a big one at Madison Square Garden. We were alone. Just before the show, Dee had gone back to the hotel, sick with some flu bug, and Charles had gone with her. Charlie was shooting somewhere in New Mexico, I think. I remember this new panic in Jessie's eyes just after Deirdre left, before I escorted Jessie to the stage. This was, like, after six years of working with her. Six years of an almost complete silence apart from quiet requests or responses. The way she looked at me in the dressing room—it was like she was seeing me for the first time. I think I said something like, 'Hey, kid, it's okay. We got this.' She just nodded, and I walked her to the stage. That whole show, she kept looking over to the wings, to see if I was still there, I think. Like she was scared I was going to leave her." A choking sound escaped his throat at the memory as a new, lonely future away from Jessie bloomed.

"She was thinking what a circus her life had become," Josh managed. "That she was at the top of her game and yet she was as alone as ever."

"And with Charles and Dee gone…the only person left was me." Matt shifted his stance and sighed heavily. "Jessie walked off that stage trembling. Those big tears of hers we see sometimes?"

"A lot, lately." Josh bit his lip and winced as he tried to get comfortable. Matt helped him adjust his pillow.

"Well, it was the first time I saw them. Or that she let me see them. One at a time they fell down those pretty cheeks, big slow ones that Jessie didn't even bother wiping away. I didn't know exactly what was going on, so I did what I always did, which was try to stand back out of the way and just watch so the powers-that-be at the venue could laud their post-show praise on her, but she never took her eyes off me. She pushed through them and wrapped her arms around my shoulders, and buried her face in my neck. It shocked the hell out of me. And I think that was the day I surrendered my heart completely to that beautiful, sad girl of yours. Holding her like that, trembling in my arms, whispering to her that everything was going to be okay, I could feel just how acute her loneliness was. How badly she needed me."

"And?"

"I know you know what I'm talking about here, Josh." Matt's voice was rough, raspy. His worried gaze bored deeply into Josh's cloudy, hurt eyes.

"Course I do." Josh watched Matt while the man tried to regain his composure.

Matt took a quick breath before he said, "I swear to God, Josh. I could feel her pain. It gutted me. It was like she opened a little window to her soul that night. Like she took ownership of my heart. That's the kind of history I have with your wife. She's everything to me. When her world devolves into chaos, she turns those beautiful eyes on me and I crumble. I've loved her for a very long time, but it's not like I ever fantasized about being with her. I had Julie. I trusted that Jessie loved me back in a way I could handle. Part of that became the pure, simple joy of seeing how happy she is with you, when things are good between the two of you."

"I'd ask what changed but that's obvious."

"It started with Morgan and Nadia, Josh. It escalated with Jacob's reappearance in your lives in a way neither of you could have predicted. But you've had your space. You need to let her back in. She's going to need a new rock, Josh."

Josh struggled to speak but he couldn't. His heart sank for Matt as the man begged Josh for a difficult favor.

175

"Tell her goodbye for me." Fighting back waves of emotion, Matt locked his eyes in Josh's. "Please. I can't do it. Years, Josh," he said, his voice barely audible. "Years, I've watched over her. Years, I've loved her."

Someone down the hall dropped a tray and cursed. Josh's eyes didn't leave Matt's, which now were more light grey than hazel. And they were swimming.

"All right."

Matt extended a hand and gave Josh's good shoulder a light squeeze. "Don't fuck up," he managed to mumble. "You need each other. What you have is worth fighting for, Josh."

And with that, Matt sucked in a breath, swung around, and left the room.

Up the hall, he paused outside the small waiting room where Jessie was curled into a ball on the sofa. Hugging a pillow, she was snoring lightly, one arm wrapped around a cushion, but she didn't appear happy. Her jaw was tight, her lips turned down.

Watching her sleep, Matt let his gaze drift over her body, the body that had loved him so fully and completely for almost twenty-four hours.

Arnie met his troubled eyes. Matt saluted him, and Arnie saw him go.

By far, the hardest thing Matt did in his entire life was force his feet to propel him forward, and walk him—for the third time in their long history—far, far away from Jessie Wheeler.

Chapter Twenty-five

A blossoming sun was just peeking over the horizon, turning Calgary's buildings indigo blue and the sky blue-black, edged with pink, when Jessie woke with the need to pee. Groaning, running a hand behind her neck, she stood and stretched quietly, and tiptoed out of the room so as not to wake the finally slumbering Arnie.

In the hallway, she looked both ways, hoping Matt would have found a chair somewhere close by, but he wasn't in sight.

There was a 'one-er' down the hall, a single toilet in a single room. Yawning, Jessie moved towards it, stepped inside, did her thing, and washed her hands before padding softly down to Josh's room. Charlie was still there, snoring away, looking every bit as uncomfortable as Jessie figured he felt, and she absently wondered how he managed to sleep half-sitting and half-slumped in the wide chair. Film sets, she figured in the end. Early morning calls, like at five a.m., were often the norm. Actors often had to grab catnaps here and there, wherever. It was part of the biz.

Josh wasn't sleeping any better than his assorted watchers. A combination of pain and drug-related nausea were keeping him awake. As Jessie's vision adjusted to the dim light in his room, she scanned every corner before summoning up the courage to focus on her husband. When she did, she jumped, surprised to see him awake and watching her.

Making her way to his bedside, Jessie clutched the rail and looked down at him.

"You must really hate me," he said.

"I just miss you," was her answer, spoken from somewhere between *I'm sorry* and *you suck*.

"You have a funny way of showing it."

Jessie's lips were quivering. Raising her shoulders and giving him an *I don't know what to say* look, she shook her head. "I'm at a loss, Josh. I can't apologize for being with Matt. I know it's not really a surprise to you."

Josh waited a few seconds before shattering her world. "He's gone, Jessie. He asked me to say goodbye for him."

Her throat got so tight Jessie had trouble catching her breath. Dropping her head backwards, she closed her eyes and then opened them to spy a ceiling she couldn't see for grief. "Sometimes I think," she lamented to Josh as she pressed a thumb and forefinger to the outer corners of her eyes to soak up the tears before they could waterfall down her cheeks, "that he's my only friend. And now he's gone. For good this time."

Matt. Josh replayed their last conversation. He truly had been—and was still, tonight—a guardian angel. Jessie's rock. For years. His last few words to Josh were about reconciliation and love. Forgiveness. Hope. For Josh and Jessie.

Extending his good arm to his wife, Josh asked, in a quiet tone, "Do you want to lie down with me?"

"Really?"

"Yeah, Jessie. Little one…I know what Matt means to you. What you mean to him. I'm sorry things have been so tough this last little while. I kinda feel like I pushed you into his arms. In a way, I'm glad he was there for you. To hold you."

Hesitant, Jessie walked around the foot of the bed so she could be on Josh's good side. Searching for the button to lower the rail, she admitted sheepishly, "You didn't push me. I went willingly."

"You remember when we got married?" Josh spoke while Jessie settled on her side next to him. "Ouch," he said, and adjusted her left arm so it wouldn't lie on his hurt ribs. She laid it on his good arm instead. "When we got married, we said we would try to work together and not be apart for too long. Yet I feel like we're always apart."

"Seems that way. It sucks."

"We need to do better."

Jessie turned her face into his arm. A quake in her shoulders alerted Josh to the fact that she was sobbing. Clutching his arm, she curled her legs up tighter and let the tears come.

"Hey, little one. Don't cry. Please."

"You said we need to do better."

"I did."

"Are we finally over that split rail fence? On the same side now, Josh? Because I really can't handle any more waiting and wondering and having no friends around and, and..." She sniffled, "Loneliness. I love our kids but I need friends my own age. I need my husband."

"We're over the fence if you want to be over it, Jessie."

"And...and Matt? Why aren't you more mad?"

"Like I said. I know what he means to you. Not that I ever want to share you, but in some way I'm relieved that it finally happened between the two of you. Your surreal night, as he put it."

"That's not probably something you and I need to talk about, Josh." The sniffling quieted.

"Then we'll let it rest. It's done. It's over. I'm sorry that he's gone. Life is never the same when Matt's not with us. And I know how bad this is going to suck for both of you."

Jessie was subdued as she pondered that agonizing truth. But for Josh's sake, she suffered in silence and took the high road. "Thank you for understanding. I mean it, Josh."

For a while, they laid together and listened to Charlie snore.

"How did you ever sleep with the guy?" Jessie could tell by the way he said it that Josh was trying to grin.

"He's worse when he's drinking," she sighed, wanting to force a smile out but simply too done in to manage the task. Pushing herself back a little, Jessie took a good long look at her husband. "How bad is it?" she asked. "The pain?"

"Worst of my entire life. Longest night of my life."

"And day," she added.

"Nope. Don't recall much of the day."

They were silent, reflective, on how bad things were, and on how bad they could have been.

The moment Josh had pulled the trigger and watched his horse die was going to haunt him forever. He cringed, and a small moan escaped his lips.

"What is it, Josh?" Jessie asked in a whisper.

The words escaped alongside the anguish Josh held inside all that long night and day. "I shot Blue. I had to kill her."

"I know, babe." Snuggling closer to him, Jessie kissed his bicep. "I can't imagine how awful that must have been for you."

"She wasn't what they said she was. Wild. Incorrigible. She was just lonely."

"Yeah."

"I know a woman like that."

"Yeah." She paused. "I hope you never have to shoot me."

The comment drew a tiny upturn to Josh's lips. "If I do, you may as well just shoot me too. I don't want to live without you, Jessie. Let's just keep figuring this out, okay?"

"The whole you and me thing?"

"Yep. That's the one. The marriage thing. The grief when we're not together is too much. You know?"

"I know."

"I know you know."

"I'm real sorry about Blue."

He was silent for a moment. "Me too." Then he added, "I'm real sorry about Matt."

"Me too," she said.

When Charlie awoke and saw Jessie in bed next to Josh, holding his hand, her breath on his skin as she snuggled into him, he wasn't at all surprised to see big wet tears trailing down her cheeks.

But what Charlie didn't know was that, in the safe and comforting arms of her husband, Jessie was mourning the loss of her rock. She was mourning the loss of her cherished, beloved Matt.

Chapter Twenty-six

"Jessie's moving the kids to the ranch," Kayla told Jacob as she studied an email on her phone. "Zach says Josh is getting out of the hospital tomorrow. He's not going to be very mobile for a while, but they refuse to hire help. They're duking this one out on their own."

"Jessie's keeping her schedule pretty free, Kay. Three small kids and a needy husband…" The light flecks in Jacob's blue eyes had Kayla laughing.

"Douche," she said, pretending to hit him before refocusing on Zach's email. "Us Sawyers aren't needy." Her eyes narrowed. "Oh."

"What?" Jacob was just lowering himself onto a narrow padded piano bench at the workshop tour's last venue, a small theater in Kelowna, British Columbia. Just for fun, Kayla had asked him to surprise their audience with his ballad, played live on the piano, as accompaniment to her post-intermission dance. They had arranged with the theater to do a private morning rehearsal. Facing him, she was leaning over the glistening piano as she checked her smartphone messages.

"Zach says Josh and Jessie are cutting down on using security, except where the kids are concerned or for big events." Wide-eyed, she looked up at Jacob. "Matt's gone."

"Ah. That's gotta suck." Jacob wiped his palms on his jeans and met Kayla's narrowing, curious gaze. "But Jessie's moving to the ranch."

"Yes." Tossing her phone in her bag, which she'd set just beneath the piano while they fine-tuned their number, Kayla surmised, "That's gotta hurt. Losing Matt."

"There's only one way to love Jessie Wheeler. And that's from a distance. Unless you're Josh Sawyer."

"Apparently. Although he may disagree with you on that last point as well. Loving her has, on occasion, been equally excruciating for him." Quiet, Kayla held Jacob's gaze until he allowed a small smile, which encouraged her to smile back. "Good thing you've found the next best thing."

"No," Jacob grinned and said honestly, "I found the best thing. I must have been out of my mind to ever think a woman who is so in love with a guy that she wears his ring around her neck, could possibly ever love another man. Matt's always known that. I'm glad I'm past the kind of pain he's in right now. It sucked, Kayla."

"You're preaching to the choir, Jacob." With a seductive flourish, she moved behind him and bent to encircle his shoulders in a big hug.

"You Sawyers," he added lightly as he covered her fingers with his, "must have some kind of superhuman power. Some kind of witchy love potion or something. Loving you is surreal, Kayla. I mean that. I was blind but now I see."

"If you're going to get all romantic on me, Jacob Ryan, I'll be too mushy to do any more dancing. And I think those lyrics are taken, by the way. So don't go trying to use them."

Throwing his head back to laugh, Jacob was amazed at how good life was in Kayla's company. Truly, if there was some kind of Sawyer power at play, he was downright grateful that he'd been sucked in. Jacob and Kayla were adjusting to their new life together, and as yet the youth on the tour respected both of them enough to keep the relationship on the down low, away from prying media eyes, although tonight's live accompaniment would most certainly raise a few interested eyebrows.

"We should go see them. Josh, Jessie and the kids. We need to mend fences, and you need to establish a secure relationship with your son."

That sobered him. Jacob's shoulders sank. "Josh won't go for it, Kayla. He's terrified of losing Dylan."

"And Jessie."

"Well, it may take some convincing, but that's no longer an issue. Hasn't been since New York."

"He loves his baby sister. Josh will listen to me. He wants me to be happy."

"Josh is not the same guy from the *Mystic Nights* days, Kayla. Something broke in him when Jessie and the kids disappeared, and it got damaged beyond repair when I…" He gulped. "The whole Florida thing. Fear is a part of his everyday life now. It controls him. I doubt there's any reasoning that will allow me back in Dylan's life."

"The Josh I know and love is still in there somewhere, Jacob. Jessie going back to the ranch is a good sign. Dylan's your son, and my nephew. We'll figure this out together. Deal?"

"Okay. Deal." Closing his eyes, Jacob soaked up the wise, talented, sexy woman hugging him now. "You're adorable," he murmured.

Her smile vibrated against his neck before Kayla kissed Jacob's cheek and moved to the center of the stage. "Okay, lover boy," she commanded. "Let's do one last pass and make some magic here. Then maybe we can go back to the hotel and make some more magic before the official rehearsal with the troupe this afternoon. You in?"

"Hell, yeah!" he agreed with a happy grin. "Ready?"

Wiping his hands on his jeans again, Jacob curved his fingers slightly, as if he was holding bubbles—or maple bacon cupcakes—in both hands. With the grace of an experienced, very musical player, he edged into the ballad with a restrained refinement.

At center stage, watching Jacob lose himself in a piece he wrote, Kayla almost forgot to start dancing. When Jacob peeked up at her over the polished beauty of the elegant baby grand on which he was playing, his shy grin reminded her that she had musical beauty to offer today too. She just had to separate herself from Jacob's puppy dog eyes, first, which wasn't easy to do since they had only been reconciled and together for a few short weeks.

She moved with a poise that perfected Jacob's lovely ballad. The highs, the lows—it was as if she was filling the song out for him, making it complete.

As if she is completing me, Jacob thought as he started to sing.

Dancing her own unique blend of styles—ballet, B boyz, jazz, modern—made Kayla an original. She had her own voice and she was confident enough on stage to use it. Jacob reflected as he watched her that she was also confident when it came to lovemaking, so much so that she was taking control of him more and more, riding him and urging him towards climaxes as rich as their musical climaxes. She was also into experimenting with, well, toys for one and, she had told him although they had yet to go there together, multiple partners. Jacob was intrigued, had some experience in that department, and shared Kayla's interests. They were a good pair in a lot of ways.

Jessie was usually more about being responsive, he remembered. She'd liked it when Jacob took control, although she certainly had her own sexual voice too, when she felt like using it. She was into toys to a point, but sharing her man was a thing of the past, for her, relegated to the Downtown Eastside days, with the exception of that crazy night in Scotland years ago with Katrine when Jacob and Jessie first hooked up.

Now, Kayla brought her dance to its pinnacle just as Jacob reached the satisfying highest notes of his ballad. The effect, to both of them, was an otherworldly spiritual kind of passion elevated above all other, that got a rise out of both Jacob and Kayla, and which made him ache to hold her and bring their bodies together the way the music brought their souls together. She complemented him the way Jessie did, musically, but Jacob could watch Kayla interpret his music with her body and soul, whereas with Jessie there was a sacred kind of beauty, but it always came with a limit once they left their musical stage. Even in the bedroom, where they often ended up in the old days. It didn't matter how much they loved each other or how incredible their music was together. Her soul only opened so far for him. It stopped when her longing for Josh took over and that, Jacob knew, was like some kind of glass ceiling he would never surpass, could never shatter.

Talia? Beautiful, sweet, funny, kind. Jacob could not conjure up his memories of her without feeling completely gutted. Guilt, mostly, ate him alive over her, but he was learning to let her go with some kind of healing light. The Caribbean had helped over that first while—sailing on Sarah May had offered a certain kind of freedom. Now, recognizing that Kayla fulfilled him in ways that Talia would never have been able to, Jacob was crossing that threshold, and when he hurt the most, in the middle of the night usually, Kayla held him and whispered all the right tender thoughts to help him through the toughest memories, the ones imbued in twisted metal and splintering glass.

The song came to an end, and Jacob's fingers hovered over the keys for a few moments before he removed them and laid them on his lap. Kayla was still in her secret place, lost in the final strains of a ballad so lovely and sublime that she could not let go.

It was the theater's lighting tech who burst the perfect bubble.

"How was that special?" he asked, referring to his name for the light. "The color okay? Or do you want to try magenta?"

"I like the blue," Kayla managed, reminding herself that she was not floating above the earth any longer. A sideways look to Jacob told her that he, too, was still lost in the music and in the dance.

Jacob was also lost in the woman. "I never would have believed it," he murmured inwardly as he watched this silly girl with the cranberry-tinged hair, tight tank, baggy B boyz pants and Converse Chucks step out of the light and glide towards him. Not many months earlier, he was almost suicidal, the world felt so damned dark.

But most surprising of all, was that the girl that saved him was Josh Sawyer's sister.

Kayla. A woman Jacob would hold dear for the rest of his life.

~ ⌣ ⌣

Vancouver walkers, joggers and cyclists were wearing T-shirts and sundresses by the time the weary workshop dancers and musicians were delivered back to their grungy East Hastings parking lot. It was a brilliant evening; an orange sun was laying itself to rest by melting into the Pacific, silhouetting the many cargo ships waiting patiently for access to Burrard Inlet, and subsequently putting a big fat 'period' on the tour.

These young mostly twenty-somethings were, like the cargo boats, changed. Tired and ready for rest, they were now things of beauty, fueled by Kayla's dream of hope, of her belief in their talents and potential. The brief time on stage, powered by a backdrop of music and dance, had sparked a new energy. The youth would do better now; they had the confidence to move forward, to create lives of passion and purpose.

Humbled at the effusive hugs and praise of her new friends, Kayla swiped at tears that grew more profuse with every goodbye hug. Jack Deacon was present with his wife, Lydia, and by the time the last dancers were ready to leave they, too, were overcome by the overwhelming success of the workshops and the spring tour.

"We'll do it again," Jack said, offering the last hug of the day just as the sun disappeared and downtown Vancouver became a tableau of rich indigo blue buildings accented with its own music of rolling buses, light beeps, and the occasional homey seaplane. "Gas up and we'll talk, Kayla."

While Lydia gracefully held Kayla's fingers in hers and invited her for dinner next week, Jack took a step forward to shake Jacob's hand. "Jacob. It was a surprise to hear you played on stage last week for Kayla. I understand it was quite a spectacular event. A video or two snuck up onto YouTube."

"She's a special woman, Jack. I couldn't help myself." Glancing down at his boots, Jacob added humbly, "I hope Charles was okay with it."

"Okay with his artist expunging a bad rep by making a charitable appearance on this tour? He and Deirdre couldn't have planned it better themselves, son." Jack tossed in a note of concern Charles had voiced to him when they talked the day before. "They may have preferred to send some security along with you."

Looking up, Jacob shrugged. "I'm hearing they're shorthanded these days. We were fine."

"Losing Matt was inevitable, from what I understand," Jack lamented. They all liked the man and were sorry to see him go. "Apart from what happened with you and Jessie, I hold onto my hope that you remain one of the good ones, Jacob."

Cringing, Jacob felt the need, as he always would, to cement his acceptance of responsibility for what happened around New Year's. "What I did was wrong, Jack. I've been talking to Charles and Dee about how to make right. We're working on some fundraisers and speaking engagements. Education. That kind of thing."

"I'm glad. Now, take this young lady home. She looks exhausted."

"I will. Thank you, sir. For everything. You changed lives by sponsoring these workshops."

Interjecting, Lydia smiled broadly. "That's his mission, Jacob. My husband is a kind man who uses his good fortune to help others. Jessie, of course, being the most famous of those. And we are glad you are doing the same. Good night, son."

As they strolled away arm in arm, Jacob was about to reach for Kayla when her eyes, looking beyond him, alerted him to the fact that someone else remained. Wheeling around, a wide grin lit up his cheeks.

Casey. Benjie, too, was by her side. Striding forward, Jacob swept her up into a big hug.

"You are going places, Casey," he told her, as Benjie moved to Kayla and held her tight, which unleashed a new torrent of grateful, exhausted tears. "You are one amazing drummer, and a pretty darn good dancer too. We'll be staying in touch."

A cloud washed over the dark, soulful eyes of the stunning aboriginal girl who'd shed her slouchy image and emerged as a confident, beautiful butterfly over the course of the workshops. "I wish I could believe ya, Jacob. But I'm scared. What if I mess it all up? What if it all just…disappears? Like a dream? A bad dream," she added.

"It won't if you have a good attitude and continue to work at it, Casey. You have talent."

Pulling at Jacob's sleeve, she glanced at Kayla, saw that she and Benjie were engrossed in happy tears, and she spoke quietly. "Jacob, you're the only one who knows about what happened on the reserve. I trust you. I just don't know if that will ever come back to haunt me, ya know? What if I have some success and then it all just gets pissed away by my past?"

"We all make mistakes, Case. Look who you're talking to." Jacob pointed a finger towards his chest. "And look at Jessie. She's gotten past those erotic photos and films she made back when she lived on the Downtown Eastside."

At Jessie's name, Casey blanched. "Don't remind me," she growled and studied a caterpillar struggling across the quickly darkening asphalt.

"You're gonna have to let this animosity against Jessie go, Casey. She may be able to provide you with one of your biggest opportunities. Or if not her directly, you mentioned that the Keatings talked about getting involved with you. You can't continue to hate Jessie and expect things to work out in their camp."

Her big eyes peeked up at him from beneath long, wet eyelashes. "I guess you've learned that too over time, huh?"

"What I've learned is that good things can happen if we open our hearts to let them. I can't erase the past, or the fact that I'll always be in love with Jessie. But trying to let go, trying to forgive, makes room for the future."

"You and her were so good together, Jacob. Your music was unreal." Casey was pouting, her lips turned down.

"We're still making music together, Casey. Jessie and I are still trying to salvage a friendship. She's a good person. You need to cut her some slack."

"I dunno. I just hate what she did to you."

"Dylan, huh?"

"She used you, Jacob. And then she took your son away from you to go back with someone who the whole world is waiting to completely lose it. With your little boy around."

A sharp twinge almost caused Jacob to sink to his knees but he held his cool. "Josh is a problem. Yeah. In some ways. I hear you. I guess I'm hoping that now that I'm with Kayla, he'll be more open to access."

"Access is not the same thing as raising your own kid."

"It's better than nothing. It's better than lying awake at night listening to Jessie try to smother her tears with her pillow. She'll never love anyone but him. Not like that."

"Jacob…?"

"Yeah?"

"We're friends, right? We can be honest with each other?"

"Yeah, Case. I hope so."

"Is that why you're with Kayla? To try to win over her brother? To stay close to Jessie and Dylan?"

A chill shot up Jacob's spine. "No! Jesus no, Casey. Don't start that rumor, please." He glanced over at Kayla, who was saying goodbye to Benjie. "I just got her back."

Softening, Casey said, "You two are good together."

He grinned. "I know. She's amazing." Holding open his arms, he added, "C'mere, kid."

With a sad smile, Casey disappeared into Jacob's embrace. He held on tight.

"You call me if you ever need anything. Got it? Although I'm sure I'll be seeing you around La Casa anyway."

"La Casa?"

"It's what the Keatings call their house. I think Jessie named it years ago or something, I'm not exactly sure. But you'll love it there. It's cozy."

"Okay." With a final hug and a happy grin, Casey took Benjie's arm and they grabbed their bags and shuffled off down the sidewalk towards Benjie's brother's car for a ride to Casey's small abode to grab some things. She'd be spending most of her nights at the charismatic Benjie's from now on.

"Let's get you home," Jacob said to Kayla with a smile. "You need sleep."

Near Benjie's brother's car, Ulysses was waiting for them. Jacob waved and signaled 'one minute.'

"I could use some sleep. But maybe some playtime first, hmmm?"

"You never have to convince me," Jacob laughed, as they grabbed their bags and said their goodbyes to the bus driver before starting to move towards Ulysses.

"So, Jacob?"

"Yep?"

"I guess we'll have to start mending fences with Josh and Jessie, huh? Now that we're back to reality?"

That sobered him. "They're in Alberta. Jessie finally moved the kids there, remember?"

"Then we'll take a trip. I think I owe her an apology."

"We need to warm Josh up before I land on their doorstep, Kayla. The last thing we need is a big altercation in front of the kids or on set or something."

"I'll call him. I want to see how he's doing, anyway."

"All right. In the meantime…" Jacob dropped his bag in Ulysses' trunk.

"Hmmm?" Yawning, Kayla stretched and smiled a greeting at Ulysses.

"I need to buy a better place so I have room for my girlfriend," he winked. "I've had a realtor looking on my behalf. How do you feel about doing some condo hunting tomorrow?"

"Can I sleep in just a bit?"

"A half hour. That's all."

"Dictator." Flinging her cranberry accented hair in his direction, Kayla slid into the back seat of Ulysses' car and sank down into its luxurious leather. "Home, James," she joked. "So tired. So happy, but so tired."

Closing her eyes, she nodded off before Ulysses turned onto Burrard a half mile away, and dreamed of a future filled with children, hope, and Jacob.

Chapter Twenty-seven

"We're going to live the waterfront lifestyle," Jacob told Kayla when he snuggled in beside her the next morning, after setting a mug of home brewed coffee on the nightstand. "Keep your place if you like for those PMS days when you want to bite my head off for no reason, but stay with me as much as you like. I found a place in the Olympic Village with access to False Creek so we can go kayaking. It's off the Seaside Bikeway so we can take leisurely Sunday afternoon rides with our kids. Good?"

Rolling over to cuddle with him, eyes still closed as she slowly started to wake, Kayla murmured, "Kitchen?"

"Separate temperature controlled wine fridge."

"Important. And?"

"Built in espresso machine."

"And outdoors?"

"Huge deck with a garden. Oh and two fruit trees. Don't ask me what kind of fruit. What even grows here?"

Her smile was enough to convince Jacob that he was on the right track. Circling her nipple with his finger, he added, "I've also got a Yaletown loft booked to see. And a house in Dunbar because I know you love the neighborhood, but I thought the access to False Creek and the bike trail would be awesome. Plus there are lots of cafes in the area and it's close enough to East Hastings to walk to, or to bike to, for the next series of workshops."

"I have my scooter," she slurred sleepily as she eased over onto her back and stretched both arms above her head so Jacob could shuffle lower in the bed and smother her belly with kisses.

His tongue grew more adventurous, and he leveraged himself up to lie on top of her, placed his hands on Kayla's hips, and made an *mmmm* sound to acknowledge that he heard her comment about the scooter.

She took the *mmmm* as Jacob's pleasure as he explored her body, and reached down, eyes half-open now, to smile at him and push back his dark curls so she could watch him.

"What time?" A frisky light in her eyes telexed playful thoughts.

"We have time." Jacob's words were rather smothered because he wasn't feeling ready to ease away from the increasing sizzles that pleasuring his girlfriend's willing body transmitted to him, and he lifted her hips to bring her closer to his lips.

Moaning softly, Kayla's face flushed pink with sweet desire. Pure contentment and joy lit up her dusky, dreamy eyes. "Take your time," she demanded. "Your realtor's going to do just fine by you. He can wait."

"She." Sinking lower on Kayla's body, Jacob got back to work. He looked up and pretend-scowled at her. "What'd I tell you?" he teased, a mischievous grin replacing the scowl. "Wider. For me. You don't listen very well."

"Oh God, I think I'm in Heaven." With a low, happy *rrrrr*, Kayla complied.

The realtor checked her watch three times before Jacob texted *running late*.

Jacob bought the condo in the Olympic Village, pleased when he and Kayla arrived for their initial viewing to discover that Steve and Sophie lived in a nearby building. The new condo was vacant. As soon as the paperwork was finalized, Jacob moved in.

Once they did some furniture shopping and he was settled, and Kayla had moved a few things over as well—her computer and some fave kitchen tools, mostly—they decided it was time to plan the 'mending fences' trip to Alberta.

Coincidentally, their timing was perfect. The smallest Sawyer was turning three in June. Kayla made the call to Josh, and a date for a visit was set.

～～～

Stubborn as always, Josh had gone right back to work the week he got home from the hospital. The writers on *Sacred Peace* scrambled but since he was playing a sheriff in a contemporary western town, it wasn't a stretch to 'roll his truck' in an episode. Jessie was less than thrilled, but she understood the rigors of TV making as much as he did, and the honest fact was that the production suffered every day he was off work.

The night Josh got the call from Kayla, which came in after Arnie'd driven him back to the ranch after a day on set, Josh removed himself from Jessie and the kids and limped out to the sun porch to talk. Afterwards, he sat quietly, the phone in his still slinged hand and the opposite thumb and forefinger absently scratching his chin. His view was of the corral where Blue used to roam happily. When Jessie joined him after settling their children for the night, she wondered whether his pensive mood was due to the call from Kayla, or from the loss of Josh's special horse. Perhaps both.

"Hey, babe," she said, easing down next to him on the wicker loveseat. "You okay?" Sighing in contentment at the opportunity to put her feet up on the antique trunk they were using as a coffee table at the end of her long day with three busy kids, she rested her left hand on his thigh. "We've hardly had a chance to talk. The kids go nuts when they see Arnie's car in the driveway."

Josh's King Ranch was parked in the same spot where he'd left it the night he was hurt. Nodding at it, he grimaced. "I can't wait til I can drive again."

"That day will come soon enough," Jessie admonished him. "Don't be in a hurry. Arnie's only too happy to drive in from Calgary for you. What's his news, anyway?"

"He's wondering about taking a week off. His wife wants to fly to the Maritimes to see her mother."

"Oh. There's a thought."

"We'll get to P.E.I. again one of these days, Jess. And we'll stop in Peterborough on the way. Okay?" Moving his left hand, he entwined his fingers in his wife's. "I'll talk to Charles about letting Arnie go for a bit. Now that you're here, and with Dan and Sam taking turns with the kids when you're on the move, I don't really think we need Arnie around as much anyway."

"I know. I want to keep cutting back our security, Josh. As long as the kids are covered and you get to AA meetings, we're golden. Don't you think?"

"Appearances notwithstanding, yes. I'm with you on that front."

"So. The phone call. What's Kayla's news?"

"Kayla." Josh sighed. "I suppose I should be glad the two of us are back on speaking terms."

"But you don't seem happy."

Josh was still staring absently at the corral. Sinking lower into the loveseat, Jessie leaned more on her side and switched hands in his. With her right hand, she massaged his thigh gently and listened attentively.

Her husband's voice was subdued. "Did you know she hooked back up with Jacob?"

Apprehensive, Jessie hesitated before speaking. She didn't admit to being in touch with Jacob via texts. "I saw a video on the Internet. He played piano and sang live on stage for her solo dance during one of the last tour dates. His latest ballad. So I guess you could say I assumed."

"I don't know what to make of the two of them together, Jessie. I can't say I like it."

"And that's putting it mildly, isn't it, babe?" Rubbing his thigh, Jessie moved her hand closer to an area that might appease her husband a little. Anything to get rid of the old sadness that seemed to cling to him like a shadow.

"Jacob's not ever going to be my favorite person, Jessie. I can't seem to shake him off."

"If he makes Kayla happy, then why can't they be together?"

"I don't think I need to spell it out for you, little one."

Okay, he called me little one. So he can't be that mad...

"What about Dylan, Josh? I think we need to talk about Dylan. With or without Kayla...Josh, Jacob has the right to see his son...um, to see him. He's never tried to establish any legal custody arrangements. You have to admit he's been okay."

"Look, Jessie." Josh's voice was rising in pitch. Jessie tensed and stopped moving her hand, although Josh didn't seem to notice. "First of all, it sickens me to hear you call Dylan 'his' son. There was a time I wanted Jacob to be a part of Dylan's life. That time has come and gone. He didn't have any interest in him then, and now that Talia's gone I feel like his interest is more of a ploy to see you."

"That's not fair. Kayla's bound to be an influence. Dylan's her nephew. Sort of."

"Okay, the fact that you added 'sort of' kind of freaks me out." Emitting a low growl, Josh eased lower into the loveseat.

Jessie stilled her movements. "I just mean biologically he's not. But yeah, he's her nephew as much as David is, as far as I'm concerned."

"Jacob needs to give up his rights to Dylan. He needs to let me officially adopt him."

"You know he'll never do that, Josh. We all agreed to keep the courts out of this. He'll be happy as long as we allow access when and where he wants it." *It's like talking to a mule,* she thought, lines of worry furrowing her brow. *Jacob. None of this is fair to him. It's never been fair to him.*

"Dylan's turning three. Pretty soon he'll understand more of his weird parentage, Jessie. I just don't want to confuse him any more than he's already confused."

Frustrated, she jumped in. "No, let's be honest here, Josh. You're scared of losing him. Which in some ways makes me happy because at least it means you accepted him."

With a quiet *mmpphhfftt,* Josh turned his face away from her.

Leveraging herself up with her left arm, Jessie moved to the antique trunk in front of her husband so she could face him and read his emotions more clearly. She took his good hand in both of hers.

Josh exhaled and refocused on her.

"Babe," Jessie started carefully. "I've got news for you. Little boys have big hearts. They can fit all kinds of love in them. The more, the merrier."

"And if Jacob fucks off again? Or is just using Kayla to get to you?"

"Doesn't matter. He and I are done. You need to trust me on that account."

Josh shook his head. "You lost that trust, Jessie. I'm sorry. It went out the window with your little trip to Florida, regardless of how that ended up. Look," he sat up straighter, but at least lifted her knuckles and kissed them, which helped Jessie relax and not worry that this would become a full fledged fight, "I just don't want Jacob around. Period. I want him out of our lives."

"What you want and what you might get are two different things, Josh." She mellowed. "Babe, look. If you value your relationship with your sister and want her around, you're going to have to let Jacob come around as well. Despite what you think his intentions may or may not be."

"It's bad enough that the two of you recorded together. You'll be playing shows to support *Sacred Peace* and in support of your new album that's emerged from that soundtrack." Josh's eyes darkened.

Detecting a small flash in the somber brown eyes she knew well, Jessie sucked on her bottom lip and waited. "What?" she finally asked him, breaking the uncomfortable silence.

"I don't know," Josh said quietly. "Maybe having Matt in the middle was a good thing, huh? As a buffer. Of sorts," he added sarcastically.

Tears pricked Jessie's eyes. "Can we not bring poor Matt into this mess?"

"Matt's a part of this mess, Jessie."

"Matt was the glue that held me together, Josh."

"Shoulda used your old Jim Beam."

"Okay, now you're playing dirty." Rising, Jessie shoved his fingers away from her.

Josh stood too, leaning on his good leg. "Jess, stop," he called to her back. Pausing at the doorway, Jessie half-turned back to him. "I told them they could come, okay? One visit, to see how we all do. That's all. I'm just a glutton for punishment, apparently."

"No." A tiny curve formed on Jessie's lips and her eyes lightened. "No, you're just a really good man, Josh Sawyer." She reached out a hand to him. "Come, babe. Let's go lie down. These kids are exhausting and you know Dylan's not going to sleep through the night."

Taking her hand, Josh limped along next to his wife across the open concept one story space, past the kitchen area, towards their large bedroom. "You were with Jane today?"

"Yes. Stella and Emily-Grace are joined at the hip. We did the kids' schoolwork and then Jane and I took them on a short hike, which tired them out enough for her and I to grab coffee at The Summit Café. Dylan slept the whole time we were there. Small mercies. But by the time I got home he was wired again."

"Maybe we should get TV."

"Never. We fed the horses and I continuously defended our decision not to get them a puppy. They've got the barn cats for pets."

"You'll cave one of these days."

"Our lifestyle doesn't leave room for a puppy, Josh, unless you want them to have a lapdog, which just doesn't match the whole ranch vibe. Discussion over. Now come here, big boy. Let me help you remember why you married me."

Wide-eyed, happy, chewing playfully on one corner of her lip, Jessie stepped backwards and sat down on the edge of the bed. Grasping Josh's belt with her right hand, she urged him slowly towards her. He limped over, and used his left hand to push back her hair. Jessie lifted his T-shirt and kissed his belly button, wrapping both arms around his back and pressing her palms into his skin. Sighing at the simple sweet pleasure of loving him, of holding him, of finally being with him with some sense of confidence that they would be okay as a couple, she let her lips trail up to his nipples. His ribs were healing, yet he winced as she touched him.

"It still hurts," she murmured, touching his side as if she could impart some healing energy into him.

"One body part doesn't." A diabolical grin lit up Josh's cheeks as he bent forward to kiss his wife's forehead.

"Good thing." Undoing his belt, Jessie exhaled slowly. Unbidden, a memory of doing this for Matt slid into her mind. She paused and closed her eyes as a hot flash of memory launched itself into her heart.

Josh caught the pause, although he didn't see the pain that crossed her face.

His next words were a whisper. "I'm not going to ask what that was," he breathed.

Jessie let out a long, quiet Yoga breath and encircled him with her arms again. Turning her cheek to rest it against his belly, she didn't answer.

Quietly, Josh grabbed her arm and pulled it away from his body, then repeated the process with the second. Moving backwards away from her, Shanda crossed his mind—cute, blonde, perky, willing, head over heels in love with him...Or this. A wife whose alliances seemed, of late, murky and grey, even though Josh knew he trumped them all.

"You did that for Matt," he snapped, standing a few feet away from her. "How'd he like it? What kind of sounds does he make? He turn you on?"

"I was just missing him. That's all," Jessie whimpered, staring at the floor, wishing she could disappear.

"Making love to me makes you miss Matt. We're off to such a damn good start here, Jessie."

Tilting her face up to search her husband's eyes, Jessie whispered, "I've been with a lot of men, Josh. In good times and in bad. It's what I know, to make them feel better. I've never known a man not to like it. So yes, Matt liked it. And I liked doing it for him. Right now I'd like to do it for you. But it's your call. I understand if you need more time."

Hesitating, Josh studied his wife and considered what she was telling him. Yeah, he knew about her Downtown Eastside history. He was aware her stepfather had likely asked for—or forced—the same move from her from the time she was twelve, although Josh had never really asked her about those dark days. Deuce McCall? No doubt. Maybe being good to him saved Jessie from other kinds of grief. Got the tension over with, per se. Picturing her with her other men, the ones she loved—Sandy, Charlie, Jacob…Well, they were lovers with some continuity. Boyfriends.

Matt was a conundrum. He was a safety net who put his own life in danger to save Jessie and who would do it again at the drop of a hat. There was a deep, deep love there, something almost indefinable for its longevity. Did Jessie service Matt with a sense of detachment as she would have the men from those long ago Downtown Eastside films? Not hardly likely. Although Josh sensed there was some of that there, some wanting to make him happy as a kind of weird entitlement.

I'm her husband, he told himself as Jessie sat on the bed with her shoulders slumped. Jessie—an international star, a loving mother of three children, a woman who helped heal the world after a shooting by singing John Lennon's *Imagine* in the very location where people lining up to see her show were killed…

"Why?" he managed, his eyes moist. "Why do you like to do that for men?"

"To show love," she whispered without missing a beat.

Josh padded softly back over to her and, with his good hand, lifted her chin. "Look at me, Jessie," he demanded. "I love you more than any man on this earth could ever possibly love you. I love you more than life itself. But I have to tell you. It hurts to hear you say that sucking on a man's dick is a way to show him love."

"I've never been turned down before," she answered softly. "I like doing it, so why should I mind? What's the big deal?"

"The big deal," Josh replied, "is that when my wife wants to make love to me, I want her to make love *to me*. I don't need her recalling what she did for other men, especially one I trusted not to take my wife to his bed." He paused. "Was it his bed, Jess? Tell me it wasn't ours."

Hesitant, Jessie nodded. "Yeah. We were at Matt's place." She started wringing her fingers together the way Emily-Grace did when she was anxious. She did not admit to being with Matt in the guest bedroom of the UBC house.

"Jessie?"

"Yeah."

"Tonight you're being turned down. I don't need sex from you to know that you love me."

Rising slowly, Jessie stood and faced Josh. Defiant, she raised her shoulders and bit her lip. "Josh, I appreciate what you're trying to say. I really do. And I know what you're thinking about Matt. That maybe I slept with him as some kind of thank you. But that's not true. I was with him because I needed the connection. I needed to be held, and there's no way to feel closer to a man you love—yes, love—than by having sex with him first. So you can take your high horse and stop treating me like the sex I had with other men was dirty. Even in the old Downtown Eastside days it was, most times, pleasurable. You know why? Because I got to explore sex in my teen years with a boy I loved desperately and whom I still miss today, with no parents around to tell us that what we were doing was wrong."

Walking closer to Josh, Jessie finished undoing his belt, and she pulled down the zipper. Easing his jeans down over his hips, resting them there, she reached up and undid the sling over his arm as she spoke.

"Not until Deuce McCall first raped me in Charleston did things get really mixed up in my head again. Not until Charlie started cheating on me did I realize how much I missed being with someone I could derive pleasure from, whom I trusted with my life and who I felt soul-connected to. And so yeah, you. You big dork. And Jacob, yes, and Matt. Soul-intimacy, Josh. Not just sex."

Jessie lifted her husband's T-shirt over his head and let it drop to the floor. Slowly, her eyes locked in his, she watched a new pleasure and desire settle across his face—in his eyes, his mouth as his lips parted, in pink flushes on his cheeks—as she lowered her hand and wrapped her fingers around him.

As he widened his stance, she had a little more to say. "So take whatever honor it is you're trying to stuff up my ass and let me show you—yes, show you—how much I love *you*." With that, Jessie started to massage him.

Powerless to walk away, Josh closed his eyes and leaned his forehead against hers. His breath turned a little ragged, and Jessie smiled a small smile of satisfaction before she eased down onto her knees and took him in her mouth. She felt his good hand run through her hair, and his hips start to move.

"I'm sorry," she heard him whisper.

When she stood a few moments later and pulled off her own top and bra, Jessie said, "I'm not. I love sexing you, and I'm not apologizing for it or for what I did with other men I wanted to make love with when the time was right. But that being said, Josh, from now on…" Her eyes filled with tears as she gently turned him and eased him onto the bed on his back so she could crouch over him without hurting his shoulder, ribs or leg, "I only want to ever make love to you from now on. Okay? We need to move forward knowing we love each other and that we are committed to each other. No more messing up for either of us. You good?"

By then Jessie had her jeans and panties off and was rubbing him a little more so she could ease her body down over him and start to rock. Josh gasped when he felt her clench around him and, looking up into the pale blue eyes of the woman he loved more than life itself, he was glad she had the confidence and self-esteem these days to take charge and love him in a way he was beginning to understand was both a gift to him…as well as a gift to herself.

"I'm good," he managed, and didn't last long before he was really good, and quite satisfied with his wife, and feeling more and more comfortable with her love for him as they moved away from the fiasco of Jacob's actions in Florida, Josh's violence at the Grammys, and Jessie's desperate plea for connection from Matt.

He kissed her full on the lips, long and hard, before saying, "I love you, Jessie. Always and forever." For good measure, he added a soft, "Thank you."

"For what?" she asked him, smiling as she stroked his cheek and gazed upon her man with a sincere and abiding, and most of all trusting, love.

"How about for everything?" he replied, light in his eyes and love in his heart. "How about just for letting me be the man who gets to love you?"

Jessie almost couldn't answer. Her voice was thick with emotion when she did. "I cannot even…Josh…we've broken each other's hearts enough, babe. But always always always I wanted you. Always. Never anyone but you, babe. Never."

"Always and forever," he murmured, kissed her again, and held her.

They fell asleep when their eyes got too heavy to keep them open; when the stars came out and aligned themselves the way they were meant to; and as the northern lights filled the skies with vibrant hues of rainbow color that reigned over Josh and Jessie and their little family with a dreamy wonder and a vibrant glow.

Chapter Twenty-eight

"Um…Monday?" Holding onto a vegetable tray of cut carrots, cucumbers, and green peppers, which was about to be taken outside to the children, Jessie stared at Charlie. "They have a love scene in two days?"

"Yep." Reaching for the tray, Charlie grabbed a green pepper and bit off the end. "Hence the reason you and Jane need to choose another day to visit set."

"We were planning to meet the kids' tutor Monday. She's taking them for three hours so Jane and I can get some shopping in with our stylist for that big fundraiser. I even convinced her to take Dylan!"

"No. Not happening. You are not welcome on my set while your husband is shooting love scenes. I know you, Jessie, you'll worm your way in with the Third A.D., find out what time the love scene's happening, then you'll crash us and upset Shanda. We don't need that stress."

Fuming, Jessie slapped his hand when he reached for a carrot. "These are for the kids, Charlie. Josh is gonna hear it from me. He needs to tell me this stuff."

"Ha! I sure as hell wouldn't have told you if I was Josh. Some things are really not your business, Jessie. Like it or not."

They were in Canmore at Charlie and Jane's house, on a Saturday afternoon, to celebrate Dylan's birthday earlier in the week. It was June now, and Josh was finally sling free, although he was doing physio for his shoulder and to regain better mobility in his leg. He was back to the gym and recuperating well overall, but Jessie was ready to kick his arse after finding out he had a love scene scheduled for Monday that he hadn't bothered to tell her about.

"Like I needed any other stress today, Charlie. Thanks for that."

Storming outside to the back deck, Jessie anxiously scanned the tree line. Charlie and Jane lived at the highest point of homes on the mountain, where cougars were occasionally seen meandering the yards and streets. After Josh's experience with Blue, she was terrified. Jane and Josh were with the kids, though, playing Frisbee, and so were keeping a good eye out for any unwanted super large kitty cats. The family no longer retained security for days such as this, when they were just hanging out with friends, albeit famous friends.

Canmore was a quiet outdoor sports town—an NHL player lived next door and an Olympic cross-country skier resided just down the street, so Charlie figured rather haphazardly that if any problems arose he would just go knocking on doors.

Another reason Jessie was feeling stressed was the impending arrival of Jacob and Kayla. They were due later in the evening, after making the drive from Vancouver. Josh was anxious too, Jessie could tell, judging by the way he was becoming more and more quiet as the day went on, and the last thing she wanted to do was stress him out more, but Jessie being Jessie, she was bursting. So when she finally got close enough to him where she could speak without the children overhearing, she rattled him with, "So I hear you and Shanda are getting it on in two days."

"Thanks, Charlie," Josh called sarcastically across the lawn to his friend, who was taking his infant son from Jane to soothe him.

"You got it, Josh. Any time." Frustrated, Charlie fired Jessie a hard look of warning, which she responded to with a haughty stare.

Turning to fix a steady gaze on Josh, Jessie crossed her arms and stuck out her bottom lip. "It wouldn't be a big deal except that this woman's crazy about you. I wish you wouldn't hide this kind of stuff from me."

Groaning, Josh tossed the Frisbee back to David, who ran after it with the glee and freedom of a five-year-old boy while Dylan, squealing, trailed him. Stella and Emily-Grace had disappeared up onto the deck with their dolls, where Stella had a big pink sit-in playhouse in one corner.

"What difference does it make?" Josh asked her. "I tell you, you get upset, I don't tell you, you get equally upset." Pausing, he took a closer look at her. His petulant wife's eyes were floating.

"Jessie, I'll arrange for the tutor to meet you and Jane and the kids at the Calgary condo instead of at the soundstage's classroom. It's no big deal."

"Fine." Her pale eyes were wide and nervous.

Josh couldn't resist a small smile. From up above them on the deck, Charlie relaxed when he saw Josh pull Jessie close and press her to him. She was being sulky, but her husband's reinforcement of his love for her was helping ease the tension after the discovery of what *Sacred Peace's* shooting plans were for Monday.

"Stop worrying. You're a worrier." Josh leaned forward and kissed his wife's forehead just as the Frisbee, accompanied by the two Sawyer boys, crashed at his ankles. "Ouch," he laughed, and limped off after the kids so he could grab Dylan with his left arm and swing him up and around, to the little boy's delight.

Scowling, Jessie followed him and reached for her son. "Give me that child. You're gonna hurt yourself. Dweeb." But she, too, was soon giggling, and her heart was happy despite the nerves surrounding Jacob's visit and Josh's Monday schedule.

That night, all of the children were in bed before Jacob and Kayla darkened the doorstep, but the couple hadn't been expected early, so it wasn't a big deal. They were planning to stay overnight with Charlie and Jane, to avoid any awkward discomfort at the Sawyer ranch, and they would have all day Sunday to visit with the kids. Josh's defining rule for their first visit was one day. That was about all the stress he could handle.

Before they arrived, the conversation steered to healing. It started with Josh's physical wounds but, in the company of good friends, quickly gravitated to psychological healing. The couples were sitting in the Deacons' large cathedral ceilinged living room at the front of the home, where a sizeable stone-framed fireplace, not lit tonight since it was warm enough, created a very ranchy-western vibe.

Josh was seated on a deep black leather armless modern chair with his back and side to the fireplace, with Jessie snuggled into a similar chair next to him. Opposite them, against the north wall, Charlie had Jane tucked cozily under one arm; like Jessie, she had a leg folded underneath her butt. The girls and Charlie had drinks in their hands, so did Josh, but his was his old standby, ginger-ale, although, Jessie noted as he kept glancing towards the doorway, he was clutching the glass tightly and likely wishing for something more potent.

Jane, with her genuine interest in healing the planet, was the one to gently suggest to Jessie and Josh that they consider either writing to or visiting… Morgan. "Think about it," she said, to their utter surprise. "Go see him. In person. A conversation with him might unload some of the old pain."

"Jesus, Jane," Jessie mumbled, shocked at the very idea of staring into Morgan's blank eyes again. A creepy shiver shot up her back and rankled the hair at the back of her neck. "We're still trying to pick up the pieces here. He destroyed us."

Josh remained silent. No way could he even consider going anywhere near the dark memories those days brought forth. Even now they came at him like cars on a fast moving train, one after the other, all sinister and terrifying—hearing that Jessie and the kids were missing, Nadia's deception (and her sizzling lovemaking), Jessie leaving him and taking up with Jacob in New York, shuttling kids back and forth, alcohol, cocaine…

Jessie, glancing sideways at Josh to see him staring at Jane, incredulous and frightened, thought he looked like a little boy and not the striking man he had grown into. Surreptitiously, she shook her head at Jane and mouthed *no*.

Thankfully, Jane took the hint and didn't press the issue. Jessie made a point to bring it up to her maybe on Monday while they were shopping. Seeing Morgan…maybe it would put some things to rest, for her. Maybe she would even go see Nadia's grave. Maybe Josh could in time, but he was pale now, and it wasn't the time to discuss Morgan and Nadia's deception.

The night was starting to get the best of Josh. The tense wait for Kayla and Jacob, who none of them were even remotely used to seeing together, was interminable. Besides, the last time most of them saw each other was when the tour bus pulled out of Vancouver, the day Kayla made the very public announcement that Jacob had raped Jessie in Florida, and the last time Jessie saw Jacob was after two stilted weeks of working together at the Robson Street studio. No way was this meeting tonight going to be comfortable, for any of them, although it was certainly a wise decision to hold their gathering here, with the somewhat neutral Charlie and Jane present.

The streets outside were quiet. When Jacob and Kayla finally pulled up—Kayla driving a rented SUV, although Jacob did do some of the driving, of which he hated every moment—the arrival and parking of the vehicle may as well have been the appearance of a Lear jet carrying the Duke and Duchess of Windsor, Josh and Jessie were so wound up.

No one moved until the doorbell rang. Charlie disappeared to let his guests in. Wisely, Jane got up to check on the kids, which left Josh and Jessie alone for a few minutes, since the house was four levels, and Charlie actually had to meet Kayla and Jacob down on the bottom level and walk them up to the main living area via an inside staircase.

"You okay, babe?" Jessie took her husband's hand and gave it a gentle squeeze.

"Nope." Josh was staring at the glass he held in his right hand. Leaning forward, he switched it to his good hand, extended his arm, and set it down with a gentle thud.

"They're not here to fight, Josh. Remember that Kayla really cares about him."

"You gonna be able to remember that, Jessie?" Josh sent her a hard look. "And that supposedly he cares about her?"

Taken aback, Jessie nodded. "Yeah. In fact, hell yeah! I'm happy for them." In a softer voice she added, "We can do this, Josh. We can manage to have some kind of friendship with them. They're both good people."

"Are they." Josh frowned and glanced towards the staircase. Voices were drawing closer. Hearing his sister's bubbly laughter floating up towards them, Josh realized it was a sound he greatly missed. He swallowed, and blinked. Jessie gave his hand a harder squeeze, and then she rose and faced two dear people she knew it would hurt to see.

Kayla emerged from the stairwell first, with Jacob behind her, and Charlie behind him. The couple appeared tired but surprisingly buoyant.

Love, Jessie thought with a pang as she spied Jacob in his usual tight black jeans and grey T-shirt. *They're in love.* Her eyes melted down to Jacob's belt. It was the old worn one he used to wear, and Jessie couldn't help but feel a physical reaction at the memories of all the times she undid that belt and pulled him close. She pushed the thought away at the realization of how sad those days always were, and of how complete she finally felt with Josh by her side again.

A trickle of air drifted up her back as she felt and heard Josh stand behind her. Kayla stepped tentatively forward, raising a hand to brush back loose hair in her Sawyer way. Her hair was now just blonde. Both Josh and Jessie were surprised—they could hardly remember a day when Kayla seemed, well, herself.

Charlie sauntered casually off into the kitchen and started to prepare drinks for their new guests.

"Hey, Jessie," Kayla managed, apprehensive but trying for a hug anyway. Jessie graciously accepted.

"Hi," Jessie responded brightly. "How was the drive?"

"It was fine, it was good," Kayla replied, eyeing her brother over Jessie's shoulder. Smiling, she let go of her sister-in-law and stood back and studied him as Jessie's eyes locked on Jacob's. "Josh, you scared the crap out of me. I can't imagine being on this planet without having my big brother on it with me."

With a nervous look to Jacob, who Josh was not happy to see was lost in a Jessie-Jacob bubble, Josh frowned before taking in Kayla's grey leggings and flowing, floral top. She was very 'naturally' pretty, and had a glow about her today, which was quite the opposite of the way she looked the last time he saw her, the day she left on the tour.

"I'm okay," he mumbled, not unfriendly but not exactly over-the-top gracious and welcoming, either. "Sucked for a while but I'm okay." Kayla walked into his arms and gathered him into a mostly one-sided hug, since he was still eyeing his wife's back, straining to hear the quiet dialogue that seemed to be passing from Jacob's lips to Jessie's.

Following Josh's stare, Kayla pivoted around on her summer flip-flop.

There was a light in Jacob's blue eyes, despite the tension he and Jessie had parted with back on Robson ages ago. His cute grin had Jessie crossing her arms and leaning on one foot, angling her head and, Josh realized because he was very familiar with that stance, she was likely also sending Jacob one of her ridiculous teasing half-smiles that both men thought was so cute.

She had her back to Josh and Kayla, but they could see Jacob clear as day, and he had no regard for anyone in the room but Jessie at the moment.

It wasn't like the old days, though, when Jacob was filled with longing and a pouty sadness. Instead, he was grinning from ear to ear at Jessie's obvious playful acknowledgement that he was in love.

"You big nerd," she said aloud to Jacob now, waltzing into his arms and burying her face in the familiar neck. "Kayla, of all people. It's perfect. I'm so glad the two of you sorted things out."

"I doubt your husband thinks so." Breathing in the lavender he loved and would forever miss, Jacob closed his eyes and pressed Jessie's body to his. With a nervous laugh, though, he wiped a sleeve underneath his nose and released her when he looked up to see Josh firing dynamite sticks at him, one at a time, all lit. Kayla was rolling her eyes, not even remotely concerned at the old intimacy at play between her man and his ex. Jacob tossed up his hands and shook his head in jest anyway.

"Ne touché pas," he said to Josh with a light laugh. "Not touching. I swear."

Flipping around, Jessie, who still had one hand on Jacob's waist, laughed outright, ignored her husband's death ray stare, and purred to Kayla, "Oh, I'm done here, honey. This brooding musician's all yours. Want me to tie him up with a big red bow?"

"He's not yours to give away." Kayla's cheeky response was accompanied by a happy wink.

"He'll always be mine." Jessie's equally tongue-in-cheek response was greeted with a chorus of wails and laughter from Jacob and Kayla. "I found him."

The good natured teasing lasted the way all good greetings go between friends who've been parted but who can easily pick up where they left off. The only difference in this case was that, with Jacob and Kayla's new romance leading the way, the couples were able to leave the old tensions at the door. All, that is, except for Josh, who descended into an uncomfortable silence as Jane approached and welcomed her visitors.

"Come, sit," she offered, leading the way to their seats in the living area. Jacob and Kayla dropped down next to each other on a west-end loveseat, at a sort of nine o'clock to Charlie and Jane's twelve o'clock on the larger couch against the north wall. Jessie and Josh remained across from Charlie and Jane in the black leather chairs on Jacob and Kayla's right.

"How was the tour, honey?" Jessie asked Kayla comfortably as she snuggled into her chair. Josh, in the black leather seat to Jessie's right, was kind of behind her as she spoke to Kayla, so Jessie couldn't read his expression or thoughts.

"The tour was a little different than the usual," Kayla admitted honestly. "I had to train them up. This group had to learn to be professionals, to act like professionals. There were a few issues but nothing we couldn't surpass. Everyone made it through."

"The usual PMS stuff, huh? Tension between women, that kind of thing?"

"We had a talk on the bus between Calgary and Regina," Kayla laughed. "I told them I had a supply of chocolate and chips and that when anyone was feeling hyper-sensitive for no reason they were to come see me. I used a fair bit of our budget on PMS emergency measure junk food, Jessie. Sorry."

"That's much more important than replacing costumes or hairspray, Kayla. I'll allow it."

"Jack might not like it." Kayla's lively spirit was back, all bouncy and play-ful, like the old Kayla.

Relieved and thrilled, Jessie blushed happily at her while Charlie jumped in to defend his father. "Is that a line item in the budget? PMS? Because my dad has no clue what PMS even is. I'm an only child, remember? No girls. And Jane's easy."

"Are you now?" Jessie pointed a finger at Jane and raised an eyebrow.

"Depends who's asking." Jane bent her lips to Charlie's ear and whispered something that was apparently seductive, and Jessie found herself floating in a rather weird moment when she remembered she and Charlie had once been engaged, and that she'd slept, numerous times, with all three men in the room. A pink flush crested the tops of her cheeks and she ducked her head, embarrassed.

A few more minutes of easy rapport passed between all of them with the exception of Josh, who sat back feeling very removed from the others in the room, and wishing for some pain meds since his healing leg was starting to ache, as it often did when he was tired. Drugs were still not his friend but he did take over-the-counter painkillers on occasion when he felt really des-perate. Tonight was approaching that level of pain, exacerbated by anxiety and the threat of rain for the next few days.

At one point, Jessie watched Jacob and Kayla swap stories with Charlie and Jane about one of the cities on the tour where the theater was supposedly haunted, which launched a whole diatribe about the existence of ghosts. It got a little strange when Jacob said he smelled Talia's perfume from time to time. Kayla admitted she'd caught a whiff of the floral fragrance one time at the workshop space.

"Maybe she was looking out for you and me," Jacob told her, grasping Kayla's hand.

"Maybe she was," Kayla agreed, with a sweet smile for him.

The two lost themselves in each other then, and Jessie sat back and watched them, her lips parting in wonder. The room got quiet, and suddenly she felt lost in the old bubble with Jacob, who looked over at her and treated her to a little *I'm the luckiest man in the world* grin.

Leaning forward in curious wonder, Jessie bounced her thoughts right back to him. *You're happy.*

It was as if he knew exactly what she was thinking. Blue flecks passed across Jacob's eyes as he lit up and answered with just a simple look Jessie easily recognized. *Damn straight I am. Finally.*

Biting her bottom lip, Jessie couldn't help herself. Reaching further forward, she took his hand and lifted it, held his gaze, and brushed her lips across the beloved fingers.

Charlie cleared his throat, which made Kayla toss back her ponytail and let out her jolly laugh that everyone missed and treasured.

Josh stilled and sucked in a breath. *I can't stand it,* he was telling himself. *I can't stand seeing the love that still exists between them. I can't stand that I will always think he's a better match for Jessie than I am. I can't stand that we have to share our son with him, and more than that, I can't stand that my sister has now fallen under his charms. I can't stand him. Period.*

He turned his head away, towards the grand stone fireplace, but made the mistake of emitting a tense exhale that came with a quiet, "Jesus Christ."

Realizing what she'd done in terms of how Josh would interpret it, Jessie closed her eyes and picked a spot on the floor to stare at while she gathered her wits. Jacob sent her an *I'm sorry* with a genuine look of condolence, and Kayla looked over at Josh with a semblance of surprise on open lips. Concerned,

Charlie placed an arm around Jane's shoulders and frowned at Josh. Jane, ever the sweetheart, touched Jessie's wrist, which motivated Jessie into action.

Standing, she moved over to her husband's chair and, carefully so as not to hurt his sore spots, squished her butt in between his legs. Picking up his good arm, she wrapped it around her belly and leaned carefully back against him. To his credit, Josh accepted the gesture and bit his tongue.

Half an hour later, a small cry came from the top of the half dozen stairs that led up to the bedrooms. Jacob straightened. All evening he had been considering asking if he could go see Dylan, at least peek in at him, but Josh's subdued, bitter countenance towards his appearance in Charlie's home was growing darker by the minute, and Jacob lost his nerve, although he could sense Kayla's support. Now, though, Jacob wondered if the awake child was Dylan or David—he figured Dylan, since the child sounded younger than five, but it was late in the evening and it wouldn't surprise him if David were up. Holding his breath, he was afraid to turn around to look.

Jacob had his answer, though, when Josh's lips parted and his gaze darted from the top of the stairs down to Jacob. Swallowing nervously, Jacob locked his eyes in Josh's and waited for a cue. With a start, he was sorry to see that the hostility in Josh's eyes had at some point been replaced with fear.

Jessie felt Josh's entire body go rigid the second Dylan cried. It was no surprise that the child was up—he was their usual non-sleeper, their fussy boy.

"I'll get him," she murmured softly to the assembled crowd, all of whom were tense and wondering how this would go. Before she eased herself upright, though, Jessie twisted around to her husband and placed a warm palm against his cheek. As usual, her simple touch calmed him, and both Jacob and Charlie wondered at how she did that, at how she could simply look at Josh and let her energy meld into his body and soul and offer a sweet, gentle, confident calm. They saw it happen, the moment Josh registered that he wasn't alone here tonight, that there was a deep wisdom and maturity at play now in his often childish wife.

"Love you," Jessie whispered to Josh just before she stood. The others heard her say something, but couldn't make out the words. Still, they all knew what she was telling him.

As she rose and her footsteps echoed across the floor, Josh let his gaze drift downwards before he summoned up the courage to meet Jacob's searching eyes again. This time he conveyed a different message. It wasn't fear, or anger. It was more like a *please please please.*

Jacob just nodded, a barely discernible nod that was, more than anything, a simple *thank you.*

Charlie scooted past Jane's legs and followed Jessie to the bottom of the stairs. As she scooped up her son and made her way back downstairs, he said, "Hey, Dylan. Do you want a drink of water?"

Instead of answering, Dylan whined and buried his head in his mother's neck.

Chuckling lightly, Jessie rubbed his back and held him against her heart. "Yes," she said to Charlie. "He will want some water. Thank you."

Moving into the kitchen, where the others couldn't see them, Charlie started to run some filtered water from the tap. While he was waiting for it to cool, he asked Jessie if she wanted him to find an excuse to remove Josh from the room so Jacob could see if Dylan would warm to him, since it had been Christmas since they'd spent any real time together.

Thinking about it, Jessie sucked on her lip and finally said, "No, I don't think so, Charlie. Let's just keep everyone in the same room and see how it goes. Josh promised me he would behave."

At Charlie's raised eyebrows, she sighed sadly. "I know what you're thinking. Do we really trust him? You know something? I do. Tonight I do, anyway. I can feel his fear and sadness. It's soaking through me."

"Oh, Jessie." Charlie paused in his pouring of Dylan's water and just looked at her. "He's going to be okay. Josh is dealing with everything bit by bit. He's holding up, isn't he?"

"Yeah, I think so. He's trying, Charlie. He really is."

"It was a bad time. You should think about that whole forgiveness thing, with Morgan."

"Not right now, hon. My man still needs to be held together with invisible rope. He's not ready for a step that big. Not yet."

"Okay." With a gentle brush of his lips against Jessie's forehead, and a second kiss for Dylan, Charlie added, his voice a little dusky, "Let us know if and when we can help you two with anything. In the meantime…are you ready?"

"Into the breach." Inhaling to the count of seven, Jessie wheeled around and padded out to the living room with Charlie close behind her, Dylan's water glass clutched in one hand. Without looking at either Josh or Jacob, Jessie lifted Dylan away from her body, which was no easy task since he was always whiny and a bit of a cling-on when he awoke. As she sat in her original chair, she repositioned him so his back was to her chest.

Intimidated by all the adult faces looking at him, Dylan twisted sideways towards the fireplace on the east wall so he could bury his face in his mother's arm. Immediately, the little boy perked up. Raising both arms and extending them out to Josh, he said, "Daddy."

Like a burst balloon, the tension in the room instantly dissipated. A tiny smile curved upwards on Josh's lips, and his scared eyes brightened. Alight, Jessie stood and set her son in Josh's arms, being careful to watch his sore shoulder and still tender ribs. Dylan ended up snuggling into Josh's side, facing away from Jacob, but as Jessie sat back down she said to her musical partner, "He'll come around. He always needs a few minutes to really get woken up."

The adults continued their conversation while Kayla got up for a pee. When she came back, after disappearing out to the car post-pee, she had a big three-foot high stuffed white polar bear in her arms. Shrugging, as she sat she said to Jessie, "We figured Dylan didn't really need anything, but I've made it a tradition to get my niece and nephews something when I'm on tour. It's Dylan's birthday week, so he gets an extra big gift. We got this guy at the Aquarium in Quebec City. He took up his own seat on the bus."

"He's awesome," Jessie smiled gratefully. With her head, she gestured towards Josh and Dylan. "He'll know you, Kayla. Try him now."

"Okay." A zig-zaggy breath later, Kayla leveraged herself upright by leaning one hand on Jacob's thigh. Watching her, Jacob wiped damp palms on his jeans.

Josh wrapped his left arm tighter around his son's shoulders, and used his right hand to steady Dylan's water. "Auntie Kayla's got something for you, Dylan," Jessie heard him say to the little fellow.

A moment later, Kayla appeared in Dylan's frame of vision. "Hello, sweetheart," she said softly, her heart almost stopping at how much, as he grew older, he resembled Jacob more and more. "I love your curls," she whispered, biting back *you look so much like your daddy.*

Jacob's heart was stopping too, and a pulse was pounding in his ears. There was not a damn thing he could do to change anything, to take back all the lost time with this child and a woman he loved beyond all reason, with whom he had created Dylan. All he could do was suck in a deep breath and try to live in the present, but it was damn hard.

Sweet Jesus, he thought, *I want to know my son.* Squishing both hands under his thighs was the only way he could keep from vaulting forward and grabbing Dylan, and disappearing into the ether with him.

Jessie wasn't watching him. Her eyes were locked on Josh, so she could read him and interpret his actions, and hopefully intervene if necessary. Right now, he was studying Dylan—it was almost as if he was assessing everything about the child, memorizing him, even. Jessie frowned.

Without looking away from his son, Josh was tucking a dark curl behind Dylan's ear. "Auntie Kayla brought you a present, Dylan," he was saying. "I think it's a big cuddly teddy bear. Do you want to see?"

To the amusement of all of the adults, and bringing a tear to Jessie's eye, Dylan straightened. Eyes widening, he pointed innocently to himself. "A pwesent? Me?"

Josh leaned forward and tried to set down the child's water glass with his bad arm, but he winced. Charlie jumped up and rescued it. Josh's hurt shoulder wasn't quite ready to go the distance yet.

With a big smile, Kayla lifted the large stuffed polar bear. "Jacob and I got this guy for you," she said to her nephew. Her smile grew wider when Dylan, who had his left thumb in his mouth now, extended his right hand and drew his fingers through the teddy bear's fur.

"Soft," he whispered in his adorable little boy voice.

"Yes, he is, isn't he? He's very soft."

"Mine?" Dylan still wasn't sure.

"Yes. He's yours, sweetheart. Want to come see him closer?"

At Dylan's slight nod, Kayla glanced at her brother and sent him a silent *thank you* smile. Josh didn't help her lift Dylan, so she effectively took the boy right out of his arms. The moment he was gone, Jessie stood quietly and climbed back in, sitting with her back against Josh's chest again.

From across the coffee table, Charlie and Jane mused at her effect on Josh again. He almost completely relaxed as his wife's body settled against him.

Josh buried his face in Jessie's hair, avoiding the thing in the room that had hurt him so badly in the past. Namely, Jacob, whose power to hurt Josh and erode his confidence and faith in the world seemed to just go on and on.

Kayla took Dylan back to her seat and set him sideways on her lap to face Jacob, to whom she handed the big teddy bear. Jacob knew his role; he'd practiced it well with Emily-Grace and David in New York when the other two Sawyers were younger. Soon the polar bear was dancing and singing, and Dylan's laughter was pealing up to the cathedral ceiling and beyond.

Charlie jumped in once in a while, just to keep things light and moving along, but Jessie was spellbound. Dylan was the image of Jacob. She felt Josh move, she felt his warm breath on her neck, and knowing that he was stealing peeks at the joyous activity on the loveseat, she ached for him. But there was no winner here tonight. No matter how she looked at this situation, some-body was hurting. They were all doing the best they could to patch up the horrific damage Morgan and Nadia caused.

But we wouldn't have Dylan at all, she caught herself thinking. *We wouldn't have this beautiful child if Jacob and I hadn't gotten together.* The other side of the coin, the more she thought about it, was that she had that sacred time with Jacob. Yeah, it had hurt like hell the whole damn time, being away from Josh and all, but there were good memories too, of snuggling in bed with Jacob, of playing music and writing songs with him, of slipping her hand up under-neath his T-shirt and melding her skin into his. Of caressing, and brushing her lips over, that sad but sexy cross inked on his back.

No doubt about it, Dylan came from a deep, shared love, and both men who called him theirs knew that. In some ways, it made things a little easier. In some ways, it hurt worse.

Laying a hand over Josh's on her thigh, Jessie met Jacob's eyes as he relaxed the polar bear on his lap for a moment and looked over at her.

Catching her anguished look, recognizing its sorrowful intensity, Jacob knew where it was going to lead.

Spotting the panic on his face, Charlie's hawk-like gaze darted over to Jessie as well. Catching his concerned look, Josh tensed. Jessie being Jessie, it was apparent that this time with Dylan and Jacob was undoing her. The nefarious events surrounding how the child was conceived—all the pain, all the loss, all the heartache, coupled with this new coming together, with Kayla now part of the package, was simply overwhelming.

Leaning back against her husband, Jessie stuffed a fist in her mouth, but it didn't help. Above and beyond all was guilt, and it was washing over her like a rogue wave at a north shore Prince Edward Island beach. Shoulders shaking, she turned her face away from Jacob, twisted her body halfway around, and curled up into a tight ball in Josh's lap.

Shocked but not surprised at this outlay of emotion, Josh responded the way Jessie knew he would. First there was a quiet, "Sshhh, Jessie, it's okay. We're dealing with it." And then there was his comforting breath on her cheek, his lips damp against her eyes, his thumb brushing the pain as it escaped and left wet trails down her cheeks. "Little one," he murmured, "it's okay. It's all okay."

The thing was, though, that as much as they were all growing and trying to deal with the mess it seemed they were always trying to clean up, nothing felt okay. Jessie wrapped an arm around Josh and buried her face in his good shoulder. He didn't look up. He just held her and soothed her and let her weep.

Taking Jane's hand, Charlie had to fight off his own emotion. More than anyone, except maybe Steve and Matt, he felt Josh's agony back when Jessie was missing, and then he helped hold him together when she was with Jacob. This, tonight, was not an easy evening for any of them, and at the center of it was a three-year-old boy who was well loved, but whose sheer existence left two men and a woman they both loved trying to figure out how to cope.

Jacob had to turn his head away from Jessie and Josh. Scrutinizing them together was painful. Jessie was expressing what Jacob knew was her guilt and pain, and watching her cling to Josh, who was loving her with whispers and tender touches, was too much to take.

"All right," Kayla said quietly to Dylan after a bit, "let's you and me and Jacob go see if Jane has any good kid-kinda snacks in her kitchen. Maybe some of those bear paws or goldfish or something. Jane?"

With a fearful nod, Jane got up and accompanied them to the kitchen, where Jacob could take Dylan in his arms and talk to him without hearing Jessie sob over a past that was dead and gone and a present that sometimes still hurt like hell.

Touching her back as he moved, Charlie made his way past Jessie and Josh and hopped the steps to go check on his two sleeping children, and David and Emily-Grace. Grateful, he kissed each child and tried not to let his own tears and stifled sobs wake them. In the ensuite bathroom off the master bedroom, though, he lost it. A few minutes later, Jane, always calm, always his light, came in and took him in her arms.

"It's over, Charlie," she said, her patience and wisdom imbuing her words with hope. "It's only up and up from here on in. It's just hard tonight, that's all. For everyone."

"I know, I know," he managed, wiping a sleeve across his eyes and taking the Kleenex she handed him so he could blow his nose. "I just can't stand to see them in so much pain all the time. It's a lot, you know?"

"Hey," she said, grabbing his chin roughly and forcing her husband to look at her. "That little boy has a lot going for him. He's fed, he's clothed, he'll never have to worry about where his next meal is coming from or where he can lay his head. Neither will his parents, ever again. Jessie, I mean, who knows what that kind of bare-bones existence is like. He is well loved, and you and I will help the people providing that love navigate the troubled waters that surrounded his conception. You got it?"

"I do." Charlie nodded. "Really, Jane, I do. I just need a minute, that's all." He smiled sadly, his eyes still leaking a little. "How did I get so lucky, huh, to find you?"

"That's easy," she said softly. "Jessie ran away, and you went looking for her. Instead, you found me."

"I wasn't looking for her on the Downtown Eastside," he said.

"Sure you were. Her essence, at least."

"I guess. She does have a way of changing people, doesn't she?"

"Only the ones willing to change, Charlie. She has a lot of love and light to share, and although a lot of that leads to the things that hurt people, like loving Jacob, and Matt—yes, she told me about Matt—she's also got the capacity to show everyone else how to love. She'll make sure Dylan gets the best of both of his fathers. Dry your sorrows, Charlie, and come back downstairs when you're ready."

Charlie had grown a lot over the years. He knew his wife's advice was worth listening to. When he stepped quietly back downstairs ten minutes later, he wasn't surprised to see Jessie still snuggled up in Josh's lap, but facing Jacob and Kayla now, her tears dried and a respectful, quiet laughter dancing across her eyes. Kayla and Jacob were telling more tour war stories, and even Josh was allowing a small smile here and there. Soon, he was even joining in with a word here and there.

Dylan fell asleep in Jacob's lap, and nobody suggested moving him. Josh, who earlier might have slugged Jacob, had in his lap the woman who gave birth to the child, and she belonged to him. There were days, weeks, even a few months very recently when he'd thought again that they were destined to live apart, but now she was here, on his lap, in his arms.

His.

Dylan would always be a part of his life. Jessie was teaching Josh that there was enough love to go around, even, as much as it hurt, to Jacob still, and to Matt, who everyone lost because of an impossible situation.

I'm grateful, Josh managed to tell himself before the night was over. *My sister is here and she is happy. My good friends are here, my children are here, I'm sober, I'm healing, I have a great job, and I have a wife I love beyond measure who loves me back equally as much.*

The night came to a close with laughter, yawns, and the movement of protesting, sleepy children and, at the Kananaskis ranch, intense lovemaking that said *I love you* and *thank you* more than words could ever even begin to express. Josh and Jessie were just dozing off when Dylan awoke again, and soon there were three little bodies slumbering in their big bed. Still, they reached across the children and held hands, and it was in that glorious pink-dawned perfection that they drifted off to sleep.

Chapter Twenty-nine

At five a.m. Monday morning, Josh slipped out of bed quietly so as not to wake Jessie. He had a seven a.m. call and needed to make the drive from the ranch to Calgary, but he was accustomed to the series' demanding schedule and always enjoyed the drive, especially now that his leg and arm were well enough to allow him to handle the big truck. Unlike Jessie with her iPhone tunes, Josh was a radio guy. He liked the announcers' playful banter, and it was always a fun bonus when one of Jessie's melodies filled the truck. Josh listened to Jacob's tunes too, when they came on, but usually with a frown and an ear for the lyrics to see what he had to say, since many of his songs were in some way about his love for Jessie.

This morning, just before Josh padded towards the bathroom to grab a shower, he paused to consider his wife as she slept. Hugging a pillow, Jessie was on her right side. Her pink lips were parted slightly, and she seemed so at peace. So many times in their shared past, Jessie's restorative sleep was rare and colored by nightmares. Josh exhaled slowly as he watched her breathe, grateful for his wife's simple presence in their big bed.

The sound of the water rushing through the pipes woke Jessie when Josh started the shower. Stretching, she snuggled under their light summer quilt and waited until her husband reappeared, then she pulled back the quilt and scooted over so Josh could snuggle with her before he had to go.

"Time for a quickie?" she asked him with sleepy eyes as his body, still warm, and damp in places from the shower, cuddled against her.

"Nope. I wish." Josh brushed his lips against Jessie's and sighed as she lovingly moved his rogue hair back behind his ear. "Gotta make set by seven."

"I wish you could stay here with us today." Pouting, Jessie buried her face in his chest.

"Not today."

"Mmmm. I know. Big Shanda snuggle day, right? She gets more of you than I do today?"

"Yyyeeppp." With a final kiss and a squeeze, Josh eased off the bed. He pulled on jeans and a T-shirt. "I'll call when I can. Tell the kids Daddy loves them. See you tonight, Jess."

"Grrrrr." Pressing her lips into a tight line, Jessie sulked.

Stopping at the open doorway, Josh couldn't help but laugh. "Stop worrying. If you and Jane are still planning to take the kids to Calgary today to see the tutor, text me and maybe we can meet at some point. I can drop out to the condo if you want."

"Fine."

"Promise? You'll stay away from set?"

Burying her face in the pillow, Jessie groaned. "I hate this part. The love scene stuff. The 'you leaving me' stuff."

Unable to resist, Josh sauntered back to the bed and eased down on top of the quilt to lay his body over his wife for one more minute. Tenting his arms around her, he buried his nose in the cherished sacred hollow of her neck and breathed her in. "I love you, Jessie. Have a good day with Jane and the kids."

"All right. I love you back, Josh." She rolled back onto her side as he left her one more time.

Before he turned to walk away, Josh smiled sadly at the big, wide eyes watching him.

It didn't get easier to part. Ever. After everything, every second Josh and Jessie were together was precious.

As the King Ranch faded off into the distance, Jessie said a whispered prayer for Josh's safety, and dozed until David crawled into bed beside her.

"Hey, handsome," she welcomed gladly, snuggling him in close. "You're my early boy. Shall we go start some breakfast before your two lazy siblings decide to join us?" Jane and her children weren't expected until nine. That would leave plenty of time for the kids to join Gary, Jessie's Aunt Evelyn's husband, to do the rounds—he had taken up the duty about a year ago—which included feeding Josh's remaining horses, Toby and Misty. Gary, a long-haired ponytailed hippy, was great with the children. He taught them tons about herbs and wildlife and the history of the area. Today, his welcome appearance would grant Jessie enough time to tidy up the breakfast dishes, pack the kids' knapsacks for the trip into the city, and take a short run.

At five to eight, Emily-Grace took Dylan's hand and, with David skipping along behind them, they marched out into the farmyard to meet Gary, but he peeked inside the door before he took the kids off on their rounds.

"Here, Jessie," he said, holding up a clear Tupperware container. "Muffins from Evelyn. I'll leave them here since my boots are muddy and they're a drag to remove. They're still warm."

"Your boots are still warm? Uhh…that's kinda disgusting. Thanks for sharing that delightful tidbit of info with me, Gary."

Spotting the twinkle in her eye, Gary laughed, a boisterous loud laugh that filled the one level rancher. "Chocolate chip," he winked. "Eat one now and burn it off on your run while I watch your little monsters."

"Two. If I'm running I can have two. Thanks, Gary. Don't let Dylan out of your sight. He'll climb his way into the stall before you can blink an eye and we don't need another horsie accident anytime soon."

"Gotcha." Saluting her, Gary left, letting the screen door shut cozily behind him. Jessie grabbed two muffins and deposited the container on the kitchen island before she threw on a pair of running shorts and a sports bra. Pausing at the doorway, she sorted out her fave iPhone exercise playlist before she stuck earbuds in her ears and headed outside.

The summer day was already starting to heat up but it was early enough to hit the trail before it got too hot. A thirty-minute run would do today—that would give Jessie enough time for a quick hop through the shower before Jane's expected arrival. Circling the barn widely so Dylan wouldn't spot her and come after her, Jessie did a few warm-up stretches just past the two Sawyer ATVs, then adjusted the volume on her iPhone (louder, of course) and jogged up the main trail behind the ranch.

Mildly, she thought about the cougar that had attacked Blue, but Jessie pushed the large cats out of her mind and focused on her run. She'd tucked a can of bear spray in the small pocket inside the waistband of her shorts, just in case. Josh had a neat tan leather Back-Packer Jessie'd got him for his birthday in April. From the Okanagan Saddlery in British Columbia, it was a cool and comfortable rig, worn over the shoulders like a backpack. It carried Josh's 1912 Winchester 94 short-barreled rifle in a scabbard-like interior. On the outside was a pocket and loopholes designed to securely fasten in an axe. Jessie could have chosen to take the backpack for extra security on her run, but the day was hot and she decided to go it alone with just the bear spray. In the end, she was harassed, but not by four-legged animals.

Since Matt's abrupt and painful departure when Josh was injured, Jessie and Josh had conferred with Charles and, against his wishes, cut back on their family's security. Privacy was an issue, and Jessie just wanted alone time to process what had actually happened with Matt, and to grieve his loss from her life. Her argument was that nobody would know where the Sawyer family was living in Alberta anyway, and with her taking time off while Josh worked on his series, she could safely watch the kids. Spending a lot of time with Jane would help, and Josh would be around some since he was not scheduled to work all day every day. His character, Bobby, was in a lot of *Sacred Peace* scenes, but not all, which granted him some free time.

"Besides," Jessie had argued, "Charlie and Jane don't have security with them every day."

"Jessie, you and Josh have a level of fame unequalled by most couples. You've already suffered by not having security. I won't take that risk again." Charles was adamant.

Jessie almost caved. But in the end, with Josh's hesitant support on a trial basis, Jessie moved herself and the kids to the ranch without constant shadows, although Dan and Sam were there when outings like today demanded it, and Arnie too, was close by if need be, but the guys generally only met the family in the city, and were not present at the ranch.

Today, Jessie found herself facing an issue Matt or one of the others would normally have dealt with. Just as she was finishing her run, she slowed down and, breathing from the exertion, waved to Gary and the children, who were bent over the garden Gary was helping Jessie and Josh get ready for planting.

"Momma, come see," David called to her in his excited little boy voice. "Slugs! And worms!"

"Oh, yummy," Jessie grinned, her heart bursting with happiness. "I'll be there in a bit, sweetheart," she called. "Momma needs a quick run through the shower before Jane gets here! Okay?"

"Okay! But Momma, Gary says I can hold a worm. Can I hold a worm?"

"Yes you can, David, but we have to wash your hands before we go. Deal? With soap. And don't let Dylan stuff any in his pockets."

At that, Jessie scooted off down the little hill from the garden and was about to go inside the house when she spotted a blue late model Dodge Caravan wheedling its way slowly up the long laneway to the ranch. "Hmm?" she wondered, stepping back from the half open screen door and staring, puzzled, at the van. It pulled in by Jessie's SUV, parked, and the two front doors opened. A man and a woman got out and started towards Jessie.

"Um…do I know you?" Jessie asked the woman who, it appeared, according to the vehicle's license plate, was from California. In her later middle age, the woman was a little on the heavy frumpy side, and her light cotton capris and button up short sleeve top were sadly wrinkled. Birkenstocks on her feet and a straw hat crowning her pseudo matronly look made her purposeful stride and straightforward, serious face almost intimidating.

By contrast, the man with her, whom Jessie presumed to be her husband, was dour and sour faced. Thin and wiry, he slumped when he walked, as if he was accustomed to being the woman's shadow.

The woman approached Jessie with an air of authority. "Are you? Yes, you are. You're Jessie Wheeler-Sawyer."

"Ummm…yes. And you are?" Trying to be pleasant, but rather annoyed at the interruption to her day when Jessie had to grab a shower and ready herself and her children for nine a.m., it hadn't really occurred to her that these people might be fans. The implications of that—of realizing that her and Josh's quiet presence in the area might be threatened—was sobering. Even Josh's accident on Blue, and the fuss and news it created, had not resulted in fans rushing their door. In fact, the reaction had been quite the opposite. Nearby Canmore was accustomed to celebrities living in their midst. The people there were outdoor folk, rustic and down-to-earth. They lived their lives with quiet purpose, and didn't resort to stalking or hunting down their neighbors.

"We're John and Mary Dakota. We're visiting the area and heard you lived here. We would like to say hello and grab some photographs."

It wasn't a question. It was a given. Jessie was used to pushy fans, though, so she swallowed and chanced a glance up the hill towards her children, who were just out of sight. "I can do a photo with you, sure," Jessie agreed lightly, hoping these people would grab their photo and leave her in peace.

"But what about the kids? We want some of the kids."

"Um, the kids are with their father," Jessie lied. "We don't allow photos of them anyway. We're trying to keep their lives private."

"You gave up that right when you became a public figure, Jessie," the woman scolded, an entitled, haughty stare accompanying the blatant remark.

"No, um, I…" Jessie was at a loss for words.

Mary stood next to her and posed while John nodded and grabbed a few photos.

"Thank you for, uh…um, actually, this is our home. We don't usually meet with fans here. Maybe I could ask you not to share our location with anyone you happen to meet?" Swallowing nervously, Jessie glanced back up the hill. She could hear David nattering happily now, and surmised that Gary was bringing the kids back down to the house. Mary and John heard the little boy too, and both looked up.

"Is that Josh Sawyer?" Mary asked when she saw Gary, her voice rising in pitch.

"No, uh…it's a family friend. Um, I thank you for dropping by, but we need to get on the road. We have some appointments to keep today." Jessie could feel her blood pressure start to pound in her ears. The last thing she needed or wanted was for her children to be looked over and photographed by this pushy woman.

Mary was one step ahead of her, closely followed by her tall, gangly man. "Oh look, John," she called loudly. "It's Jacob Ryan's kid. Not hard to tell."

"Jesus." Cursing under her breath, Jessie waved at Gary, hoping he'd take the kids to the barn, or into the house at a quicker pace than he was moving now. Mary was already snapping pictures, and there was no doubt all three of Jessie's children heard the remark referencing Dylan's parentage. "Please, ma'am, please," she begged, jumping in front of the woman and forcefully pushing down her digital camera. "No pictures of the kids. And please don't refer to our child as Jacob's. Please."

Mary stopped short as, behind Jessie, Gary got the jest of what was happening, and moved to usher the kids to the side of the house so they could enter via another door. He kept one watchful eye on Jessie who, he could see, was losing it with this woman. Next to him, Emily-Grace stood stock-still and stared up at the imposing woman in the funny hat. Beside her stood Dylan, but Gary scooped him up and reached for Emily-Grace's hand.

"But he is Jacob Ryan's son. Isn't he?"

Emily-Grace was frozen. Jessie heard her small voice ring out. "Dylan has two daddies."

"Honey," Jessie twisted around, "go inside with Gary, please. Take David and Dylan." She turned back to Mary. "Please leave," she asked in as kind a voice as she could muster. "My children and I…we really need to get going."

"But we want to see Josh Sawyer. Or…" Mary pointed to Gary, who was struggling to make Emily-Grace move. "Are you sleeping with that man now?"

"Jesus Christ." Squeezing her eyes tightly shut, Jessie tried to maintain some semblance of sanity in dealing with this woman who obviously felt Jessie and her kids were some kind of public display meant for her entertainment. "This man is my aunt's husband. He takes care of the ranch for us when we're not around. Ma'am, you need to leave."

Sidestepping her, Mary started snapping more photos of the children.

Finally, Gary grabbed Emily-Grace around the waist and tried to hoist her, but she started kicking. She was wearing a pretty cotton sundress with a skirt that flared a bit, which she loved for dancing. It was slippery, and Gary lost his hold of her as she struggled. Slipping to the dirt, Emily-Grace twisted her wrist when she landed, and she started to cry. David bent to help her. Jessie could hear his small voice, consoling, whispering, confused and concerned, as his sister spoke to the weird lady.

"Momma sleeps with Daddy," Emily-Grace was mumbling between sobs. "Momma sleeps here."

"Where is your daddy?" The woman knew no bounds. The little girl near her feet was sobbing and rubbing a sore wrist, sitting on the ground with her pretty skirt flared out over rain-refreshed, steamy Alberta dirt. But Mary didn't flinch.

Jessie turned to Gary. "I need your help here," she said, tears of frustration pricking at her eyes. "Please." She also appealed to John. "Please take your wife and go."

To her surprise, the man straightened and glared at her. "Not until we get pictures of Josh Sawyer too. We have a bet on with some friends."

You have friends? Jessie thought in a wacky way as she struggled with what to say, what to do. Moving past her, Gary grabbed each intruder by an elbow and, with his muscular outdoorsy body, ushered them back to their vehicle.

"Josh is in the barn," he said, in no way willing to let them know that Jessie was sometimes here alone with the kids. "But he is busy with his horses and would not be happy to know you were out here snapping photographs of his children."

Oh shit, Jessie thought, closing her eyes and wheeling around to help Emily-Grace up off the damp ground. *Here it comes.*

"Two of his children. The little boy is not Josh Sawyer's son. He's Jacob Ryan's son. What's his name? Dylan?"

Cringing, Jessie lifted her sobbing seven year old. "Come on David, Dylan," she said softly to the boys as she carried Emily-Grace. "Into the house."

As the screen door squeaked on its hinges, she heard Gary arguing with the couple, who were refusing to get into their vehicle. "I will call the police if you don't leave," he was saying. Next thing Jessie knew, the woman was screaming. Turning, Jessie saw Gary stomping on the camera, his hard boot easily crushing it into bits.

"I'm calling the police!" Mary was threatening. "I'm pressing charges against both of you!"

"Oh, Lordy," Jessie breathed. "Emily-Grace, are you okay, honey? Let Momma see that sore spot."

"I hurt my wrist, Momma," her daughter sobbed. As Jessie dropped her onto a bench inside the door and bent before her, David tapped her on the arm.

"Why did that wady say Dywan is not Daddy's son?"

"Oh, honey," Jessie sighed. "Emily-Grace understands. It's because we were living with Jacob in New York, remember? When Daddy was sick? And so Dylan started growing in Momma's belly when we were in New York. But now we live with Daddy. So Dylan kind of has two daddies." Carefully touching her daughter's wrist, Jessie was convinced the girl was more upset over the intruders than over how much her wrist hurt, so that, at least, was good news.

"But Emiwy-Gwace and me wived wif Jacob too. So don't we have two daddies too?"

Smiling tenderly, Jessie took David in her arms and hugged him tightly. "Jacob would love that. I know he loves all three of you very much." That seemed to be enough to settle the children for now. "Go wash up from those worms, you little monkeys. Jane will be here any minute."

Emily-Grace, being the little mother she loved to be, wiped away the last of her tears and went off to help her siblings clean up. When she emerged a few minutes later, Jessie held out another dress, a light summer cotton sleeveless yellow one. Sulking, Emily-Grace grabbed it and went off to change.

Gary stormed into the house. Behind him, Jessie saw the blue van chug off down the lane just as Jane's fancy SUV made its way into the yard. Gary had the main body of the smashed camera in his hand.

"They say they're going to the police, Jessie, but they won't get anywhere. They were on private property, for one."

"Oh, shit." Sighing, she sat on the arm of a big couch.

"I wouldn't want to see this happen again, Jessie. You need to get your security back on duty. You can't be alone here at any time, not with these children in your care. Not with crazies like those two around."

"I thought I only had to worry about bears and cougars." Slumping, Jessie looked up as Jane came in carrying Lucas in his carrier. Stella was by her side. The little girl immediately ran off to find her best buddy.

"Who was that?" Jane asked, her pale lips twisted in confusion.

"You don't want to know." Rising, Jessie left Gary to explain. "I'm sorry, Jane. They slowed me down. Can you wait while I have a quick shower?"

"Sure, Jessie. Go. I'll keep an eye on the kids."

"There are muffins Evelyn made on the counter. Help yourself." Moving off to the shower, Jessie grabbed one and wolfed it down on the way in, grumbling all the while about the need for security and wishing for the umpteenth time that she was 'normal.'

Chapter Thirty

Later, in Calgary, Jessie peeked in her rearview mirror to spy Jane pull in behind her. They had to take separate cars on their excursion since they had so many car seats and booster seats to manage. Jessie had parked at the soundstage.

Confused, Jane rolled down the passenger side window when Jessie jumped out of her Lexus. "What is this? I thought we were going to the condo."

"I need to grab some workbooks for Emily-Grace and David. Won't be a minute, Jane."

"Uh-huh." Jane's brief sarcastic retort left a downturn to her lips. "I'm counting. Starting now. I would prefer to be at the condo before hungry lips here wakes up." Gesturing behind her, she was clearly referencing her infant son.

"Hurrying," Jessie called behind her as she started to sprint away. "Going now. Back in five."

"You said a minute!" Groaning, Jane considered texting Charlie to warn him. Jane knew damn well that Jessie knew damn well Josh's love scene was being shot this morning. This unexpected visit from his wife would not go over well.

Inside, Jessie ran up the stairs to the classroom two at a time. It only took her a second to grab the two workbooks from a wooden cubby built into the side wall. Naturally, at the bottom of the stairs her curiosity got the better of her. With a glance to the parking lot outside to her left, she took a hard right and ventured into the soundstage where a hubbub of action and hustling bodies told her that the electricians and grips were likely gathering gear so as to have it ready once the new scene was blocked.

With a pointed finger, a gal from wardrobe directed Jessie towards the set where Josh was supposedly waiting for blocking to start. Knitting her eyebrows together, Jessie considered it interesting—it was the sheriff's office set. Maybe the love scene was finished?

"Jessie?"

Cocking her head, Jessie took in Shanda, who had just called her name. The actor was clad in a skimpy silky pale cream bathrobe that only went as far as the tops of her perfect thighs. "Oh," Jessie said stupidly. "You're still on the love scene."

"Yes. We are."

We. Hmmmm. Without meaning to, Jessie felt her blood pressure spike. Tossing her curls, she crossed her arms and threw a guarded smile towards her husband's co-star. "And how's it going, Shanda?"

"It's going just fine." Shanda took a right turn. Shoving a carrot in between her lips, since she was standing by the craft table and the vegetable tray was handy, she crunched on it and said, "I thought you weren't coming in today."

Raising her hand, Jessie showed her the kids' workbooks. Somehow, the colorful animal stickers on David's and the yellow minions on Emily-Grace's just seemed wrong in this space. "I had to get these," she mumbled.

The First A.D. appeared and hollered, in a deep, booming voice, "Blocking's up! Cast and keys only, please."

"Must run," Shanda said, munching on her carrot and watching Jessie over her shoulder as she sidled away. "Work calls."

The blonde curls bounced as she walked. They were cute and perky, like the girl, which annoyed the hell out of Jessie. With another glance at the exit leading to the parking lot, she rather thoughtfully ran a forefinger over her top and bottom lip and then followed Shanda to the set just in time to see her settle beside Josh and say, "Did you know your wife is here?"

Jessie could see Josh's panic at hearing the words she couldn't hear, but could sense what they were by the way Shanda followed them up with a nervous glance in her direction. Josh, too, twisted around and stared at Jessie in complete disbelief. Unsure of what to do, but unable to convince her feet to move in the opposite direction, Jessie lifted the workbooks and mouthed, "Needed these."

"Bullshit," Josh mouthed back, his eyes narrowing.

Trying to appear non-plussed, Jessie shrugged.

The A.D. tried to get the blocking underway, but Josh held up a hand. "One minute, please," he requested.

As he strode towards Jessie, she gulped. Bare feet, with the hems of his faded jeans hanging over his toes, and a white T-shirt rimming his hips, he was about as adorable as he got. Swallowing, she looked at her husband the way she knew Shanda—and every woman on set—was seeing him. Tanned, muscular biceps he was working hard to bring back after his accident on Blue, strong abs, the chestnut hair Jessie loved to touch, the full lips she loved to kiss, to run her tongue over…he was the whole deal. This was the man who came back to her this morning for a second quick cuddle before he had to leave for work. This was the man who exchanged vows with her on a sandy Prince Edward Island beach. This was the man Jessie shared children with. This was the man she loved beyond all measure.

And he was angry.

Grabbing her shoulders, Josh twisted Jessie around and, frowning, pointed her towards the exit. "Out."

"Ouch!" Jessie cried, twisting out of his grasp the same way Emily-Grace struggled out of Gary's earlier. She turned to face him. "I just wanted to say hi since I had to run in to grab these for the kids."

"Jessie, sometimes I don't know what the hell to do with you! I made it quite clear that I don't want you here right now!"

"Yeah, because why, because Shanda's going down on you to give you a nice little suck, is that why, Josh? I hear the love scenes are pretty raunchy on this set."

"Your mind always go there, Jess? Some fond memory of what you did for Matt, is that it?"

"That's low, Josh." Angry red spots formed on Jessie's cheeks. "Don't bring up Matt to me. Not today."

"Why not today? Why not every day? We may as well keep his memory alive, at least, eh? We won't have a kid like the one you brought home after your love affair with Jacob!"

"Josh! What the hell?" Incredulous, Jessie was so lost in this new hostility flaring from Josh's usually soft brown eyes that she didn't see Shanda approach Charlie to her right.

Josh changed his weight to his other foot and stared his wife down. "I asked you not to come here today. Yet here you are. Not much fucking wonder Matt left. Again. Apart from an uncontrollable need to sex my wife, I mean."

"Okay, this isn't fair! I just wanted to say hi and you're getting all defensive and stupid! You want your time alone with Shanda, is that it?"

"Yeah, her and me and seventy crew. Yeah, you hit that nail on the head, Jessie."

"No." Jessie lowered her voice as Charlie stormed over with Shanda tailing him. "You want her alone, that's what. Without the crew."

Something flickered in Josh's eyes that Jessie recognized. Truth. Desire. "Oh, for fuck's sake," she muttered angrily.

Charlie, in producer mode, touched Josh's arm. "Go," he demanded. "They're blocking for the reverse. They need you."

Josh didn't move. He stared at Jessie, and wondered what was going through her head, what she could read. There was desire, as far as Shanda was concerned. It was unexpected and Josh had no plans to follow through with it, but nor did he want his wife present to distract him from the scene, from the little bit of fantasy he enjoyed disappearing into with the lovely and desirable Shanda in his arms.

Charlie blew up. "You two are impossible! Josh, go! Now!" Glaring at Jessie, he threw up his arms. "Sometimes, and not very often I have to admit, I am glad you are Josh's problem and no longer mine!"

Jessie blinked and raised her chin. *Ouch.*

Grimacing, without looking at him, Charlie gave Josh a hard shove to get him moving. To Jessie he glowered, "You know the rules, kid. No wives allowed on set today. You need to leave."

Jessie was still lost on the sheer anger and frustration in her husband's demeanor. It was a complete reversal of his cuddles from the morning. Some of it she recognized as nerves, but knowing that didn't help settle her rising unease at all. Tossing her curls one last time, she blinked away her tears and turned to go, throwing one final remark at Charlie as she did.

"He's hurting. Look at his eyes. Get him some Advil, at least."

"Jessie, wait," she heard Josh call to her back. But Jessie kept on going, raising her finger behind her back in an upside down third finger salute as she started to jog.

Backing up, heading back to work, Charlie cursed and turned to Josh. "I mean it. She's a fucking handful sometimes."

With a low growl, Josh pushed by him and strode towards the set. *Yeah, but she's my handful,* he thought, a quiet gratitude surging upwards in his heart at the same time a new fear set in. Shanda, next to him, was clearing her lungs and mind with a long Yoga breath. The morning had been intense, so far. Something had happened that threw both of them. And now, both Josh and Shanda were extremely relieved that Jessie had left the set. Taking Shanda's hand, Josh brushed his fingers against hers and tried to get into character as Charlie strode up behind him.

"She right? Your leg hurting you, Josh?"

"Could use some Advil," Josh mumbled.

"You're sore today?" Shanda was surprised. Josh hadn't said a word.

As Charlie went off in search of something to ease his friend's discomfort, he was humbled at how easily Jessie could read her husband. One look in Josh's eyes and she recognized that he was in pain.

Pissed, unaware of the quiet love both Charlie and Josh were sending her way, Jessie ducked into the ladies' room near the exit. Seated on the toilet, she hung her head and forced herself to breathe slowly and deliberately. A few minutes later, a couple of women from the crew popped in and did their thing. At the sink as they were washing and drying their hands, they remarked on Jessie's appearance on set.

"Thank God she didn't see what happened this morning. She'd be completely losing her shit right now."

Inside her small cubicle, Jessie stopped breathing and raised her head to listen.

The second woman jumped in. "Which part? God that was hot, watching him go after her on the desk like that. I'd take him any day. Jacob Ryan be damned."

"The part after the bell. After the director cut. That part."

"Oh, yeah. When he kissed her. That long, tender kiss. I guess Josh was still in character."

"Still hard and wanting her, you mean."

"I'd love to know what she said to him to earn a kiss as sweet as that one."

"She looked like she was going to cry."

"Wouldn't you? Loving a man you can't have, and having to practically sex him in public like that? In front of a crew? He's breaking her heart."

"Yet Josh kissed Shanda like there was no tomorrow. Like he wanted her."

"After the bell. After 'Cut.'"

"Yep."

At that, the women left the washroom.

By the time Jessie collected herself and made a break for the grey day outside, Jane was almost frantic. Now Jessie wasn't on anybody's good side, but she hardly cared. She put her SUV in reverse, ignored her kids' whines and complaints that she took too long, and she steered towards the production's rented condo that Josh and Charlie shared for five a.m. calls and late nights.

Her tears fell freely but she convinced herself that Josh was committed to her, that he would not overstep any more boundaries with any woman apart from the work he had to do on set. *I'm here,* she told herself, pounding her chest lightly for effect. *I'm here in Alberta and I know he loves me. We'll be okay.*

Their recent renewed commitment to each other cemented the thought. What remained jarring, though, was the conversation Jessie overheard in the restroom. What frightened her was the thought that something had transpired between Josh and Shanda that set the gossips on the crew chattering, that was tender and sweet, and that happened after the director called 'Cut.'

Swinging into a parking space at the condo, Jessie paused and wiped away her tears before she turned off the ignition and twisted around to referee a fight between Dylan and David.

There would be time to discuss this unsettling news later. For now, she had kids to care for, a tutor to meet, and a friend to apologize to. Also, Arnie was walking towards her. He would accompany Jane and Jessie on the shopping trip with their stylist, Samantha. Dan was already upstairs to keep an eye on the children during their outing. The day was mostly grey but steamy and warm, and the tutor, a young twenty-something Asian girl, would be taking them to a park later to burn off some energy.

"Hey, Arnie," Jessie said as Arnie approached. She took a chance. "I was just wondering. Have you heard from Matt at all?"

Arnie reached out a hand and placed it behind her head, then drew Jessie towards him for a chaste kiss on her forehead. "No, I have not," he lied. He was in touch with Matt on a regular basis. "Have you?"

"Nah. I don't expect to. C'est la vie."

Reaching into the vehicle to retrieve Dylan from his car seat, Jessie paused, her face hidden from view from everyone except her youngest child. "But I sure could use his advice right now," she thought, as a surge of world-weariness washed over her. "I miss him, Dylan. Today I really miss old Matt."

Dylan smiled widely, and hugged his momma as Jessie lifted him out of the car. "I miss him too, Momma," he said in his little boy way. "And I miss Daddy. And Jacob."

"Well, that about sums my thoughts up too," Jessie mused, laughing despite herself. "You're some wise old kid, you know that, Dylan?"

Shaking her head, she ushered the older two into the condo as she carried Dylan, and soon, the busy-ness of her young family took her mind off Josh and Shanda, and Jessie didn't find herself worrying again until she was back home, after Jane was gone, when the three young Sawyer children were sound asleep.

Chapter Thirty-one

$\mathcal{A}$ quiet knock came at Charlie's office door late in the day, after most of the crew had already said their goodnights and headed for home or to the nearby bar for a drink.

"Yo," he called, secretly hoping his visitor only had a quick question. The day was long and stressful, from his point of view, and Charlie was regretting his thoughtless comment to Jessie about being glad she was Josh's handful, and not his. All day he cursed himself up and down for that one. The hurt in his friend's eyes was enough to sink him for the entire day. Kicking her off the set was necessary, but Charlie's insensitive comment was not. Now he just wanted to make the drive to Canmore, preferably with the radio on loud enough to drown out his thoughts, or to at least distract him from dwelling on the long day. A snuggle with his wife was in order. Jane's calm voice and loving touch would set Charlie's rattled nerves straight.

From all perspectives—camera, director, producers—the love scene had gone extremely well. The lighting—thin lines of light separating the actors from the dark background, today—was exquisite, and the hot chemistry between the actors was obvious, practically steaming up the prime lenses that were being interchanged for distance and close-ups. Charlie had watched the master takes and snuck back later for some of those closer shots. By then, the sparks and nerves had mostly dissipated into the drudgery of adjusting lights and multiple takes, but still, Charlie had found that watching Josh and Shanda work together in such an intimate scene was extremely captivating.

Lately, the two were spending more and more time together off set. In the early days, when the series was first ramping up, Josh almost always chose to be alone, eating lunch in his trailer studying lines, or simply avoiding cast and crew during lighting, when he wasn't needed, while others gathered around the craft table and swapped weekend warrior stories or the sad state of their love affairs—whatever. But now Josh was often in Shanda's company. Just last week they had their heads together almost every day at lunch, choosing to laugh and chat during the entire duration of lunch instead of going their separate ways to prep for the rest of the day. It seemed the two had become very good friends over the course of *Sacred Peace's* production run.

When did that happen? Charlie wondered. Josh was doing better, emotionally, so that was part of it. With Jessie and the kids at the ranch, he seemed to be coming out of his shell more, as if their everyday presence in his life was lending him strength for both physical healing as well as giving him the much needed injection of psychological healing his marriage required.

Too, Shanda had been around Josh a lot while he was in the hospital. At the time, Jessie had needed to fly home to be with the kids and to pack them up for the move to the ranch. Charlie dropped in to see Josh a lot back then, since he, Charles and Jonathon had put most of the production on standby while they sorted out how to shoot a series without its lead. Often Shanda was there when Charlie popped around, sitting on Josh's bed with her back against his pillow and her legs stretched out, ankles crossed, laughing about one thing or another, and swapping tales from work on other productions. She accompanied him to physio, too, assisting him with movement from his bed to his wheelchair, and the other way around.

Their comfort level was far too relaxed and intimate to suit Charlie. But in terms of set rapport and relations, it was exactly what *Sacred Peace* needed. And it was definitely apparent that Josh was blossoming with Shanda's easy friendship.

Now, Shanda was at Charlie's door, according to the pretty blonde curls that peeked around the corner.

"You have a minute, Charlie?" she was asking as he poked papers from his messy desk into a worn leather messenger bag.

"Shanda, hi, sure."

Striding around to the padded office chair in front of the second hand wooden desk the pre-production team had acquired for his use, Charlie removed the few items he'd placed there so he wouldn't forget to take them home—a thermos, a pair of dress shoes for the occasional social gig or for meeting with Calgary's interested dignitaries, a small blue insulated lunch bag he'd used for carrying a yogurt and fruit to snack on in his car on the drive from home early this morning.

"Thanks." Grateful, Shanda eased into the chair and crossed her legs at the knees. Folding both hands on her lap, she sat with her back straight, and watched Charlie drop into the swivel chair opposite, across the desk from her.

Charlie moved a tall wooden giraffe so their eye line would be unimpaired. "Africa," he explained, his cheeks a little pink. "Jane does humanitarian work there, with a few different organizations. This guy came back with her after her last trip."

"She's a remarkable woman." Shanda shuffled a little nervously.

"Yes, she is. Jane is constantly teaching me to become a better person."

"You're completely devoted to her." Shanda said it like she was almost surprised, the words rising and falling in pitch as she raised her eyebrows.

"I am. Astonishing, isn't it?" A sparkle of light danced through Charlie's tired, bloodshot eyes. "Who would've thought Charlie Deacon would settle down with a wife, two kids, and a house in the suburbs?"

Pointing at him, Shanda added, in a serious tone, "And I've seen the mommy car."

"I still have the Porsche," he winked, leaning back. "Jane knows her limits."

"I've seen that too." Forcing a smile, she wasn't fooling Charlie.

His smile did an about face. "What is it, Shanda? What can I do for you?"

"Yes. Well." Running long, tapered fingers through her loose, bobbed curls, Shanda glanced up at him but quickly looked away. "It's a bit of a tough one," she said.

"Oh." *Crap. So much for hitting the road.* Charlie snuck a peek at his phone. *I oughtta text Jane and tell her I haven't left yet.*

He was about to pick up the phone when Shanda said, "I thought I was going to lose it today, when I saw Jessie on set."

A quick burst of anger flashed up Charlie's body and ended in a red bloom across his face. "Jessie knew better than to come to set today. She was asked to stay away."

"She goes a little rogue at times, huh?" Sometimes Shanda's voice was girly-quiet and feminine, as if it lacked strength. Like little bell-peals. Now, after such an emotional, taxing day, she was tired and the hushed voice seemed to be all she could muster.

"Lots of times." Charlie's lips turned even more down at the corners. Grabbing a pen off the desk, he twisted it in his fingers. "I would like to guarantee that won't happen again, Shanda, but all I can say is that when it comes to Jessie, sometimes all we can do is try to cut her off at the pass. She can be pretty damned stubborn."

"Is that because she was a runaway? She was alone from a young age, right? Homeless?"

Unable to help himself, Charlie bristled. Jessie was, and always would be, someone he would want to protect, despite her tendency to run rogue and piss him off on occasion. All of them, all of the people in her close circle, felt that way about her. If they could, they would constantly form circles around her and close ranks, just to keep the big old bad world at bay. Yet sometimes it was *her* strength that kept *them* going. She was a conundrum, at the best of times.

"Jessie missed a lot of her teen years, yes, in terms of parents offering guidance. But that freedom also is part of her charm. She's got a certain 'je ne sais quoi,' you know?"

"A mystique? Yes, I suppose you can call it that."

Chuckling, Charlie responded with, "But you'd rather call it something else. Like maybe something with a few curse words attached."

"Charlie," Shanda sat up even straighter and searched for the words. "I didn't necessarily come here to talk about Jessie Wheeler."

Emitting a small sucking pop from between his lips, Charlie pointed his pen at her and said lightly, "Sawyer, actually. Jessie Wheeler-Sawyer. She just uses Jessie Wheeler professionally."

"Point taken." Uncertain, Shanda held Charlie's focused gaze. "I guess it's pretty clear which side you're on, Charlie."

"I'm not taking sides. There are no sides to take here, Shanda."

"You know, for someone who got clearly screwed around on back when Jessie and Josh were doing *Drifters*, I'm surprised you're all such good friends today."

"Forgive and forget, Shanda."

"You don't want to live your life without Jessie in it."

A shocked silence soaked through Charlie's body. He went rigid as the blood left his face in a rush. A steady illumination took over the earlier playful, fatigued eyes. To Shanda he said, his voice subdued, "I only really got to know Jessie after we split up. Josh and I were friends as kids. I like these people. They make my life interesting."

"You can say that again. From what I've read—"

"Shanda." Gently, Charlie sat forward and leaned his elbows on the desk, on a few call sheets and production schedules he'd printed out and tossed there. There was a script there, too, mostly white with colored pink, yellow and green pages in between—the colors representing the changes made by writers after the original episode was released to the cast and crew. "Why are you here? It's been a long day, and my wife is promising me a hot bath and hopefully some good sex when I get home, and that's after an hour-and-a-half of driving. I'd like to hit the road soon."

"I'm sorry, Charlie. I wouldn't be here if I didn't…There's a problem."

"Uh huh."

"It's serious, Charlie. It's a serious problem."

"Meaning?" He clasped his fingers together, white knuckled them, and waited.

"Meaning I think…I think I may have to leave the show."

There were tears now, points of light that Charlie knew meant visible moisture wasn't far away. With a loud frustrated *grrrr* sound, he sat back and looked away, and started drumming one set of fingers on the arm of his office chair. "I'm not surprised," he said. "In fact, I've considered having to let you go." Looking back at her, he asked pointedly, "Josh?"

Emotion was getting the better of Shanda now. Her voice was thick with angst when she spoke. "I didn't plan it. I told you when we started production that I was afraid of him. Remember?"

"And I made the mistake of telling you he is one of the kindest, most generous men you would ever meet. I should have told you he has a long Viking history and carries a spear."

"I'm in love with him. Charlie…it hurts like hell."

Charlie paused and held his breath. He tested her. "Should I be glad you're not telling me you're having an affair with him?"

"I'm not. Charlie, I never thought I was that person. The one that could break up a family. As if I could, I mean." Shifting her legs, Shanda grabbed the arms of her chair and pulled it closer to the desk, closer to her boss, one of her co-stars, a man she had sincerely grown to love and trust since the beginning of the season one shoot. "That's the thing, Charlie. Today I realized I just can't do it anymore. I can't go to work and be naked with this man…and have him love me the way he does, in character, physically…then have him be Josh again, someone whose friendship I've come to adore on such a deep level…and then have to leave wanting more, you know? Being desperate for more? Knowing he is trying to patch together his relationship with his wife after going through hell with her, and with three small kids…" Shaking her head slowly from side to side, Shanda was crying freely now. "I don't want to be that person. But I feel like I can be. Like it's going in that direction."

The admission was not a surprise to Charlie. He'd seen it coming, hell, the whole crew saw it coming. Yet hearing her say the words today of all days, after Josh's tender post-bell kiss, which had the entire crew gossiping, and after Jessie's nervous visit to the set, freaked Charlie out. He felt his heart sink. There was no question which way this would have to go. It was like Matt all over again…in order for the Sawyers to have the support they would need to continue to figure things out in their marriage, Shanda would have to be removed from the equation.

"Shanda."

"I can't," she gulped, using a forefinger to wipe away a tear as she interrupted whatever he was going to say. "I can't do this, Charlie. I can't work with him this way. I want him. All of him. Not just the *Sacred Peace* him."

"Josh, huh?" A slight twist of his lips conveyed what Charlie was thinking, although Shanda didn't get the whole picture until Charlie voiced it. "What the hell is it about that guy?"

She laughed, despite her tears. "You still haven't figured that out, huh? After all these years?"

"I know why Jessie and I had trouble. She was so distant, so removed, and I was a party boy. And I know Josh is a really great guy. But I still don't get why women fall for him the way they do."

"It's because they want to save him, Charlie." Shanda's eyes were wide now, and in her mind she was in another place as she explained this to her boss. "Look at yourself. You've got your shit together. You're Mister 'all-married-and-happy-movie-star-life-is-perfect.' Josh is this guy who the world is still trying to destroy. He's like this little boy sitting on a cracked sidewalk in shorts and a dirty T-shirt who just watches the world move around him while he nurses a cut on his finger. Who has this sad frown on his face that says he's got all this hurt inside. We all just want to bandage that finger. Charlie, it's like when he walks onto set with that long hair falling over his ear, he's hiding. He doesn't want anyone to really see who he is but the thing is, some of us have figured it out. We know who he is. And we know why he hurts."

"Jessie…knows why he hurts, Shanda. You can only guess."

"I know." Charlie could hardly make out the words because Shanda's voice was so choked with emotion. "That's why I have to go. I want to know all of him, everything about him. I want to be the one Josh turns to when he needs to be held. And I want the physical release that lovers get when the world becomes too much and all you have left is the pleasure you take in each other, in each other's bodies. But I know…I know I can't have that. I knew it on set today when I begged him for it, after the bell. When he kissed me, Charlie…I knew it was his way of saying goodbye. That he and I…just can't *be*."

Good on ya, Josh, Charlie was thinking. Aloud he said, "I need to talk to Charles and Jon about this, Shanda. But I know what they're going to say."

"They're going to say I have a contract. I've shot half the season already, and I have a contract. Look, I've got other offers, Charlie. I'll get my agent to pay out the contract and I'll move on."

"Finish the season, Shanda. At least."

She wiped a hand over her forehead and let out a frustrated yell. "Charlie, it's like you're laying the wood and asking me to build the fire! I know you care about Jessie. You still love her. You don't choose to spend your life with your ex-fiancée of eight years close by and just shut off those feelings. And

I'm begging you, since I know you don't want to see her hurt, to let me go. Release me from my contract and find someone else. Let me go."

"I can't see Josh going for this either, Shanda. You two have built up a rapport that works for *Sacred Peace*. It won't be easy for him to lose you."

"Damn it, Charlie, just kill Olivia off and get Bobby to cry. Big tough guy like that crying? Imagine the ratings." She said it with a flourish of one hand. "You'll score huge. It won't hurt the show to lose me. All the big shows are killing off their main characters these days."

Charlie stood, indicating their meeting was over. "I need some time to think about it. You need some time to think about it. Let's talk in a few days."

"I mean it, Charlie." Her voice was low. "If you care about Jessie, you'll find a way to let me go." Turning, Shanda headed for the door.

Charlie's voice stopped her.

"Shanda…"

"Yes?"

"You said it won't happen. That Josh isn't going for it. For…you."

"Yes." Her voice was a whisper.

"So why should I be worried for Jessie?"

Her eyes darkened. "Because, Charlie. You said it yourself. Jessie goes rogue. She hurts him again and again. And one of these days Josh is going to need somewhere to turn. And when it comes to me versus you, guess who's got the most welcoming arms."

"So why would you go…if you think there's a chance…"

"Because guess who will end up with the broken heart. That's why. Good night, Charlie. Drive safe."

When she left the office, and her footsteps faded down the hall, Charlie sank into his chair and studied a crack in the old desk. He didn't move until Jane texted him with a brief *where you?*

He had the Porsche with him today. Outside, sinking into it, he found himself super-pissed at Josh until Shanda's description of him sobered Charlie. It was true. And Jessie was the same. They were a perfect match. It was just unfortunate that sometimes neither seemed to have the capacity to help the other.

"Good thing there happens to be a lot of other people who care about the two of you," Charlie thought as he piloted the sweet little car out of the parking lot and pointed it west towards the snow-capped Rocky Mountains. Matt crossed his mind. Matt, Jessie's best friend and security and, recently, the man to whom she turned when she felt lost and alone, adrift in a sea of confusion and hurt. Had she intended to hurt Josh via her liaison with Matt? No. Never. Josh was simply collateral damage. In all their years together, Jessie had never crossed that line with Matt, a man who could have tempted her many times. No, she turned to him finally because the hurts and loneliness between her and Josh got too big, and the great love and trust between Jessie and Matt easily facilitated a physical coupling.

Welcoming arms, Shanda had said.

I suppose that's something in itself, Charlie found himself thinking, pondering the fact that Jessie and Matt had only recently hooked up after so many years together. *But Josh…he doesn't need that temptation, especially with a woman as sweet and kind and giving and pretty and talented as Shanda.*

Shanda was right. She would have to go. Josh was a good man, but he was only human and, judging by the way his wife ignored both his and Charlie's wishes and showed up on set today, Josh was dealing with a firecracker. Jessie was, at the very least, unpredictable. Set her off and Josh would have a new flame on his hands.

Literally.

You're laying the wood and asking me to build the fire, Shanda had said. She'd also said *You still love her.*

"Yeah. Of course I do," Charlie mumbled now, hanging right and passing a rusted Toyota that could only have made the trek out west from eastern Canada. Charlie peered sideways and squinted. The license plate read 'Nova Scotia.' He chuckled. There were a lot of east coasters in Alberta, most working in the oil fields. That kind of rust on vehicles generally appeared after being exposed for long periods of time to the salt air of the Atlantic ocean.

Back to loving Jessie…Well, for Charlie, it was no longer a physical thing and hadn't been for years. But Jessie was indeed someone he cared deeply for, and for whom he would move heaven and earth to protect.

Even if it meant potentially damaging his new series, which Charlie had worked hard for years to develop.

Jon, with all his fears about working on a series featuring his sometimes unstable son again, must have had a sixth sense about this one. They would lose a lead cast member again, only it wouldn't be Josh. It would be Shanda, and her heart would be heard breaking all the way back to Vancouver.

The mountains loomed in the distance now, all black and craggy and enigmatic, silhouetted against the setting sun, which left a thin line of light purple and pink and orange behind each mysterious peak. Above were dappled clouds, lines of grey-white cotton against an indigo black sky, like quilt batting being stretched apart.

Groaning, Charlie put the pedal to the metal, and the spirited little sports car ushered him into an unknown future which included, when he got home, a whole new earful about Josh and Jessie and which, when all was said and done, brought back old fears that outweighed the stress of Shanda's request ten thousand times ten thousand times more.

Chapter Thirty-Two

With a mighty roar, the King Ranch zoomed up the lane at nine p.m. The kids were asleep, and Jessie was in the master bedroom folding a load of kids' clothing when Josh approached the house.

The one-hour drive from the set had given him plenty of time for reflection on his day. The physical urges he experienced while working with the pretty Shanda were catching up to him. Every time he thought about her body—the way she arched her back and raised her hips so his lips could brush her tight stomach, her breasts, that moist spot between her legs—Josh shivered.

Delicious, he'd thought as he drove. *She's just delicious.* And he'd instantly pushed the thought away, only to start a new cycle that started with slow, wistful tunes on the radio that encouraged him to lapse into thoughts of Shanda lying beneath him, tremors scaling his body as he remembered their shared scene, which took six hours in total to shoot once you counted close-ups and reversals, with lighting breaks in between.

The most intense part of the scene was the desk part, since that was when Shanda's character pulled Josh to her and their lovemaking built to a point of explosion. Yet…as actors, they didn't go the distance this time, and had to fake it instead. Remembering, Josh winced as he recalled Shanda's earnest eyes boring into his, moments after he'd 'acted' his climax, while he was pushing sweaty strands of highlighted blonde hair off of her forehead. He was leaning on his good arm, but the sore shoulder was acting up, and Josh's ribs hurt too, from all the activity. He was on his knees on the hard desk (on cushions during the close-ups), and the metal in his leg ached. Yet what hurt the most was Shanda's plea just after the bell went, after the director called 'Cut.'

"This isn't enough for me," she'd wept. "I need more from you. I want more, Josh."

It hit him when she used his name, and not his character's name, how deep Shanda's feelings ran. Josh had nothing to say that could change their status. He and Jessie had just reconciled and no way was he messing that up again. So he'd bent to Shanda and offered her all he had to give—a long tender, passionate kiss that he somehow hoped would help ease his co-star's hurts.

"Thank you," she had whispered to him, her body naked underneath him, his jeans hiked low around his hips, his bare chest soaking up the warmth of hers.

Now, walking towards the ranch house Josh shared with the woman who was now, and always would be, the lone recipient of his deepest capacity to love, Josh felt a certain angst crawl up his spine and land in his heart.

Jessie had not been a happy camper when she left set today. But Josh's day had been intense and painful, both emotionally and physically. It was long and exhausting, and he was beat. The erotic hangover from his pure physical attraction to Shanda's flawless body had stirred up his emotions and left a potpourri of swirling feelings Josh really couldn't deal with tonight. The Advil was doing nothing to ease his aches, and he was likely in for a nasty fight with Jessie.

He limped slowly up the walk to the screen door.

Jessie heard him come in. Suspending Emily-Grace's now clean dress in front of her, she paused in her folding and cocked her head to see where her husband would land. She heard him set his coffee thermos on the kitchen island, sigh heavily, and then make his way to the bedroom.

Limping, she reflected inwardly. *He's super tired. Go easy on him.*

When the light changed at the doorway to the bedroom, Jessie inhaled quietly and looked over. Josh was leaning against the doorframe, body and soul, pretty much. Exhausted.

After a last fold on their daughter's dress, Jessie delicately placed it in a clothesbasket. To Josh she said, without looking at him, "You hungry?"

"Nope."

"You still mad?"

"Nope." His tone was lighter the second time. "You?"

"No."

She was struggling, though. Josh could read her like a book. He moved into the room and picked up one of David's T-shirts. Folding it, dropping it into the basket, he said, "It's done now. No more intimate scenes for a while."

"Glad." Jessie couldn't bring herself to ask about what she'd overheard in the washroom. In the end, she didn't directly have to. Josh started them down that road.

He let out a heavy breath and set down the small jeans he'd just picked up. "Look, Jessie," he started, sideways facing her. "The feelings Shanda has for me…they're not reciprocated, okay?"

"I think maybe they are, a little," Jessie managed, trying to keep her voice even.

Josh tilted his head and bit the corner of one lip. "Why do you think that?"

Unsure, Jessie paused in her folding.

Josh took Dylan's T-shirt from her, finished folding it, and set it in the basket. He laid a palm against his wife's cheek and forced her to look up at him.

"Tell me why you think that," he demanded quietly, giving the question the reverence it deserved.

"I know you kissed her. After the bell. Apparently while she was lying beneath you on a desk. Naked. After…things were intense."

A light blazed like a rocket across Josh's eyes. It disappeared as quickly as it appeared. "She said something to me," he told his wife. "I reacted."

"Hmmm. Are you going to tell me what she said?"

"Does it matter? I'm not hooking up with her."

"She tell you she wants you?" A wide-eyed innocence played itself out across Jessie's face. She was back to her childlike self, the girl Josh figured Jessie often reverted to when she was scared. When she felt threatened.

"It doesn't matter." Closing his eyes, Josh drew up his shoulders and pressed his wife against him. "I only want you. You know that."

"So why were you so freaked out today?" Her words tickled his neck as Jessie tucked her arms around the waist of the man she loved with a desperation that often hurt more than it healed. "When I was on set."

"It was intense, Jess. What we were being asked to do. You didn't need to see that, and I didn't want you to see it."

"Especially because there are feelings between you and Shanda."

"I won't deny that she and I have grown close over the duration of the shoot, Jessie. But let me say this for the very last time. I am not going down that rabbit hole with her. I'm sorry that things have gotten mixed up between you and me. I'm sorry if in some weird way you think your thing with Matt might somehow make me feel entitled. You need to know that I don't feel that way, as if I deserve my turn to mess around."

Stiffening in his arms, Jessie turned her face into the hollow of his neck.

Josh continued. "Shanda has strong feelings for me. That's what she said after the bell. She wants more. But she knows she's not getting it."

Leaning back, Jessie faced her husband with a stricken expression. Resting her hands on his waist, she said, "But the kiss. After you cut. Shanda's likely thinking otherwise."

"It was like a hangover from the take, Jessie. You know what it's like. Things were a little crazy. She said what she said, I kissed her. It won't happen again."

"I'd rather you were working with an actor you hated."

A small tired laugh eased her worry. "Me too, little one." Bending his forehead to hers, Josh let out a long, contented breath. "This is the only place I want to be. Ever. You are the woman I want to grow old with."

With a gentle smile, Jessie ran her tongue over her husband's lips. "You too tired to play?"

Josh was about to answer when his cell phone rang. He fished it out of the chest pocket of his vintage shirt. "Charlie," he said. "Probably making sure we're not killing each other."

Tapping the 'answer' icon, Josh dropped slowly down onto the bed, wincing and straightening his aching leg with his right hand as he did so. "H'lo Charlie," he said. "Didn't you get enough of me today?"

Jessie tensed. She hadn't had a chance to mention their intruders today. Maybe Jane had…

"Is Jessie there?" Charlie skipped the formalities.

"Yeah. I just got home. We're sorting through today. Why? You don't need to bring up her visit again, Charlie. We're figuring it out."

"Put your phone on speaker."

"Charlie?"

"Just do it, Josh."

Eyeing his wife, Josh tapped the phone's speaker icon. Jessie sighed and perched her butt on the edge of the bed next to him.

"Hi, Charlie," she said quietly.

"Jessie, Jane told me what happened today."

Josh sucked in a breath. "What happened today?"

Leaning against him, laying a hand on his thigh, Jessie said to the phone he was holding on his lap, "I haven't had a chance to talk to Josh about that yet, Charlie. He just got in."

"Josh, your ranch had visitors today. Jane said a couple of folks showed up and demanded pictures of Jessie and the kids. And that there were some… vocal reminders of Dylan's parentage that frightened the kids."

"Jane wasn't here, Charlie. She passed the van as she was driving in." As briefly as she could, Jessie explained the incident to Josh and Charlie. She summed it up with, "Gary took the woman's camera and smashed it. There were threats about involving the police for harassment or something."

"You are the one who should have gone to the police, Jessie. These people were harassing you."

"I know, I thought about it later, but we were late and—"

"And you wanted to crash my set." Charlie was firm and unyielding. "Look, listen closely, the two of you. I've had a pissy long day. It ended with an actress in my office crying on my shoulder because she's in love with her co-star. Shanda's beside herself, Josh. She's finding it hard to continue working with you."

Josh sank deeper into the bed and wrapped his free fingers around Jessie's. "I didn't know it was that bad. I'm sorry."

Jessie laid her head on her husband's shoulder and closed her eyes.

"The thing is. Shanda's a big girl, but that just makes her have big girl hurts. Today was rough. But I trust you, buddy. I know you're not going to be stupid and take a chance on losing that beautiful girl who's beside you right now. Not again. But after today I sure as hell didn't like coming home to my worried wife telling me that some lunatics were running around your ranch harassing Jessie and the kids. It freaked me out. I want both of you around for a long time so you can live that happily-ever-after you both so desperately deserve."

He gave them a few moments to let that sink in before delivering his coup de grace, his reason for calling at the end of their long day. "This is not your producer and co-star calling. This is your friend. You need to re-engage your security."

"Matt's not coming back, Charlie. Ever." Jessie didn't have the heart to look at Josh as she said that, but she felt him tense.

"Not Matt, then. Although it sucks because he knows all of you best. Talk to Charles and either hire someone new or just do some serious scheduling. No more of this rogue thing, Jessie. You're not living a normal life and you never will be. And by the way, just for interest's sake, what happened today—I called Gary, I got the whole scoop—scared the living shit out of me. I'm hiring security for my family as well, as long as they're isolated back here in Canmore. Three more months on *Sacred Peace* and then we're good to go."

"Charlie?"

"Yes, Jessie?"

"I hear you. I got a bit scared today too. Those two were a little bit off their rockers."

"A little bit!" Charlie's guffaw was loud and obnoxious. "Gary checked with the police. They don't appear to be pressing charges. They never went in to the station at all."

"Well, that's good, I guess."

"Josh, you're quiet. What are you thinking, buddy?"

Lifting Jessie's fingers to his lips, Josh kissed her and considered what to say. "I think I'm tired and I want to go to bed," he said almost inaudibly. "I think I don't want to think anymore today."

Charlie softened. "Listen, we've moved call an hour tomorrow since we finished late today, and you're not due in til noon anyway. Sleep in and enjoy that family of yours. I'll talk to Charles and get him to send Dan out from Calgary in the morning. Okay?"

Josh chuckled but his eyes were darkening, although Jessie could still see that they were cloudy with pain. "So you're not only my friend, producer, and co-star. Now you're also Keating camp security."

"I'm your friend, Josh. And Jessie's too. I didn't think it was a good idea in the first place for the two of you to live out there alone in the wild."

"You were happy to disown me earlier today, Charlie." Trying to lighten the mood, Jessie joked lightly but her words fell flat on tired ears.

"Jessie, if I ever see you on my set again, it will be too soon." Yawning, Charlie signed off with, "Get some meds into your man and sing him to sleep. Tomorrow we shoot until midnight. Josh will be staying at the condo tomorrow night, and you and your family will have security 24-7. Good night, you two."

After he was gone, Josh and Jessie sat in silence. Finally, Jessie got up and padded into the washroom. She came back with two Advil and a glass of water.

Josh shook his head. "I've already had too many today. No more, Jessie."

"They'll help you sleep, babe."

"I know what will help me sleep." Lightening a little, Josh sent Jessie a look he meant to be sexy, but which ended up being more of a wince.

"Let me check on the kids, and I'll see what I can do." Jessie set the Advil down on the nightstand and started to move away but Josh stopped her.

"I'll go," he said. "I haven't seen them all day. Leave the laundry. I'll help you with it in the morning. We'll talk about the security tomorrow too." With that, he limped off into the main open concept area of the home and made his way over to the kids' bedrooms.

Watching him, Jessie frowned. Tomorrow Josh would be staying over-night in Calgary after working til midnight. Three more months of this. Would Shanda be sticking around? She could easily imagine the pain Shanda was going through but Jessie also knew the woman had no idea how bad it could get. Loving Josh for as long as she, Jessie, had, and being apart from him as often as they were, was often completely debilitating. At the same time, even those early days had really hurt.

And Jessie being Jessie, she actually felt a pang of sorrow for Shanda.

Ten minutes later, she climbed into bed next to the man who caused so much pain by virtue of being a kind, generous, sexy soul who was very easy to love. Jessie brushed back his hair and peered anxiously into Josh's liquid eyes.

"You're in pain," she whispered. "I think you should go back to the doctor, Josh."

"I'm just tired," he said. "It was a long day."

"Sleep, then." Snuggling into him, Jessie waited for the usual, "Come play first." It didn't come. Josh was snoring within seconds. Holding him close, she listened to him breathe, and prayed she could love him forever, and never again feel the agony of loss the way she knew Shanda was feeling it tonight.

Jessie let her eyes drift closed, and she, too, put the crazy day behind her.

Chapter Thirty-three

In mid-July, just after the Sawyers, Deacons and Keatings celebrated Jessie's birthday with a low-key gathering at the ranch, the producers of *Sacred Peace* bought two tables at a fundraiser for the Alberta Children's Hospital, where Josh and Jessie's oldest two children were brought after being found by a jogger in a freezing park four years earlier. Gracious to the core, when Jessie was approached to sing at the upscale event, she easily said 'yes,' although the horrific memory of the dark day her children were snatched from her arms in the Langley basement was one of the lowest of her life.

The night of the fundraiser, Charlie and Jane landed at the ranch in a sleek black stretch limousine chauffeured by a hired driver from Calgary. They popped into the ranch house and waited for Jessie to put the finishing touches on her makeup before Jessie and Josh would join them for the drive to Calgary. Arnie was coming along to watch over his celebrity charges; he would sit in the front with the driver. Dan and Sam were staying at the ranch to keep an eye on the home front.

Carlotta and her sister were also present; their good-natured appearance earned a few dramatic eye rolls from Jessie. In their bags, next to a motley assortment of kids' craft supplies, were cupcake mixes, ready-made icing, and candy sprinkles.

"And you're expecting my kids to go to sleep at what time tonight?" Jessie asked Carlotta with a happy grin. "You're digging your own grave here, Carlotta."

Stella and Lucas were part of the crowd too—Carlotta was thrilled at having a baby to care for. A real old Sawyer ranch party was well under way before Josh and Jessie joined Charlie and Jane in the limo, making it much easier for the two sets of parents to leave their offspring for the night.

Through the nighttime oasis of Alberta ranch country they drove, under inky starlit skies that promised a perfect grown-up night out. Chatter was fluid and friendly, with everyone on his and her best behavior. For Jessie, who was already yawning after her early morning with David, with Dylan up right after him, it was an emotional night long before she was delivered to the upscale Hyatt Regency Hotel in Calgary. Josh, too, was feeling the soul crushing, melancholic effects from a low-spirited time in his life he preferred to forget. Even Charlie and Jane were quiet and subdued as they entered the ballroom hand in hand and spotted a large digitally projected sign on the stage announcing the Alberta Children's Hospital fundraiser.

This was Jessie's second time in the space today—she had been in to meet Jacob and their back-line band in early afternoon for a sound check. The plan was for her to perform her own half hour set, ballads and slow songs, mostly. Then she would step back while Charlie took the stage to introduce *Sacred Peace*, to provide some background on the series, which was a hot topic in the city these days. Jacob would join Jessie then, and they would sing three songs from the soundtrack album they recorded months earlier. The songs would play out while, behind Jessie and Jacob, digitally projected images from the series would act as teasers for the new show.

Earlier, while they were dressing at home, Jessie had remarked to Josh how strange it was going to be to sing while knowing he and Shanda would be featured in the images just behind her. From her vantage point looking out at the audience, she would not be able to see the screen, but she planned to turn around during the instrumental parts of the songs and sneak peeks when she could.

At the same time, all she would really see of the audience when facing the ballroom would be silhouetted heads and bodies, since the ballroom would be in semi-darkness in order for the images to display properly.

Now, the two couples were led to their round table, which also seated Shanda and her casual date, a divorced thirty-something Calgary city councilor the actor met when the good-looking, assertive muscled black man toured the set one day. Jacob and Kayla, who'd flown in from Vancouver the night before, were also at their table.

Neither Jessie nor Josh noticed the hard look that passed between Charlie and Shanda as Charlie took his seat. At the next table, though, were Charles and Deirdre and Jonathon and Giselle, with two Calgary dignitaries and their spouses. And both Charles and Jon were hyper-aware of Shanda's presence at the table, because earlier in the week they had finally agreed to release her from her contract with *Sacred Peace,* and both were just sick about it.

The news would come out tonight. Charlie would be making the formal announcement during his preamble on stage after Jessie's solo set and before Jacob would join her to perform the songs from the *Sacred Peace* soundtrack. Glancing now over to Charles and Jon, he nodded a 'hello' and let his gaze drift back over to Josh, who was reaching across Shanda on his left to shake the hand of her date, whose name both Josh and Charlie remembered as Joseph. Charlie, too, half-stood and reached across the table to shake the man's hand. Joseph had a friendly aura and a viselike grip. The gregarious, friendly man was known to be a generous and vibrant supporter of film and television production in the city of Calgary, and was immediately likable.

As, over Shanda's lap, Josh and Joseph broke into an easy chat, and Jane eased into light conversation with Jacob and Kayla, Charlie leaned an arm over Jessie's shoulders and quietly asked her to accompany him for a few minutes. Somewhat surprised, she stood and let him escort her to the far end of the ballroom and out into the hallway to a smaller room she and Jacob were using as prep green room space.

Josh twisted his head slightly to watch them go, and Jane, who knew Charlie wanted to catch Jessie and give her the heads up about Shanda's departure from the show so Jessie wouldn't have to hear it while she was quite visibly on stage, shrugged her shoulders at Josh and said, "Something about his introduction to the *Sacred Peace* tunes." Josh bought it outright, and casually leaned back to continue chatting with Shanda and Joseph.

As the green room door *oompphhed* closed behind Jessie and Charlie, Jessie eyeballed her reflection in the mirror before she turned back to her good friend. Tonight's designer dress was a mid-thigh deep forest-green Zuhair Murad, with a plunging lace neckline and tight lace sleeves. The skirt flared out a little, accentuating the strong quadriceps muscles Jessie earned through home gym workouts, Yoga and dance. A gracious updo was her choice of hairstyle tonight, fashioned with Carlotta's help since, over the years, Carlotta had become much more than a housemaid and babysitter, and instead more of a personal friend and rather versatile assistant.

"You are stunning," Charlie ascertained, a somber twinkle in his eye. "Stop admiring yourself, your highness, and cop a squat. Please."

"I'm checking my hair, you dope," Jessie recoiled. "Nerd." Curious, she caught his serious vibe, and slipped onto a high chair. "What's up, Charlie?"

Exhaling slowly, Charlie looked away before finding the strength to meet Jessie's eye. She held her breath and listened, angling her head as if the position would make whatever this apparently momentous news was easier to bear.

Charlie opened with, "There's something we agreed to make public tonight that I wanted to let you know about in advance, so it wouldn't come as a complete surprise to you."

"Ummm...*we* being? You and Josh?"

"No, Jon and Charles and me. I'm telling you because—"

"Oh." She wilted. "Because this has something to do with Josh." Without knowing what was going on, Jessie's heart hit the floor with a dull thud. "Uh, Charlie...why do I have a bad feeling about this?"

"I think you'll have mixed feelings," he said honestly. "Josh might have his own warped perspective, though. You need to be prepared."

Silent, Jessie studied him. Then she broke the quiet with, "You're giving me news that you think will upset Josh. That you're making public tonight. You're telling me because you think he might go off the rails."

"I'm telling you because this might upset him, yes."

"Jesus, Charlie. Are you guys firing him? He loves working on *Sacred Peace*."

"Not him, Jessie. And not exactly firing."

It took her a second to clue in. "Oh, shit. You're letting Shanda go."

"The day she was crying in my office she asked us to release her from her contract. She's agreed to do two more episodes. The writers are going nuts trying to make it work for the show. A search for new cast is going public on Monday."

"Why?" Breathy and barely coherent, Jessie tried to understand. "Charlie... did something happen between Josh and Shanda?"

"Josh has done nothing, Jessie, if Shanda can be believed, but you know she has strong feelings for him. Shanda maintains she can't work with Josh anymore. It hurts too much."

"Oh. Um. That serious, huh?"

"I don't think you're surprised."

"He's an easy man to love, Charlie." Jessie eyed him closely as he bit his lip and regarded her. "That is in no way a dig at you, honey."

"Humph. You suck anyway." Inhaling, Charlie continued, "What I'm worried about with respect to Josh, Jessie, I say to you as a friend, not as Josh's co-star or producer."

She straightened. "You don't need to say it, Charlie."

"He's not the same guy, Jessie. From the first of the season. He socializes, he's happy."

Swallowing, she managed, "I kinda thought I might have something to do with that." Jessie was twisting her fingers together in her lap.

Charlie laid a hand over hers so she would stop the anxious movement. Some old reflex from their long ago intimacies made him want to kiss the downturned pouty corner of her lips, but, inwardly, he laughed it off. "Of course you have something to do with it. You have a lot to do with it, you and the kids. Your husband is the happiest I've seen him in a while."

"And he spends most of his time at work. So obviously a good chunk of his happiness is coming from his involvement with the production."

"It's like this, Jessie." Sighing, Charlie itemized what he figured were the secrets to Josh's contentment these days, as if he needed the right number and combination of keys in order to unlock the deepest, most intricate parts of the man. "First, he likes the part of Bobby. And he's damn good at playing the guy. Bobby's challenging for Josh, and he's the lead. Lots of screen time, which as you know us egomaniacal actors crave. His character has the opportunity for long-term continuity to evolve and grow, unlike short film stints. Second, we've got a fantastic cast and crew. It's like *Drifters*, he says. Everyone's family now. And we've got some of your old *Drifters* crew, recruited via Jonathon, so that helps."

Jessie winced, and lifted a hand to twist a ringlet in her hair as she sucked in her stomach and listened. Unfortunately, since her hair was swept up for the evening, which she had forgotten in her quest to listen carefully to Charlie, she had no choice but to let her hand fall uselessly back down to her lap. *Drifters. I miss everyone*, she thought with a pang. *I miss that cast and crew family feeling.*

"Third," Charlie was saying, "Josh has the ranch close by, and you and the kids with it. He's got a good life going here, Jessie."

"And four, he has Shanda, a woman he works intimately with who has become his very good friend. Who worships the ground he walks on."

"Shanda is leaving, Jessie, because she and your husband have grown far too close. This is going to suck for you to hear, but you should know they spend hours together on set. Lunch, lighting…they're always together."

With a small shrug, Jessie shrank in her seat and challenged Charlie. "So this is you getting back at me for my unintentional dig earlier, is that it?"

Choosing to ignore her comment, he made a small *pfftt* sound and dove in a little further. "Shanda had the good grace to come to me and admit that things are out of hand for her. She's afraid of what might happen if…if…" He sighed and let the sentence drift off.

"Ah. If Josh and I mess up again. And he needs a warm body."

"He's going to be lost without her around set, Jessie."

"Love your honesty there, Charlie. Thanks for that. Just what I needed to hear."

Reaching forward, Charlie gave Jessie a gentle hug. "Would you rather I lie? Like I said, I'm certain Josh has done nothing other than nurture what has become a strong friendship. But he'll be angry, Jess. At her for leaving, at us for letting her go, at himself for feelings I'm sure he doesn't even really understand, and—"

"At me for getting in the way." Sitting taller, rigid, she blinked and stared him down.

"Not just that." Frustrated with having to spell it out for her, Charlie paced in a circle, pinched his bottom lip, and added, "You slept with Matt, who was your good friend."

"Yes," Jessie whispered, slumping over slightly. "And I lost him forever because of it. But he is a helluva lot more than just a good friend to me, Charlie. He always has been, since…well, pretty much since the Deuce McCall days."

Charlie reached forward and entwined his fingers in hers. "So Josh will be angry at you for having had what he has the decency not to pursue. He'll lose her for doing nothing, in his eyes."

"S'okay, Charlie. My husband found out I was a whore a few years ago. We're so over that now." Tears pricked at her eyes, but Jessie remained stock still, one knee folded over the other, her spine straight and long again, and her elegant manicured nails, the fingers held by Charlie, in her lap.

"Oh, for Christ's sake, Jessie. That's not what this is about." Yanking his hand away from hers, he said, "Get over your princess syndrome. Not everything is about you."

"Ah, but this is. Shanda's really leaving the show because she doesn't want to see me get hurt. She doesn't want to take that chance."

"You're very perceptive for a whore." Charlie's attempt at lightening the mood failed miserably, crashing to the floor with Jessie's heart.

"So that's what this is really about. And that's why Josh will really be angry. His anger will be pointed at me. Wow, that makes Shanda a very honorable person, Charlie. Not much wonder Josh is crazy about her."

"As a friend, Jessie." Charlie's shoulders sank. "The whole production team is crazy about her. She's a very special lady."

"Oh."

The small voice alerted Charlie to something he hadn't really considered. Now, he kicked himself and tried to backpedal. "No, Jessie, don't…Look, you cannot take all of this on your shoulders. That wasn't my intention."

"You just told me the entire production is going to mourn her loss. Essentially because of me." Slowly, Jessie slipped off the high chair. "Lovely. Fucked up Jessie fucks up the entire *Sacred Peace* dynamic. I'm not even on the show and yet I managed to fuck it up."

She started to brush by Charlie, but he grabbed her elbow and stopped her, although she didn't look at him. "Jessie, wait," he tried, but she raised a hand to stop him from speaking.

"Sometimes, Charlie, you know what?" Jessie pondered what to say. Finally, she swung around so she could meet his worried gaze straight on. "I get really, really tired of being the reason everyone else hurts. D'you ever think…that maybe I'm not worth it?"

"Not for one second, sweetheart." Charlie held her arm and lost himself in those sweet pale ice-eyes until Jessie pulled her arm out of his grip, moved forward, and pushed open the door.

"Well, I do," she breathed, and made her way to a private cubicle in the public restroom for a silent, lonely reprieve before forcing her feet to spike their high-heeled way across the floor back to her table.

Chapter Thirty-four

*B*y then, Josh had clued in that something was up, because Charlie was back at the table, not making eye contact with anyone but Jane, who was rather sympathetically studying him. So when Jessie sat down with an oversized pout and a rather ungracious thump that didn't in any way, shape or form suit the chic Zuhair Murad, he grabbed her hand and asked her what was up. At his urgent tone, the rest of the table went quiet.

Jessie glared at Charlie, pissed at him for ruining a night that was already historically overwhelming and painful in nature.

In the end, it was Shanda who spoke up.

"Josh," she said, a slight tremor in her voice giving her nerves away. "I'm guessing that Charlie just told Jessie something that might…well, that might upset you." She glanced over at Charlie, her blonde curled bob daintily highlighted by the overhead chandeliers, her stunning red dress with its sweetheart neckline perfectly accenting her small breasts. "Am I right?"

Charlie had no answer beyond a pissed-off, sorrowful stare.

His look alone alerted Jessie to how much Shanda meant to *Sacred Peace*. Growling under her breath, she furrowed her eyebrows, sank deep into her chair, and stared at her strappy heels.

"What?" Josh asked, rather annoyed at being left out, that people at the table seemed to know what the hell was going on while he was left in the dark. Kayla and Jacob seemed equally confused, but even Joseph was contrite and staring uncomfortably at his feet.

"I'm…I'm done in a couple of weeks." Once the words were out, Shanda shut up. Her throat had closed over and she had nothing more to say. There

261

was, in fact, nothing more to say anyway that could possibly ease the angst her departure was causing for everyone, including herself.

"What do you mean done?" Josh had forgotten Jessie was even at his side.

Charlie watched her anxiously as Jessie closely observed her husband's reaction to news that she knew would hurt him.

Apologetic, her shoulders curving slightly forward, Shanda couldn't help laying a hand on Josh's thigh, which, from Jessie's hyper-interested perspective, did not go unnoticed. She raised her eyebrows and frowned as Shanda struggled to find her voice.

"I mean...I mean I can't work on *Sacred Peace* any more. With you."

From diagonally across the table, both Jacob and Kayla waited for Josh to clue in as to why. Both were well aware of the attraction Shanda had for Josh. It was old news, and it was something that had been talked about the few times the couples had gotten together over the past few months, although always in Jessie's company, and never to Josh's face. Now, they saw him pale.

"You'll find someone else," Shanda was saying just as the emcee for the evening took the microphone, leaving the table hanging in an uncomfortable silence.

Sitting back, staring at the charismatic dreadlocked Jamaican emcee but not hearing a word he was saying, Josh couldn't look at Jessie. He understood now why Charlie had taken her aside. It was to prepare her, in case he, Josh, lost it. To let her know that he would, on some level at least, blame her for his loss of Shanda. Unknowingly to him, too, Charlie was right about the flood of mixed emotions that suddenly soaked Josh's body as if he were a sponge. There were so many things running around his brain and heart now that he almost couldn't breathe. The blood pressure pounding in his ears didn't help, nor did the sudden wave of nausea rolling around in his belly.

Shanda had come to mean something to him. She wasn't just a co-star. She was a good and trusted friend, one Josh looked forward to seeing each day after he kissed his wife and children goodbye and made the drive to the set. Shanda was a happy voice, a steady wisdom, and an even-tempered, attractive co-star whom everyone adored. In the world of actors, many of whom had anxious hang-ups and the need for constant praise and attention, she was a rare and coveted individual.

In many ways, she was Josh's Matt.

Jessie's eyes were locked on Josh's left thigh. Shanda's hand was still there, and Jessie noted that Josh was now wrapping his fingers tightly around hers. Charlie noticed too, and cleared his throat, hoping Josh would look at him and clue in, but Josh was now just in some confused, angry place in his mind. He was so accustomed to Shanda's presence nearby that the fact that he was holding her hand didn't even compute. He didn't let go until the first course of his meal arrived, and then most of the table ate in silence.

When Jessie was summoned to the green room to warm up her voice an hour later, she was only too happy to go. But by then her mind was a maze of whispered hurts and harried accusations, and she was less than thrilled to take the stage to sing ballads in such an anxious state.

But take the stage she did.

The first song was hell, but she got through it.

Six bars into the second ballad, she waved a hand to Christian at the grand piano to her right. "No, no," she demanded. "Stop." Rising from a tall, cushioned stool near the front of the stage, Jessie threw a look of apology to Christian, and another to the full band and the backup singers behind her.

The audience fell into a shocked silence. Everyone present realized this was not the norm for a Jessie Wheeler show. At Jessie's vacated dinner table, which Jacob was about to also leave to hit the green room to warm up his voice, everyone froze. Josh met Charlie's eyes. *What the hell?*

Wide-eyed, Charlie just fidgeted. *No clue,* he gestured with raised hands.

Jessie was quiet for a moment before she started to speak. Even the servers on the ballroom floor stood as still as statues as her words started to emerge, slow and subdued at first, until she built some confidence in what she needed to say. At Charles and Deirdre's table, desserts were being consumed. Every spoon was lowered, and Charles grasped his wife's hand. This couldn't possibly be good.

There was one more person watching, from an Internet stream in an aged stone hotel in quaint old Montreal.

Matt.

Jessie's beloved Matt.

If Jessie knew he was viewing the concert part of the fundraiser, she may have chosen her words differently. Because what she said impacted him greatly.

She started by holding up three fingers. "There are three things I know well now, at this point in my life. One is friendship, one is love, and the other is loss."

As the room took that in, a low rumble acknowledged that most people in the expansive ballroom knew Jessie's story. Some glanced over at Josh, and watched his uncomfortable gaze never leave his wife's face, which was lit by a soft pale light that left a gentle shadow melting over the stage floor behind her.

Her eyes were glistening, partly from the light, and partly from emotion, Josh knew. Jessie's first song had been a love song she had written for him, that she often sang in his honor. It seemed it was that song that set her on this track, as if she needed to explain some things about it in order to continue to pleasure the wealthy patrons with her sensuous and loving voice.

He raised his chin and listened.

"In my life I have known great friendships," she was saying. "But they took me a while to find. Now, many of my friends are scattered around North America. I still see them, I'm still in touch with them. Mostly, that is," she added tenderly, and if she dared, she would have said Matt's name. "I have known and received great love, starting with a boy in my teen years who I lost in a very bad way. In the most horrific of ways."

Looking down, Jessie went back there, to the house on Tradd Street in Charleston where Deuce McCall heartlessly killed Sandy, her first love, in front of her. Josh saw the wave of pain cross over her, and so did Jacob and Charlie and Charles and Dee. All of them were poised to vault to her aid. But she was stronger now. Jessie raised her chin and continued as, behind her, Christian sat rigid and poised, ready, at her cue, to re-count her in to the next planned melody.

"The next boy I loved—a man—was everything a woman dreams of for her lifetime love." She smiled sadly down at Charlie, whose concerned face she could almost but not quite make out in the dim light. "But I wasn't accessible to him and I lost him too. Today he is a cherished friend."

Before her, Charlie exhaled slowly as Jane exerted a gentle pressure on his nervous, sweaty fingers.

Jessie paused and licked her lips before she found the nerve to seek out Josh in the capacious space. He was sitting stock still, frozen, afraid to breathe. Behind the table where Jessie's eyes couldn't go, Shanda grasped his hand when she saw Josh's wife's eyes light upon his apprehensive gaze.

"The next man I loved took me over the edge in every way possible. I'm still there with him. I will always be there with him, hovering over that edge trying to hang on no matter what the world decides to throw at us. What we have was built on a deep, abiding friendship and mutual respect for the tough times we'd both been through in our lives. Our love was, and is, anchored in truth and honesty. It's not a Hollywood thing. We fight. We make mistakes. But I cannot imagine my life without this man in it. I cannot imagine raising our three children without him by my side. Yet..."

And she looked at Jacob. "Yet there were times in our life together when we had to walk away from each other. And then came my island to float on. Sweet, sweet Jacob."

Josh winced, and Jacob swallowed as Kayla's grip on him tightened. Charlie would have been amused if he had some idea where Jessie's moving monologue was going, but as it was he just stared at her, entranced, and listened.

"Jacob and I are passionate, musical soul mates. We write amazing tunes together, as you will hear when he joins me in a bit. I will love him til the day I die. But I've learned, the hard way, that there is a limit to my love for him. A physical limit. It hurts like hell at times, at least it used to, but I know that sometimes when it comes to love there are lines that have to be drawn in the sand. So I have a line. And Jacob's on the other side."

A slow Yoga breath and a count of seven preceded Jessie's next statement to her captive and breathless crowd. "There is one other man I love with a desperation and pain that will never leave me. His name is Matt, and he was my security, right from the very beginning, when Charles and Deirdre Keating took me in and started me on this incredible journey."

Another low rumble took over the room, only this one increased in intensity and length. Josh fought the urge to stand up and run. Shanda gripped his hand with a viselike strength.

On stage, letting her gaze land on Shanda this time, Jessie continued in a hushed tone. "Matt was with me for several years. Next to my husband, he is my best friend. He is my soul mate in so many ways. He took care of my family's safety for years at great risk of losing his own. In New York," she paused, struggling to retain control of her emotions, "Matt leapt in front of a gun and took a bullet for me. With no regard for his own life."

Again, Jessie glanced down at her fancy sky-high heels, and took a few deep breaths as she struggled to get out what she needed to say. Clearing her throat, she reached for enough strength to continue. Gripping the microphone, she refocused on Shanda. "Matt's dedication to me and to my family knew no bounds, and evolved into the most beautiful, rewarding, unequalled, steady friendship of my life. I am stubborn, I can be difficult, and I can be a real handful."

A small titter filled the room like a wave, undulating, rippling, falling.

Jessie smiled, but there was a wet sheen across the diaphanous eyes now. Still, she held on and raised her shoulders high. "Friendship," she whispered into the microphone, "became love." The room buzzed a little louder now. Josh shrank into his chair. "And then love became loss because I crossed that imaginary line in the sand. And I had to let go."

The audience fell silent.

"Matt is no longer in my life," Jessie continued, stronger now, still holding Shanda in her gaze. "And I miss him. I miss him every second of every day. I miss the friend who put up with me even though sometimes I behaved like a spoiled princess. Who took a bullet in his shoulder and whose wife left him…because he spent so much time watching over me. I crossed a line and it ended a beautiful friendship. I crossed a line and lost the one steady person in my life who I could always depend on. That kind of friendship is rare. It's a deep kind of love. And it's worth holding on to."

At that, Jessie left the room reeling while she stepped back. After a moment, she glanced back over her right shoulder at Christian, and nodded to him. He took a quick scan around the stage to signal the other musicians, and counted them in. A light touch on the ivory keys set the music back in motion, and undercut the heavy emotion now layered in the grand ballroom like a hazy fog. It took until the end of the song for the fog to lift, and even then it just settled up near the ceiling, above the wealthy patrons, above Charles and Deirdre and Jonathon and Giselle, above Charlie and Jane and Jacob and Kayla, and above Joseph. And most of all, above Josh and Shanda, who quite clearly understood Jessie's message, but who were powerless to know how to deal with it in practical terms.

A half hour later, when the privileged guests in the luxurious space were transfixed by the passionate lull of Jessie's ballads, she stepped back from the microphone again as the evening's emcee welcomed Charlie to the stage. Jessie, too, was under the spell of her music, and barely heard what Charlie had to say as he introduced his new television series to the crowd. His announcement about Shanda exiting part way through season one was met with a quiet hesitation. He didn't offer a reason, and the crowd, who had yet to see Josh and Shanda's magic together on screen, was only mildly concerned.

By far the biggest roar of the evening came when Jacob headed towards the portable metal stairs at the side of the stage that the hotel's crew had assembled for the evening's gala event. Jacob and Jessie singing together was a rare and coveted treat these days. Jogging up the half-dozen stairs behind the grand piano, he stopped at Jessie's side, lightly touched her arm, and gave her a tender kiss on the cheek before he took his usual spot at stage left or, from the audience's perspective, to the right of the stage.

Charlie, too, who had welcomed Jacob to the stage on behalf of *Sacred Peace*, leaned in to his old girl for a chaste kiss while Jacob accepted his guitar from a technician and shouldered it.

"Okay?" he asked her, aching to discuss Jessie's earlier public foray into the loves of her life.

"Fine," she murmured, covering the mic and breathing him in, wishing Charlie wasn't one of the folks she always ended up hurting. "We'll talk later, okay Charlie?"

"Okay," he said, studying for the briefest second the sad pearlescent baby blues as they searched his eyes. It seemed all their assembled baggage was playing at the surface tonight.

Jessie took a small step closer to the mic after Charlie's back disappeared down the metal steps. A pensive glance to Jacob, and one to Christian, and she stood ready. As he did in the old days, Jacob would count them in. In the pregnant silence before Jessie heard his husky voice to her left, she peered into the audience and caught Josh's silhouette in the half-light. She couldn't see his face clearly, but he was sitting back now, slightly rigid still but more relaxed than he'd been earlier. His arm was stretched easily across Shanda's shoulders, not tight, just in a casual friendship kind of way, but their hold on each other was obvious.

What must Shanda be thinking? Jessie wondered as Jacob's counting launched the first song. *Maybe she's pretending that my man is hers. Maybe she's ready to sink into a puddle of despair.*

The first song, and Jacob's presence on stage, injected a new energy into the evening. It was the one Jessie and he had written together that first night when she went against Charles' wishes and brought Jacob into the Robson Street studio. Tonight, another guitar player was playing Jessie's part, but she had the lead vocals, and there was always something about sharing the stage with Jacob that elevated her mood and catapulted her into the stratosphere. The only things missing were faded jeans and Jessie's old brown boots.

The song was a slow, almost metal ballad along the lines of Metallica's *Nothing Else Matters,* with pumping guitar and heavy percussion. It had a long intro that gave Jessie time to watch her husband settle deeper into his chair. She wondered if he could see her eyes—their table was close, and she was bathed in light. Jessie sent him a barely perceptible nod, and a quick gesture—the *I love you* she knew Josh relied on at the end of her performances. She knew he got it, because Josh shifted in his seat and sent her a right-handed salute. It was comforting to see that sign from him as he sat there with his left arm draped across his co-star's shoulders. It was an affirmation, a link, a trust in who they were; it was a trust in their heart to heart connection that meant it was okay to sit there in the company of a good friend without threat, without risk of rising jealousy or anger.

Jessie half-smiled at him before she stepped forward and grasped the microphone. As she lost herself in this new song, knowing that images of Josh and Shanda as *Sacred Peace's* Bobby and Olivia were dominating the screen behind her, she was aware of Jacob's presence at her left, and of the others on the stage—Christian, the band, the back-up singers—but Jessie let their presences fade. Letting the music swallow her whole, she disappeared. Josh always said she was raw on stage, that she left nothing behind, and tonight's songs for *Sacred Peace* were more raw than usual. They suited the show, which was gritty, a contemporary western that often had Jessie's husband out on location, sometimes on horseback, although of late, with his injuries, more often than not in an old range rover.

Harmonizing with Jacob was one thing; it was easy. Jessie and Jacob intuitively knew what the other was thinking on stage, and it gave their songs a fine-tuned perfection. What was tough for Jessie was going to a necessary 'dark place,' to a rare, red, visceral hole deep in her soul where she could draw from old pain. She needed that connection in order to do the heavy ballad justice. This was the raw edge Josh recognized in Jessie's music, which set her apart from other, more average singer-songwriters. Metaphorically in the feral music tonight were unwelcome rough hands on her body—Deuce McCall's and Jessie's stepfather's. Also edgy and raw were Jessie's helpless screams the night Sandy was murdered; the agony of aching for Josh and her children when Morgan and Nadia took over their lives; the loss that left her numb that Vancouver pink dawn when Josh came home smelling like sex and told her he was flying out to Toronto.

Jessie was soaking her lyrics with deep pain tonight. Those who knew her best easily discerned the difference in this song compared to her earlier, lighter love songs. They knew their girl well. What they were seeing and hearing in the ballad with Jacob was a new, savage ache.

The rest of the audience was clueing in too, that they were experiencing something rare, something wild and untamed. They could see the stunning images behind Jessie and Jacob, all timed to the music—Josh as Bobby on horseback galloping into a shot, drawing the reins, his long hair windblown; meeting Shanda inside the Sheriff's office, kneeling by a body to investigate a murder, Josh as Bobby struggling to adjust to his wife's death…

There were more, too. And they were all stunning, offering a glimpse into the *Sacred Peace* TV series and into the rough, rugged landscape of the Alberta heartland that had everyone present sitting on the edges of their seats wanting more.

Combined with the music, those who understood that what they were seeing was special were elevated to new heights that left them with suspended breaths and a resurgence of all their own old hurts and pain. It was as if Jessie opening herself to them in such a primeval way was making all of them see her, and their own souls, in a whole new light. Sharing her own pain was lending a depth of emotion to the show featuring her husband that was, to the more astute patrons present, both shocking and serenely beautiful.

Josh was transfixed. By the middle of the song, Shanda was sobbing.

Near the end of the heavy ballad, a primitive wailing guitar took the room by storm. It was Jacob, doing his thing, his guitar resting against his thigh as he made it literally sing, as he encouraged the most perfect, satisfying notes from it. He was playing an instrumental bridge at this point, so Jessie turned halfway around so she could watch the screen. She was just in time to see the edited clips build the raw sexual tension between Josh and Shanda…or Bobby and Olivia…to see them explode—literally explode—at the song's climax, when Josh shoved Shanda against the wall and brought her to orgasm in front of the crew that first time.

In the onscreen images, as the song peaked, Josh was faking his own climax. His arm was around Shanda, his forearm tensed across her belly. As this was happening, Jacob was playing a 'denouement' of sorts, a few notes after the highest peak. As he picked out the notes, on the screen Shanda turned back to Josh as he sank to his knees and gripped her tightly, both big hands clutching her hips, her desire-dazed eyes locked into his before he let out a low, throaty choking sound and pressed his face into her abdomen.

Watching, what got Jessie the most, was the way Shanda was looking at Josh on screen. Besides desire and her post-orgasmic flush, her face read both shock and surprise. Her expression was truth; an honest realization that the man who just brought her to climax was rare, special. As Jacob's guitar melody sank lower, Shanda, on screen, was almost melting; Josh's chest and back were heaving as he clung to her. A last note from Jacob was perfectly timed with the edited shots—a medium shot of Shanda, tenderly pushing back Josh's hair so she could see his face.

Jessie had to turn back to the microphone to finish the last stanza. It was hard to turn away from Josh, from them, but she had a song to finish for the mesmerized guests spread out below her. So many nameless, faceless persons.

Jacob's fingers on the guitar slowed, and Josh's and Shanda's images faded into the series' title branding and a website address.

When Jessie tried to come out of the depths where the tune and the images sank her, her eyes settled on one set of fingers loosely grasping the mic. Oddly, she wondered how it got there. Letting go, her fingers trailed away slowly, almost one by one, as she tilted her head up to fix Josh in her gaze, to find Shanda completely in his arms, both hands over her face and her shoulders shaking.

For Shanda, it was too much—the images, the music, the love of Josh's life onstage between the Josh she had here at her side tonight…a friend… and the Josh she had at work…her man, in her eyes, even though he was only hers in a fantasy world, as Bobby.

Shanda was leaving a job she cherished and a man she loved.

Watching her, Jessie swallowed and stilled as Josh buried his face in his co-star's hair and whispered softly to her. Raising her chin, she stood stock-still as the applause rang out and the song filtered its way to its melodic, satisfying, and yet somehow unfinished end.

There were two more songs to go. Charlie was back in his seat now, and he caught Jessie's lingering look towards Josh and Shanda. Twisting in his seat, he saw what she saw—the kind of sorrow that comes from an imminent, forever kind of parting. But he couldn't know what she was thinking, which was *Matt Matt Matt I miss you. I miss my friend. So much.*

Jacob saw what was happening and looked to his right as Jessie backed up from the mic and balked. Even knowing her as well as he did, he couldn't discern that it was a combination of Josh and Shanda's connection and imminent parting along with her loss of Matt that was destroying her up here on stage tonight, but he was well aware that heavy emotions were getting the best of her. A glance towards Christian ended up in a shared silent telegraph that Christian knew meant *one minute,* and Jacob stepped over cables towards his ex-lover.

His hand on her elbow jarred Jessie out of the reverie where the feral music, the stunning images, and the unexpected announcement about Shanda had taken her. Jacob's warm breath and the familiar, comforting green apple scent of his hair as he bent to her stirred Jessie. Fixing her eyes on his chest, she reached out and touched him, just because he was here and she could. Eyes moist and sorrowful, she gazed up at the tenderness in his loving cobalt blues, and let him draw her back from the difficult cobwebbed corners of her heart and mind that hurt.

The last two songs went better—it was the first that really brought Matt to mind, because he had stood in the Robson Street studio and listened to Jessie and Jacob premiere the song. It was the day they fought, when she left the studio in a huff. Jessie hadn't seen him again until the night with Miranda at La Casa, the night Matt and Jessie made love. The night Josh was alone, injured and cold, immobile on polished stones, by the side of a creek near their ranch, staring at the dead bodies of his beloved horse and the cougar that felled Blue, as his body spiked with fever and his hope for rescue dwindled.

It was a lot to process.

It was a lot to endure.

Chapter Thirty-five

After the final bows, Jacob placed his arm lightly around Jessie's waist as they stepped down the stairs to the floor below, where Arnie met them and walked the two to their shared backstage room. Arnie closed the door behind them and took up a stance outside, as Jessie slipped back onto the high chair from which she'd faced Charlie earlier, and stared at Jacob, who moved towards her for a tight, friendly squeeze, before letting go and leaning against the counter.

"It's okay, Jessie," he said to her in a hopeful voice he wasn't sure he believed. "I think they're just saying goodbye."

"I know," she agreed, pressing knuckles into the corners of her eyes as she used a foot to propel her around towards him. "I think what got to me is just that I hate goodbyes, you know? I hate them with a passion, Jacob."

Jessie was sitting crossways on the high chair, with her long legs hanging down over one side instead of dangling from the front. She leaned her forearms on the back and laid her cheek on the top arm.

"Matt?" he asked her quietly. "I take it you're referring to Matt."

"Y-yeah. Matt."

"I'm sorry about him. He's one of the good ones."

"I'm sorry too. I miss him."

He paused. "I'd think you'd want to be rid of Shanda." Jacob wasn't accusing, just honest.

"How can I want her to go? Josh adores her. Charlie needs her. She's a friggin' good actor. Jacob? I think it's time I put everyone else ahead of me for a change."

He considered that. "Are you sure about that, Jess?"

"You think I could lose him to her. You're wrong, Jacob. If Shanda takes Josh to bed I'll be right there with them. She'll be orgasming so hard from me that when he goes inside she won't even notice."

"Uh, Jessie. I don't think that's such a good idea—"

"I'm kidding, Jacob. I'm talking metaphorically here. Better the devil you know, right? I'll get to know her so she won't even consider taking my husband to her bed."

"If you say so." He was doubtful, but Jacob remained silent.

After a reflective moment, Jacob reached over to a small bar fridge and opened the door. Retrieving two bottles of Guinness, he laughed. "Someone knows us," he said, raising a bottle like a trophy before twisting off the cap and handing it to Jessie.

"Charlie," Jessie told him. "How much do you want to bet he tipped them off?"

"He probably stashed the Guinness here for himself." Jacob took a hefty pull on his beer and leveraged his butt up on the counter that ran across the back of the small room.

They talked about the set they'd just mesmerized the audience with until a quiet knock came at the door. It was Deirdre, with Charles in tow, coming to offer congratulations on a stunning performance. Wisely, neither brought up Jessie's passionate and touching mini-speech early in her set. Instead, they focused on the incredible *Sacred Peace* tunes. Charles was literally vibrating, counting his new millions, while Dee pooh-poohed him and Jacob laughed at their easy rapport. Jessie remained quietly pensive.

After they left with hugs and waves, Jacob and Jessie finished their beer before heading back out to the main ballroom.

The evening was moving into a relaxed dance mode. Couples traded off partners and moved through the next hour and a half with grace and a calm formality. Throughout the dancing, Jessie looked for an opportunity to talk to Shanda. She found it at the end of the night.

The couples were standing around their table saying goodbye when Jessie brought the farewells to an abrupt silence by saying, "Hey, Shanda, walk with me for a minute? I need to grab a few things from the green room."

Josh sent her a look of warning and a subdued but firmly voiced, "Jessie."

"S'okay, Josh," she told him, squeezing his hand and then letting it go as she started to move away. "I got this."

Shanda paused and tensed, and met Josh's apprehensive gaze before moving. In the end, she took up a solemn stride beside Jessie.

Inside the small room, seeking an opportunity to gather her senses, she asked if she could use the private restroom while Jessie gathered a few things.

"Yes, of course," Jessie replied, and moved around the space grabbing her belongings while Shanda disappeared for a few minutes.

Inside the restroom, Shanda stared at her reflection in the mirror and wondered what Josh's wife was up to. Was she going to utter some kind of threat? *I'm leaving already,* she mumbled to herself. *I'm fixing this. It's done.*

When she finally got up the nerve, she flushed the toilet and washed her hands, then pushed open the door. Looking up as she passed through it, Shanda met Jessie's eyes. She sobered quickly at the hard-pressed lips and concentrated gaze aimed in her direction.

"What?" Shanda asked uneasily, taking a step backwards.

Placing a hand on the back of one of the high chairs, Jessie turned it towards Shanda. "Sit," she demanded.

"Why?" Shanda didn't move.

"Because we need to have a chat, Shanda. Just the two of us."

"I don't think so, Jessie. I don't think there's anything further we need to say to each other."

"Actually, there is." Sighing, Jessie made her way to the counter and leaned back against it.

Shanda remained still. "Earlier tonight, on stage. What you said. Was that for my benefit? Because you should have just saved your breath, Jessie. It doesn't change anything."

"It changes everything, Shanda. You'll see. Just listen, okay?"

A barely perceptible nod followed thirty seconds of silence.

Jessie repositioned her legs, crossing her feet at the ankles, and she dove in. "The thing is, Shanda. I've given Josh enough sadness. Enough...darkness. I want to give him back some light."

Uncertain, Shanda touched her lips nervously and watched Jessie with an air of caution. "I think having you in his life is light, Jessie. You and your children. Period. The bad stuff sometimes comes with the good, right?"

"I've given him more than his share of the bad, Shanda. The whole world knows that."

"So what are you saying?"

"I'm saying you see something in Josh that few people see."

Shanda's tone was sarcastic, as if she was waiting for Jessie to drop a bomb. "What do you think I see in him, Jessie? Why do you think I…love…your husband?" She said the word 'love' as if hoping it would bait Jessie, piss her off, maybe.

The music tonight—Jacob's presence—Charlie's announcement that Shanda was leaving the production…All of it had conspired to bring Jessie to a point where the air seemed thinner, like she'd reached the top of a mountain after months of struggle and pain to get there. It was hard to breathe there, hard to just sit and consider the thin blue air around her without gasping, without choking. But there was a certain peace about it too. There was something sacred at the top of that mountain that said *let it go. Let the worry go. Let the worry down.*

Almost without noticing, Jessie opened a hand and gently turned it over to face the floor. Slightly dazed, she watched as an invisible nothingness dropped from her palm and floated, like dust motes on a downward drift, to the floor.

Her words were robotic, tired. "You love him because you see the broken-hearted part of him. You see all the damage. The invisible scars that encircle his body like tracks from a needle. The visible ones, too. When you made love with him on set, did you kiss the scar on his side, where my stalker knifed him? I'll bet you did. Because you wanted to heal him with your touch. With your lips."

Stunned, Shanda sucked in a breath. That was all the answer Jessie needed.

"You're a good person." Jessie exhaled again, from the top of her lungs, and not completely, so her voice got a little high in pitch. "You're kind, Shanda. You want to put Josh back together. You want to wrap your arms around him, and hold onto him forever to keep him from breaking again. That's what you think of when you see my husband, Shanda. His brokenness, and how you can fix it. That's why you love him."

"I don't...I don't...know..."

"Yeah, you do. You know. It's why he responds to you. Because you have this air of patience and understanding with him, when you're around him. You know how special he is. And how much the world has wronged him. Mostly because of me. Because I let the world believe he hurt me, and because I left Jacob to go back to him. And because who I am and what I do made us targets that destroyed him for a time. That took away an essential trust, and that built walls I don't think will ever come down."

Shanda's whole body loosened up then, as if she were suddenly made of Jell-O. A small moan escaped her lips. "Stop this," she pleaded. "Stop reminding me why I want him so bad." Her eyes glistened as she added, "I know how selfish I am."

"It's not selfish to want to help someone, Shanda. It's selfish to want to leave them when they need you."

A hushed silence filled the room. Outside, muffled sounds reminded the women that the party was ending; the fundraiser had come to its natural close, and hotel staff were standing at the perimeter of the grand ballroom waiting for their guests to depart so they could start the cleanup. Absently, Jessie wondered where the boys were, and Jane. Had Jacob and Kayla left?

She blinked back at Shanda when Shanda spoke, her voice dusky and unsure. "You don't know...where this could end."

"Oh, yes I do. I know the risks. I also know and trust that my husband loves me."

"So if he cheats on you?"

"He won't. You know how I know?"

"Because Josh is better than you. You did it to him, with your security friend. But Josh won't stoop that low." Shanda's tone was biting.

"You're half right. My 'security's' name is Matt. Years, Shanda. For years Matt was there for me. Seven years before I even met Josh, Matt was my constant shadow. He was there for us, for Josh and me, and then for our family. He was my best friend all through my Charlie years, my most steady friend. I hardly even spoke to anyone then, but I spoke to Matt. Not much, but he was always there if I needed something. He became an even better friend after I met Josh, when I started to open up, finally."

Jessie held up a finger. "One night." Choking with emotion, she said it again. "One night, and years of friendship were erased. Gone. A man I love beyond all measure is no longer a part of my life because I took him in my arms and loved him on a night when we were both feeling lonely and lost."

"Josh won't cheat on you, Jessie, unless...unless things go bad with the two of you. Which means if I stay around I still won't have him the way I want to have him."

"You already get him more than I do, Shanda. You're with him all day and half the night too, sometimes. And you know what you give him? You give him friendship and love, which I know he gives you in return. You give him happiness, because he goes to a workplace every day that he cherishes, where Josh is surrounded by love, by people who love him and who he loves back. Josh is no longer shy and quiet, a man who wants to just disappear into the character he is playing so he can hide from all the 'real world' hurts. Where he can hide inside his heartache and sadness. I see how happy he is on *Sacred Peace*. With you. That happiness translates to us at home. You know what you give him, Shanda? You give Josh a safe place to land. A safe place that's exempt from the chaos I bring to his life."

"Jessie...are you...is this for real? Are you actually asking me to stay?"

"I'm not asking, Shanda. I'm begging."

A new silence overtook the room. This one was so intense that although the outside sounds were shuffling in under the door, they were not heard by either of the women inside, who may as well have been facing each other twenty-paces away in a gunfight, waiting, with hands poised, for someone nearby to holler, "Shoot!"

"You're asking a lot from me."

"I'm giving a lot to you. I'm giving you back your friend."

"You're asking me to look but not touch. You have no idea how impossible that has become for me."

"You keep telling me you love him, Shanda. If that's true, if you really do love Josh, then be there for him in a way he really needs right now."

Shanda eyed Jessie quizzically. "Jacob. Am I right? You're referencing Jacob?"

"And Dylan. It's not impossible to be around someone you love and not cross that line."

"But it was with your friend Matt."

"In the end, yes. Like I said, I know the risks."

"I'm sorry, Jessie."

"Not as sorry as I am. For a lot of different reasons."

A weak smile was Shanda's response to that, which came with a legion of understanding. "You, Jessie Wheeler-Sawyer," she emphasized the Sawyer, "are every bit as remarkable as everyone says you are."

"No, I'm really not," Jessie answered softly, the overhead lights in the small space highlighting her pupils and giving them a misty, gauzy aura. "I'm just a woman in love with a man. I would do anything for him. I would do anything for Josh, to see happiness in his eyes every second of every day." Garnering the last bit of courage she had left, Jessie poised a question to Shanda that she was almost afraid to ask, which Shanda already knew was in the cards, but which Jessie needed to voice herself, to affirm that it came from her heart. "Shanda, will you stay on *Sacred Peace*? Please?"

Shanda smiled. "Apparently you will also do anything to make Charlie happy too, huh?"

"Don't forget Charles and Jon. And a crew that adores working with you. And the future audience of this amazing show."

"Okay."

"Okay?"

"Yes. Okay. But I might need to call on you and Jane for some marathon wine binges."

"I'll bring the Haagen-Dazs."

At that, Shanda stepped forward and gave Jessie an effusive hug. "You really are something else. Any other wife would want me tarred and feathered."

"Light and love, Shanda. There's no place in this world for anger and hostility."

In the hallway outside, they found a quiet Josh and a somber Charlie leaning against a wall, heads down and hands in their pockets. Jane was farther down the hall chatting with Deirdre, while Charles and Jon were engaged in serious conversation with Giselle and Joseph. Jacob and Kayla were nowhere in sight.

Jessie stopped ten feet away from the boys, and let Shanda approach them on her own.

Shanda was smiling. Both Josh and Charlie eased themselves away from their leaning post, and watched her with undisguised curiosity. Before she spoke, Josh peeked over Shanda's shoulder at Jessie who, he was rather alarmed to see, looked absolutely drained. It was a look he knew well, which instantly worried him. Swallowing, he straightened.

Shanda's voice drew him back to her. "Josh," she started. "I get it now. I get the whole mystique about your beloved Jessie Wheeler."

"What?" Josh asked with a naïve innocence that further cemented Shanda's adoration of him. "What do you get about her, Shanda?"

Charlie studied her, then turned his face towards Jessie who, now, was leaning side-on against the wall, arms hanging at her sides as if she couldn't muster up the energy to bring them to her chest and cross them. He frowned.

"What I get about her, Josh, is that she loves her men with a deep love that goes beyond passion. That goes beyond desire, and that goes beyond sense and reason. Because she gives them what they need, sometimes at great loss to herself. She went to Jacob when he needed her the most. He took what he needed from her and she suffered for it. And then she forgave him. She gave your security friend, Matt, what he needed, and she lost him. She lost her friend. And tonight, Josh, she is giving you what she believes you need. Charlie, too."

Josh was quiet as he took that in. His answer didn't surprise Charlie. "She asked you to stay."

"She did, Josh. For you."

Biting his bottom lip, Josh couldn't bring himself to look at Jessie. If he did, he figured he would crumble in that very public venue. Charlie went to her instead, clapping Josh on the shoulder of his leather jacket first before he made his way to her and gathered her into his arms with a husky, "Thank you."

Grinning like a schoolgirl, Shanda stood in front of Josh. It only took him a moment to catch up to her as far as his mood went. Laughing, he reached for her and gave her a generous squeeze.

"All right," he said. "We'll be okay. Right?"

"I hope so." She sighed, and relaxed her hold on him. "Joseph's a pretty good guy. Maybe if I get enough sex from him or from some other sexy man I won't be so damn attracted to you. You're likely just a mirage, anyway. All package and no contents." She winked.

"Is that what you really think?"

Josh's eyes were about the happiest Shanda had ever seen them. Smiling, she stood on tiptoes and brushed her lips against his ear. "No," she whispered. "But all of a sudden I have so much respect for your wife that I'm no longer interested in trying to find out." The conversation took a serious turn. "I mean it, Josh. If I'm staying, I'll rewire my thinking. I'll have to. I hope you'll respect that I might need some boundaries. And I might have some tough days."

"I'll be right there with you, Shanda. Because you're right about Jessie. She's 'all that and more,' as they say."

"Take her home, okay? I think she's beat. I'll see you on Monday."

With that, she stepped off down the hall to give Charles and Jon the good news, while Charlie collected Jane and Josh approached his wife.

Josh pulled Jessie into his arms and, slightly alarmed, was surprised at how light and limp she felt to him. "You did a good thing, little one," he murmured into her fancy updo. "I don't know what you said to her, but the entire production will thank you for it. The images on the screen tonight were stunning. The audience was completely transfixed. The world needs Shanda in *Sacred Peace*."

"That was Jacob. Not you. It was his presence on stage, I mean, that left the audience transfixed."

"Ha ha, Jessie made a funny. Nice try." Leading his wife down the hall, one arm gently wrapped around her shoulders, Josh couldn't resist a playful dig. "As if that little runt has any Oscars on his shelf."

"What, Grammys don't count? And I hear he's got a new movie coming up. With Montreal director Denis Villeneuve. He just might catch up to you."

"As if." Josh frowned, and looked down at her. Jessie was forcing a smile but it wasn't quite reaching her eyes. "Hey, Jess, are you okay? You look completely done in."

Deirdre echoed the sentiment before Jessie got up the energy to answer. Soon, Dee and Josh escorted Jessie into Charlie's rented limo. Once inside, Jessie hunkered back into the deep leather seat with half-closed eyes and a glass of Baileys and milk. All the starlit drive home, she never spoke. Her mind was elsewhere. Her mind was on Matt.

That's where the top of the mountain took Jessie. It gave her a viewpoint she knew was relative to Shanda and Josh, but it wasn't one she necessarily wanted or felt strong enough to handle after the powerful, emotional evening. As Charlie, Josh and Jane talked quietly, reflecting on the evening, and laughing about texts Carlotta had sent about the kids and their busy evening at the ranch, Jessie stared out of the window and watched the barren Alberta landscape fly by as their driver, with Arnie's steady voice beside him, left the cacophony of the city's multi-colored lights and rushing traffic.

To Jessie, it felt as if she'd been trying to outrun the confusing emotions surrounding Matt's sudden departure. Talking to Shanda, singing those songs—they were a skid to a halt, a slide to a stop, the end of a nightmare and the beginning of remembrance. At one point, Matt's memory was so strong it became completely overpowering. Jessie could smell him, his usual aftershave, the cologne that seemed to imbue his expensive clothing, his musky body-scent. She could see him teasing her, or gently offering wisdom, playing with the kids or, at work, watching every corner with eagle eyes, focusing a serious gaze on Jessie as they walked to or from a stage that meant every nerve in his being was tense, every fiber was on alert.

She almost said his name, almost whispered it there in the car, Matt's essence was so strong tonight. Across from her, Charlie saw Jessie's lips move; he didn't know what she was saying, but her eyes were closed now and he knew she was in another world, in that place deep inside where Jessie retreated when the emotional stakes got too high.

"Josh," he said quietly, gesturing to Jessie.

Raising his eyebrows, Josh looked over at her, and removed his hand from her knee. He placed it around her shoulders instead, which alerted

Jessie to the real world. Josh took the glass of Baileys from her—it was empty by now anyway—and he set it on a glass tray in the limo. "You okay?" he asked her.

In answer, Jessie twisted her body slightly and buried her face in his side, sinking deeper into the seat and wrapping an arm around his stomach. No verbal answer was forthcoming but Charlie and Jane chalked up her disconnected weariness to the intensity of the night and the fear they knew she would hold onto with regard to Shanda's continued presence on the *Sacred Peace* set.

Josh knew better. After what Jessie had said on stage and, likely to Shanda later, he discerned it was the absence of Matt that was setting Jessie off tonight, that was propelling her into a deep, dark, lonely place. There was no jealousy in that thought. Josh took responsibility for his part in Jessie's need for Matt, in the man's essence, in his body. And he also clearly knew how much she was missing him, the man who demonstrated his absolute commitment to her, his unfailing love for her, by diving in front of a loaded gun. For her.

Pulling her close, pressing her to him, Josh's heart ached with the tiny mewl that escaped from Jessie's closed lips. It was an anguished sound of despair.

At home, Charlie and Jane collected their two children while Josh helped them with the kids' things. Carlotta and her sister were already sound asleep, and the security was changing shifts, utilizing trusted crew referred to them from the Albertans on the *Sacred Peace* crew for the switch off.

Jessie managed a wistful goodnight to her friends, but it was slurred from the effort to speak. Charlie nodded towards her as she hugged Jane and padded off, her heels hanging from one hand, towards her and Josh's bedroom. "She's having a spell, Josh. Will you two be okay?"

"Sure, yeah. It was the hospital, the memories...the music, the whole Shanda thing...Matt." He sighed. "I'll keep an eye on her. Sleep will help."

"I'll come by tomorrow, okay?"

The anxious tone to Charlie's voice actually brought a small smile to Josh's lips. He shrugged. "Sure, yeah. Fire me off a text when you two get moving in the morning and we'll plan a ride, if Jessie's okay and if Jane doesn't mind letting you go."

Jane's voice cut in. "He can only go if you take that leather backpack with your gun in it."

"Charlie can wear that and I'll have my scabbard. That cougar attack was rare, Jane. As Jessie always says, we can't stop living our lives because we're scared. We can't let fear run us."

"Just take the right precautions, that's all I'm asking." Jane wheeled in under Charlie's arm. They were outside now, and the kids were settled in the limo, Stella half-awake and rubbing her eyes, and the baby in his carrier. "This man is loved."

Charlie's cheeks turned an interesting shade of moonlit pink as he clapped Josh on the shoulder and turned to usher his wife into the limo.

Josh couldn't resist. With a shy grin he said, "I don't think I've ever seen Charlie speechless before, Jane. Well played."

Her eyes dancing, Jane pecked Josh lightly on one cheek. "You're not the only man who makes women's knees go weak, Josh."

"Yeah, I've learned that the hard way. 'Nite, Jane."

"Goodnight, Josh. Take care of that girl of yours. Extra hugs tonight, okay?"

That sobered him. "Yep. Fer sure, Jane," he mumbled, pocketing his hands as Charlie ducked into the limo behind Jane with a wave and a sleepy goodbye.

Inside, Josh made it to the entrance of the master bedroom before he heard Jessie sobbing behind the closed door of the ensuite bathroom. The house was now in darkness, with the exception of the odd digital numbers here and there announcing the time, like on the microwave or a clock radio, and there was a thin line of blue light from a nightlight peeking out from under the bathroom door. Staring at it, Josh could barely make out a shadow; at least, that's what he thought it was until he realized that what he was seeing was his wife's body, likely in a fetal position on the cool tiles.

Debating what to do, Josh decided to let Jessie have some much needed privacy before he went to her aid. Pulling off his socks and shoes, he pushed them aside, ripped off his belt and stripped down to unbuttoned pants instead of his usual boxers since Carlotta and security were in the home, and he made his way to each of his children's bedrooms. Even from across the open concept space he could hear Jessie's muted grief-stricken cries, and they tore at his spirit that, only that night, was lifted with Shanda's renewed commitment to their series. In the end, after brushing his lips across the top of each beautiful young forehead, and after lifting Emily-Grace's singer-dolly and tucking it under her arm, Josh halted in front of an antique ladies' secretary desk. His laptop was on it.

Flipping open the lid and poking the power button, Josh waited until the screen lit up before he lifted the wooden chair in front of the desk, set it farther back as quietly as he could, and opened his Gmail.

Selecting 'new email,' Josh waited til the window opened and then he started to type in an address. The email application picked up 'Matt Kelly,' filling in Matt's address.

"Hope you haven't changed this, buddy," Josh thought as he considered what to say. In his heart, though, he felt Matt would not have changed his address. Come hell or high water, if Jessie ever really needed to reach out to Matt again, there would have to be a way for her to find him. No way would this address ever change, although Josh was well aware that Jessie and Matt had cut off all communications. Her despair tonight pretty much confirmed that.

Ten minutes later, Josh hit 'send' and exited the email application. With his right hand, he closed the laptop and stood, trying not to screech the chair on the wooden floor. By the time he made it back to the master bedroom, Jessie was half-asleep on the bathroom floor, on her side, completely worn out.

"C'mere, sweet girl," he whispered, crouching behind her so he could lift her. He was building strength in his shoulder, but it still hurt to lift her. Jessie remembered his injuries when Josh groaned as he stood, but he shook his head at her when she tried to protest. "No," he said, carrying her into the bedroom. "I'm fine. Tonight I think you need me for a change."

Whimpering, Jessie leaned her cool cheek against her husband's shoulder, and let him set her down on the bed. Josh reached both hands around her neck and undid the clasp of her designer dress. Pulling down the elegant zipper, he hesitated when he saw new tears form and start to trail down her pale cheeks. At the same time, she averted her eyes from him.

Instinctively, Josh knew his movements somehow were echoes of her night with Matt. A sharp pang almost sucked the breath out of him, but he continued his ministrations anyway, lifting the hem of her dress and pulling it over his wife's head.

Tucking her in, Josh watched her curl up on her side and close her eyes. Sleep would hopefully not be elusive tonight. Jessie would need this time to restore her body and soul. Gently easing into bed behind her, Josh wrapped his body as close around his girl as he could manage.

"Sleep, little one," he whispered to her. "And Jessie…thank you. I love you."

A few minutes later, her even breathing alerted Josh to the fact that Jessie was asleep. He continued to cuddle her anyway, and wondered whether his email made its way to Matt, wherever the man's pain had landed him.

$\mathcal{I}$n his old stone heritage hotel in Montreal, Matt had streamed the entire fundraiser live on the Alberta Children's Hospital's website, then re-watched Jessie's performances numerous times. He knew about the event…because he and Charles were in touch almost every day. Although Jessie was completely unaware, Matt was still on the Keating payroll, coordinating Jessie's security from afar.

Just about to close his laptop to go find a sunrise breakfast after his all-nighter—that had included some good booze—Matt heard a ping that alerted him to an incoming email. Scrolling to it, he was taken aback when he saw that it was from Josh. He paused, one finger hanging over the computer's track pad, before he got up the nerve to try to focus on the fuzzy words.

Matt didn't answer right away. He shut the lid and grabbed his card key to the room. As he strode towards the elevator, he pondered Jessie's performance, and what she said about him. It had hurt to the core to see her, to hear her, to remember their bond and that incredible intimate night and day with her. Time wasn't really easing the pain of his absence from her life, from the life of the Sawyer family in general. Acute twists in Matt's gut came at odd times, like when he saw a woman with 'Jessie-hair,' or a family with small children. Hearing Jessie's music was enough to send him to bed with a bottle of scotch and, lately, Jessie's old brand of cigarettes.

Strolling down the street towards a crepe place he'd discovered that was open 24/7, Matt pushed away thoughts of Jessie as Josh had described her in the email, overcome and sad at her loss of him. That image of her was too painful to bear; not that Josh had gone into any detail, but Matt knew Jessie better than anyone, even Josh. So he was well aware that she was likely in a puddle somewhere. In Josh's arms, he hoped, the second Josh got off the computer.

Should I tell them where I am? he wondered as he banana'd past a keen busker already out on the sidewalk holding a sign advertising 'free hugs.' Free hugs. *I need a whole body, not just a hug.*

Should I tell them where I'm going? Matt and Charles had an agreement. Jessie was not to know exactly where he was, or that he was still in charge of her security. He and Jessie needed distance between them, and that would be hard to maintain if things got tough again and Jessie came flying in to see him.

After inhaling a Spanakopita crepe with lots of wilted spinach and extra feta, topped with a Greek yogurt dip, Matt made his way back to his hotel. He planned to spend most of the remainder of his day in the attached 24-7 bar, which had become a pattern of late, with the exception of his work with Charles, some of which Matt accomplished via Skype, and the few hours he tried to smother his memories of holding Jessie in his arms by taking nameless women to his bed.

Two hours ahead of Alberta time, it was now six a.m. in Montreal. Hesitating, Matt opened the laptop lid and navigated to his email account. Re-reading Josh's email, his shoulders sank. He started to type.

~~~

Jessie was still quiet in the morning. With Carlotta and her sister Helene, as well as Josh in the house, she slept in while they dealt with shushing the kids, and breakfast and dressing. Now, though, she was drying dishes after saying goodbye to Carlotta and Helene, which left a new sad ache in her heart. The women were picked up in the same limo the Sawyers and Deacons had shared last night. They would meet Deirdre and Charles in Calgary, and fly back to Vancouver with Dee. Charles would stay to spend some time in the *Sacred Peace* production office.

Josh was in the barn with Dylan. Jessie could see Emily-Grace bossing David around at a shallow outdoor inflatable pool, which served the family well on blistering hot July days like this one was shaping up to be. The kids weren't in the pool, they were kneeling beside it, floating Barbie dolls around in a motorboat. They had a little city built next to it too, complete with a lunch truck and a parking garage. In short, they were content.

A low *rrrrrrrr* alerted Jessie to the presence of an approaching vehicle. Charlie's newest Porsche. Jessie knew the sound well, plus there was no way the security guy now at the end of their laneway (likely doing Sudoku or checking his iPhone Facebook) would let anyone but Charlie or Arnie, Dan or Sam up to the ranch. No more weird Johns and Marys. No way.

Charlie pulled the sleek little car up next to Josh's King Ranch, and Stella was out and up to the pool before he even eased his tired body upright. Jane and the baby would come along after the baby's nap, which Jessie was grateful for, since the boys were going riding. She knew from experience that Jane's presence would, if not lift her brooding mood entirely, at least relieve it somewhat. Jacob and Kayla were expected by as well, later in the day, *after they drag themselves out of bed*, Jessie thought wryly.

Setting down the plate she was drying, Jessie watched Charlie make his way into the barn. A few minutes later, the boys would emerge and Jessie would have to go take Dylan—pry him from his father's arms, more likely, since the little boy was attached to Josh at the hip and would want to go riding with him. Josh was willing to take him on the ride, by setting him on the saddle in front of him, but Jessie was adamant. Bad enough Josh barely survived a cougar attack on his horse. No way was she taking any chances letting her children go into the woods.

She settled into the rest of the dishes and tried not to dwell on Matt, or her meltdown in the washroom last night and what Josh must have thought of her, losing it like that.

In the barn, Charlie paused by Blue's empty stall and stared at a large framed photo on the back wall. The picture was a close-up of Josh with his right hand on the horse's neck, nose-to-nose, a happy, trusting look passing between the two of them.

"Jessie and the kids hung that while I was in the hospital," Josh told him as he busied himself with saddling Toby for Charlie. With one eye on Dylan, he gestured to the little boy. "Keep an eye on him, will you?" Dylan was seated on top of Josh's chestnut horse, Misty, on the saddle, and he was rifling his hands through the horse's mane while he talked baby talk which, oddly, Misty seemed to appreciate, since she was calm but her ears were alert.

"Yeah, hey Dylan, how are you, buddy?" Charlie's voice was distracted.

He was humbled at the presence of the photograph. The day after Josh was forced to shoot Blue had been a long and frightening one as Charlie and Arnie searched for their friend. An icy fear shot up Charlie's legs at the remembrance of finding the dead horse with a gash in her neck and a bullet in her head, the hungry cougar nearby, also stretched out, lifeless, on the polished stones of the creek bed. To Josh he said, "Doesn't it bug you?"

"What?" Josh looked up from tightening Toby's girth. The horse snorted its disapproval.

"The picture. Being reminded of her."

"She didn't do anything wrong. Blue was a good horse. There was honor in that horse."

"How so?" Charlie laid a hand on Dylan's leg. On top of the tall animal, the busy little guy was moving around a little too much for Charlie's comfort. "The honor, I mean."

"Even after she was bit and I was tossed, she stood as long as her knees would hold her. In between me and that big cat. She could've made her way into the woods to die. Honor."

"I see. Reminds me of someone."

"Yep. Hence the picture. I like it."

A tiny upwards curve formed on Charlie's lips. "Me too," he said simply. "So...she was really out of sorts last night."

"Yep. Didn't get any better after you guys left." Josh didn't have the heart to look at Charlie. He knew what he would see. Hurt and worry. The usual, as far as Jessie's meltdowns were concerned.

Charlie was crushed. "You have a fight?"

"Nooopppee. No fight. No words. A closed bathroom door and a puddle on the floor. I carried her to bed around three."

"Oh. All because of Shanda, Josh? I don't know why she'd ask Shanda to stay if she was that scared you were going to fuck her over."

"Nothing to do with Shanda. Not really, when you strip away the layers, anyway." Josh finally got the horse's saddle and stirrups adjusted. Turning to face Charlie, his voice softened. "She's missing Matt. He was her shadow for years, Charlie."

"Oh. I'm guessing that sucks for you. Knowing that."

"Some, yeah. But I get it. I get how much it hurts not to have him around anymore. Hell, I miss him too. The asshole." Slapping Toby gently on the rump, Josh moved to Dylan's big horse and took the reins. With his left hand, he reached for and gave Charlie the leather back-packer with the short-barreled Winchester and axe in it. "Put this on. You do remember how to use the thing, right?"

"A backpack? Who the hell do you think I am?" Charlie grinned and worked the backpack over his shoulders. With his free left hand, Josh grabbed it and adjusted it.

"The gun, loser."

"Got yours?" Charlie sobered as he spotted Josh's other gun sticking out of the scabbard by his saddle. "All right. We're good. What about this fella?" He gestured towards Dylan, who stared at him implacably.

"I go widing too," Dylan told him from his mighty perch.

"Daddy will ride you around the barnyard for a bit, Dylan, then Momma will come get you, okay? Jacob and Auntie Kayla are coming by later, and so's Jane with baby Lucas."

An angry pout washed over Dylan's face and he crossed his arms. "Dywan go widing with Daddy and Chawwie."

"Nope. Not this time, buddy." Josh's heart swelled though, and he grinned at Charlie. "I can't interest the other two in riding," he said by way of explanation, as Charlie laughed outright.

"This one's your ranch buddy, I take it," he said, following Josh out to the barnyard with a set of reins and a big, lumbering animal behind him.

"Right down to the worms," Josh joked, pointing to their sprouting garden. "Although I admit, David likes the worms too. But he has no interest in the horses. Dylan and I do the feeding rounds when I'm here. Don't we, buddy?"

Dylan's frown turned into a happy smile. "Yep. Me and Daddy."

Laughing, Josh hoisted himself up into the saddle behind his son. Gathering the reins in his hand, he looked back at Charlie. "We'll just go around the yard a few times. Make yourself comfortable on that beast."

Secretly, he was hoping Jessie would see him and come out to get Dylan so he wouldn't have such a big scene with Dylan when he tried to get him off the horse. Jessie's soft manner with the children was something to behold. Rarely did she lose her temper with them, although they did frustrate her from time to time. But usually she just walked away and settled her nerves rather than raising her voice and fighting with them. She would be able to soothe Dylan down and away from the horse, although Jessie had told Josh that Dylan always waited with baited breath for his daddy to return from his rides.

They jogged around the yard and a ways up the main trail three times before Jessie finally came outside, her hands in her back pockets, and flip flops on her feet. She was wearing one of those backless halter-tops that stopped Josh's heart every time he saw her in one. Glancing at Charlie as he reined the horse back towards the barn, Josh couldn't suppress a grin. Shaking his head, he chuckled. "Charlie's still a sucker for your momma, too, Dylan," he said. "Look at him. He can't take his eyes off her."

At the barn, Jessie had reached Charlie on Toby, and was looking up at him while he made small talk about Jane and the baby, who had given them about two hours sleep in total last night, between the time they got home and when the sun came up. She turned to Josh when he approached. They still hadn't talked about last night, and she was still pale and quiet.

Josh dismounted before fetching Dylan from Misty's saddle. Emily-Grace saved the day by calling to her youngest brother. Dylan squirmed down and went running over to the other kids.

From his nearby vantage point, Charlie watched Jessie and Josh. It couldn't be easy for her, letting him go off riding like this after what happened months earlier, but at least Josh wouldn't be alone on this ride. There was something else at play here now too, though, and Charlie knitted his eyebrows together while he tried to figure it out. Josh still had one hand around the reins of his horse, but he was approaching his wife with a small smile that seemed almost peaceful. Jessie's lips were curved downwards. She was still upset, apparently, and not her sort of usual happy self.

With his free left hand, Josh touched her elbow. "Hey," he said, too quietly for Charlie to understand anything but his movements and expressions. "He's in Montreal."

Jessie's lips parted. "Wh-what?" It took a moment for Josh's meaning to sink in.

"He's in Montreal, and last night he watched you sing. Streamed it. He's been drifting, but Jessie—he's booking a place in P.E.I. til the end of September. On your little island. To heal. Like we did."

"Matt?" The name was barely audible. Jessie tilted her head to the side while she said it, and her eyes deepened into a wet, saturated ice blue. "Really, Josh?"

"Yeah." His smile got wider. "Every gorgeous Prince Edward Island sunset Matt sees will have your name on it."

Struggling with something appropriate to respond to him with, Jessie swallowed and reached for her husband's hand. "I'm sorry," she whispered to him.

Josh shook his head slowly from side to side. "I'm not," he said softly. "He saved your life, Jessie. If it weren't for Matt…" There was no point in completing the sentence. They both knew what he was saying. Josh touched her cheek with his gloved hand. The cracked leather reins tickled her, and smelled like home. "If it's not going to be me by your side…well, I'm glad it was someone who really loves you. That's all."

Chewing on her lip, Jessie stepped forward and wrapped her arms around her husband. "God, I love you," she breathed.

Charlie had to look away. He laughed lightly, though, at where life had brought them since that momentous day when he first met Jessie at his father's Downtown Eastside workshops.

"Love you back, little one. Always and forever, remember?"

"Y-yep. You got it, Josh. Be careful today, okay?"

"We will." With one last kiss on her forehead, Josh swung up into the saddle. "Give us a couple of hours."

"All right." Sighing, Jessie blew him her usual post-performance kiss, and Josh grinned before urging his horse forward.

Charlie was right behind him. As he passed Jessie, he said, "You two are absolutely sickening. You just make me sick." He was laughing happily.

Brightening, Jessie waved him off.

Matt. He was in Montreal. And he was heading to, of all places, Jessie's beloved healing island on the east coast.

A load lifted off her chest, and she felt like she could breathe again. She sent Matt a telepathic note.

I miss you. I miss you, and I love you. Stay safe.

In Quebec City, two hours east of Montreal, Matt took his foot off the gas pedal. One of Jessie's ballads had just come on the radio. *I miss you and I love you* was its message. He could hardly drive for the tears that filmed over his eyes, but he used the back of his hand to wipe them away, gripped the wheel, and envisioned the glorious Technicolor Prince Edward Island sunsets that were calling him towards Jessie's much-loved home.

Chapter Thirty-seven

*T*wo weeks later, Jessie was wrangling kids and sorting out food and drink that was quickly taking over every spare inch of space in the ranch's kitchen. She and Josh were hosting a gathering at the ranch that had started on Friday night. Today was Sunday, and they were capping off the weekend with an outdoor bonfire. The weather was perfect, not blistering hot, just summer-comfortable, and the annoying bugs were tolerable with strategic placement of citronella candles. Even the kids were cooperative, right down to Jane and Charlie's bouncing baby boy, who ate, slept and cried like the model child Charlie always joked that he was.

Their guests were special—Jacob and Kayla had flown in from Vancouver for the weekend and were bunking in Canmore with Charlie and Jane. But they were lowest on the totem pole of this gathering. The main event was a *Drifters* cast reunion. Maggie was here, from New York, with her regular man John in tow. Carter and Ashley had arrived a week earlier, since Charlie and Jon had put their heads together and cast Carter in a supporting role as a regular on *Sacred Peace*. Carter, with regular visits from his L.A. lady, was living in a Calgary condo but planned to spend as much time with Josh and Jessie at the ranch as possible, to help 'exercise the horses,' he told them. Sue-Lyn had flown in Friday at noon with her new girlfriend Leia. But of course the highlight was Steve's arrival with the sweet, gentle Sophie and their two boys, Caleb and Cole. They came in Friday around dinnertime on the Keating jet, only days after moving back to Vancouver once Steve's latest project wrapped up in the states.

Jessie had been watching the lane all morning for Josh's King Ranch to swing in. Josh had gone to work early Friday morning and was bringing Steve and Sophie and the boys back with him that night. When the truck finally pulled up and drifted to a stop in its usual spot by the barn, Jessie went running. Steve didn't disappoint. Grabbing her by the waist, he swung her around and hollered in her ear until, laughing, she had to tell him to stop or she'd be sick. Sophie, too, was a blessing to see on their Alberta property, all dainty and pretty and pink and pale.

The weekend was crammed with wild kids and carefree adults and now, tonight, the mood was a little mellow, infused with a combination of exhaustion and a sense of impending departures, which would happen scattered over the next day. Already all of them were feeling the loss of each other. There was just no comparison for the friendships the group had built up over their time at *Drifters*, and the ensuing heartaches and challenges that time wrought.

They left the older generation to their own party. Jonathon and Giselle and Charles and Deirdre were back in Vancouver for the weekend, attending an industry party for producers that Charlie was skipping to be with his friends in the Kananaskis.

Midway through the evening, with the smaller children tucked in bed, and Carlotta and Helene back to watch over them, Jessie looked over at Jacob and Kayla to spy Emily-Grace snuggled up in a light blanket in Jacob's lap, her head bent in conversation with Stella on Kayla's lap. All four were laughing and carrying on about something that Stella, who had a real 'Charlie-like' flair for the dramatic, was telling them. Jessie discerned it had something to do with the guitar lessons she'd given to the two girls earlier that morning. Kayla was looking at Jessie and pointing a finger, and it seemed there was some kind of challenge about the dancing she'd done with the girls the night before at the Deacon place in Canmore. Some kind of lighthearted rivalry between the students and the teachers seemed to be happening.

Watching them, Jessie felt removed, as if she was on the outside looking in. It seemed that never had there been such sheer happiness on the faces of Jacob and Emily-Grace. Always, even in the New York days, there was a price on the bits of happiness they took from each other. Always there was a sadness, a loneliness, a sense of loss, a sense of impending doom. Only now, with

Josh and Jessie together and their family reunited, and Jacob safely a part of the picture in a way nobody expected, was their happiness full and complete.

Of course a lot of that had to do with Dylan, and Josh's acceptance of Jacob as a full and equal partner in the child's rearing. There was only one complication besides distance, as far as all of the adults responsible for Dylan were concerned, and it came up now when Emily-Grace cried out and held up Kayla's left hand.

"What will Dylan call you now?" she asked in her effusive little girl way. "Like, stepmother? Or are you still his aunt?"

Kayla had just slipped on a ring she'd tucked carefully away in the pocket of her light summer jacket. Now, she waggled it in front of the gang who, thanks to Emily-Grace's earlier exclamation, were now all paying attention. She was rushed by the women in the group, all except Jessie, whose eyes were lost on the happiness lining Kayla's face.

Next to Jessie sat Josh. Their eyes met and he smiled. Kayla had bloomed over her months with Jacob since they met up in Summerside, P.E.I. during the workshop tour, and she was radiant. *How can I get in the way of that?* he seemed to be asking Jessie. *I've never seen her this happy.*

A blue melancholy washed over Jessie as she took his hand. She could feel Jacob's eyes on her now, watching, waiting, wondering, and she was afraid to look at him for fear of what she might give away. Always, always, always he would be her musical soul mate and her past lover, at times in her life when she needed his love and understanding. Did it make sense for him to end up with Kayla? To be happy with Kayla? Hell, yeah. It was a perfect match in Jessie's eyes. The union had already brought Dylan back into his life in a way that Josh approved of. And…it kept Jacob in Jessie's life, too, at a safe distance that left no room for any more sexual entanglements, and which helped alleviate some of the horrific, soul destroying guilt Jessie carried with her since leaving Jacob for Josh after the Nadia standoff in NYC. Pregnant with his child, in fact.

There were a lot of emotions at play, but the overriding one, from Jessie's perspective, was sheer joy.

Swallowing past the cotton suddenly stuck in her throat, she finally allowed her gaze to drift over to Jacob, who was at a twelve o'clock to her three o'clock, as far as their campfire circle went. The cobalt blue eyes she would always deeply love were tinged with an orange hue from the flames of their cozy fire, just like on that first night years ago in Scotland when Jessie figured out his difficult guitar bridge for him. He was that youthful twenty-six-year-old guy again, only wiser and more hardened by life, and much less pouty and lonely. The peace in his eyes stretched over the fire and enveloped Jessie, who closed her eyes for a few seconds, raised her face to the starlit heavens, and whispered, "Thank you." Talia crossed her mind, as she knew it did Jacob's then too. Sweet, kind Talia, whose last thoughts only seven months earlier were that she could never fully have Jacob because his heart belonged to someone else.

Rising, Jessie made her way past Josh's knees over to Jacob. Easing down behind her daughter on his lap, she wrapped her arms around his neck and breathed in the familiar and much-cherished green apple scent, while Emily-Grace jokingly complained and while the smile on Kayla's face almost split her in two.

"So happy," Jessie murmured in his ear, her cheek tickled by his curls. "You did real good, Jacob Ryan. Loving a Sawyer is the ultimate reward. I promise you."

"You told me before that there would be crazy fights." He was chuckling as he held her close.

"And crazy make-up sex," she whispered back. "The fights will be worth it. Ah, Jacob. I can't tell you how sweet it is to have you back in my life. In our lives. Forever."

"My fans are really gonna hate me now," he grinned. "But I don't give a shit. I don't care if I have to leave this crazy business forever."

"Liar," Jessie laughed and sat back on his lap, cradling her daughter against her belly. "You have a film job starting next month. Apart from that, you're not going anywhere else except on a mini-tour with me while we promote *Sacred Peace* for these other doofuses." She nodded behind her towards Charlie and Josh.

"I would still go anywhere with you, Jess. Only," he grinned and grabbed Kayla's hand, "this dancer comes with us. Always. Deal?"

"Best dancer I've ever worked with."

Kayla let go of Jacob's hand and high-fived Jessie. "Thank you," she said with a sincerity and love that had Jessie cover her own chest with a happy sigh.

"Truth." Jessie took Kayla's hand and kissed her knuckles. "I'm so happy for you both. Really."

An emotional silence followed, but dark-haired Stella broke it by throwing her hands dramatically out to the sides and saying, "But we still haven't figured out what Dylan will have to call her! People!"

"How about just Kayla?" Kayla suggested happily. "No Aunt, no weird stepmom thing…"

With a final squeeze around her daughter and a kiss on Jacob's cheek, Jessie left them to their discussion. Moving back towards her folding lawn chair, she stopped instead by Josh.

"Hey," she said, reaching up to tuck a big curl behind her ear.

"Hey." Josh's eyes were liquid brown, all flickering melted chocolate in the sparks rising upwards from the campfire. And they were happy. "Need a seat?"

"Well, I have one." Jessie angled her head to the right, glanced at her vacant chair, and bit her bottom lip. Her voice softened tenderly and her blue eyes grew serious. "But it's lonely over there alone."

Widening his knees, Josh patted his right thigh. He opened his arms. "You don't ever have to be lonely again, Jessie," he whispered, his gaze not leaving hers. "Just melt into me."

A small moan got caught in Jessie's throat at the way he said that, and at the way Josh was looking at her now. *For real?* she asked herself. *We can be happy? Together? Forever?*

Easing herself down onto his lap, into her husband's welcoming arms, Jessie ignored the rousing teasing that started from the mouths of all of their friends and which even resulted in a few marshmallows tossed their way. Emily-Grace and Stella quite vociferously hollered a few *eeewwwwwsss*, and Charlie and Steve met each other's eyes and floated off to some happy places in their hearts they hadn't felt for quite some time.

Jessie stayed on Josh's lap, on her side with her face buried in the hollow of his neck, until someone gently poked her with a stick and offered her a marshmallow.

Steve. He had dropped into her vacant chair. She rolled around and laid her back against Josh's chest while Steve popped a marshmallow onto the sharpened stick he was using for roasting. Steve handed her the stick and warned her not to let it catch on fire.

Leaning forward, Jessie found a spot near the edge that was more coals than flame. Skillfully, she rotated the marshmallow until it was an even brown and started to droop. Bringing the marshmallow back towards Steve, she let him maneuver two graham wafer crackers sandwich-like over it. The bottom one had a square of milk chocolate on it.

"You've done this before," he told her and, behind her, Jessie felt Josh's body quake slightly as he chuckled.

"She lost more to the fire than she ate back in P.E.I. that summer we stayed on the north shore," he told his friend. "This one's a fluke."

"That's because you always shook my stick and made me lose focus," she teased him as she laid back against his chest again to eat her S'more. "You're not exactly the easiest campfire buddy to have around."

"Who, Josh?" Rolling his eyes, Steve handed him the stick. "Let's see you do it, smarty pants."

As the good-natured teasing continued, Jessie let herself back out of the conversation and once again become just a happy observer. There was no comparison for the company of the cheerful group gathered around the fire and the sheer joy of their laughter as it drifted upwards on the stillness of the perfect summer night. And there was no comparison for the sweetness of being held by the man who, in Jessie's lifetime, had caused her no end of pain when they weren't together, and who brought her the greatest joy when they were able to put the world's hurts aside and just love each other.

Only one thing—one person—was missing from this equation now, and his absence left a hole in Jessie's soul that may as well have been a bullet's path, its searing pain was so intense.

Matt. Matt, who was now settled into a cottage somewhere on Prince Edward Island. Who was alone, likely staring at the same stars, likely watching the ashes of his own campfire drift off into an endless black sky.

Matt, who, like Jacob, Jessie would always love for his friendship and for his devotion to her when she needed him. Matt, whose pain Jessie could feel from across the country, as he sat alone under Atlantic skies and cooler, sea breezy winds.

I was your downfall anyway, Jessie thought now as a new guilt wrapped itself around her. *I was your bullet. And I ripped you in two.*

She turned her head to the side, and closed her eyes. Josh felt a tremble course through her body as Jessie sank deeper into him, curling marshmallow-sticky fingers around his and breathing in his essence.

"I love you," he thought he heard her whisper.

"I love you back," Josh breathed into Jessie's neck, not knowing that her tender words were meant for more than just him on this warm Alberta evening.

Around them, their circle of friendship seemed complete. Above them, an inky sky winked in beauty as an unknown plane drifted on some mysterious path towards an unknown future.

Far to the east of them, twenty-nine hundred miles away, a lone man told himself it was enough; that one night was enough, the fact that she knew he loved her was enough. The years that were his to watch over her and then her family were enough. Those years weren't without their challenges, no, she was stubborn and she was a child, sometimes, but she was Jessie and so she could be forgiven for the things she did wrong, for the rogue choices she made, which were usually made to protect others. Which were usually made to protect one man, the man she loved beyond all others.

Josh Sawyer, Jessie's raison d'etre. Jessie's everything.

Without planning to, as he sat by his own fire late into the night on the east coast, Matt echoed the question Charlie had posed to Shanda more than a few weeks earlier. *What is it about that guy?*

He added, *why is Jessie so hopelessly in love with him?*

That's easy, Matt answered himself. *One look in those sad eyes and any woman would be hopelessly lost. Any woman would want to hold together a man who is that broken.*

Sprinkling a full watering can onto his fire, Matt watched as the steam he created sizzled and made its way upwards. Then he went inside his small one-and-a-half story loft cottage and made his way into the washroom. There was a white-framed mirror above the sink. As he brushed his teeth, he gazed at his reflection, and paused.

Matt's eyes were a light hazel-grey. They were absent of light tonight, after a lone night of drinking and smoking and watching airplanes full of people who were going places come and go through the sky above. The eyes staring back from the mirror looked tired to him. They looked dead.

He dropped his toothbrush on the counter and spit, wondering why he even bothered to brush his teeth when he rarely saw anyone more than a storekeeper, or someone walking their dog along the cliff below his cottage, who waved from a distance.

In Alberta, Jessie was remembering the last time she saw Matt. It was that night at the hospital when, through the glass window in Josh's room, Josh saw her holding Matt. Jessie was recalling the stricken look on Matt's face that night, the hopelessness she too was feeling at the time, knowing their brief time alone together was over, that he had to go.

But more than anything, what struck her now, was the memory of looking into Matt's eyes that night. They were floating, for sure, with tears that a strong, proud man like Matt would rarely shed, and they were intelligent, smart, quick, loving and kind. Gentle. Those were Matt's eyes. Always gentle, even just under the surface when he was angry with her for doing something stupid, which Jessie knew she did a lot over the years with Matt as her shadow.

But what jumped out now, as vivid as if he was still in front of her, searching her soul and aching for a piece of it, was the deep sadness in Matt's eyes. His loneliness was already forming then, like cement in his spirit, weighing it down like the rusty iron anchors clawing at the heavy wet sand lining the bottom of the ocean near where he was hanging his head these days.

As in P.E.I. Matt laid his head on a pillow damp with the nearby ocean's salty moisture, Jessie laid her head back into the curve of her husband's neck. Matt turned his lips to a cool, solitary existence, and Jessie breathed in the warmth of Josh's love.

It was worth it, they told the universe in a simultaneous, serendipitous exhalation. *Love. That one night, and all the years that led up to it. It was worth it.*

Even though Jessie had told Shanda otherwise.

As Josh pressed Jessie's body closer to him, he wondered why she was quaking, and why his neck was damp. In Prince Edward Island, Matt closed his eyes against his own dampness, and slept.

The stars continued to twinkle in their merry way above the heads of all of them, and despite empty holes and shattered hearts, airplanes continued to drift eastward and westward. Somewhere in Darnley, P.E.I., a dog barked, its call hollow in the echoing bliss of summer on the healing island, and somewhere in the back woods behind the Sawyer ranch a cougar crouched and growled, its call muffled as it resonated throughout the unknown wild.

At the Sawyer campfire, vibrant orange bits of flaming wood morphed into lifeless grey ash. Lifted towards heaven on an unseen breeze, they disappeared forever into the night, lost like souls shattered by time, and vanquished like spirits destroyed by love.

The End.

Thank you!

Please remember to rate and review *A Sacred Peace*—self-published authors rely on our readers to help spread the love!

P.S. You've made it this far...so you're officially a 'Drifterite!' Term coined by reader Amanda Grady of Ontario, Canada.

CLAIM your free excerpt from *A Song For Josh* by joining the Drifters readers' group at **www.susanrodgersauthor.com**

Happy reading!

Susan

www.susanrodgersauthor.com

Facebook: search **Susan Rodgers, Writer**

Twitter: **@srbluemountain**

www.bublish.com

email: **fatcat@pei.sympatico.ca**

About the Author

Susan Rodgers' first novel *A Certain Kind of Freedom* was a Finalist in the Writers' Federation of Nova Scotia Atlantic Writing Awards for unpublished manuscripts. Her short story from the novel of the same name, published in two anthologies, has received rave reviews, as have the Drifters novels, Susan's all-time favourite books to write.

Owner/Operator of Bluemountain Entertainment, Susan is a 'Diploma With Honours' graduate of Vancouver Film School. She produces mostly documentary style client films and short dramas with plans to one day shoot a Feature Drama based on the novel Atlantic Blue.

Formerly a Museum Curator, in winter Susan lives with her partner Steve and her striped cat Oliver (Lucy Maud Montgomery once said the only good cat is a striped cat) in Summerside, Prince Edward Island, Canada. In summer, she hides in a small trailer in Darnley, P.E.I., where she writes novels, paddles kayaks, and crafts sandcastles on the beach. She makes frequent trips to Vancouver to visit her son Christopher, where she enjoys life in the hippie city while listening to great music and sipping on good espresso.

Books by Susan Rodgers

Drifters series:
A Song For Josh
Promises
No Greater Love
Riptide
Whispers of Home
And Then There Was Silence
Let the Music Cry
If I Could Sing You Home
After the Rain
Into the Blue
A Sacred Peace
Watch Over Me

Coming Soon:
A Certain Kind of Freedom
Seasmoke
Atlantic Blue

Feature Screenplays:
The Story of Jack & Emma
Atlantic Blue
Beautiful Jane
They Were Dreamers (adapted)

Short Stories:
S12
A Certain Kind of Freedom
A Gentle Peace

www.ingramcontent.com/pod-product-compliance
Lightning Source LLC
Chambersburg PA
CBHW060551030726
47498CB00005B/1355